D0427245

THE BEGGAR'S CUP

ERIC BLAU

THE BEGGAR'S CUP

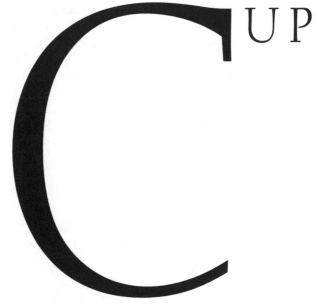

ALFRED A. KNOPF   NEW YORK   1993

THIS IS A BORZOI BOOK
PUBLISHED BY ALFRED A. KNOPF, INC.

Copyright © 1993 by Eric Blau
All rights reserved under International and Pan-American
Copyright Conventions. Published in the United States
by Alfred A. Knopf, Inc., New York, and simultaneously
in Canada by Random House of Canada Limited, To-
ronto. Distributed by Random House, Inc., New York.

A portion of this work was originally published in *Reform
Judaism.*

Library of Congress Cataloging-in-Publication Data

Blau, Eric.
  The beggar's cup / Eric Blau.
     p.   cm.
  ISBN 0-679-42557-8
  I. Title.
PS3552.L393B44   1993
813'.54—dc20   93-18365
                                                          CIP

Manufactured in the United States of America
First Edition

for Al, my cousin,
without whom there might not be an Israel,
and for Paul, my son,
who died there

THE BEGGAR'S CUP

PART ONE

1.

John Wayne blew his nose into a large tissue. I always get these goddamned colds in the summertime, he said.

Vitamin C, Morris Albert Cohen said.

What does that mean, Moe? Take it or avoid it?

Minimum five thousand units a day, Cohen said in his Polish accent. Come on, I'll show you the stream.

They walked together over a meadow that ended at the tree line. Entering the grove, they pushed through the bushes and branches.

Why didn't you cut a path through the woods, Moe?

I like it this way. It's a good feeling. Too rough for the cowboy?

Shit, yes! Wayne said, laughing. I ain't wearing boots. Look at the scuff marks on my shoes, Moe.

They emerged from the woods. Wayne listened for a moment.

Cohen studied the intense face, then smiled. You didn't expect to hear a live stream?

No, Wayne said, but I heard about it. You can't go to a party without someone asking if you'd heard about Moe Cohen's trout stream. Wayne walked with long strides toward the sound of the rushing water, stopped at the edge of the high bank, and looked down at the current. The water was swift and clear, swirling around exposed boulders.

Moe Cohen, inches taller than Wayne, stopped alongside him. Well, John, what do you think?

Wayne blew his nose again. Damn if it doesn't look real! How long is it?

Half a mile, maybe. Something like that. It runs from up

there by the rise, and it goes back into the woods and turns around and comes out. It's a loop, like.

Damn if it ain't real! How long did it take to build?

A few months, I think. I was in Transylvania. *The Wife of Dracula*, we were shooting that.

Good box?

Unreleased. Soon. It's a summer picture. Horror goes good in the summer.

You should know, Moe. If anyone knows horror, Moe knows. Another smash?

Well, we have confidence, John. Horror goes as big as Wayne goes.

My guys tell me horror, your kind of horror, outdraws me, John Wayne said. He quickly slapped leather and drew his thumb and forefinger, pointed it at Cohen, and said, Bang! Bang!

Well, said Cohen, I have to do good. I make three screamers so I can do one good film. On that one I always take a bath.

Well, pilgrim, artsy-fartsy makes no bread. You should know that. Besides, art is so fucking boring.

I could argue, John, but let me put it this way: there's got to be cowboys and Indians, and there's got to be art. Plus, somebody's got to do it.

Hey, I appreciate art, Moe. You know that. I've done it once or twice myself. Wayne stepped down the bank to the stream, where he kneeled and cupped some water with his hands.

Cohen noticed his hesitation. You can drink it. Pure. One hundert percent pure.

Wayne drank. What'd it cost you?

I don't know. That's for the accountant. You want to try for a fish?

Sure. You got a rod?

Morris Cohen walked back to the trees and returned with a split-bamboo eight footer that he handed to Wayne. A fly already was tied to the leader.

You do that, Moe? Wayne said as he examined the beautifully tied Royal Coachman.

No, my man did. He knows those things. He fishes.

For a few silent minutes, Wayne cast into the dark pool. A trout took the fly, and Wayne worked the fish in. Then he gently removed the hook from its jaw and returned the fish to the water. Two pounds, he said. You fish much, Moe?

Boring. I tried, but for a conversation piece, it's first-class. For cowboys and your assorted *goyim* it's a sensation. You know something? A few weeks ago I had a dream about you in a role where you're wearing a full beard.

Never happen. I'm too old for beards, Moe. An artsy-fartsy film?

Don't worry, Johnny. From that dream I woke up laughing, and I dropped you from the project.

Thank God, Morris! Wayne made a long, delicate cast. Listen, I came here to talk business. The party's building a war chest and I drew the short straw. The chairman said, You go see Morris Cohen. Well, I'm not very good at these things.

How much?

They told me to leave that up to you.

You know why?

No.

Because Goldwater was over here last week. He knew the amount I should give. So that's what I gave.

How much?

Secret, Cohen said and chuckled.

Christ, Moe! That's really embarrassing. They should've told me Barry was out here.

Cohen slipped his arm around Wayne's shoulders and

pulled him close. Someone made a mistake. Hey, it happens. So you shouldn't waste your time, Johnny. I'll do something extra because of your wonderful pitch.

Goddamn embarrassing, Wayne muttered.

Well, give 'em hell when you see the sons a bitches. Tell 'em you had to explain to me the state of the nation or something. Come inside, Johnny, so I can write you a check.

2.

After Wayne had left, Morris Albert Cohen went out to the patio and sat in the big wing chair facing the distant hills. To the west, in the afternoon sun, the ridge tops were deeply red. Cohen was less aware of the surrounding embrace of the land than he was of himself. He felt depressed. That was the right word: *depressed.*

Why, he asked out loud. Why? Tears formed and traced down his furrowed, nearly scarred cheeks. This experience had been repeating itself in the last few weeks—tears following emotions he could no longer control.

This was the doctor's doing, he thought. Too many damned tests with no conclusions. In inconclusive matters, Moe Cohen always thought the worst; he was sure he was going to be given fatal news. So that was it: the end was near—although maybe it would be welcome. Death, depression—why? I can reach out and pluck any fruit from the tree of life. Anything that makes me feel good: Women. This house. The Porsche. The Rolls. The film company pouring money into my pockets. Money that comes and comes—I can't give it away fast enough. Ah, America! There's no joy in it. No joy.

He waved his hands through the air as if to disperse the heavy darkness of his emotions as he would a cloud of gnats. Cohen opened the buttons of his shirt to feel the sun on his chest. The house in the valley had become his sanctuary, his hiding place. Sometimes a Goldwater or a Wayne would visit, but always infrequently and mostly for a few minutes. Cohen wished they wouldn't call here at all. They could visit him in his offices or in his hotel suite. This was his private place, the only place where he didn't have to be charming, to be Big Moe, the King of Horror. Here, in this place, he could remain the young man who'd driven a horse-drawn wagon out of Kolkowicz. All the way from Kolkowicz into the sun-drenched San Fernando Valley.

So, he wondered, why am I so down, so depressed? I am only fifty-four. Top of my life, it should be the top of my life. With his eyes closed against the sunlight, he said, What do you think, Mama?

Images of his mother—tall, redheaded, big breasted—filled his memory. Only here in this place, when he was alone, could he invoke her, call her to life merely by saying her name. Mama! Mama! he chanted until the tears coursed down his face. He spoke to her out loud in the fluent Yiddish he rarely used anymore. *Forgive me, Mother! I would not have left you, Mama, if you had not insisted. Even so, even so, I should have known better! Mamenyu, Mamenyu, tell me where is your grave? I will go there and cover it with flowers.*

The two-hundred-bucks-an-hour shrink had listened to Cohen's account of this cancerous anguish—the result, said the Titless Analyst in her soft, deep voice, of his deep feelings of guilt. I need a shrink to tell me that? Guilt? Guilt! By the thousand weight! I know that, dear lady! What I want you to tell me is how to get rid of it.

Five sessions a week but no results. Sometimes it takes years to work through a problem, she had said, a deep problem like yours. She had said that many times. This was an *expensive* asshole!

When he told the Titless Analyst that he had begun to dream that he was lying in a shallow grave in the forest, she said it was a good dream. He was finding his way back—to a cold and loveless womb. Into an unbearable coldness. Is it possible, Morris, that your mother did not want you to be born! That she was, so to speak, locking you in? Burying you in a cold grave?

You're crazy!

Think about it, Morris. Don't just abreact. Let you find yourself.

Listen to me! I dreamed about being in a grave. I was dreaming about a real grave. I *was* lying in a real grave. I dug this grave with my own hands! A real grave, in real dirt, in a real forest thick with trees. With my hands. Many graves.

In the ensuing silence, Morris Cohen had concentrated on her thin smile. This was the first time he'd spoken of the graves to anyone.

Yes, she had said, I see. We will continue with this to-morrow.

But that session had been the last of ten. This was many months ago.

The graves had been real. Twilight in the Polish wood, a rustling of leaves, and out of the grave rose a tall, gaunt figure: the Jewish vampire who could not face the rising sun and live. Maybe one day he would make a movie about an avenging Jewish vampire who flies through the night draining from the world the blood of anti-Semites. His eyes still closed, Cohen smiled.

He got out of the chair and went inside, returning with a glass of scotch. He regarded the hills again, then spoke: *How much you would have enjoyed this place! And the kitchen, Mama! It has things of which you have never dreamed. What you could have done with a Cuisinart!* The memory of her in the kitchen of their restaurant in Kolkowicz surged up like a movie in a screening room. Miriam Cohen dripped with sweat. Her hair, which she pushed back constantly, fell across her flushed cheeks. She tended several saucepans at once. Toward the back of the huge stove simmered two large pots, one with a cabbage soup, one with the thick stew for which she was famous. Morris saw himself, dressed in his black pants and white shirt, entering the kitchen and calling out the orders he'd taken. Smiling, his mother repeated them. *My chief,* she said, handing him a plate of sausage with sauerkraut, *Here, take!*

As Moe pushed through the door to the dining room, he glimpsed his mother lifting one of the stove lids with an iron handle and jamming a log into the red embers. How much easier it must've been for her when his father was alive, but for eight years he'd pretended to take his father's place, and she not only had allowed him to do so but also had taken pleasure from it. *Moishe,* she said. *Never could I do the work without you, darling Moishe!*

That night the restaurant was filled. Thirty-six people. Rigo, the Hungarian fiddler, played without letup. *Play, Gypsy! Sing, Gypsy!* Music made the food taste better. Leibush, the drunken miller, sang at the top of his voice, protesting the squeaky sound of the violin. The last of the entrées had been served. Now Morris prepared the dessert tray: three different cakes, baked by his mother that morning, and the compote of cherries, apricots, and grapes that he'd made himself. After he served the dessert and tea, he reentered the kitchen. His mother sat exhausted on the stool; she was wet with sweat, her apron spread over her knees. She stared toward the stove, her hazel eyes empty. *I see you so clearly! Mamenyu, Mamenyu, where is your grave?*

Again Morris began to sob. He walked down the patio steps and followed the flagstone path to the swimming pool. Scotch in hand, fully clothed, he leapt into the tinted, shimmering water. He floated face down, staring at the bottom of the pool. He felt his mouth shape into a smile; then he burbled,

Am I dead now? I am dead, he thought, in the truest sense. Then he swam to poolside and placed his empty glass on the ledge.

Schmuck! he shouted into the hot sky of the Valley.

3.

Moe Cohen poured himself another drink but did not change his clothes. He stood on the hot, bright flagstones, swaying with the ancient rocking motion of Jews in prayer. He sensed himself standing, rocking, in the rude *shul* of his childhood. *Baruch Atah Adonoi!*

He prayed louder to drown out distant explosions. The Germans had come. The Russians had met them. The men in the *shul* had rocked rapidly, anxiously. Young Cohen, taller than all the others, had sweated profusely. Suddenly the rabbi shouted, Go home, everybody! And in a moment the *shul* had emptied.

Even as Morris rocked and dried on the flagstones, the prayer books on the benches of the empty *shul* entered his mind. He could still see the heavy pages of the old books being lifted by the wind coming through the unclosed door: yellow pages on gray benches.

How far away are the guns? That was what his mother had asked the Red Army colonel who was eating the fish she'd prepared for him. How far away are the guns?

Twelve kilometers.

And we can hear them in the town?

I can hear them; you can hear them, the colonel said. There are hundreds of artillery pieces—some big cannon, too. Put your hand to the floor and you'll feel them.

I can feel them in my feet. Who will win, Colonel?

They will win, he said, sucking the flaking flesh from a long, white bone. They will win, Madame. Most of the thunder is theirs. Stalin has sent the 112th and the 113th Infantry Battalions to die for the Motherland. The 19th Artillery has fifty inferior guns and not enough shells. And also please consider, Madame, they have been here for some time. Excuse me, that is unfair. Their *surrogates* have been here for a very long time. They are fighting to be free from the U.S.S.R. To show how sincere they are, they eat a Jew or two a day. But Marxism-Leninism will triumph in the end, hoorah! What's for dessert?

Compote. Cake? Apricot torte.

The torte with tea.

You will lose?

Did I say we would lose? Quite impossible. That would be quite impossible. But, I would suggest, Madame, if you have a small flag with a swastika, hang it on your wall.

Morris Cohen walked out of the poolside sun to the patio, then fixed himself another drink and swallowed it. He directed his thought to Marcus, his son. Morris Cohen sighed: their only connection was a monthly check, and they hadn't spoken for almost three years. Marcus had informed him then that he, Morris, was a hopeless philistine, the purveyor of violent filth. Big MAC Pictures was a laugh track throughout the land; people bought tickets to sit in the movie house and giggle. *Even your so-called serious films are pretentious shit. The only thing you succeed at, old man, is making money. I had more respect for you when you were a sewing-machine mechanic.*

Maybe if his son had loved him, Morris Cohen would not have felt his life was so empty. Even if he were a gangster, shouldn't his son love him and give him respect? Did he not respect Marcus? Had he not supported his career as a composer? Why, then, all this venom directed against him? The answer had remained unspoken: no talent. Marcus knew it, and could not tolerate the idea that his father also knew it but would never acknowledge it. His father—smiling, towering above him—would listen to Marcus's new composition and inevitably say, Marvelous! We've got to record it. We'll get a good orchestra. The London Symphony, Marcus. It must be done by the London Symphony with Pavarotti singing. But neither the London Symphony nor Pavarotti would accept the engagement, and the reason was clear.

When Morris asked Marcus to score one of his films— *Don't cover me with your shit, Dad. How insulting can you be?*—Morris had almost struck him. He'd raised his hand but held back; Marcus had simply smiled. Such hatred! Such contempt! I can give you everything I have, my son, but we will have to settle for a check I don't even sign personally. A MAC check, my son, which every month you will accept. Moe accepted the truth of his feelings: he did not love his son. Blood, he thought, might be thicker than water but too often was thickened by bile and hatred.

Moe Cohen tried to recall his own father, Solomon. But his memory produced only the shadow of a man who stooped. A smile with a missing tooth. The waiter his mother had praised so much. The father who had coughed into corners. The man who every so often had pinched his cheek and had said: *Morris, my beautiful son!* Solomon had said that many, many times. Had he ever said anything else? Morris could not remember. He did remember his father carrying the heavy serving trays and sometimes doing the baking or cooking. Smoking cheap cigarettes—coughing, coughing, departing that night with the rest of the diners but never returning. Where had he gone? When Moe tried to visualize Solomon's face, it would not present itself. Why couldn't he remember more? Yet he *had* felt the grave loss, perhaps because Miriam so mourned her stooped lover who had coughed himself away.

Now Morris Cohen strained to hear the distant guns of memory, and the rumbling came again. The small panes of the restaurant's window glass trembled. The Red Army colonel finished his tea and departed.

What does it mean, Mama?

Moishe, you know.

The Germans will come?

Yes, yes.

Is it really true what they do to Jews?

I think so. We will have to leave.

Morris gazed out the window as a solitary airplane roared over. It had swastikas under the wings.

Leaving would not be so easy. A plan! A plan! Miriam said. We need a plan.

In the dark restaurant was a meeting of whatever Jews hadn't already fled Kolkowicz. Plans and tactics were exchanged that night. The idea of Leibush, the miller, was ultimately accepted: the young men, all the young men who had been bar mitzvahed, should leave immediately, in a group, and go as students to Warsaw, where they could join relatives. In his opinion, Leibush said, it would be a safe journey. The remaining Jews of Kolkowicz would take a day, two at the most, to pack up everything of value and then leave. As for himself, the miller said, he would stay behind.

About that there had been protests. He would be in danger! He could lose his life! Leibush shook his head. Nonsense, he had said. There was no danger. And besides, he could never desert the mill. His mill had been the first in the history of Kolkowicz. Had not his grandfather built it? Had not his father made a living from this mill on the river? If he quit the town, what might happen to the wind that turned the blades?

You're mad, Leibush! Think of your wife, your children! I will send them to Warsaw with you, he said with his familiar gold-toothed grin. Listen, even the Germans bake bread and appreciate good flour! Then the laughing miller delivered his final argument: Doesn't everybody always say, if I don't pull out my *schmeckel* everybody will swear I'm a *goy*? Leibush would suffer no more protests. He would stay with the mill the Wollachs had built. Final!

As a further part of his plan, Leibush gave the boys his large wagon and two gray horses. A loan, he said.

In the darkness the young men let out a cheer and had to be quieted. I expect you, the miller admonished them, to care for the horses and the wagon. It is a loan, not a gift.

At dawn, it was agreed, they would assemble outside the restaurant. Morris—at eighteen the tallest (a giant!) and strongest, with a good head on his shoulders—would be in charge. Leibush had left the wagon for them behind the restaurant in a grove of trees.

4.

How distinct was Morris's memory! Nine young men, each with a suitcase or a sack. How strange that each wore his Sabbath clothing as if he were about to go to *shul* or a wedding.

Morris Cohen rocked on the flagstones in the California sun. How clear it all was! Each face and name. Yes, yes! The boys from Kolkowicz.

Heshey Wollach, a redhead with a big nose, the miller's eldest son. Sixteen.

Asher Zabinsky, a peanut who shifted from foot to foot as if his shoes were filled with water. Thirteen.

Duddy Levy, a champion farter who said that he had *shtupped* all the Kolkowicz girls, and sometimes had a black eye for it. Fifteen.

Yussie Glatter, the clubfoot, a very good mathematician, a future doctor who bit his nails constantly. Sixteen.

Mendel Moscowitz, good-looking but cross-eyed. Who would ever marry him? Nineteen.

Simon Chiliwicz, the ritual slaughterer's son, occasionally allowed to cut the throats of chickens. He stammered. Sixteen.

Simon Gershowitz, always quiet. Was he bright or dull? Of him the rabbi had said, Still rivers run deep. Maybe yes; maybe no. Fourteen.

Yiddle Abramowitz, the brightest of them all. He spoke Hebrew and knew the Talmud backward and forward. Ruchel Glatter had caught him masturbating in the miller's barn. Eeech—disgusting! Seventeen.

And himself, of course. Just eighteen.

Miriam had given Moishe, her son, an envelope stuffed with currency, half in United States dollars, which had been sent from New York by rich Uncle Axel, who owned a grocery store on 9th Street. (All the streets had numbers there.) In Warsaw it will be all right, an almost breathless Miriam whispered to her son. The Russians will never let the Nazis get to Warsaw. You have my brother's address. Be useful, my son. Don't let your relatives do for you.

All right, Mama, Morris Cohen answered with a broad smile. Don't worry. You'll be with me in a few days.

She threw her arms around him, and he could feel her breasts against him. She kissed his mouth; never had she kissed him so hard. An hour later, as he drove the wagon, Asher Zabinsky alongside him on the wooden seat, the others in the back, Morris still felt his mother's kiss.

As they traveled they sang songs, but only Polish ones. They were students going to the university. All was well! That is, until Yussie Glatter went to buy some milk from a farm where he'd overheard some farmers saying it might be smart to seize some Jews as a way of impressing the Germans when they arrived. At this news Simon Chiliwicz became quite disturbed. No good, he said, traveling in a group was dangerous! They all could be captured at once and given over to the Germans. You know these crafty peasants! There ensued a noisy argument in Yiddish.

Finally Morris yelled out: Shut up! You want the Germans to swoop down on us?

Quieted, the boys of Kolkowicz turned to him and asked what to do.

Morris tapped his cheek with a closed fist. Let me think. He walked to the side of the road and pissed into the bushes. What should he do? What should he say? Even after he had emptied his bladder he remained at the roadside. Why should he be the leader, anyway? But when Morris Cohen rejoined his friends, he said they had to split up. Warsaw was not so far—maybe two days on foot. Because there would be no wagon, Gershowitz and Chiliwicz, the two Simons, decided to go to Kraków, where they liked their relatives better. Because of his clubfoot, Yussie Glatter wanted to know whether he could walk to a town with a train station.

Morris said he thought that would be all right. Then he cautioned them to speak Polish, *only* Polish! He would take the wagon on for a distance, leave it on a quiet road and then release the horses into a pasture. At night. He would have to wait for night to fall.

The boys listened in silence. When Morris said, Understood? they merely nodded and muttered their acquiescence. Mendel Moscowitz wiped his eyes.

At staggered intervals, they selected separate paths of the triple-tined road that divided them one from the other.

5.

Once alone, Morris had asked himself, What do they want from us? He climbed up to the wagon seat and spoke to the broad-beamed dray horses in Yiddish: Get along! Get along!

Very soon you will have Polish masters. Don't let on that you're Jewish. After a time he fell silent, letting the horses plod slowly ahead into nightfall. Unhitched on the edge of a cultivated field, they immediately began grazing in the dark.

Suitcase in hand, Morris strode purposefully through the bright, moonlit night on a road he did not know, looking frequently from side to side. Perhaps two hours had passed, but he could not be sure.

He stopped abruptly. Someone, probably a drunken peasant, was lying on the road. Morris came closer. It was a naked person. His heart pounded. He knew: it was one of the boys. He stood over the body for a moment, then squatted down and turned it over. Mendel—it was Mendel all right! By the bright moon he counted eight puncture wounds; four in the chest, four in the abdomen. A pitchfork. The blood no longer flowed, although dried, caked rivulets traced down to Mendel's thin thighs. The genitals had been hacked away. A shriveled piece of scrotum remained attached to the abdomen.

Still rocking in the motion of prayer, Morris Cohen's tears came again, and the deep racking sobs. Although his clothes had dried, he trembled in the chilly light of the sun that now had fallen behind the hills. He went inside for an old cardigan and another drink. He sat in a chair facing the long window until the light had vanished. Are you sure you have not dreamed this, Morris Cohen asked himself. He felt his testicles draw up. No dream. Mendel it had been, dead on the road.

How heavy Mendel's slight body had seemed when Morris had dragged it into the potato field. He had pulled up the new green shoots, whose roots were grasped by clumps of earth. Now, forty years later, the odor of the field filled his nostrils. The earth had been soft. He had hollowed out a deep pit with his thick-fingered hands. He had placed Mendel's body gently into the ground. Mendel's crossed eyes had stared up at him. He covered him over with the earth. He replaced the young potato plants as neatly as possible. With a clenched fist he beat his heart and intoned the prayer for the dead.

Kicking the bordering grass of the road with his heavy shoes, Morris Cohen walked through the night. The bright orange moon dispelled the tall shadows of trees. His shoe kicked a thin, straight branch from the grass. He picked it up. He could not quite make out what was at the end of the branch. He turned from the shadows into the moonlight and saw, pierced through by the sharp point of the branch, Mendel's penis, scrotum still attached, hanging there like a hairy rag. Morris hurled the branch into the shadows across the road, struggled to breathe, and vomited.

Had *that* been a dream? No, this was no dream. Not the body of Mendel in the potato field, not the circumcised cock like a sausage on a stick, ready for roasting on an open fire.

In the morning, some miles away from Mendel's grave, Morris Cohen realized that he'd left his suitcase behind. With the horses? With the wagon? With Mendel? He felt inside the pockets of his pants and jacket. The money and identity papers were still there. He considered discarding the latter because they clearly marked him as a Jew. On the other hand, Morris reasoned, the papers might prove useful—if the Russians triumphed—but useless if the Germans arrived in Warsaw before him. Who were his friends? Who were his enemies? Who might stop him on the road? There were no answers. He was far away from Kolkowicz, on a sunlit road filled with peril. Morris Albert Cohen turned off the path and entered the forest that suddenly appeared around a wide bend.

Was that forty years ago? In another life?

6.

He walked through the sweet-smelling shadows. It had been more than a day since he had slept and longer than that since he had taken any food or water, but he was neither sleepy nor hungry. A great distance off he heard voices. Polish. He listened intently. He was able to make out the voices of three women, one man. From the man's complaints that he already had walked far enough and that no mushrooms had been found, Morris guessed he was old. Just a little distance more, said a woman's voice, there will be plenty. Then the voices drifted upward, as if caught by a wind.

The sounds of these unseen mushroom gatherers filled Morris Cohen with terror. Almost without thinking he fell to his knees between the spread roots of a large tree. He tore away the earth, digging a trough, just as he had dug Mendel's grave. But here the earth was much harder, and Morris's grave was longer than Mendel's but shallower. His hands had become raw, his fingernails broken, from the digging. He lay down in the trough and covered himself with twigs and leaves, praying that this grave would not be seen. He praised God for His mercy. How weary he was. He struggled to keep his eyes open. No hope. The sleep of the dead overcame him. When he awoke, the day still dappled his eyelids. Morris lay in his makeshift tomb until twilight came and no more voices were to be heard in the forest. All was still. He sat up, pushing the leaves away; he stood up, listening; he walked, stealthily as a Red Indian. In a shaft of moonlight he came upon a clutch of white mushrooms growing on a fallen tree trunk. What was the blessing to be said before eating a mushroom? He decided on the *brucha* for vegetables. Was a mushroom a vegetable? What if they were poisonous? What difference did it make? He had to eat. He devoured a handful of the white conical forms, then awaited some sign from his stomach. Nothing. He ate some more of the mushrooms. He was still hungry, thirsty too. Later his stomach issued a warning rumble. When he dropped his pants, his bowels were loose.

All night he walked through the moon-pierced forest. When day came, Morris Albert Cohen dug himself a fresh grave. In these daily graves sleeping did not come easily. The forest was filled with noises. There were animals—deer, fox, squirrels, rabbits, and game birds. The animals saw and smelled him; he had not bathed in more than a week. One morning the wet nose of an animal probed his blanket of leaves, but Morris's startled jerk sent the gray fox racing away. Sometimes there had been the sound of axes and the clattering of leaves as a tree fell. Sometimes he heard shots, single shots. These he thought came from the guns of hunters. The rat-tat-tat bursts, he supposed, were military.

Polish voices in the forest, it seemed to Morris, were less frequently heard. Subdued. The dominant voices were German, loud and laughing. Why were the Germans in this forest, and for whom were they hunting? Certainly not for Morris Cohen. So, there were others in the wilderness. Poles. Jews. Russians. *Who?* Machine-gun fire. Trees falling, or men falling?

He had restricted his gleaning to dawn, when the forest was deeply silent except for the rising birds, when there was enough light to forage for fallen nuts, berries, mushrooms, wild cabbage, garlic, and onions. But Morris was constantly hungry and growing gaunt. One night, aching with hunger, he quit the forest and walked through an adjoining field, beyond which sat a farmhouse. Slowly he crossed the sea of grass and stood silently before it. Once he was sure that no one was awake, he moved toward the porch. He heard the soft clucking of chickens. Guided by the sound, he found the coop. Searching for eggs, he reached inside the feathered darkness—and the hens set up a racket. Somewhere a door opened and shut. A firm Polish voice shouted: If that is you in the chicken house, my dear fox, I have a big gun to shoot you. Go home, fox, go home! Leave Olek's chickens alone! Morris withdrew his hand from the coop, and the hens settled down to soft cackling. He was sweating, and his breath sounded like a sawmill. Again Morris heard the door open and bang shut. So near, so near, to food. Eggs or your life! This he could not risk, and he retreated from the henhouse.

Next Morris groped around in the darkness of the barn. He could smell the tethered cow before he touched it. He stroked its flank. Near the cow was a cask half filled with water. He cupped his hands, scooping up the water and drinking it down, not minding whatever was floating on top. There was a second cow, smaller. A heifer? There was a peaceful goat. Also, two horses.

Outside the barn stood a structure not much larger than an outhouse. Morris pressed his face to the door and sniffed. The smokehouse! He slid open the rusty latch as saliva sprang up violently in his mouth. His hard fingers recognized a hanging goose, then another and another. A rope of sausage. This he lifted from the long nail from which it dangled, and he devoured two links as he slid away into the shelter of the forest. It had been good sausage! Forty years later, in the dark room in the house in the San Fernando Valley, Morris Cohen could taste it still. But if God saves your life with a link of sausage, he thought, He might also visit you with new afflictions. Thus came the Time of Ghosts and Fever.

A short while after Morris Cohen reentered the forest he became intensely feverish. Soon he had lost track of time. Events had no definition. Drenched with sweat, he breathed heavily in the darkness. Feebly, he rested his back against a thick birch. He said Kaddish for himself. The forest seemed alive with apparitions. They glowed in the darkness and were easily seen. At first these shining ghosts had filled him with terror. But after a while he accepted them as welcome company. When Morris would sing a feverish song, the ghosts joined him in chorus. One night, under the glare of the moon, he saw his mother. She wore a thin garment through which her large breasts were visible—also the hair between her legs. Morris, she said, what are you doing alone in the forest? Where are the others? Have you done something wrong, Morris? No, no, he protested, I did what I could, Mama! I swear to you I did my best. What are you doing in the forest, Mama? Are you all right? The apparition sobbed and evaporated. Morris Cohen trembled and said over and over into the forest air, It's not my fault, it's not my fault, it's not my fault, it's not my fault.

Then Theodor Herzl appeared, sitting with his legs crossed on the trunk of a fallen tree. Why are you weeping, Morris, Herzl asked.

My mother thinks it is my fault!

I will tell her it is not your fault. It is the fault of the anti-Semites. Are you a Zionist, Morris?

A Labor Zionist.

That's all right. But no ideological debates until we establish the Jewish state. Look at you, Morris! You are filthy. You need a bath.

I know, Morris said. He looked at Herzl sitting on the tree trunk with his top hat, fancy suit, and spats. In his left hand Herzl was holding a pair of spotless white gloves; in his right, a black walking stick with a silver knob at the top and a silver tip at the bottom. Sir, Morris said, the forest is filled with Germans, and I must sleep every day in a grave.

Take a bath, anyway. If the enemy captures you, you must be as neat as a pin! You must stand erect. You must speak as an emissary of the Jewish state.

But sir, I'm afraid. Comrade Herzl, I'm afraid!

He smiled. I know, Morris. I, too, am afraid. What if the Jewish state is not established?

Morris Cohen stared at this ghost and finally said, Are you really there? Is this not a dream?

Herzl lit a thin cigar and blew some smoke into the forest air. The smoke shaped itself into a great halo over Herzl's head. No, Morris, he said, if you will it, it is not a dream.

Will you explain to my mother, Morris said, that it isn't my fault? She is in Kolkowicz.

There was no Herzl on the tree trunk. I am going mad, Morris thought. He trembled in the grip of a chill that did not in any way reduce his fever. He stumbled forward. The trees seemed so tall, reaching, reaching, the crowns bending inward. Where did the sun rise or set? Was he walking east toward the border? Which was the way to Warsaw? Was the forest as immense as an ocean, or was he tethered like an ox to a pole that was embedded in a grave? Did he walk in circles, moving the millstones to grind the dusty bones of the dead? Days passed. Perhaps weeks. What had he eaten? Where was water? Had he left the forest at night to raid farms? Vaguely Morris remembered sitting in a thick bush, swallowing the yolk and white of an egg. Some of the slimy white had run down his lightly bearded chin. Was it a stolen egg or that of a forest bird?

The fever seemed to have lifted his brain above his head. He had the constant feeling that his legs were endlessly long as they dangled weakly from his hips. His torso seemed to have shrunken; his head felt as tiny as a walnut. For all that his body had the sense to dig a grave each morning. Walking in patterns directed by his fever, Morris would sometimes find himself at the side of one of his previous graves. He had no memory of having slept, although sleep must have been part of the light and the dark of the forest. He remembered lying in the earth and shaking, his teeth rattling inside his head. There was the pale memory of praying—to God, to his mother, and to Theodor Herzl, who on many nights had hovered above his grave rattling a *pushka* as if the blue tin box was a beggar's cup.

The ghost of his mother came several times more, but she always kept her distance. She had not answered his calls. Once came naked Mendel with his crotchless body. Behind him stood the boys of Kolkowicz, shaking and *shuckling* as if praying in *shul*. Are you all dead, Morris asked them very softly. Are you all dead? Are you dead in the forest? Am I dead in the forest? Suddenly Herzl appeared among them. Morris, he said, promise me that you will do your duty.

What is my duty? Morris shouted into the moonlight. What is my duty?

All the ghosts disappeared. Morris, his long legs wobbling beneath him, stepped forward on the cushioned forest floor, singing the Yiddish song "Shicker Iz a Goy."

Rain. Rain had not cooled his fever. Rain—falling into the grave. The wasting body of the boy rocking from side to side in the pool of his own grave, the earth turning to mud. By morning the sun was pouring in through his shroud of leaves, and a sheet of mud had dried like stone on his back. The fever had broken, leaving little blisters on his lips and inside his mouth. German voices fell into his grave, as if they were birds sitting right above it, on a branch. Laughing voices, something like Yiddish. Morris half understood the German words—soldiers making fun of their commanding officer. Morris Cohen instructs his body not to shake, not to disturb his cover. He hardly breathes.

There is a little animal rooting between his thighs. It mounts his stomach and scurries up his chest, then lifts itself onto his face. A rat looks right into his eyes. Morris twitches his cheeks and jaw, and after a moment the rat retreats to explore his armpit. It moves down to his hand and discovers the wound on his little finger. It chews off the top joint. Morris will not scream; will not respond. He had no memory of the pain—had it been great? No memory at all.

The fever returns, but it is less intense. A pale memory of scooping cool, fragrant water from the bowl rotted out of a tree stump. Graves. Long mornings of bird song high up in the dappled air. More graves. Another grave. A woman's face is staring down at him. Her skin is dirty. Her front teeth are missing. She cackles softly, neither human nor animal. She seizes his crotch and unbuttons his fly. The shrunken worm of his cock is in her hand. He pulls himself out of the grave. He seizes the woman by her hair, beats her face with his fists. He throws her to the earth. She rolls into the grave. She cackles wildly. He runs. The heavens are wheeling. The leaves of autumn rattle around him. That day he had slept outside the sheltering grave. He had not been discovered. The fever returns. His little strength was gone. He could barely stand.

In the naked daylight he sat on the ground, leaning against a tree. Fever again. Morris Cohen talked to himself out loud. He saw Miriam walking among the trees. Here I am, Mama. She did not turn toward him. Theodor Herzl appeared before him and shook his blue tin beggar's cup.

Shemah Yisroel! Save me! Save me, Comrade Herzl! Take me home to Israel!

He could not stand or walk. All through the night, he sat against the tree singing songs from home. He could hear Rigo scratching away on his fiddle. He thought of Yehudit and what they had done in the barn of Wollach's mill. His fingers had found her spot. They almost had done it. They should have done it. She had been ready. He was as hard as iron, and she had been holding it. Why hadn't they done it? They should have. No! Yehudit was a nice girl, a good girl.

Morris pulled himself to his feet. His lips were thick, cracked. The blisters inside his mouth had begun to burst. He spit out blood as he stumbled forward. Toward a friendly border? A German outpost? Occasional gunfire. The sound of engines. Polish voices. German voices. His heavy shoes pushed like boats through the dead foliage, until he came to a clearing among a circle of old trees whose naked roots were fiercely exposed. The ground felt soft and velvety beneath his feet. He got down on his knees and slowly, painfully, excavated another grave. For the first time since the onset of the fever, Morris Cohen fell into a deep and dreamless sleep.

He was awakened by a slow shifting of the earth, the undertow of a great ocean. The sea of earth curled up, grasped his hand, and sucked it down voraciously. He had awakened with a start, his mouth filling with earth. The earth was eating him up! Morris was struggling like a swimmer against a demon tide when out of the black deep a weight fell upon him. It was a leathery corpse, its skull resting on his face. He looked into the hollow eye sockets. Dirt slipped down his throat as he screamed. He beat at the heavy black sea with his arms. The earth slid and shifted. Dry bones churned up—skulls, arm bones, finger bones, hip bones, foot and leg bones! Entire skeletons with the tattered, leathery remains of flesh. A loose hand of fingers hooked onto his ear. He imagined himself a single breath away from death when his hand finally caught hold of a clump of tangled roots, and he pulled himself up and out of the roiling grave.

I don't care any more! Morris Cohen shouted, his voice no more than a hoarse whisper. Do you hear me? I don't care any more! Take me! Kill me! No more living in graves! No more living with skeletons!

He had lost more than sixty pounds. He was a walking, lurching skeleton. All that day he marched on long, weak legs in a random direction. The forest night slowly gathered him in. Ahead, beyond the trees, he made out the lights and the shape of a small building. Morris walked out of the forest and up the wooden stairs. Without knocking he pulled open the door and entered.

7.

A uniformed man sat at a table. A pistol lay there before him. Morris Cohen wanted to speak but was unable to issue a sound. He regarded the man in the uniform. The man in the uniform looked up at Morris Cohen. In Polish the man said, Aha, another Forest Jew!

Morris reached inside his torn, mud-caked jacket and placed his identity papers before the man at the desk, next to the pistol. Then, without warning, his legs collapsed. He was sitting on the floor. He heard himself laughing. Loudly, hysterically. The man at the desk laughed. Jews, he said, Jews are crazy!

Morris Cohen drank some more scotch. The trembling life he had relived in the dark suddenly stopped; the screen of memory faded to white. Although he could not see his stunted finger in the dark, he held it before his face and smiled. The whole history of the forest with its graves was contained in the top of his little finger, eaten by a Polish rat.

He switched on a light near the chair. His glass was empty. Why did he drink whiskey when it did him no good? He was as sober as Rabbi Henry Hoffman. Perhaps it was his size. Morris Cohen was six feet, seven inches tall and weighed almost three hundred pounds. If he consumed a gallon, would *that* make him drunk? *Shicker Iz a Goy.* In the re-frigerator a broiled chicken had been left for him by the black maid who, thank God, went always to church but never to the cinematic dens of sin. He sat on a stool at the white Formica serving counter and separated the chicken with his huge hands. He ate in silence.

8.

The building outside the forest was a border-guard outpost. The guard at the table helped him into a small room, a closet, where there was a cot. Morris Cohen lay down and slept until the next day. The man who woke him was another border guard, younger than the first.

The next year of his life was eventful, unforgettable, but strangely routine. For money, the border guards—you Jews always have a little money—turned Morris over to two Lithuanian smugglers. The clean clothes they gave him were too small; the coat tight, the pants short. Speaking accented Polish, the Lithuanians thought the ill-fitting clothes (included in the smuggling fee) were a blessing in disguise. One of them said he looked like a badly made scarecrow, sticking out all over. If they were stopped by police or Germans, they told Morris, they would say he was the village idiot, mentally retarded, cuckoo. Money in advance, please. And don't say a word!

There was a character note for you, Cohen thought. Mental defectives wear short pants. Frankenstein's monster.

The Lithuanian wagon with Morris Cohen and a load of potatoes rolled along back roads for five days. No one stopped them. The cargo was unloaded at a small fishing village, where a rickety fishing boat awaited him. Only after the smugglers gave the pilot some of the zlotys he'd paid them five days earlier was Morris beckoned aboard. As the slightly listing boat putt-putted away from the dock, one of the smugglers shouted, Jew bastard, you'll burn in the ovens!

After eight or nine hours, Morris Cohen was put ashore on a busy pier in Riga without knowing where to go. His mind was clouded with weariness. He wondered if he now, indeed, was free, but he was too tired to care.

He seated himself on a weathered keg and closed his eyes.

The voice he heard was very clear: *Bist du a yid?* The speaker was a middle-aged woman with a scarf over her head. She wore a coat-length heavy gray sweater.

Yes, Cohen had answered.

Come with me. I am from HIAS. You are safe here, she had said. Are you hungry? Come, come! You look like you haven't eaten since Yom Kippur.

Cohen so clearly remembered her round little face. Ruchel Amberg! Sweet Ruchel! It was in her name, although she had died many years before, that he gave his annual check to the Hebrew Immigrant Aid Society.

Morris remained in Riga for almost a month. Ruchel had found him a room and instructed him not to go out except with her. Moishe, she had said, you're a little bit conspicuous! Even with clothes that fit, my child, you are more Goliath than David! I will bring you food in the room.

Isn't it safe here in Riga, he had asked.

When I get you a passport to leave, then it will be safe.

A few evenings, Ruchel Amberg had taken Morris Cohen for short walks. On these occasions she had advised, Stoop a little, Moishe, stoop a little!

In his room he ate and slept dreamlessly. Awake, he had recounted the days from Kolkowicz to this place. He gained weight. He gained strength, but his joints ached, and he couldn't walk without pain. Much of the time he was anxious and would break out into sudden sweats. He wondered what had happened to the boys from Kolkowicz. Whether his mother was all right. Had anyone reached Warsaw or Kraków? Perhaps Morris Cohen was the only one of the Kolkowicz Jews to survive—an awful possibility that made his heart pound.

The time in the room passed neither slowly nor quickly. For hours on end he studied the roughly plastered white ceiling. There was nothing to do, which was fine with him. Waiting, when he was not anxious, Morris floated pleasantly like a log in a warm, benign sea.

Ruchel would always arrive with a piece of fish or a cutlet and, best of all, freshly baked bread. Had anyone from Kolkowicz arrived in Riga? She did not know. Was there a way to reach his mother? She did not know. These are hard times, Moishe. We must pray for the best. Finally, Ruchel Amberg arrived with documents from HIAS. In a few days he would be on his way to Sweden, where it was much safer. Through HIAS, Ruchel purchased his airplane ticket to Sweden with some of his American currency. Two days later, in clean clothing that was still too small, Morris Cohen got off the plane in Stockholm and was greeted by another woman from HIAS. She walked up to him and said, Please, Mr. Cohen, come with me.

He was boarded in a rooming house where he shared a room with two rabbis—one old, the other quite young. They were pleasant enough and did not badger him, even though he would go to the synagogue only on Friday nights. Later HIAS got him his own room in an apartment belonging to a Jewish family. Because he'd been apprenticed to a Kolkowicz mechanic who repaired sewing machines, they found him work in a Jewish shop that sold and serviced bicycles. Bicycles were much simpler to repair than sewing machines.

The constant news about his mother was none whatsoever. Morris considered writing a letter to the restaurant in Kolkowicz but felt this might be a mistake. Maybe his mother was in hiding or, like Wollach, pretending to be a *goy*. No, sending a letter was too risky.

In many Stockholm neighborhoods, Yiddish was the language heard on the streets. Morris would ask every Jew he encountered for news from Kolkowicz, news about Miriam Cohen. He had copies made of the small photograph of his mother he carried in his wallet. These he tacked to the message boards of HIAS, synagogues, Jewish restaurants and social halls, with a carefully printed note headlined, HAVE YOU SEEN MIRIAM COHEN OF KOLKOWICZ? There had not been a single response.

Morris mastered the simple mechanics of bicycles with no trouble. From the shop owner, with difficulty, he learned a few words of Swedish. He read the two Yiddish newspapers, one a weekly and the other a daily. He ate voraciously. He gained back his lost body weight. At night he tried to block out the thoughts of Kolkowicz, of the murder and mutilation of Mendel, of the forest of graves, and sometimes he even succeeded. He was most successful when he entertained erotic images. Yet excepting the most furtive and unfulfilled experiences, Morris knew little of sex. Like the other young men of Kolkowicz, his sexual knowledge came from watching a horse or a cow being serviced. Eroticism came mainly from the tales they had told each other about their own sexual experiences—suspecting, of course, that each purveyor of such tales was lying. They did, however, believe Simon Gershowitz when he told them without embarrassment that he masturbated daily.

What did a vagina look like? Morris wondered. Did you stick your *schmeckel* into the peepee hole? Did it hurt the woman, or did she like it? Was doing it from behind a sin? Why did he get so many erections? His fantasies almost always centered on Yehudit. Fully dressed, they would lie down in the grass or in the hay of Wollach's barn. They would kiss and kiss and feel and feel until, at last, she would pull down her underpants and he, without looking at her nakedness, would bring forth his erect penis. And, mysteriously, it found its way inside her. Lying on the brown-blanketed bed, Morris Cohen masturbated and caught his ejaculation in a handkerchief. Emptied of his passion, he filled with shame.

Morris met Pauline Cronowitz at a HIAS party. She had a pretty face. She was Polish. They danced. Her laundered perfume filled his head. Her body was already in his arms in this sea of music. The unbearable language of love was Yiddish! And so Poli became the central figure of his nightly fantasies. Within weeks they were doing everything except *it*.

She had taken out her beautiful, large-nippled breasts. He fondled them gently, kissing the nipples and, at last, taking them into his mouth and sucking them. Poli held her breast firmly to his mouth. Suck, suck, my darling! I love it! Put your hand down here! Poli's pink hand went inside his pants. Unbearable, unbearable, wild, and unbearable! Poli, he had whispered, Stop, please. I can't hold back. Poli! Poli!

She had embraced him fiercely. It's all right, she said, because we love each other. Did he love her? he wondered. Did sex cause love? Had Poli ever done this with anyone else? Would her mother discover her soiled underpants? Embracing him, Poli repeated over and over again, I love you, Morris, I love you. Then she would chatter about her dream of America. She hoped when she got to the city of Chicago —would he like to see the photo album of Chicago?—she would already know English. She was studying with a Mrs. Elbaum, who once had given English lessons in Warsaw. *How do you do? My name is Poli Cronowitz. I am sixteen years old. What is your name? Do you live in Chicago? My name is Poli Cohen. Mrs. Poli Cohen.* Then she laughed lightly and kissed his mouth. If you did sex with a Jewish girl, he wondered then, did you have to marry her? In Kolkowicz he had been told never to dishonor a Jewish woman. Had he dishonored Poli? *In Chicago there are tall buildings,* Poli Cronowitz said very crisply.

In the darkness of his room, Morris Cohen was aware of the smile on his mouth. A sweet moment, as he recalled it now. *My name is Poli Cronowitz. I am sixteen years old.* And I was Moishe Cohen, nineteen, so how could I do those things to such a nice Jewish girl?

With Livia Lundborg sex was pure pleasure without a hint of guilt. When she'd purchased a rebuilt bicycle, it hadn't occurred to him that this blond Swedish woman could be attracted to this tall Jewish boy. The next day, his boss sent him to Livia's house to take a look at the brake, which had been acting up. Morris Cohen rode his own bicycle to her redbrick house, where everything would happen.

They shared no language between them. She took his hand as soon as he entered the house, then led him to an upstairs bedroom. Undressed him. Laughed at the suddenness of his erection. Brought him to the pillow-laden bed, the first bed he'd seen that was longer than he was. There she gave him sex in such a way that Morris never again wondered about the mysteries of women. She had been made of molten gold, Livia Lundborg. She was perfect. He came to her twice a week, each time more wonderful than the last. He wondered what she was like, aside from sex—not a complaint, merely a curiosity. Had she been married? How old was this perfect woman? Thirty-five, forty? Her Swedish was almost always incomprehensible, and, for his part, Morris spoke in a Swedish so sparse that he could barely ask for a glass of water. Yet there was another strangeness: he easily gave her what she wanted of him. Her orgasms were so intense that Morris had to hold her hands away; the first time she had clawed his flesh and drawn blood. While they made love, Morris watched Livia and listened to her sudden cries. Watched her and molded himself to the desires of her body. He was with her, intensely, but he also was looking at her golden, glistening body from a distance. Even as he was deep into her beauty, Morris Cohen felt that he was *not* there. Somehow he had not been involved. Sex with Poli had never been as complete or satisfactory, the act always interrupted, although he had felt involved with her.

The news arrived more quickly than anticipated. HIAS had completed arrangements for Morris Cohen to go to the

United States, where his Uncle Axel with the grocery store on 9th Street would receive him. It was only the matter of a short flight to the Soviet Union and then the Trans-Siberian Railroad to Vladivostok. Finally a Japanese freighter to Seattle. America!

Poli was devastated. How could he leave her? Didn't he love her? Would they ever see each other again? Morris reassured her as best he could. Surely it wasn't far from New York to Chicago. Still, Poli wept. That night in his room her passion and anger raged. It had excited him. Poli demanded that he enter her. She wanted him to have her completely, to take love's prize, her precious flower, before he went off to the American Diaspora, to consecrate their love forever. She pulled his sex toward her openness. Morris pushed into her as deeply as he had into Livia, meeting her passion and anger with a sense of triumph. He poured his strength deeply into Poli Cronowitz, and she wept in his arms. He said, Shah! Shah! But in that moment he knew, despite his tenderness, that he did not love her.

He didn't depart Stockholm for two months. In that time Poli had announced she was pregnant, and he had continued his visits to Livia's house. Livia was married, he learned, her husband a volunteer member of the RAF in England. Morris did not tell Livia about Poli; nor, of course, did he tell Poli about Livia. He accepted the fact that he enjoyed sex with the dark Poli and the blond Livia without shame.

When the time came to leave Sweden, he was happy and relieved. The farewell to Livia was tender, not unhappy. It has been very good, she said. I will cherish these days, Morris. She gave him a pocket watch as a gift of remembrance. The days of parting from Poli were filled with pain. What shall I do? Poli wept one night in bed. What shall I do, Morris? Soon I will begin to show.

It's all right, Poli. We will marry.

With that Poli was contented with the wages and rewards

of passion and sin. The next day she revealed the situation to her short, round mother, who had said, simply, As long as he stands beneath the *chupah*. They were married in a brief ceremony attended by her mother and a handful of Sweden's transient Jews. *Mazel Tov! Mazel Tov!* and sweet wine all around! During their last night, as they were making love, he found himself distracted and thinking of Livia, which in turn had excited him. Poli had asked, as she always did, Morris, do you love me? And Morris had answered, Yes, Poli, I love you, as he had always answered.

When he arrived in Seattle, he had seventy-four American dollars left. HIAS provided a train ticket to New York, where Uncle Axel from 9th Street fell weeping into his arms. It was late June 1940. Morris Cohen was not yet twenty-one.

9.

Morris Cohen pulled his great frame out of the chair. He turned on all the lights, something he did each night. The house was in the center of his eighty acres and it pleased him to think that his was a beacon shining beneath the California night sky.

On the East Coast it was dinnertime, so he made his weekly calls to his daughters: To Carrie in Westport, Connecticut. To Emily in Rye, New York. He always felt strange making these phone calls and had to summon up his maximum robust, hearty, loving, information-seeking self. Not too different from the images he was called on to project at negotiations and in various business and administrative matters. The deadly charm of Big Moe.

Speaking to his daughters always brought his son, Marcus, to mind with regret and bitterness. Carrie and Emily were tall, dark women he found dull and proper. They were in every sense the offspring of their mother. In them he could find nothing of himself. They had married very average young men, for whom he had provided enough capital to establish careers. Carrie's ex-husband, Charles, had a small chain of major-appliance shops. There was one child, a surprisingly lively boy. He enjoyed seeing him, though twice a year was about the average. Emily's husband, Wallace, was Catholic and as successful as a chiropractor could be. Boring, boring. They had a daughter from whom he received a weekly letter. *My Dear Grandfather*. Well, at least that one could print and spell. She was eleven. And a son, one year younger, who had a curved nose like his own, who giggled too much.

He suffered through the telephone babbling without a letdown in his paternal and grandfatherly energy. The end of all phone calls: When will you come East again, Daddy? Are you sure? Four weeks isn't so long! Miss you. Love you. He had hardly known them as children; as adults he knew them less. And Poli? He hadn't spoken with her in almost a year. Remarried—a dermatologist, retired—and living in West Palm. Sure that she'd made her match, Morris was pleased. Sometimes, some things turn out well.

He made a cup of coffee and thought about calling Cinci Adams. He'd given her a role in his last opus—a tiny woman but well formed and amusing to play with, an above-average sexual athlete. But, he sighed, not tonight. She could bring him no comfort. What would, what could? More and more he found himself in the grip of a vicious, relentless depression. Maybe it was his age. But he had the strength of a bull! He had conquered Hollywood! The King of Horror—a position even Hitchcock admired. *Well, Moe, you have the good sense not to refine what you do. Whenever I find myself aesthetically trapped in a scene, I ask myself, Well, what would Moe do. Then I do the proper gauche thing. You, sir, are a buccaneer standing on a mountain of shit!* And Morris had smiled at the round-faced man. *Alfred, the only difference between you and me is the size of the mountain.*

He put his hand on the phone. Maybe Cinci? No. He walked out to the patio with its blazing lights and gazed up at the star-filled skies winking down at his illuminated refuge. He looked upward and shouted: Here I am, Moishe Cohen from Kolkowicz! What am I doing here? How did I get here? Tell me, God, is this a real place?

And although God might not have spoken, the answer came to Morris Cohen as surely and coldly as the starlight. This was not a real place. This place of lights, the beaming house, the sparkling pool, the shining stream where a flashing trout suddenly leapt—all this was weightless as a dream. Only what was real? Kolkowicz? The graves? The forest was certainly real. At the edge of the forest the dreams had begun. Each day they grew and gathered speed.

America was a dream, and everything in America was a dream! There was the dream of his uncle's grocery store. Had Axel gotten rich from bags and cans and bottles? Coca-Cola. This was a name known in Kolkowicz. Campbell's Soup. Such a royal name for a soup. Heinz Ketchup. Only in America such a name! Del Monte Herring in Tomato Sauce. What did Del Monte know from herring? Kellogg's Corn Flakes. Sustenance made of cobwebs and rainbows, smoke and mirrors. And like smoke Morris Cohen had drifted through each day, living dreams within dreams.

The sideshow mirrors! The fatherhood dream—and here comes round Poli with the bundled, circumcised dream whose name is Marcus. The sex dream! Poli receives all of him now in a dream, and in the dream he hurts her. The American dream: a daughter named Carrie, of whom a dream neighbor says, *Carrie. That's an American name.* The home dream! Five freshly painted rooms at 649 East 9th Street, corner of Avenue C. Beds floated in through the windows; tables and chairs rose up out of the floors; the dresser drawers filled up.

The big dream of enterprise! Dreaming Uncle Axel comes

out from behind the store counter and says, *Moishe, I have a bicycle partner for you. A place on 26th Street!* And, lo and behold, there is such a place. Bicycles bought, sold, rented, repaired! And WE ALSO REPAIR ALL TYPES OF MACHINES. The machinery of dreams purrs, an endless hymn.

The HIAS dream! My mother, Miriam Cohen, is there any word? *No, Morris, no word. You don't have to come to the office, Morris. If there is word, we will call you on the telephone.* But this is a dream. I come to you on dream feet. My mother, is there any word? The dream of war. The Japanese drop bombs on Pearl Harbor and all the trees in the grave-filled forest fall down. *You are too tall. You're not in the army, Mr. Cohen. That's a sad story about your mother, but we'll look for her.*

Dream of the big bank! *Morris! Morris! Hand over fist! Look at this! The bottom line, it piles up like Russian snow in the winter! Partner, my partner, we are rich! From bicycles and all types of machines we are rich!* Yes, the dream of the dead partner. Walter Berkstein, partner of Morris Cohen, passed away on October 23, 1944—heart attack—at the age of sixty-seven. Lawyers come with dream papers, and they say, *Sign here, Morris Cohen.* The lawyers say, *We have given the widow her share. You're the boss, so here's the bill.*

America was filled with bicycles, and each one needed parts and repairs. On birthdays and major holidays, every child in America needed a new bicycle! Singer sewing machines with foot treadles or electric motors—every American woman had one. Every kind of machine ever sold needed to be fixed. In a big parade, with a thousand electric fans blowing like trumpets, the bicycles marched with the sewing machines into Morris Cohen's shop. Day and night, night and day, Morris was there with his two workmen, his six workmen, his twelve workmen. When he got home the children were asleep, Poli half asleep. In the large bed she was content to be close to him; he, too, was satisfied with that.

But he could hear the cannon outside Kolkowicz. Dream cannon, dream flashes of artillery that emitted no sound, the *Daily News* reporting the dream. From the East come the Russians, from the West come the Germans; to the East go the Germans, out go the Russians. And Poland—where is Poland, and where are the Jews? What is Auschwitz? Dream feet walking from 26th Street to 9th Street. Dream smoke. Floating dream. Where is Miriam Cohen? Dream soup, the taste of Kolkowicz. Morris on dreamy feet carrying the tray through the door to the man in the corner. He is Theodor Herzl. He is shaking his blue tin beggar's cup. The bomb falls. Wollach's mill explodes, and Cohen's restaurant along with it. The dream blows away and lets in the wind. Another dream. Theodor Herzl shakes his cup. The RAF flies. Lieutenant Lundborg fires at the lead Heinkel. Lundborg explodes. Livia weeps. The Fox Movie-Tone world turns over. Wading ashore, the Japanese splash the dream waters with their papier-mâché dream boots. The Nips carry their smoking zeros under their arms. Unpiloted bicycles roll through the shop doors. Red, white, and blue ribbons flow out over the needle plates of a million sewing machines. The workmen fight their way through the stringy red, white, and blue confetti. The Japanese are singing: *Banzai Apple Pie!* Pearl Harbor goes up while the U.S. Navy goes down, and Davey Jones sings dreamily: *Subcontract! My Uncle Sam needs you, Morris. Make a million dream widgets. Deliver them tomorrow. For Miriam Cohen's sake! Win the war and make a fortune! But don't go to the bathroom. Pissing is not permitted during work hours!*

Meanwhile: *Morris, I am pregnant with a girl named Emily.* Poli, when did I *shtup* Poli? *Good! We will move to Long Island, Poli. We will buy a house near a temple! I am a rich man. I live in a dream filled with banks. I am a subcontractor punching out nine-pronged widgets.* Omaha invasion dream. Silent armada. Rafts of corpses crashing ashore, the dead lapped by foaming waters where white bones ring like bells.

Once I built a tower to the sun. . . . The sky is falling. The air is burning. The napalm is bubbling. Poof, Coventry! Voilà, Dresden! *Auf Wiedersehen,* thousand-year dream! *Sayonara,* dreamers of Hiroshima! *Mamenyu, Mamenyu, are you the bones which once carried you, are you the ashes scattered across the fields, are you the light-gray smoke lost inside the rain?*

Morris Cohen sucked in the warm air of the Valley. He said to himself, as he so often had said: I should not have left you, Mama! There was room in the wagon, Mama.

10.

The ringing phone prickled his skin. When the phone rang out here, it was almost always a crisis call from one of his children, or from Archer Doty, his CEO, and that only if the studio was in flames. Only a few people had this number, and they did not include Poli or the President of the United States. Of course, a tape machine was permanently engaged: *This is Morris. I am out of town or out of the country. Leave your message and where you can be reached. Wait for the beep.*

Beep. Morris, this is Hal Wiederspiel. When you get this I'll be—

Morris picked up the phone and cut off the machine. Hal! Morris shouted with a surge of good feeling. What's happening? It's a long time! How are you?

Getting older. I'm fine. What about you?

Same shit.

Horror?

Horror.

Losing or winning?

At all the wrong things I win. You're calling about money.

That, too.

You got it. For what did I pledge? Don't laugh, Helmut. I just gave John Wayne a taste, but I knew what I gave for.

I always tell you, Moe. I have a bunch of nuclear physicists who've convinced me they can bring in a nuclear fusion process.

Am I supposed to understand this, Hal?

Yes. It's the opposite of fission. Oh, shit. A process that allows the production of nuclear energy with no radioactive waste and no production dangers.

I'm not big enough for nuclear games, Hal.

What I need is a small amount to develop some papers and have a few meetings. That's when I'll need the heavy money—and you're right. Only governments can play.

Israel?

Yes, full partner. If we succeed, fossil fuel's the twentieth-century dinosaur, and the cost of energy falls ninety-five percent. Plus, the Arabs are out of business.

How much?

A hundred and fifty thousand.

Millions, I thought you were going to say. Where do I send it?

My post office box in Orford. You have the address?

Yes. And when do I get to see you?

A half hour later, when he put down the phone, Morris Cohen felt elated. God, how he loved that man!

11.

He found himself smiling as he turned on the sound system, selected the Israeli Symphony's recording of Mozart's *Die Zauberflöte* and said aloud: Mama, what a life this is! Look at your son in California. Rich and, in a way, famous. People already complain about me, Mama. They want me to do bigger things—well, that's not exactly true. That's part of the publicity: What will the King of Horror do next? Ah, Mama, you don't know what publicity is? In America, dear mother, if you're the government or you have a big business or lots of money, you buy all the press, newspapers, radio, and television you can afford. Even when they know you're lying, they'll print what you say. There are so many lies in the world today, Mama, that nobody even has the time to count them. So in my business I have a publicity department that tells all the lies that are good for Big MAC Pictures. So, what will the King of Horror do next? Let's say we'll do a beautiful, serious film with Marilyn Monroe starring as the virgin queen—a lie. But no more Draculas, no more werewolves. No more aliens from Mars. Just beautiful films, Mama!

What he had very much wanted to do was a film about Helmut William Wiederspiel, an American Jew, widely known as the Dutchman. But what he got from Hal was a broad smile and a joke. *Ask Moshe Dayan—he'll love it!*

Listening to Mozart, Morris Cohen recalled the day early in 1947 when Wiederspiel entered his plant on 26th Street. At that time, more than a hundred workers were employed by MAC Machinery to assemble and pack the components arriving from Japan. Wiederspiel, a former major general in the U.S. Air Force, had walked directly into the shop and watched the workers assembling machines on order. Morris had spotted him from his mezzanine office and immediately went down to the factory floor. Are you Wiederspiel, he asked.

Wiederspiel had nodded and then put a number of questions to Cohen about changes that had been made in the design and function of the machines being assembled. For almost an hour they had spoken about machines and motors.

You know a lot about these things, Morris had said.

I'm a mechanic. I used to fix cars when I was a kid in Orford. I was born to be a mechanic.

You're still a mechanic, Wiederspiel.

I have an airplane company.

You make airplanes?

Trouble shooter. Test pilot for airlines and manufacturers. Overhaul and rebuild wrecks. Things.

Wiederspiel said this so naturally that Cohen became wary. How can a Jew be in the airplane business?

In a restaurant down the street, Wiederspiel explained his business over lunch. There was reason to believe that within months the United Nations would pass resolutions permitting the establishment of a Jewish state in Palestine. Wiederspiel said this as if he were discussing the future of sewing machines, but Cohen felt his heart leap into his mouth. This is for real? he said.

Wiederspiel nodded. There's a very good chance. Truman wants it. I need your help, Morris.

How much?

No, no. I need more than that.

What?

You. I have been meeting with David Ben-Gurion. He thinks it will not be easy. When the U.N. passes the statehood resolution, a lot of hot shit's going to hit the fan. So while we're waiting, I'm putting together a sort of support operation. Israel—the state of Israel—will need lots of help, you see. Things.

Cohen's eyes filled with tears. What do you want me to do?

I'm not sure. But your shop might be useful to make stuff. *Things.*

Anything you ask, Cohen said in Yiddish.

Thank you, Morris. Wiederspiel pressed Morris's huge hand, then went back to talking about motors. He had an idea about reducing the vibrations, and Cohen knew it was perfectly sound. Son of a bitch, Hal, I swear you are a fucking mechanic!

Believe me, Morris, that's my true profession.

It happened as Wiederspiel had said. With Truman's support, the United Nations passed a resolution for the establishment of a Jewish state in November 1947. The Arab states ringing the U.N.-designated area quickly positioned their armies and warned the Jews that no such state would be acceptable. In May, Ben-Gurion convoked an assembly of Jews which pronounced the existence of the state of Israel, and a few days later Wiederspiel asked Morris Cohen to manufacture bazookas. Design plans arrived the next day, and within a month a group of Cohen's men had produced a thousand bazookas. Three trailer trucks rolled onto 26th Street, and by dawn the trucks had been loaded and were rolling away.

In the fall of that year, Helmut William Wiederspiel had asked Morris Albert Cohen to come to California to set up a small manufacturing plant. In fewer than three days, Moe had placed the management of MAC Machinery in the hands of Louis Shute, his first executive officer. It was the first time he'd delegated any major responsibility, and he'd done it without hesitation.

In a small, freestanding building outside Chico, Cohen geared up a little armaments industry for the embattled State of Israel. Together with six men and two women, Los Angeles Jews, he fashioned rigs and jigs and workbenches that produced mainly spare parts for rifles and artillery pieces, and a few for airplanes—all designed by Wiederspiel, who would drop into the Chico shop every other week, always managing to work at the bench himself.

How the products he turned out got to Israel, Morris did not know. Either a vehicle came to make a pickup or he dispatched his own truck to some anonymous location. Once he'd driven a shipment himself to a hangar on the perimeter of the Los Angeles airport, where it had been quickly off-loaded onto one of Helmut's reconstructed commercial airliners. It had been a little after 3:00 a.m. The rebuilt plane had taxied out slowly with no lights, found a runway, rolled up to speed, and disappeared into the sky. Cohen's heart had thumped with an unknown pride. For Israel, he had murmured into the engine-purring darkness. It had been Wiederspiel who set all this into motion. Helmut William Wiederspiel, a Jew for great occasions.

By year's end Cohen was able to return to New York. MAC Machinery had thrived under the direction of Louis Shute. Feeling redundant in both endeavors—the fight for Israel and the small industrial wars—Cohen became depressed. From a psychologist he got a little help; from a psychiatrist he acquired a prescription for Valium, but it made him feel too dopey and he gave it up. He started an affair with Dottie Kumel, a bosomy young artist in his marketing department. She was not sexually interesting, willing to lend herself to any of his needs or inventions but like a child committing a delinquency. After a few months it had become plain that Miss Kumel had serious things such as marriage on her mind, though Morris quickly disabused her of that notion. When she said it might be best for her to leave the company, since everybody knew about them, Morris agreed this was a good idea. He sent her on a luxurious trip to Bermuda, then bought her a well-established chocolate shop in Greenwich Village. She wept for joy.

On July 20, 1949, the war against the Arab League ended when Israel signed an armistice with Syria. Similar accords had been signed with Lebanon, Egypt, and Trans-Jordan. On October 7, 1951, Morris Cohen was indicted by a grand jury in California for high crimes and misdemeanors—a case known as *The United States* v. *Helmut William Wiederspiel et al.* Morris Albert Cohen could hardly restrain his joy! Maybe, if someone from Kolkowicz was still alive, he would say, Do you see what Moishe Cohen has done for Israel, for the Jews? It is a great thing he has done! We should forgive him for being rich and famous and alive!

In February 1952, Cohen sat with the others in the federal courtroom. Although the bill of particulars against the de-

fendants was as sensational as it was long, it had been presented in a songless monotone. Cohen managed a smile,
though, when the shop in Chico had been cited.

The defense attorney didn't dispute the hundred-odd
charges against Helmut William Wiederspiel et al. Instead
he made an impassioned speech about the circumstances,
about the war, about Hitler and the deaths of the six million,
about the anguish and pain of anti-Semitism, and about Jews
living in actual and historical exile from their ancient homeland, not to mention the U.N. resolution, the establishment
of the State of Israel, the perfidious attack of the Arab states,
and in consequence the defense of the new state by Jews
from every corner of the earth, and in particular the Jews
from the United States. It was an extraordinary speech, and
many in the courtroom wept. For himself, Morris Cohen had
restrained his strong impulse to applaud.

Next came a parade of Hollywood character witnesses for
Hal Wiederspiel, more than a dozen taking the stand and a
hundred more in deposition: Danny Kaye, Clark Gable, Bette
Davis, John and Lionel Barrymore, Greta Garbo, Ludwig
Donath, Chico, Harpo, and Groucho Marx, Louis B. Mayer,
and two Hungarian directors whose names Cohen did not
quite catch.

This was not a jury trial, and the judge explained he would
announce the sentence in five days—an interval filled with
receptions and parties, mainly around swimming pools.
Wiederspiel insisted on introducing Cohen as the well-
known film producer, so of course he became a point of
intense interest to directors, writers, executives, and starlets.
Before the five days had passed, Morris had been to bed with
three of the most beautiful bodies in the world.

What do you think of Hollywood, Morris? Hal had said.

Crazy, Morris answered, but I think I'll open a branch out
here.

High on his bench, the judge pronounced Helmut William

Wiederspiel et al., eighteen men and women, guilty as charged of high crimes and misdemeanors ranging from treason against the United States (a required technicality) to the illegal manufacture of arms, the flying of planes without license or clearance within and without the borders of the United States of America, the forging of various federal and state documents, dealing in contraband, smuggling both goods and persons, etc. For the defendant Wiederspiel, death by firing squad and one thousand, one hundred, and eight years in a federal penitentiary. Only Hal got the death penalty as well as an eternity in prison; the others had received somewhat shorter sentences.

After the judge had spoken, a great silence descended over the courtroom, then an excited undercurrent. The judge hammered his gavel for order, and silence again prevailed. Sentence, said the judge, is suspended. Cheers filled the air.

Less than a year later, Morris and Louis Shute established MAC Machinery of Los Angeles. Shortly after, Morris Albert Cohen went into the movie business, although he wasn't certain whether his sole reason for doing so wasn't to keep his bed warm. His first production, *The Mistress of Dracula*, was his own idea, concocted for a ripe starlet who gave marvelous head and cooked amazingly well. Her last chance, she'd said. Morris hired a twenty-two-year-old screenwriter who had been impressed by some of the producer's images. Then he hired a director whose credits consisted of two failed films. Cohen observed the production with interest but little excitement. Any of his suggestions were accepted with alacrity by both the director and the writer. When the fifteen-day shoot was completed, Cohen sat in the editing room and worked with Oscar Bellini, the cutter. Now this *was* exciting; the nonsense of the footage was turned into a flowing intelligence. Tawdry, perhaps, but except for one or two impossible sequences, not as incomprehensible as the writer and the director had made it.

Quietly released as the lesser half of double bills throughout the backlands, *The Mistress of Dracula* became a spoof-
able horror hit. *Your blood, my darling, is the best I have ever
drunk.* Vampire laughter. Blood trickling from the corners of
the mouth. In its first eighteen months, the picture earned
more money than MAC Machinery had in the previous two
years. This was Hollywood?

Two years later, Morris Albert Cohen sold the machinery
company to a Japanese firm for nine million dollars and
opened the offices of Big MAC Pictures. In the same year,
Hal had divested himself of his airplane business and made
Israel his permanent home. Twelve years later, in 1967, after
the Six-Day War, he acquired an apartment in Jerusalem
overlooking the Old City. On a quick business trip to Los
Angeles, he stayed at Morris's place in the Valley. Yet breakfast was the only time they could spare each other.

Listen, Morris told Wiederspiel over coffee, I'm what you
said I was. I'm a mogul. He placed a *Daily Variety* before
Wiederspiel. Look at that, he said. MAC PICTURES CHALKS
HUGE GROSSES; HORROR BELONGS TO KING COHEN. What
do you think of that, Hal?

I saw your last one. It's junk, of course. But you have the
touch, Moe. Sometimes you make my skin crawl.

You're right! When do I ever find you wrong?

Last year, twice. I know you made a donation to Menachem
Begin. It was also reported that you threw a party for Meir
Kahane.

Hal! You're a Labor man. I'm neutral. So what if Begin
wins? What if Kahane drives the Arabs into the sea and
becomes God? I'll have a direct line. Politics.

Not politics at all, Morris. Ego.

Cohen had snorted. *Ego?* What are you talking about? I
gave *your* people and *your* projects ten times as much. If it's
for Israel, I support it.

Morris, please! You will do what you want. I have no quarrel with you. Only remember this, Moe, Israel is not heaven. Just because you send money it doesn't mean God's saving you a golden seat. Israel is just a nation. It will be as good as Jews make it. I'm sure you're doing the best you can, Moe. We're all very grateful.

As much as he had tried to mask it, Wiederspiel was annoyed with him—not angry but annoyed. Talk about ego! Son of a bitch is a self-appointed angel! Fuck him! Yet there was something to say for angels: they forgive. So the telephone call from Wiederspiel was more than welcome. Why did he think that Hal was forgiving him—and why did he even think in such terms? Hadn't Morris already washed his sins away? Hadn't he fought for the Jewish state and saved thousands of Jewish lives?

But the boys of Kolkowicz were dead. His mother was dead. It was not his fault! Who could point a finger at him after all these years? He was the one who had lived in graves. He was that one! And although the house was filled with light, Morris felt as if he were again inside the dark forest of his youth. He undressed and went to bed, then used the master switch to plunge his house and his many acres into darkness.

12.

Morris Albert Cohen awoke at dawn. He did not remember what he had dreamed, but he had dreamed, and the dream had left him with a clear vision: an idea for a film. He had survived, he had been left alive, had been brought to bicycles, to sewing machines, to Hollywood, *only* to make this film!

Morris Cohen realized he was manic. After all these years, the answer had arrived. You *schmuck*, he shouted, you must make that film! In his silk pajamas he paced the floors of the house. The film filled his head, filled his body; it existed in the very breath he exhaled! He made notes on a yellow pad, and his neat, tiny handwriting decorated the pages. It was certainly doable, but everything had to be perfect. First things first.

Who would create the script? Who was capable of creating the design, the feeling, the integrity and grandeur? Cohen saw the Burning Bush with a name written in fire: Zachary Barthelmes!

In New York, Zachary Barthelmes answered his phone. Barthelmes, he said.

Zachary! Moe Cohen! How are ya?

Well, well, Moe! What did I do wrong? Kidding. How's the big man?

I'm in pretty good shape for the shape I'm in. So, you've gotten over the Oscar shock?

What shock, Moe? I won.

That didn't shock you? You do a great job, a really great job, and you won anyway. That's always a shock.

Barthelmes laughed. Well, I didn't expect it. And I haven't gotten a single job offer since I won.

So, you're living the real life.

Also no takers for the two originals I've been peddling.

They're on my desk. I like them both.

Are you saying you'll do them? One, maybe?

Not with you directing.

I *know* how to direct those pieces, Moe.

Nah. I don't like writers directing their own stuff.

And if I don't direct?

Then a very strong maybe. You there, Zachary?

I was lighting a cigarette. What makes it maybe?

A priority.

Priority? I'm not following, Moe.

First I want you to write me a script.

You son of a bitch. I want to do my own shit!

It's on my plate already, Zach. I have this job for you.

Don't tell me! Barthelmes said, his voice rising.

Temper, temper! First let me tell you about the deal.

No.

You do my deal, Zachary, then I'll back yours.

I direct?

Yes. You'll fuck it up, but yes. So?

Too easy. I'm no good at horror.

For horror I don't come to you, Zachary. This one's artsy-fartsy.

Ah, the secret shame of Morris Albert Cohen.

Why should I deny it? I'd rather do good films.

Who's stopping you?

Cheap shot, Zachary.

Yeah, it is. I'm sorry. Okay, what do you have in mind?

A major film about Theodor Herzl.

One-legged third baseman for the St. Louis Browns, 1943? The schizophrenic catcher for the Washington Senators? Okay, I give up.

The great Jewish leader. He did the groundwork for Israel, Zachary. Herzl was famous even without him writing the book, *The Jewish State.*

Laughter.

I'm serious, Zachary.

All right. Sorry. But why are you picking on me? I'm not even Jewish.

So what are you, an Indian? You won your Oscar for *Geronimo.*

Moe, that's different. Every writer's got to do at least one cowboys-and-Indians picture. I just got lucky with mine.

You won the Oscar because everybody said *Geronimo* had to be written by an Indian. At least a guy with Indian blood.

I know that's a compliment, Moe, but I think there is a difference.

Which is what?

Well, all Harvard-educated Americans have strong guilt feelings about the Indians.

But not about Jews?

I have a better feel for native Americans.

Listen, you can write about some Apache with an axe and feathers, so why not a Jew with a beard and a top hat?

Laughter.

Am I breaking you up here?

Yes. Listen, Moe, you can offer this project to six different Jewish writers with at least twenty Oscars among them.

I want you.

Seriously, Moe. Why not one of them?

Like you said, twenty Oscars and not one of them has ever put a Jew in a script.

I see. Well, look, Moe, thanks. Bad timing. I'm going off on a vacation.

When you come back.

I'll be away a year. I'm tired. And I promised my lady.

You still with that one—what's her name?

Kalia.

Take my deal, Zachary.

No. No. Big final no.

Why not?

Told you, Moe. It's not my thing. I'm taking a year off. Don't you *ever* take no for an answer?

All the time. Listen, I just thought of the answer.

Jesus Christ!

The truth, Zachary—I'm giving you the answer.

Moe!

Go on vacation. I'll front the expenses.

I'm not working that year, Moe. That's what gentiles call a vacation—not working.

I'll pay you one hundred fifty thousand not to say no.

Barthelmes whistled. A hundred and fifty thousand dollars for *that*? Not to say no for one year?

You'll have the money tomorrow. Don't say no, Zachary.

What about *my* projects?

You write mine, I'll produce yours. You pick which one.

Who directs?

You.

You're killing me, Moe. You're killing me! One-fifty, one year, not to refuse.

Yes or no?

Jesus, let me talk to Kalia for a minute.

Morris Cohen exhaled into the silent phone. His knuckles went white as he tightened his grip on the phone. Dead air. Are you still there, Barthelmes?

The phone sprang loudly to life. Yes, you bastard, *yes*!

Morris Albert Cohen put the phone gently down into its cradle, then leapt out of his chair. The fish is hooked! he shouted. I hooked the fucking fish!

PART TWO

1.

As they walked toward David Ben-Gurion, the old man smiled broadly and opened his arms. Helmut William Wiederspiel entered his embrace; they kissed each other twice, this cheek, that cheek.

How are you, Wiederspiel? You look wonderful, wonderful!

I feel fine, Ben-Gurion, and you look like a boy.

Flattery won't work. I am old. I am retired. I am powerless. Why have you come? Not that you need a reason to come. But would you come without a reason?

Sure I would, but I have a reason. This fellow is a friend of Moishe Cohen. You remember Moishe?

I forget many things now. But to forget Cohen is like forgetting Mount Sinai. Moishe Cohen I have not yet forgotten. You know the other day I forgot Weizmann's name. I kept saying, The first President, the first President, until someone said his name. Now if someone says to me, Ben-Gurion, you remember, you remember! I reply, Chaim Weizmann. Everybody laughs. But it is a terrible thing to forget. What if I forget the founding of the State and the Liberation War? So, tell me, dear Wiederspiel, why have you come?

This is Zachary Barthelmes. Moishe wants him to write a film about Theodor Herzl.

I'm thinking about it, Barthelmes said, nothing definite.

Ben-Gurion's wiry white hair was swept back by the desert wind. The old man took Zachary's hand into his own and patted it. Tell me, why do you want to write about Herzl? Why not me? I'm important!

The last syllable seemed to get lost in a wind gust. Of

course, Barthelmes said. But on this visit I'm looking for information about Herzl.

You can read all about Herzl from books. What's your name?

Barthelmes.

Barthelmes. What kind of name is that? Barthelmes. There is the well-known story that, when Herzl came to our *shtetl* in Poland, he stopped by our house. My father was a leading socialist Zionist, you know. Herzl picked me up, put me on his knee, and gave me a little horsey ride.

Is that true, Barthelmes asked.

How should I know? Not that I have forgotten it. I simply have never remembered it. However, my father always claimed it was absolutely true. That makes me famous, Barthelmes. That's why there is a movement to go to Mount Sinai and carve out the heads of me, Wiederspiel, and Herzl.

Barthelmes laughed along with Wiederspiel, who then said, Ben-Gurion, tell the man something.

What? I am not an authority. Have you been to the Herzl Institute in Jerusalem?

Yes.

They can tell you everything.

One of the institute scholars told me Herzl was a sort of historical flake—a high roller at the crap table of history, I believe is how he put it. Confidentially, of course.

What do they know! Ben-Gurion snorted. A bunch of Yeshiva *bucher* fund-raisers! Everybody has an opinion these days.

And you?

Ben-Gurion turned away, and his jaw tightened. Indeed I have an opinion, Barthelmes. Theodor Benjamin Herzl was the greatest Jew since Moses.

That's a big statement, Ben-Gurion, Barthelmes said in a soft voice.

Big, small—it is simply a true statement. He was the greatest Jew since Moses.

Okay, can you give me some reasons?

I can give you a bunch of reasons. But I'll give you one: he made one people out of the Jews. Listen, said David Ben-Gurion, I can't help you. I don't know enough to give answers. And, no offense, you don't know enough to ask questions.

Barthelmes laughed. I would like to make a movie about you.

Make one about the Dutchman here. About Wiederspiel you can make a good movie. Take it from me, Wiederspiel is the second greatest Jew since Moses.

After some cake and tea, they said good-bye. On the way back, Barthelmes turned to Wiederspiel. Did you hear what the old man said, Hal?

You mean the bit about the most important Jew since Moses?

Yes.

That is what he believes.

And you?

He was great, all right. Look what he set in motion.

Zachary looked out the window of the car as they rolled away from Seder Boker, the kibbutz in the Negev where David Ben-Gurion lived. The dunes and sand gave way to scrub growth, ragged trees, and small, shabby settlements. Is this what he set in motion?

Yes, Zachary, this.

It doesn't look like much, if you don't mind my saying so.

Wiederspiel smiled. It is everything, he said. Shall I drop you at the hotel?

No, I'm meeting Kalia in Jaffa.

2.

Barthelmes sat at a small, round table facing the sea. There was very little ice remaining in his glass—it was over ninety—but the scotch was still cold. Kalia was late again, and her hopeless sense of time gave him breathing space.

He was annoyed, an annoyance edged with anger. At whom was he angry? Himself, probably. He had allowed Moe to manipulate him. Flattery and a bundle of money will buy you practically anything; myself included, Barthelmes thought. Pressure—*Moe's* pressure—was making itself felt even here in Yafo. Wasn't that the idea behind the meeting with Ben-Gurion and the tours personally guided by Helmut Wiederspiel? Barthelmes fawned upon by heroes! These things to get him emotionally involved, to get him to commit to writing the film now, not just to think about it for a year. Fucking Moe with his Byzantine Jewish mind! Well, Barthelmes thought, I'm going to stick to the deal exactly as we made it. I won't say no for a year. And you can sweat that out, Mr. Cohen.

Swallowing some of his drink, he sensed a smile forming on his lips. Maybe the Israeli sun had touched him with paranoia. Maybe it was his own mind that had fallen into Byzantine patterns. Still, he was not going to be a Babe trapped in Jew Land. In the end, it was he who controlled the situation. The filmic life of the Big Jew, Theodor Herzl, was in the hands of Zachary Barthelmes.

He looked at the sea. He could not quite accept water so blue and transparent. The color was a little bit too pastel even for a nineteenth-century English countryside film. He narrowed his eyes against the sun echoing up from the lapping surface of the Mediterranean, and the gently rocking sea engulfed the lingering traces of his annoyance.

Herzl came ashore here in the autumn of 1898, but exactly where did the passengers disembark from the Cook longboat? Barthelmes looked to his right along the shoreline. The longboat had probably tied up against one of the stone landing docks, now crumbling into the sea. The *Russia* had sailed from Alexandria and struck anchor perhaps a quarter of a mile out on the painted sea. Herzl, wearing a cork pith helmet and dressed in English riding clothes, was one of the debarking passengers. The day had been extremely hot, and he was sweating. Barthelmes imagined the air of ancient Yafo as filled with dust and jazzy colors that denied the poverty shouting through the shabby streets of the port.

Topaz blue, a sea composed of blue air. A sky of a sea. In Herzl's diary there was no mention of the color of the waters off Jaffa. If he had been keeping a journal, Barthelmes thought, he certainly would have noted the quality of the Mediterranean that day. But it was the stifling heat that had gripped Herzl's attention. (Could it have been hotter than it was today?)

Herzl had shared the cabin on the *Russia* with four companions, and at night he had dragged his mattress up to the deck to sleep under the stars; the others had, too, Barthelmes supposed. A small cabin, probably tiered beds. A proper toilet or special latrines that emptied directly into the sea? Where did they dress and undress? Barthelmes laughed as he imagined the cabin at night. Five Zionists in white linen nightshirts pacing the small cabin floor, smoking long black cigars, and squeezing by each other to get to the WC. Replace Theodor Herzl with Groucho Marx, bring in the brothers, and there you have a scene for a true historical film. Did anyone fart?

Barthelmes ordered another scotch and wondered whether he was already getting bored with Moe Cohen's great idea. Helmut Wiederspiel probably would make a better movie; Hal was larger than life. But wasn't Theodor Benjamin Herzl? Barthelmes pondered that. Maybe he was important only to Jews, and a small number at that. Maybe, probably, Herzl had been made important by latter-day revisionist historians and mindless aficionados. Why would the greatest Jew since Charlton Heston share a cabin on the odorous *Russia* with four other guys in nightshirts? Big drama for Herzl was a meeting, a diary entry, or, in this case, an arduous trip. He was larger than life, but only in his mind—and how

do you film the mind's excitement? Helmut William Wiederspiel, on the other hand, was drama and action itself. A
builder of things from childhood. He would look at the face
of a clock and understand its wheels and gears. Planes flew
because the pilot Wiederspiel had built them. If there was
an army, Wiederspiel marched with it. He could kill his enemy. He loved women, and they loved him back. Cohen told
Zachary that he'd once asked him, How do you get all these
beautiful women into your bed. You're no movie star, no
international film mogul. What are these beauties, Zionists?
When there were free days, empty days, Wiederspiel sailed
a small boat or hunted deer near Orford, New Hampshire,
where he had a house on the Connecticut River.

Wiederspiel was neither handsome nor unhandsome. His
soft speech never hinted of his physical toughness. His will-
ingness to act seemed simple and uncomplicated. His ability
to suffer the Talmudic treks of his Zionist comrades and then
cut quickly to the heart of the matter was quite well known.
There was also the mysterious Wiederspiel smile. If Mona
Lisa had a brother, it would have been the Dutchman. He
had not been sent into history by central casting, Barthelmes
thought, but he *was* larger than life.

A Herzl film . . . difficult. The passion of Morris Albert
Cohen. What with almost all the Marx Brothers dead, maybe
too serious. Wiederspiel, four stars; Herzl, all eclipse! Passion
makes fools of us all. Barthelmes sighed. Well, he didn't have
to make the film. Moe Cohen had paid him only to *consider*
writing the script. *Listen, you can write about some Apache
with an axe and feathers, so why not a Jew with a beard and
a top hat?* Moe's check had arrived at his apartment the next
day by courier, in an envelope taped to the top of a carton
of books about Theodor Benjamin Z'ev Herzl. Not to say no
for one year! Son of a bitch. Well, thought Zachary Barthelmes, I've already earned that; earned it and banked it.

At least Kalia was having a ball in Israel, and sex at the

Basel was beautiful. Barthelmes smiled at his thought. He had never enjoyed sex so much as when he was traveling. Sex was always better away from home. Why was that?

3.

Kalia sat down. I'm so glad you're still here! Sorry I'm late.

That's okay. I was enjoying myself.

You met another woman. A Yemenite with a diamond in her belly button.

Yemenites don't put diamonds in their buttons.

A rich Seventh-Day Adventist tourist on her sixth day?

Exactly, and I screwed her right under this table.

Under this very table?

Yes. This very.

Well, I'm glad she's gone. My feet are killing me. I bought some great sandals in Tel Aviv. I should've worn them instead of these. Kalia kicked off her high-heeled shoes. When the waiter came, she ordered a Perrier with two slices of lime and ice, to the very top.

Why hadn't he been able to get his scotch that way, Barthelmes wondered.

Because you're not cute enough, Kalia said, pinching his cheek.

Once more Barthelmes engaged the sea.

What are you thinking, Zach, Kalia asked after a while.

I'm thinking, he said, that if Teddy boy is the most important Jew since Moses, which is what Ben-Gurion said, then Jaffa is the most important port since the earth began.

I love it here. *Yafo.*

Zachary turned from the sea and looked hard at Kalia. Sometimes, he said, you're such a smart ass. He knew I was considering doing the Herzl film. So Ben-Gurion says he's the greatest Jew since Custer was on the range. What do *you* think? Did he say that to encourage me or, slyly, kill the picture?

Maybe neither. Maybe he believed it. I can accept that, but the idea that he made one people out of the Jews? Too silly.

Barthelmes laughed. Too silly?

Well, my darling, just look around, and you'll see that nobody can bring the Jews together. That's why they're my favorite people. Take the Russians—I don't mean Eskimos, but those White Russians in Moscow. They're all *so* Russian. From sex to socks to vodka on the rocks.

Cute.

Once a copywriter, always a copywriter.

And what do *you* know about Russian sex?

I read a book.

Cute.

Very seriously, Zach. Only God—on the eighth day—can make one people of the Jews. They don't look alike. They don't even sound alike. They don't think alike. They don't agree on very much either.

Except that they *are* Jews and they are here.

Maybe, before Herzl, they didn't even accept that, Kalia said, and as she sipped her Perrier, her eyes seemed to darken.

A senior vice presidency for your thoughts, Zachary said.

She shook her head. For now let's just say I'm a Jew lover. I love each and every one of them. In their crazy diversities.

Don't worry. I won't tell your Ku Klux Klan father.

Across the stone floor of the outdoor deck she indicated to the waiter that she wanted another Perrier. We've already been here two weeks, she said to Barthelmes, so what do you think? To movie or not to movie?

If Moe Cohen committed a huge, *huge* budget, I'd tilt toward yes. But you know Moe.

Penny-pinching Jew?

No. A wild gambler who knows the reality of things. Can

you imagine financing a film about Herzl, and a big film at that? A dozen countries. Costumes by the thousands. Armies. Palaces. Spectacle unto the highest.

Hallelujah! Hallelujah! So why not make a small film—a chamber film, maybe even a documentary?

Barthelmes frowned. I don't think so. Small isn't Herzl, and documentaries I don't do. I'm also sure that's not what Moe had in mind. Look out there, Kale. See that freighter on the horizon?

Yes.

Now imagine that it's lying closer to the shore.

Check.

A Cook longboat, passengers coming down a fixed ladder, oarsmen rowing toward the shore.

So you're writing the movie!

No. I just want to give you an idea of the size. It's late October 1898. Hot, hot day. Some of the port you see now is just the way it was almost a hundred years ago. But a lot of it's going to have to be rebuilt if we're making a movie.

You could cheat, Zachary, my love.

What my pictures don't do is lie. You know why Herzl was here? Zachary said. He came to Palestine to meet Kaiser Wilhelm II.

Wouldn't a meeting in *Deutschland* do? Ah, I see! Herzl and Wilhelm were gay, and they needed a faraway secret closet!

Okay, smart ass, I won't bore you.

Sorry, Zach. I'm just so high about being here at all that everything comes out in jokes. Forgive me now, and tonight I'll fuck your head off.

So why's tonight different from all other nights?

Really, Zach, I know you're sharing all this with me, and I appreciate it.

What? I'm talking out loud here, that's all.

Barthelmes looked out at the sea. I believe that Ben-Gurion was probably right, Kale. That Herzl was a huge figure—

bigger than himself, bigger than Wiederspiel. I think he accepts that and resents it a little. Maybe a lot.

With difficulty Kalia suppressed a smile.

Barthelmes noticed this and smiled broadly. Maybe, he continued, the Jews are just overly sensitive about the possibility of false prophets. They've had a few, you know. The most famous one, Shabbetai something, operated in the mid-seventeenth century. They don't want to think of Herzl as a genuine prophet in case he turns out to be false.

How can he turn out to be false, Zach, when we're drinking Perrier in Israel?

Or worse, but what if he really was—in the biblical sense—a prophet? No problem for me, but maybe for the Jews. Saints and prophets, I think, are always problems. My problem is this: how does a prophet live? What does he *feel*?

Barthelmes lit an Israeli cigarette. For an instant the smoke floated between them; then a breeze pushed it over the stone wall, where it hung for a moment as a tiny gray cloud. Can I capture that on film? Or will I create a silly figure? Risky business, you see.

I see. So you tilt away.

Yep. I waffle and straddle, my basic nature. I can't commit. I don't know how to commit. Deeply, as they like to say.

I love you anyway, Zach my darling. Besides, we'll marry, and that's the biggest commitment there is.

These days, no.

You're a son of a bitch, Zachary! Kalia put on her shoes, gathered her bags, and left him sitting at the table looking at the sea.

4.

Barthelmes had not intended to upset Kalia; neither had he wanted to censor himself. And what was *commitment* supposed to mean? To Kalia even marriage wasn't a big enough commitment. No, for her it had to take place on a mountaintop in the presence of weeping angels. She had no doubt, although she'd been married twice before, that each time it was for eternity. If you couldn't commit for eternity, then what was commitment at all—a five-year deal, or five minutes?

He turned back to Herzl and the sea. Yafo. That had to be a big scene: from the landing through the meeting with the Kaiser, events, Jerusalem, reactions, Herzl (unlike Moses) actually in the Promised Land, business, more events, and then the departure from Palestine at night. This could be the heart of the film. Filled with color and dust and spectacle. To meet an emperor. How would that play? Barthelmes closed his eyes. Coming ashore, Herzl goes to a hotel. But which one, and did it still stand? His onshore contact had not secured transportation. Herzl had an appointment at Mikveh Israel, an agricultural school, so he decides to go on horseback. He did ride, though there's no accounting for how he learned, but his companions couldn't. Finally, a carriage is procured. Okay, maybe Herzl rides to Mikveh on horseback. I'll put the son of a bitch on a horse. Quite untrue, but much more filmic. Why not give Herzl that great *Lawrence of Arabia* look? Sand flying, dunes and scrub, hooves beating. Reveal something essential in his character without especially distorting history. So long as I don't put him on a white donkey, who can complain?

Brief scene at the rough-hewn agricultural school. Bring in a handsome Jewess who serves some Turkish coffee and cakes. Their eyes meet, a touch of sex. Barthelmes was convinced that Herzl needed some hornying up. Need an actor with suggestible balls. Rethink that. Part of his appeal has to be a very real physical weakness. Very touching when he and his party take the cramped, stifling train from Jaffa to Jerusalem. Herzl is near fainting on this Friday afternoon, and the train is rolling into the Jerusalem depot on the Sabbath. The moon is out. (Herzl had called it a *dusty* moon.) Herzl wants to hire a carriage, but his companions will not violate the religious ban about riding on the Sabbath. Herzl must walk with the others. He totters. Wolffsohn holds him up. The forty-minute walk makes him very sick that night.

Perhaps, Barthelmes thought, Herzl on horseback might play better than Herzl on crutches. History has no copyright on this. Why didn't he tell his Orthodox friends that he was sick, sick! Why suffer? A half hour of agony just to make a gesture. Complicated, that.

The style of the film, Barthelmes thought, can allow for a fluid and arbitrary time sequence. Not so much flashback and flash-forward as a ball of time thrown against a critical moment. Barthelmes didn't know which moment that was, but knew he had to find it. Think of history as a speeding snowball and of the moment as a submicroscopic barn door—that sort of aesthetic bullshit.

The scene with the Kaiser: Herzl must be as perfectly elegant and cool as he had actually been, or had pretended to be. God, that's a helluva scene! The crazy pastor Hechler is already on the road along which the Kaiser's procession will come, still rehearsing the choir of Jewish children to greet the Kaiser with the song "Heil Dir im Siegerkranz" ("Hail to Thee with the Victor's Wreath"). William Hechler, *important character*, one of five leads after Herzl. Donald Pleasance could take that part and should be available—doing so much crap lately. William Hechler, too, is larger than life, and Donald Pleasance plays larger-than-life characters. British clergyman, born in India, a New Testament fundamentalist and Christian Zionist who calculated that in 1897—forty-second Prophetic Year of Omar—a leader would rise up and bring the Jews back to Israel. Trumpets. Thunder. Hosannas. Reenter Emanuel, alias Jesus Christ. Enter Theodor Benjamin Herzl with *Der Judenstaat* and flourishing beard. Hechler goes to his living-room organ and composes the new and stirring "Herzl Hymn." (When I invent history, Barthelmes observed, it's never as strange as history actually is.) Hechler loads his scale model of old Jerusalem on a cart and hauls it to Pelikan Strasse to show it to Teddy boy. Hechler had tutored the deceased son of Grand Duke Friederich, and also had been tutor to the Grand Duke's nephew, now the reigning Kaiser, to whom Hechler's Harmonic Choir will soon sing.

This is all so goddamned complicated! Herzl is too smart, too intelligent, too Jewish. Can Zachary Barthelmes capture this Theodor Herzl on film? Sure I can! Who's afraid of the big bad Jews? But can Jews with big, dark beards make big box office? Maybe play him as Byron. Shave the beard.

5.

The driver—a surly, silent Jew who looked like a thug—pulled the cab onto the shoulder. Barthelmes had tried to drum up some small talk after the price for the ride to nowhere had been fixed, but the driver had kept his cigarette in his mouth and hadn't said anything, even when Barthelmes instructed him to stop at this place on the highway between Tel Aviv and Jerusalem. Maybe, by chance, this was where Herzl had encountered the Kaiser. Probably not. No one had memorialized the spot where the King of the Jews had embraced the King of the Germans.

This scene could really be remarkable! About three minutes long and a million dollars tall. Herzl trots along the highway, then reins in his spirited horse. The horse neighs and rears up on his hind legs, front legs pawing the air. Herzl calms the beast and dismounts. He removes his cork hat. *Frame Herzl against afternoon sky*. Barthelmes took out a small pad and began to write the scene that was forming so completely in his mind.

In the distance a cloud of dust. Hoofs. Louder. Pounding. Louder. Piercing the curtain of dust, reds, blues, yellows, silver, gold. Into clear sight thunder two hundred Turkish cavalry. Two hundred heavy mustaches are bent by the head wind. Swords drawn, eyes defiant. The KAISER's *advance bodyguard.*

HERZL's *head slowly turns. More noble than the* KAISER's. *"Hail to Thee with the Victor's Wreath."* HERZL *does not move a muscle. The* EMPRESS *appreciates his beauty, and* HERZL *can see her come-hither smile. The smile of the* KAISER *is there, suppressed, barely lifting his prematurely graying mustache. The* KAISER *comes forward, his horse dancing nearer. Directly toward* HERZL. *Now!* HECHLER *gives the downbeat. The massed voices of the children issue up to the heavens.* [Oh, I like this!]

TURKS *canter. The* KAISER, EMPRESS *in tow, barb-topped helmet in place, all in gray save the medals* [who gives an emperor medals?], *comes forward, his light hands on the reins of the white steed. Quick intercuts:* KAISER, HERZL, KAISER, HERZL. *Blue eyes. Brown eyes. Smiling broadly, the* KAISER *holds his reins in his birth-shortened hand; the normal hand comes down toward* THEODOR, *who bows his head and clasps the hand. The* KAISER *laughs warmly.* HERZL *smiles as the* KAISER's *eyes sweep over him.* WILHELM *speaks first.*

How are you, Theodor?

I could not be better, Your Highness. Are you yourself well, Your Majesty? It is a harsh country, sire.

Palestine is a magnificent country. All it needs, Theodor, is water. Torrents of water.

Exactly so, Your Highness. Bring water. Banish fever and malaria.

Palestine has a future, Herzl. Irrigation is the future of the new land! Do you Jews know anything about irrigation?

Your Highness, it was Moses himself who invented large-scale irrigation when he split the Red Sea.

Hmmm, that I overlooked. *(To the Empress)* Did you hear that about Moses and irrigation?

I love irrigation, My Lord.

Her horse moves close to THEODOR. *She leans down across the chestnut neck of her mount and kisses him on the mouth. The* KAISER *roars:*

Not in public, Queenie!

HECHLER *exhorts the children's choir:*

Louder, louder! Forte, forte, maxima forte!

The TURKS *fire their rifles into the air. The* KAISER *kicks his steed sharply in the flanks, and the royal entourage moves down the yellow-brick road toward Jerusalem.* HERZL *weeps.*

Helluva scene! I could milk that, thought Barthelmes. I might even leave in the business of the Empress kissing T. H. See if Moe finds it false. Actually, he didn't have to write that scene at all; there were dozens of big-scene possibilities from which to choose, and those were splashy and easy. Barthelmes already knew that the film would stand or fall on the little scenes, the intimate ones.

Barthelmes kicked at the scrub grass. Had he picked the precise spot where Herzl had faced the Kaiser to signal the world that a Jewish state was more than possible? Maybe the encounter took place a mile to the north or to the south, but one thing was certain: Here Herzl had tasted the imminent victory of the Jews, just as he would know within weeks how easily he had been betrayed. Still, here the tides and winds of history had conspired for a single, pomp-filled moment. Why hadn't the Israelis built a monument along the road to Jerusalem, or at least a bronze plaque: THEODOR HERZL AND KAISER WILHELM II STOOD HERE AND SPOKE OF THE FUTURE JEWISH STATE.

Barthelmes got into the taxi and directed the driver back to the Basel in Tel Aviv.

6.

Kalia Wiggins looked out at the sea, where the tiny lights of the building behind her twinkled on waves that stretched or cut short the reflections, sometimes washing them into star bursts. God it's beautiful, Hal!

Yes it is. I love it here. And the food is amazingly good. Are you hungry?

Haven't eaten since breakfast, except for a glass and a half of Perrier.

Give it up, Kalia, Barthelmes said. Tonight we eat! Let's enjoy ourselves.

The restaurant, owned by Arabs, was in the Sha'bazi district, on the outskirts of Tel Aviv. The building itself was designed with a sturdy wood frame on three sides. The other side was open to the sea, and platforms with cloth-covered tables were set into the sloping beach. On these, heavy, candle-bearing lamps anchored the tablecloths against the not-so-gentle wind. The chairs rested on sand and had to be selected in relation to the height of the diner. Wiederspiel had arranged for a table on the downward slope, only a few yards from where the sea lapped the shore.

So beautiful, Kalia repeated, almost to herself. So beautiful!

Well, this is where the poor people live. Wiederspiel waved his arm up and behind him. You know how it is. Tel Aviv started here on the sand. I think it was after the turn of the century—1904? Jews started it, kind of a beach colony. Then they built what we have now, a city with pavements and towers and all the rest of it. Sha'bazi is what old Tel Aviv crumbled into.

Where do you hide the poor, Hal? All I see are those two hotel towers.

Walk up there, Zachary, past where the tourists spend their money. Less than a thousand yards from this table, you come to houses below the standards of the worst slums in New York. Israelis without money live there, and in places like it.

Framed by the rectangle of light behind her, a woman appeared and kissed Wiederspiel on the top of his balding head. Sorry I'm late. But you were not expecting anyone else. Good, you have not started to eat! I am very happy to meet you both. One is Zachary and the other is Kalia. I know already which is which. I am Geula.

She always enters like this, Wiederspiel said. My colonel never has time to change into a dress.

I think it's very chic, Kalia said. I love those Israeli army caps.

It's yours. It will look very good on your hair. Burgundy and gold.

You shouldn't!

Never mind! I lose two or three hats a year to Hal's guests. Some of them neither he nor I like, and I know he likes you both. Isn't that wonderful? My old bear likes you!

Hal smiled. Don't be crazy!

You *don't* like them?

I like them! he said and put his hand up for the waiter, who arrived and took their order for drinks.

Kalia stirred the ice in her vodka with her long-nailed index finger. Hal was telling us about the poor Jews here. I must confess I never heard anything about poor Jews. It's oxymoronic—like a poor banker or a poor Rolls-Royce dealer.

Geula laughed. Good. At least you have said your thought. I believe most *goyim*—this is how I think of you—believe Jews are always from proper middle class to richer than Midas.

I put my foot in it, huh?

Of course not, Kalia! Is that how you say it—Kalia? Israel is a *poor* state. It can't really build houses, so instead of tearing down Sha'bazi we let it stand and people move in. But you know how history works: the poor in Sha'bazi will become rich. Israelis with money are buying up all the old junk and making little private palaces by the beautiful sea. So if you own a shack or even if you have a good lease on one, you will become rich. However, the junk must be on a good beach.

Same as Florida.

Precisely, Kalia. Florida. I was there a few times with *mon général.*

The waiter—a tall, thin Arab—seemed to rise up out of the sand like a genie. Pad in hand, he said *shalom* without looking at the quartet and recited the unprinted menu. Vegetable soup and a main dish of chicken, lamb, fish, or New York–style steak. They placed their orders.

Barthelmes's ears filled with the sound of the waves and the voices of scattered patrons, lofted up on the wind, but the Sha'bazi beach air magically separated their own voices from those of the other tables. He found himself looking at Geula, whose English was accented in a musical, continental way. Her hair was dark and straight. Her eyes were large and oval, although he could not discern their color by the light of the table lamp. Her nose was straight and just long enough to be interesting. But it was her mouth that excited him.

The dinner was delicious and strictly kosher. When the coffee arrived, Wiederspiel said, With coffee all the serious subjects come up. So, Barthelmes, tell us what you think of us? Have we a future?

Jesus, Hal, I'm still trying to decide if Herzl has a future. In the movies.

If so, Moe will be a very happy man.

I don't know. I'm just getting my feet wet.

He's waffling and straddling, Hal. My Zachary finds it difficult to make serious commitments.

Barthelmes smiled and leaned across the table to kiss Kalia. I commit, seriously. Please marry me.

You're not married? Geula said. Wonderful! It is the best way. If I married Helmut, I would lose my independence.

Please, marry me, don't marry me, do whatever you want. But for you I don't think a loss of independence is possible.

Really, Geula, Kalia said, how could marriage, a proper marriage, rob you of your independence?

Pity the poor gentile! Such innocence! Perhaps you are also a virgin? Helmut is my fourth serious arrangement. The other three were also arrangements. I learned about marriage from my parents—poison. Have you married before?

Kalia fidgeted and lit a cigarette.

Can we leave this alone, Geula? We hardly know these people. You yourself have just met them!

Geula glared at Wiederspiel. If she doesn't want to answer, *mon général*, she is not compelled. But please do not monitor me.

He smiled. Of course, Geula. You're right. Tell them anything you like, but not, I insist, how we make love.

Now you are censoring me!

Wiederspiel turned to Kalia. She has been reading heavily in the women's movement. I bring her the books from the States, and now she's shooting the messenger.

Geula laughed, quite abruptly. You are right, Helmut. I have been doing that lately. Thank you. I'm sorry.

Then kiss me, *mon colonel.* Now!

Helmut!

She loves it when I'm beastly.

Bastard! Geula said, laughing, then got up and walked to Hal's chair. She kissed him fully on the mouth and looked up. You didn't know this side of him, the lunatic side.

I love it! Don't you love it, Zachary?

I love it.

Geula returned to her seat. Let's talk about your movie, Zachary.

Too early, Barthelmes said. I'm groping along, still thinking about Yafo in 1898. Also, I don't know if I want to do the movie at all, you see.

Wiederspiel suddenly got up, excused himself, and walked down to the beach, away from the restaurant lights and the shimmering waves.

Did I say something wrong, Barthelmes asked.

No, no, Geula replied, looking into the darkness where Wiederspiel had disappeared. Nothing you said at all. These are his moods. Sudden changes for weeks now. Something is bothering him, I think. More coffee?

But her gaze did not shift back to the bright table from the dark beach.

7.

Hal Wiederspiel marched along under a sky heavy with Mediterranean stars. He could hear himself breathing, his heart beating. Why was he seized this way, more often and with less control? The cold sense of foreboding was, for him, a new feeling. Never in combat had he felt this impending doom. Not even past the point of no return over the Atlantic in a B-17 with two engines dead and one dying. Always there had been the belief that something could be done. He'd crawled out into the wing space and by flashlight had coaxed the failing engine alive. The tilting plane had leveled, and with two engines the rest of the flight had been smooth. Wiederspiel had never doubted that the bomber could be fixed, so he'd gone ahead and done it while the others waited and prayed.

Just a feeling—it came down to just a feeling. Almost ephemeral, this feeling that something had gone wrong in some dark and hidden place. When Golda had called to ask if everything was all right with the development of the new fighter bomber, he had reassured her. But when she had pressed him—Are you absolutely sure, Hal?—he'd answered, As sure as I can be, Golda. Listen, I've lost three pilots in test flights. I bet their lives *because* I'm sure. It's a heavy price, three good men. Two of them I knew, Golda had said. But if you're sure, Hal, I'm glad. I am very glad. Never before had the Prime Minister questioned him so closely about project development, but perhaps she was overwhelmed with her own problems.

Yet Dayan, also, had asked about the progress of the fighter bomber, even more closely and in a grave voice—Moshe Dayan, who'd once said in public, Well, I am just a general. I win a battle or I lose a battle, but I must emphasize that I am replaceable. Wiederspiel cannot be replaced. Dayan, who used to call him several times a week or send him little archeological gifts dug up from the ancient land, had changed. Now he didn't call except to question him. Why should that be upsetting? In fact, Dayan *was* replaceable. For the first time Wiederspiel admitted to himself that he'd never liked the man. Certainly it wasn't Dayan's conduct he minded but the damned changes in his behavior.

His own behavior had also changed: paranoia, a sense of deep, unknown shifts. When had all this started? Perhaps after Ben-Gurion had retired. By now all his disciples, his comrades in arms, had drifted away or were lost in the apparatus of the state. It was so many years since Ben-Gurion had called Israel into existence. Things had to change, Wiederspiel understood that. But Israel had triumphed, and he was irrevocably part of that triumph. But how anxious he had become!

8.

I thought you'd got over being angry at me. So how long are you going to smolder—a day, a week? This room's too small for big emotions. But I appreciate your not sulking at dinner.

I was brought up with good manners.

There's at least one good thing to say about the South.

Fuck you, Barthelmes. Like it or not, I'm a true believer.

You're still angry about commitment, Kale. You believe heart and soul in commitment, right?

Right. If two people who love each other agree to take vows and one of them says those vows mean nothing, then what have we got? A creaky, existentialist alliance, Zachary. Love for a day. Insects fucking in the air and dying once the sun goes down.

But I *am* committed. And no marriage can deepen that commitment.

Kalia Wiggins threw off the sheet and sat up, crossing her long legs beneath her in a yoga position. Her nipples had puckered in the night chill. She lit a cigarette. After the first drag, Zachary took it from her hand, and she lit another.

Well? he prompted.

I want the marriage. It means something to me.

Okay. That's agreed. I *have* committed.

Then why did you make fun of it?

I don't believe in the goddamn vows! I believe in a life with you, and marriage is incidental. So stop sulking. He put his hand on her breast. She removed it. He replaced it.

Then Kalia pushed his hand down, hard, between her thighs. You're turning me on, you bastard!

Zachary held her close and kissed her mouth. Her body became quiet. After a while he turned on the bedside radio, and they listened to the Arab music without talking. Want to go to Jerusalem, he suddenly asked. Hal found us an apartment for a couple days.

9.

The apartment was on Ein Rogel Street, which cut and tracked its way up a hill just outside the walls of the Old City. From the window Zachary Barthelmes looked down over the low stone wall into the compound, where history was shouldered aside by the bustling life of a November morning. The sun hurled itself up from the gold dome of the mosque, but Barthelmes was watching an Arab peddler who led a tired, overburdened donkey along an interior street. He tried to guess what was contained in the donkey's cargo of gray sacks, though he knew it didn't matter. The trek of this ass along the stone-paved street between the gray and light-brown lines of the ancient buildings was the thin thread of time. The same peddler had been leading the same gray donkey along the same street for thousands of years. Nothing had changed except maybe the contents of the sacks. Barthelmes held the Arab and donkey in view until they were swallowed up by a narrow street.

Where had Christ walked? Hopelessly he looked for the Via Dolorosa, then gazed aimlessly over the warren of streets below him. Had the Roman soldiers shopped here, and did they pay for their dates and olives or simply confiscate whatever they liked? In which rooms did the harlots entertain?

Like the rabbis and the priests, the harlots maintained the traditions of their professions. How else would we know the variety of bedroom arts and crafts mankind had perfected over the millennia, or was it possible that men and women had invented all the techniques and positions of sex in less than a month or two of ardent practice? For that matter, had Herzl found a piece of heaven during his stay in Jerusalem?

Barthelmes made a note in a small, leather-bound book with his monogram (ZWB) stamped in gold on the brown calfskin. Moe Cohen had given him seven of these, one for each of the countries Herzl had visited in pursuit of his dream (his nightmare?). Austria, of course. France—Paris, actually. England—politically important because of Albert Goldsmid, the Jewish colonel in the British cavalry. A little like Hechler—no, Vambery was more like Hechler. Italy—the business of the King and the Pope. Turkey. Abdul Hammid II. Germany. Russia—pogroms and *shtetls*. Palestine, of course. Barthelmes was writing in the Palestine book now. He had listed eight countries, but Moe had given him only seven books. Well, he could drop Germany; he had the Kaiser as the star player in Palestine, and that would be enough.

Barthelmes looked down into the Old City. He exhaled a deliberate cloud of smoke against the window. Maybe it was too big for a film. Herzl was all over the place. Either a ten-part, twenty-hour TV miniseries or narrow the focus, keep it in Vienna. The simple truth was he didn't have to do it at all. It would take three, four years out of his life, and he was already forty-eight. Did he need that? He hadn't been dishonest with Cohen. He'd told him the chances of his writing the film were somewhere between slim and none.

I'll take a chance, Moe had said. It's my business to take chances.

Okay, Barthelmes had said. I'll pack up my lady, and we'll go out and see the world.

Travel is good. But I expect a little research, too, Zachary.

For a hundred and fifty thousand, Moe, I'll do research and type up a report.

You mean if you refuse, Zach?

Either way, accept or refuse.

That's fair. Oh, by the way, I'll help out with the research. I'm sending you a crate of books about the hero.

Barthelmes had cocked his head. Books you bought for me? Books you've read?

You will notice, Zacho, that the books are not exactly new. They're from my personal library. I think there's a movie in that crate.

Ah, Moe, Zachary had thought, don't get your hopes up. The money is good, the terms are excellent, but the answer is very much in doubt.

Yet he couldn't shut out the scenes that had begun to arrange themselves in his mind.

10.

HERZL *has breakfast with his colleagues, ill at ease because they have not heard from the emissaries of the* KAISER. *Are they not to be received at the* EMPEROR'S *encampment outside the city? As a Zionist committee? Yes, that is* HERZL'S *understanding. It is not the* KAISER *who delays but* VON BÜLOW *and* COUNT EULENBERG. HECHLER *arrives dressed in flowing Arab robes* [that's cute] *having just spent a day and a night with his Bedouin brethren in the desert.* HECHLER *reports that he has told the tribesmen that* THEODOR HERZL, *the King of the Jews, is in residence in the land and that very soon the Jews of the world will sail the ocean seas and gather in Palestine.* SEIDENER *displays annoyance, but* HERZL *praises him and then asks if the pastor would be good enough to make inquiries: when will* DR. HERZL *and the* ZIONISTS *be received?* HECHLER *will be pleased to do so. Two more days with no news will pass.*

HERZL *walks through the winding, worn streets of the Old City. Odors of urine and donkey shit mix with those of spices, fruits, and confections. The odors fill his throat, and he puts a handkerchief to his mouth. Then he half runs toward the Yildiz Gate. "When I remember thee in days to come, O Jerusalem, it will not be with pleasure!"*

In his mind, Barthelmes superimposes Christ over the half-running figure of Herzl. Christ lugs his cross along the Via Dolorosa; from the halo of thorns, blood runs into His eyes. Handkerchief over mouth, Herzl runs toward the Yildiz Gate, splashing through the gutter filth. Christ, dragging his cross, slogs through the same puke. There was the real pity, the real heartbreak: Christ crucified was first Christ desecrated. No Tide-white garments clinging to His frame.

Herzl had made up his mind to remove all the selling stalls from the streets of the Old City. Only sacred buildings, only activities relating to the history and beauty of Jerusalem. Build the new Jerusalem outside the walls and install the peddlers in clean, modern shops. The Old City nestled snugly within an architectural ring of the best modern Vienna has to offer.

Barthelmes almost, but not quite, laughed out loud. The New Jerusalem as an unadorned Bauhaus Heaven.

11.

Waiting for word from the KAISER, *walking with* HECHLER *around the walls,* HERZL *says:*
When we have the Jewish state, I will ask your church to designate you Bishop of Jerusalem.

No! I am not worthy.

You, my dear Hechler, are most certainly worthy. HECHLER's *eyes fill with tears. (Costume note: Hechler dressed entirely in white, white shoes and a white helmet with white veil. Empress wore a similar costume. Maybe change hers to a gold satin outfit.)*

HERZL *visits a primitive Jewish hospital, praises it for everything it is not. An* OLD JEW *clasps and kisses his hand, then calls him the Messiah.* HERZL *recoils.*

Cut to HERZL *having tea at sidewalk café, flies and yellow jackets swarm around the honeypot.* WOLFF-SOHN *appears, whispers into his ear.* HERZL *grimaces.*

Fade out. Fade in atop Mount of Olives. Grand vista of hills, valleys, and Old City. HERZL *points with extended arm. His companions are paying rapt attention.*

Pan to pavement where BEGGARS *lie sprawled, crying for alms.* PICKPOCKET *at work. Customary filth. Dissolve to* HERZL, *pointing to sites of interest.* BODENHEIMER *enters frame. Grips* HERZL's *elbow.*

We have a reply from your father, Theo. No reports of your encounter with the Kaiser have yet appeared in the press.

HERZL *thoughtfully touches his lip.*

12.

Taste it! Kalia said. Go ahead and taste it.

Chicken soup? I don't believe this. Kalia, really. Since when can you cook?

Just taste it, Zach.

Barthelmes lowered the spoon slowly into the yellow broth thick with noodles, then glanced furtively up at Kalia's face.

His lips pursed over the spoon, breathing in the taste; a slight head tilt, then a half spoonful swallowed.

Well? Don't just sit there, Zach!

It's wonderful. I can't believe it: it's wonderful! On the level of Fine & Schapiro, I swear! Come on, you don't even do eggs! You bought it.

Hey, you watched me! Didn't you see the naked chicken? Didn't you watch me cut up the vegetables? Didn't you see the pile of parsley, the batch of dill, the celery leaves, the parsnip? And what about the onion? Did you or did you not watch me put it in the pot?

Yes, I did. How the hell did you know to do that?

A little Jewish bird told me.

More, Kalia. Speak.

I was walking through the marketplace—and look what I bought! She fished from between her breasts a thin gold chain, from which hung a six-pointed gold star. A Star of David. Isn't it pretty? The lady who sold it to me said I didn't look like a Jew. Of course I confessed I was a bona fide Christian. So we chatted. I told her how much I liked the Jewish people and the Israelis. Somehow we got to cooking, one thing led to another, and she gave me her hundred-percent foolproof recipe for the thousand-year-old national gourmet treasure. Wrote it all down in English, a sort of English, the way she spoke. She told me which shop to go to and Rina Schwartzkopf, the butcher's wife, herself, picked out the chicken. Great, huh?

Barthelmes had spooned up half the soup as Kalia spoke. I can't believe this, Kale. Now for sure I'll sincerely marry you. How many quarts of chicken soup makes you a Jew?

They were so sweet, Zach! They wanted the soup to work for your sake. They didn't even treat me like a *shiksa*! And you won't believe this, Zach.

Yes. I will.

Mr. Schwartzkopf, the butcher, asked me if I would consider becoming a Jew.

He was looking at your legs.

Kalia laughed. Actually, he was. Then I said maybe I'd consider it if I knew how to go about it.

You're out of your mind, Kale. The soup's great.

Listen, lady, he said, if you want to go about it, go see my cousin Dov Schechter in New York. He's a rabbi. He'll put some salt on you!

What the hell does that mean?

I think Orthodox Jews cover meat with salt before they cook it; that's supposed to make it kosher.

I thought it was the way they killed the cow.

They have some reason for putting the salt on, I suppose. Kalia held up a piece of the butcher's wrapping paper. Mr. Schwartzkopf gave me the rabbi's address.

Tear it up.

Kalia laughed and kissed the top of Zachary's head. Who knows? It may come in handy.

He lifted his bowl toward Kalia Wiggins. I'll have more soup now, please.

13.

Zachary Barthelmes, awake in the dark, sat in the chair by the window. The night was opaque, starless, with only a few distant lights and the dim street lamps on Ein Rogel. Although he couldn't see the Old City in its darkness, he thought he could feel it. He made a pot of coffee, poured a cup, took it to the window, and lit a cigarette. He stared into the ancient night of Yerushalayim. Dawn came slowly from the top rim of the sky, and now there were stars—where had they been?—and a pink sliver of light, the sudden round ascension of gold. Mosques, pink-gray stone, pulses of gold. His heart raced. Without thought or reason, Barthelmes wept.

Kalia appeared in the bedroom doorway and then knelt before him and looked into his face. Darling, what's the matter? Please tell me. What's wrong?

He shook his head. Nothing, he said. I was just sitting here. Coffee. I was watching the dawn.

Poor baby! Kalia stood up and, putting her arms around him, pressed his head against her body. Everything is gonna be all right, Zach!

That's the thing, though. Nothing's wrong. I just started bawling. It just welled up.

She sat on Zachary's knees as with growing intensity the dawn wiped out shadows and slowly defined objects until suddenly it was day.

At breakfast, Barthelmes made notes in his Palestine book from time to time.

How's it going, Kalia finally asked.

I haven't the slightest idea. I keep putting down ideas for scenes, but I don't have a handle yet. Runs all over the lot. One thing's for sure: if I don't find the right form, it'll run forever and never will get made.

Well, you don't have to write it.

I have to give Moe something for his money.

Well, just give his books back. And if you still feel guilty, write that report you promised.

I feel sorry for him.

You feel sorry for Moe Cohen?

No, for Herzl. He's being set up. As intelligent and as sophisticated as he is, he's walking right into the buzz saw of history. By the time he suspects it, they'll have cut his balls off.

Zachary, Herzl's been dead for, what, fifty years? Sixty years? More? I'm lousy at math. Come on, darling.

He's interesting, goddamn it.

Because he's the greatest Jew since Moses?

No. Because he's so human. Vain and brave. Genuine, but always looking over his shoulder and seeing himself riding one float in the parade of history.

At that, Barthelmes lit his fifth cigarette of the day. Herzl had been in Palestine less than three weeks, he continued. He'd already met with the Kaiser in Constantinople, and he was convinced his Jewish state was on the verge of being created.

Why? Kalia nearly shouted. One conversation and bingo?

He thought the Kaiser had bought it. You see, Herzl believed in Prussians with all his heart; if he'd controlled his patrimony, he would've been *born* a Prussian, probably complete with scar and monocle. Prussians couldn't tell a lie. He knew by his clear blue eyes that the Kaiser wanted his idea to work. Anyway, that's where they'd set up the roadside meeting in Palestine. That's the reason Herzl and his gang were there. That's one helluva scene, Kalia. I've blocked it out already.

Aha! So you are writing scenes!

Pour passer le temps, chérie.

Poop poopie doop, *mein schatz.*

Anyhow, Theo and his Zionists do some sight-seeing while they're waiting to be called to the Kaiser's encampment. All kinds of stops. We've visited most of them. They go to a place called the Russian Tower. It's about nine stories high, and tourists can climb to the top and get a bird's-eye view of Jerusalem. But Herzl only makes it to the first landing. So he sends his friends up and says he'll catch up. Once they're out of sight, he slumps against the wall and loosens his cravat. He's sweating, breathing heavily, damn near fainting.

Signifying?

Well, that even then he knew he was very ill. That he was running out of time. He didn't tell anybody except God and his diary—and even in the diary he goes tiptoe on that. Hey, if I thought I was about to die, I'd say, Fuck you, Moe, and thanks for the going-away present.

That's my Zachary, she said and kissed him. Now, darling, want to take a chance on my eggs?

Sure, why not? But what kind of man writes off his life for some stupid idea that practically nobody believes in except the Marx Brothers?

I haven't the foggiest. You want boiled, scrambled, or fried?

14.

What bothered Herzl most, Barthelmes concluded, was his failure to get information to or from Vienna. It took almost two weeks to learn from his father that his roadside meeting with Wilhelm hadn't been reported in the press. And so he was initially delighted when Count Eulenberg, one of the Kaiser's principal aides, explained that any and all accounts of their meetings would be released only through the proper bureau of the German government. Elated, Herzl had clicked his heels, in not too military a fashion, and had bowed his head, although not too deeply. The government itself would make the release! Perfect!

> HECHLER *reports that he himself had spoken with the* KAISER, *who without doubt thinks well of* DR. HERZL. *The delegation—comprising* SCHNIRER, WOLFFSOHN, SEIDENER, *and* BODENHEIMER—*will be given an audience at eleven o'clock the following morning.*
>
> HERZL *firmly instructs the delegation to make sure that their apparel is in proper order. When* SCHNIRER *snarls,* HERZL *merely shrugs. The applecart of history will not be upset by a pair of unpolished boots, dirty*

gloves, or a crooked cravat. And so the next morning, before they leave for the KAISER's *encampment,* HERZL *(in his nightshirt) inspects the four men—and only* BODENHEIMER *is unacceptable. His silk hat sags, his cuffs slide down beyond his coat sleeves, and* HERZL *orders him to correct his appearance with all dispatch or stay behind. Then* HECHLER *enters, dressed as usual completely in whites. Hanging like a* W *from his chin, his split beard is half gray and half red. He radiates joy.*

Finally HERZL *puts on his clothing—he is resplendent—and as a final touch he pins his Mejidiye medal to his label: it is the Turkish decoration awarded him by* SULTAN ABDUL HAMMID II.

In the tent of the KING, *a high shot of people milling like ants under the great canvas. The camera closes in as* HERZL *bows to the smiling* KAISER. *As he presents his* DELEGATION MEMBERS *to the Emperor,* WILHELM *salutes each of them by crisply touching his visor.* HERZL *then reads his prepared statement as* VON BÜLOW *compares his remarks with his own duplicate copy. He is satisfied that there is no deviation from the agreed-on text.*

The KAISER *thanks* HERZL *and assures him that his comments will be taken under advisement. The* KAISER, *on a loop, says over and over again:*

Water, trees, shade, water, swamps—water everywhere but not a drop for crops or for thirst.

HERZL *does not hear the babble, only the music of imperial wisdom. The* EMPRESS *(in a beautiful desert-gray costume) is looking on, smiling, from a short distance away. The* KAISER *invites* VON BÜLOW *to join his tête-à-tête with* HERZL.

Now, more confident, HERZL *says:*

To bring fresh water into Palestine for a Jewish colony will cost billions, but it is an investment that will yield many billions more.

VON BÜLOW's *smile is thin and knowing.*

Surely, Herr Herzl, you can supply the money.

The KAISER *slaps his boot with his riding crop:*

Well, money is what you Jews have plenty of. More money than any of us.

VON BÜLOW *smiles:*

Yes, you have in abundance that which is such a problem for Germany. Rivers of money, as it were.

As the KAISER's *and* VON BÜLOW's *laughter reverberates,* HERZL *speaks of harnessing the power of the Jordan, improving sanitation, eliminating the eye disease caused by the fig harvest. The* KAISER's *head bobs up and down in agreement, but* VON BÜLOW's *face freezes.*

At this point, Barthelmes knew Herzl's excitement was higher than it ever had been or would be again. Herzl wanted to pack up and leave Palestine at once, so that nothing could be spoiled. He was also eager to get back to Europe in time to act on the information the Kaiser would soon cause to be released. And so they packed their luggage in the middle of the night and left the Marx House by first light and took the early train to Yafo, in search of departing ships.

HERZL *is rowed out toward the ships lying offshore. He shouts up to an officer at the rail of the Lloyd steamer, which is ready to sail. No room available. The Arab* OARSMEN *navigate among the German battleships, making their gray steel statement for the visiting empire.* HERZL *pulls alongside the yacht of* GORDON BENNETT, *the publisher of the* New York Herald, *and shouts up to the deck:*

I am Theodor Herzl of Vienna. Can you accommodate my party and myself?
SILENCE.

Finally, a freighter taking on oranges accepts them, and the CAPTAIN *promises to speed up the loading so the* ZIONISTS *can make better time.* HERZL *and his* MEN *board this English ship heading for Alexandria, where better connections can be made.*

Except for WOLFFSOHN, *the others object to traveling on the small, ratty freighter. When* HERZL *insists,* SCHNIRER *calls him an imperious, high-handed dictator. They need not travel with him,* HERZL *suggests, if they would prefer to find their own way home. In the end, they refuse to leave when* HERZL *orders them off the ship. Indeed, the* Dundee *is very small, and their cabins are cramped and crowded with odors, so the travelers put their bedding on deck. The rough seas toss them about like the proverbial cork.* SCHNIRER, SEIDENER, *and* BODENHEIMER *eat nothing but throw up ceaselessly.* WOLFFSOHN *stabilizes after an early malaise.* HERZL *alone is unaffected, and like a figurehead he gazes across the prow toward Alexandria.*

What Barthelmes liked about this scene was the face-off between Herzl and the others. Herzl as bully—that was an insight. Barthelmes asked himself whether his real motivation was to find flaws so that Herzl might seem something less than the greatest Jew since Moses. Well, he thought, let the chips of clay fall where they may!

In the newspapers, on December 4, 1898, there appeared the first and only account of Herzl's Palestine adventure:

Jerusalem, November 2. Kaiser Wilhelm has received a Jewish deputation, which presented him with an album of pictures of the Jewish colonies established in Palestine. Replying to an address by the leader of the deputation, Kaiser Wilhelm said that all those endeavors were assured of his benevolent interest that aimed at the improvement of agriculture in Palestine, thus furthering the welfare of the Turkish Empire, with complete respect for the sovereignty of the Sultan.

I would have quit right then, Zachary Barthelmes thought. I would have become as depressed as Herzl's Zionist comrades. The Germans had played them like tin whistles. They were nothing—or, at most, nothing more than amusing, speech-making, windup Lilliputians.

Did Herzl scream? Rant and rave and rend his garment? No, he reordered his thoughts. He looked for the next pieces, perhaps the correct pieces in the puzzle of *Der Judenstaat*. An incorrigible Jew, Barthelmes thought with a smile. An egomaniacal nut. Was that why Morris Albert Cohen was so fond of Theodore Benjamin Z'ev Herzl?

15.

What can I tell you? Teddy Kollek was saying over tea in the small garden behind his home. It is a city of passions. The city of the Temple, the city of the Dome, it is the city of Christ and of Mohammed. So thank God it isn't the city of Moses! Everything would blow sky high.

Do you think Herzl was the greatest Jew since Moses?

Who believes that?

Something Ben-Gurion said.

It's my fault, Kollek said with a chuckle. Once I introduced him at a rally by saying he, Ben-Gurion, was the greatest Jew since Moses. He got mad and yelled at me. So I said, If you're not, tell me who is. And Ben-Gurion said he'd think about it. Now, indeed, I see he has come to a profound conclusion. You don't agree?

What can I say, Mr. Barthelmes? I don't think in those terms. Maybe it is Herzl. But maybe it is Wiederspiel.

Or even you, Wiederspiel said. You have my vote, Teddy. Anybody who sits on top of Jerusalem and keeps the blood from racing through the streets is one great Jew. But Herzl must be the greatest—or were your parents thinking of another Theodor?

At least they call me Teddy, not Dori. I have met plenty of Doris, very few Teddys. So listen, Mr. Barthelmes. If, when you make the film, there still is a Jerusalem, and if I'm still the mayor, you will have my cooperation.

Great!

You're getting in pretty deep, Zach baby, Kalia whispered into his ear.

He lifted the blond hair away from her ear and stage-whispered back, That's Hollywood bullshit, darling. I advise the mayor that I may make a film. He advises me that I may have Jerusalem. The real question is, *Is* there a Jerusalem?

Everybody laughed, but none longer than the host.

Once the conversation ran down, they left Kollek's home to walk through the streets of the Old City. Wiederspiel pointed out which houses were new, renovated, or reconstructed and related the ruins and archaeological excavations to biblical accounts that fixed time in its flight.

God, Kalia said, my father will fall to his knees with a million thank-you-Jesuses when I tell him about this. He's always wanted to come here. What do you think, Zach, should I buy him a ticket?

This is Jewish history Hal's giving us, Kale. Not Baptist.

My father thumps the Old Testament just as hard as the New. Thank you, Jesus.

Don't count on me to take you down the Via Dolorosa, Wiederspiel said. It's not my jurisdiction.

Inside the donkey's-width streets of the marketplace, Wiederspiel chatted up the merchants in their stalls and bought nuts and dates for Kalia and Zachary. Most merchants, passing Arabs or black-garbed Orthodox Jews, immediately recognized Wiederspiel in his worn leather bomber jacket. He replied, seemingly without preference, in either Hebrew or Arabic.

The most important Jew since—

—Teddy Kollek said, Wiederspiel, finishing Kalia's sentence. Big fish in a small pond.

There was no warning. A tall column of wicker baskets, collapsing in front of the next stall, toppled slowly through the air. Although the woven tower was falling clear of them, Wiederspiel shouted, Watch out! as three men, Arabs, rushed out from behind—the knives in their fists catching the weak light of the market street.

One blade, breaking from the steel choreography, thrust down and embedded itself into Kalia's shoulder. There seemed to be little pain. Twisting away from the attacker, she noticed the white tenseness of his eyes as he hurtled past her into the displays of figs and dates across the street.

Kalia felt her knees buckling, and she slipped to cobblestones. She was on her back, the blade protruding from her lilac shirt. Above her, beneath the slit of Jerusalem sky, a gray-bearded Arab, waving his knife above his headdress, was shouting, Death to Israel! Death to Jews! He flung himself at Wiederspiel, who caught the wrist of the knife hand as the blade descended and jerked the arm downward. On a continuing motion the knife plunged into the Palestinian's stomach; then Wiederspiel reversed its direction and opened the man from abdomen to sternum.

Why so much silence, Kalia wondered. Why didn't the man scream? Why hadn't she screamed?

Barthelmes was wrestling with the third attacker, holding the man's wrist with two hands, the knife high above their heads. Don't let go, Zach! Kalia prayed, but his arms were bending and his face had lost its color. She could hear him panting.

Then Wiederspiel's arm came across the Palestinian's chest and the blade of his knife cleanly cut the man's throat. A sudden arc of blood spurted into Zachary's face. He gasped and froze helplessly where he stood, while Wiederspiel raced after the Palestinian who'd stabbed Kalia. A dozen yards ahead, the man had slipped and fallen on the slick paving stones, and within seconds Wiederspiel was standing over him. He was a boy, not yet twenty.

The crowd gathered, chanting, Kill him! Kill him! What are you waiting for?

It's all over, Wiederspiel repeated in Arabic and Hebrew, breathing heavily. Back away! The police will take care of it!

As sirens approached, Barthelmes glanced down the emptied aisle of the market from where he knelt by Kalia. Wiederspiel, his knife in his hand, legs spread, stood above the fallen Arab boy. A clear, deep cut ran across his forehead, and his face was wet with his own blood. It dripped off his chin. Wiederspiel wiped his face with a hand and stepped back from his prisoner as booted policemen arrived. Stand back! they shouted in Arabic and Hebrew. Out of the way! There were still more sirens, howling all around them in the Old City.

Wiederspiel looked down at the Palestinian boy, who looked up into the older man's bloody face.

The boy wore blue jeans and a white T-shirt with *Coca-Cola* scripted in Hebrew across the chest.

Wiederspiel smiled and then pointed his bloodstained knife at the boy's chest. Where'd you get the shirt, he asked softly, almost tenderly.

16.

The Prime Minister lit Kalia's cigarette and then her own. I'm glad you are comfortable here, she said. It's a good hospital. The doctor isn't bad, either. Chief of medicine for the forces as well as director of this hospital. Did he do a good job?

I think so. Like they say, it only hurts when I laugh.

Perhaps you'd prefer that I tell you a heartbreaking story?

Kalia laughed. Stop, please! You mustn't break me up like that.

Something I said, no doubt. Golda Meir patted the white hospital sheet. It's lucky—a bad wound but clean. I am happy about the outcome, I'll tell you that. A few inches lower and I might have been making a grave-side speech. Thank God for Wiederspiel. Some defender! I thought he was already too old for that sort of thing. Hand-to-hand combat and not an airplane in sight! Well, I must go now. No rest for the bureaucrats, even women. And stay as long as the doctor asks, I urge you. Don't go running off to dances. Shall I leave the cigarettes?

A kiss on both cheeks and then she was gone. Kalia inhaled the strange brand of cigarette—an Israeli make called Time— and turned her head toward the white-curtained window. She was alone in the room, with the first quiet moment of the day. The routine had begun at dawn with the duty nurse putting a thermometer in her mouth. Breakfast. The doctor arriving to examine his handiwork and change the dressing over the sutured wound. Good, he'd remarked. Not a major battle wound. You can leave tomorrow. Kalia had managed a weak thank-you and smile. Later, a nurse helped her off the bed and walked her down the green corridor to the bathroom; it was the first time in two days she'd been off the bedpan, and she felt dizzy walking back to her room. Then

Zachary had arrived with flowers. How's my soldier? he said, pressing his lips to her forehead.

Like someone beat the shit out of me.

You hit the bricks pretty hard. I saw it all in slow motion. God, it was awful! The smells of the market, the sound of the street, all on a slow-motion video. Booming and bassy, you know that sound?

Kalia looked into Zachary's face. She reached up with her good arm and stroked his cheek. She loved his face. That morning she could not understand why it made her feel sad. Funny, she said, I saw it all in fast forward. Bugs Bunny. The sound of chipmunks. You remember the record? After a pause she said, How's Wiederspiel?

He's fine. Already back to work. Geula called and wants to make us dinner as soon as you're out.

Tomorrow.

Great, Kale. I'll tell her.

She became silent and finally said, I've been wanting to cry all morning, but nothing comes. Why do I feel so depressed?

Jesus! Who wouldn't? I mean, what a shock.

Maybe.

Listen, when you're up and around, come out and nose around with me a little. I've been all over town looking for the Marx House—you know, where Herzl stayed. But nobody knows where it is. Nobody's even heard of it. Not the police and not the young woman in Mayor Kollek's office.

Maybe there never was a Marx House, Kalia said.

It's in his diary.

It was then that the nurse had entered the room, smiling. Golda is here, she said. May she come up?

You're a star! Zachary shouted, hugging her. I'll take off, but I'll catch you later this afternoon. This you deserve all by yourself, Kale.

He had gone before Golda Meir entered.

Now alone, Kalia thought of the Arab boy flying through the air. Was it bassy, slow-mo, or chipmunks? Was there anything about life, she wondered, falling asleep, that was actually, really true?

17.

Built in the eighteenth century, the École Militaire occupied a huge square about five minutes by foot from the Eiffel Tower. Zachary Barthelmes walked slowly around its exterior, taking easily fifteen minutes. Wherever the stone wall was broken by one of the huge wrought-iron gates, he paused and looked into the grounds. At one end of the great rectangle sat the buildings, which lacked the despotic grandeur the French had intended; before them stretched the empty, stone-paved drill field. Two figures had focused historical attention on this place, founded as a military academy for poor, worthy French youth: Marshal Napoleon Bonaparte and Captain Alfred Dreyfus. Napoleon had triumphed over the rigid military caste system, whereas the aristocratic Alfred was destined to become, perhaps, its most famous victim. What a set! Zachary thought, gripping the iron bars of the gate. The degradation of Dreyfus right here, shot precisely where it happened. Oh, if this ground could sing the "Marseillaise" with blood dripping from every unctuous stone. How purple can you get? Herzl would be standing here, exactly where I'm standing. Gripping the same bars I'm gripping as he watched the final humiliation of the Jewish captain.

Behind him a vendor's voice announced, *Glace! Glace! Chocolat! Framboise! Vanille!* Barthelmes turned around, smiled, and asked for *de chocolat*. Digging the hard ice cream from the cardboard cup with a flat wooden spoon, he wandered off in the direction of the Eiffel Tower. Now the scene became clear, thanks to the vendor!

The silent MOB *presses against the gate, breathing in unison like a great bellows.* [Loud, hissing, rasping, wheezing. Music as sound effect or composed? Also the sound of cadenced marching.] *Close-up on black boots. Camera pulls back to show a file of* SOLDIERS, *two abreast. On command they halt. Another command and the soldiers quickstep and form a hollow square.*

HERZL *pushes through the crowd until he reaches the gate. He grips the bars. One hand is bare, and the knuckles are bloodless; the other is inside a gray kid glove that matches his top hat. A toothless* WOMAN *stares up at his stony, bearded face.*

Inside the wall, elegantly dressed LADIES *and* GENTLEMEN *occupy a crudely built grandstand. Murmured conversation and laughter drift upward, the sound rising, as the camera pans across their faces in the grandstand.* [Statesmen, reporters, wives, courtesans? Are they all *toujours gai?* No. Seated in the center is General Georges Clemenceau—ramrod straight. Stern, even angry. At the end, tears in his white mustache.]

Doors open in the École building to the left. THREE GENERALS *with attending* AIDES *step out and descend the stairs, their medals glistening in the morning light. They halt before the grandstand, and the* TROOPS *salute. Doors open in the building to the right. Two files of troops flank a single officer,* CAPTAIN ALFRED DREYFUS. *Sun glints off* DREYFUS'S *pince-nez; his bearing is erect and defiant.*

DREYFUS *and his* GUARDS *come smartly forward, and the sound drops out. The synchronized report of*

*the boots on the stone is absent. Hawks in long bank-
ing glides. The two-file* ENTOURAGE *stops in front of
the* GENERALS. *The* MOB *roars. The echoes beat
against the cold, slate buildings. The hawks wheel
and turn and fly past the Eiffel Tower and across the
Seine.*

GENERAL: Dreyfus, step forward!

DREYFUS *steps forward and salutes. The* GENERAL
*does not, and the sun burns against the gold of his
medals. From the clusters of* CITIZENS *at each gate
and from the grandstand rises a tiny sound, almost
like bird song. But from where* HERZL *stands it is a
battering roar.*

Avenge France! Kill the traitor! Chestnuts! Hang
him now! Chocolate! Hand the Jew over! Vanilla!
Honor! Avenge France! Raspberry!

HERZL *grips the bars, his forehead glistening with
sweat.*

Chestnuts! Chocolate! Vanilla!

The GENERAL *reads from a paper,* DREYFUS *standing
at rigid attention. The pronouncement is severely
amplified and filled with reverb. Quick cut—shots
of* HERZL's *face, Notre Dame, a blond* WOMAN *in
the grandstand,* DREYFUS, *Place de l'Opéra, Les
Halles,* CLEMENCEAU *in constant salute. A drumroll
comes up.*

The said Dreyfus is condemned to military degradation and to deportation to a fortress. Dreyfus,
you are unworthy of your uniform. In the name of
the French people, we deprive you of your rank.

The CROWD *roars as a* JUNIOR OFFICER *steps forward
and tears the epaulets and medals from* DREYFUS's
shoulders and chest.

DREYFUS *cries out:* I am innocent! I swear I am
innocent! Long live France!

The OFFICER *rips the buttons off his tunic, and*
DREYFUS *is marched around the formation. Each sol-*
dier turns his head sharply away from DREYFUS *as*
he passes. The CROWD *roars, and the blond* LADY *on*
the grandstand applauds. HERZL *presses his head*
fiercely against the bars. CLEMENCEAU *holds his sa-*
lute, and his constricted eyes follow the figure of
DREYFUS *as he is marched back toward the buildings*
of the École Militaire.

Zachary Barthelmes felt himself tremble. It was a well-
conceived scene. Moe would like it. He would weep. It would
make a tough guy cry! His ice cream had melted through the
cardboard cup and was dripping from his fingers. He smiled
as he wiped his hands. It's a great scene, but he knew it
probably was untrue.

Herzl had been the Paris correspondent of the *Neue Freie*
Presse, and the story he'd filed on the Dreyfus degradation
seemed perfunctory and, Barthelmes thought, remarkably
light on detail. It was almost as if Herzl had asked a few of
the authorized French reporters who'd been inside the parade
grounds what had happened, and from that had created a
reasonable account that had no balls. Barthelmes couldn't
accept Herzl's statement that the Dreyfus affair had inspired
his passion for the Jewish state, although it was only a year
later that Herzl had published his manifesto, *Der Judenstaat*,
and had begun his diary. In the feverish first pages of that
remarkable work, Herzl rails against the anti-Semitism that
was choking him, but with no mention of Dreyfus. In those
days of rage and writing in the Hôtel Castille on the Rue
Cambon, where the Jewish state was born, Herzl seemed to
be wrestling only with the weight and mystery of Jewishness.
Not with the impact of Dreyfus.

Why couldn't he give up being a Jew, Barthelmes wondered. Austrian Jews had been converting by the thousands,

so why did this elegant, witty boulevardier choose to wear a huge six-pointed star around his neck like an anchor? Or had he neglected Dreyfus out of rivalry? The French officer had been getting all the press, and even Herzl's friend Max Nordau, a well-known psychologist and committed Zionist, devoted more of his time to *l'affaire Dreyfus* than to the fight for a Jewish homeland.

Barthelmes then felt himself drifting away from the essence of the film. To hell with the interior Talmudic landscape. Stick with the École Militaire—a powerful fucking scene that ought to have been true even if it weren't. As he walked on, he licked the last of the sticky chocolate from his fingers. I've been reading too many books, he thought, about too many Jews filled with too many versions of truth. The scene itself was the thing! It was a goddamned good scene! Isn't Art a lie that *seems* to be true? If I do Moe's film, Barthelmes resolved, Dori will grip the iron bars of the École Militaire.

18.

They had an early dinner at the Hôtel Lotti, near the Boulevard Raspail. The interior of the restaurant was a narrow rectangle, the aisles just wide enough for the waiters to pass through. Kalia's healing arm was supported by a sling improvised from a silk Picasso-designed Gucci scarf.

That scene really sounds great, Zach, but aren't you getting in too deep? You keep on like this and you won't be able to say no.

Don't worry about that. If I don't feel like doing it, I'll be able to say so.

Then why are you reading Moe's books and doing these École Militaire things?

The books are interesting. And the diaries—they're incredible. Herzl was recording everything he was doing, *as he did it*, right up to the end.

But all good diaries do that, don't they?

Yes. But these were personal *and* political. All in longhand, unedited. Except, of course, I'm sure he edited a lot while he wrote it down. The main thing is, he was *convinced* he'd lead the Jews back to Holy Land. He was writing himself into history, Kale.

And he comes out smelling like a rose. How convenient!

He tries to avoid that by showing—deliberately, I think— a lot of the downside. And that gives more credence to the account as a whole. Plus, you have to like him when he reveals unflattering things about himself.

Such as?

Hates his wife, which he easily could've left out. Admits his paranoia and his ambitions in the theater. Maybe, if he'd had one hit play, he would've given up on Zionism altogether. Or if he had a happy marriage.

You believe that?

Not really. If I were religious, I'd say that God denied him a great play and a good marriage to make him adhere to the road to Jerusalem. That's what Hechler would think.

That priest with the weird beard?

That's the one.

Seems to me, my darling, that your script is the diaries, *n'est-ce pas?*

Of course you're right. The diaries are my guide. If I did make the film for Moe, I'd have to use them. But what I'd be after are the implications, the hints, the psychology. Herzl *did* write the diaries for history. From his point of view, knowing that he'd failed at women and art, he went for the big pie—his name writ large in the annals of mankind. History! I don't make films for history.

For art, then?

Who knows? For money, probably.

That's a lie.

I love making films.

Well, that's partly true. Kalia smiled. Except when you're doing it.

Okay. I *don't* love to do films. I *need* to do films. I couldn't write the great sonnet or novel, so I found my proper low level in scripts. There's no love in the whorehouse where I work. I *need* to do it. Understand *that*, sweet cups?

I do. Yes. I sure do. She lifted Zachary's hand to her mouth and kissed it, sucked it, bit it. He was startled. She'd never done that before. When he looked into her eyes, they seemed lost or at least focused inwardly. Zachary signaled to the elderly *garçon* for the check.

They strolled through the Tuileries and sat among the trees and statues. They talked about Moe Cohen and Helmut Wiederspiel, about the twin curses of Hollywood and Madison Avenue, about how lucky they were to be in Paris holding hands on this warm night and hearing music in the distance. Kalia was able to laugh without pain, and she laughed often. Zachary was mildly aware that neither of them mentioned the marketplace in Jerusalem. As they walked through the twinkling night toward the hotel, Zachary thought what a great setting this place would make for a scene, probably in another film. He turned to Kalia and said, I love you, you know, and wordlessly they made their way back to the Lotti.

The lights in the bedroom were out, the drapes slightly parted. The mixed light of moon, stars, and street lamps fell equally on the freshly woven Persian rug. Funky, Zachary thought as he studied the illuminated design. Probably a Belgian Persian.

Under the sheet Kalia explored him gently. He responded in kind. They had not made love since the incident. Having assumed that the wound made her uncomfortable, Zachary was pleased by her touch. Mmm, it's been three weeks.

I know. Why should a shoulder wound make everything

else numb, though? Still numb. I just felt like feeling you. You're not numb, are you?

Not for a minute. After I knew you'd be okay, I couldn't keep my mind out of the gutter.

Gutter?

No. Palace.

Too cold.

Heaven, then.

A little better. I think this may get out of hand—no pun, darling. I'm just not up for it.

Pun? Which one?

Kalia laughed. I wanted to hold you. But I don't want to tease you. I need another few days, I think.

Sure. I like this. Just don't get too frisky. I wish they had a radio and TV in the room instead of all this eighteenth-century tradition.

I like it. It makes you feel the dark. You can feel the pulse of lives here, can't you?

If you mean presences, no. But the dark *is* palpable.

Velvet?

Velvet, damask, whatever. You mind if I smoke?

Not if you light one for me, too.

Zachary waved his cigarette in tight, fiery circles in the dark. Would I have done this if we had a TV set?

Never.

Did I tell you that I went to the Rue Cambon? It's the street right behind us. That's where Herzl wrote *Der Judenstaat*, in the Hôtel Castille.

What's it like?

Nothing much, really, just a second-class hotel. He couldn't afford to stay in l'Hôtel Lotti.

Unlike us rich tourists.

Moe Cohen's rich, and I guess we're not exactly poor. Anyway, there's a plaque about Herzl alongside the entrance saying that Herzl wrote his manifesto there. But the desk clerk had no idea who Herzl was and not the foggiest which apartment he'd kept. All he knew was that people wandered into the Castille all the time asking questions about him. I gave the guy five francs to let me take a look at a typical room, and he tells me he'd considered calling one Herzl's and charging an admission fee. Are you still awake?

Yes. It's interesting. What did it look like?

Tacky, really. Maybe it was more attractive in 1896, but it gave me ideas.

More scenes?

That's right. Anyway, while he was in Paris working for the newspaper, he and his wife were apart most of the time. They already had two kids, Pauline and Hans. The marriage had already hit the rocks.

From what you say, Zach, the marriage was on the rocks from day one. Made in hell, I'd say. I'm surprised they ever fucked. Aren't you?

Well, yes and no. Even if he didn't think much of Julie, he'd want to prove his manhood. But I haven't really got a handle on her feelings. Did she want Dori sexually, or did she want to make him perform even, or especially, if he didn't want to? I guess I don't know if I can write from a woman's point of view. Do you think she enjoyed sex?

Women are various, Zach. Some women enjoy it for a while, then it becomes less important. After they have kids, maybe. To perk things up—pun—psychologists advise flowers, candles, mood music, and surprises. Live out your fantasies, right? I think all that leads women to fake passion.

Not men?

Your species, my darling, is rather obvious. Your passion rises up in its obviousness, and then it cools, shrivels, and dies. All within minutes. Then Kalia released him, got out of bed, and went into the bathroom.

Zachary lit another cigarette. The match fire seemed enormous, and he narrowed his eyes against it.

In the apartment in the Castille, a small, kidney-shaped table sat near the window. In that great outpouring of passion, when Herzl fashioned his vision, did sheets of paper fall from that desk onto the floor? The first burning pages of the diary, hot and bright. His dressing gown wet with perspiration, his hands trembling, while the pen lived its own life.

The tears running down his cheeks. The dressing gown melting, peeling away from his body. The man sitting naked in dim light and bright. His beard heavy with sweat and tears. Fever. Fever and words, not one after the other but in bursts of unreined thought: the soul vomiting up its fearful bile. The man in his silence screaming: This is the truth of it! This is the truth of it! I am a Jew who does not want to be a Jew who must be a Jew because that is what a Jew must be. I want you to love the Jew you will not love because a Jew cannot be loved. I am the Jew who thinks he is a man shackled to a land which is not his land! I am the Jew who—

Then Zachary felt Kalia slide into bed.

God, I didn't want to disturb you. You were universes away.

I was imagining what Herzl felt when he wrote the first pages of his diaries.

And what did it feel like?

It felt like Zachary Barthelmes, screenwriter, trying to feel like Theodor Herzl, journalist turned visionary. I think I flunked. I'll tell you one thing, Kalia: after that sort of intensity, a man's got to get laid.

You?

No, Herzl. Here's a scene: this would be the night before the École Militaire. Can I put on the light?

Yes. Of course.

Barthelmes got out of bed, found his Paris notebook, got back into bed, cleared his throat, and read.

Parlor room of HERZL *apartment at the Hôtel Castille. Wearing a smoking jacket,* HERZL *pours a few drops of cologne into his palm and pats it into his beard. There's a knock at the door, and he welcomes a voluptuous, smiling* WOMAN. *He sweeps her into his arms. She throws her large black straw chapeau onto the wing chair. They kiss, and* HERZL *lifts her dress from behind.*

Oh, Dori! You're so naughty, my sweet little cabbage!

Lulu! Lulu! Sweet girl!

They fall onto the sofa, and HERZL *paws her bosom.*

Wait! You'll tear my gown!

LULU's *hands unhook her corselet. When her large-nippled breasts appear,* HERZL *stands back and stares.*

You are the most beautiful woman in all of Paris!

DORI *and* LULU, *naked in bed, as much open sex as the ratings allow. They climax and collapse.*

Oh, Dori! I love you so.

And I love you, sweet girl.

Have you finished the play?

Only the last act remains.

My part—you have expanded it?

So far, another thirty lines. I cannot imagine that you will not be noticed! The lines are brightly honed, my Lulu. At the curtain call you will receive a standing ovation.

Oh, Dori! I'll never forget what you're doing for me. I will always come when you want me.

Believe me, Lulu, one day you will have Paris at your feet!

I have found a singing teacher, Dori. Not for singing but to strengthen my voice. I want to be like the Divine Sarah. My voice will ring through the theater! In my dressing room there will be so many

flowers it will be difficult to breathe. Fine
gentlemen—fine gentlemen like you, Dori—will
wait at the stage door. But have no concern, I will
not see them. Nor will I tell them that Theodor
Herzl, the great playwright, has won my heart! I'm
so excited! My first play, and I will say a hundred
lines! No, no, I am joking. Fifty will be quite enough!
Dori? *Dori?*

Pan across room to a gently snoring HERZL. *The
camera pulls back and shows* LULU *resting against
the pillows, smiling radiantly, her arms behind her
head. Her breasts rise and fall with her breathing.*

*Cut to the bedroom mirror. Daylight floods the
room.* HERZL *steps before the glass. He brushes his
hair, then puts on his Prince Albert coat and his dove-
gray top hat. In the mirror he observes* LULU *asleep
on the bed. The sheet is drawn up over her eyes. He
turns away from the mirror, lifts an orange tulip from
a vase, and breaks away a length of the stem. He pulls
the sheet down, revealing her breasts, and places the
tulip upright between them. She moans and stretches
as* HERZL *steps toward the bedroom door. He stops,
takes his billfold from his coat pocket, and removes
some currency. Pulling the sheet down to* LULU's
*knees, he folds some notes and slips them between her
thighs.* LULU *smiles and rolls over.*

Cut to sky over Paris. From far above we see HERZL
*striding jauntily, his walking stick swinging. Behind
him is the Arc de Triomphe; before him is the École
Militaire. Crowds are gathering, and there is a sudden
and loud rolling of drums.*

Good scene, right?
You horny bastard!

Oh, come off it, Kalia. After that scene you'll always see Herzl as a human being.

Bullshit. After a scene like that, the audience will never take him seriously. They'll be thinking cock, tits, and ass. Whenever he's about to deliver some heartbreaking speech, everybody's wondering when he'll drop his pants.

Think so?

Know so. Convince me otherwise.

Barthelmes laughed softly. You know what? Perhaps you're right, but it's the damnedest thing! The scholars have two points of view about his sexual activities: one is that he was a satyr; the other is that he couldn't endure sex because his true love was his mother. All I'm doing is keeping it clean. I'm saying that the hero, like other men, didn't mind a little nookie when he was far from home.

I *hate* that word, Zach. Please. And do we really need to see all this anyway? Everybody does it, and so what? I just went to the bathroom, and you know what I do in there. Would you like to watch me do it? Watch me take a shit?

Oh, God, Kalia, that's awful!

But the whole world does it. Men, women, children, parakeets. Why not put that on film, too? Herzl's a human being like all the rest of us. Doesn't he go to the john and take a dump?

Know something, Kale? I can answer that point. I can—

You're stubborn, Barthelmes.

Wait a minute! I can rebut, Kalia, but I won't. On the whole you're right. Let me unmodify that. You *are* right. If I want to kill Herzl, I do the scene.

You want to kill him?

I don't think so, no. Even if I wanted to kill him, that's too cheap a shot.

Hooray for me! I won an argument!

Hey, that's unfair! So you're right! Do you want me to scrap Lulu? And what about his gonorrhea?

What gonorrhea?

He had the clap. He wrote to a close friend explaining that he'd gone to a haberdashery to buy a sleeve for, well, to wear over it.

If you use that, Barthelmes, consider yourself a dead man! Moe will cut your balls off.

It's from one of Moe's books, Kalia. He gave me a box of truth.

Really? And there's another box of truth somewhere that tells a different story.

Zachary laughed and lit another cigarette. Gonorrhea isn't filmic, he said, but it was quite common, almost a rite of passage. In the middle class, men didn't marry until they'd established themselves. And that happened long after they got these awful urges.

I bear witness, darling.

Whores. Shop girls. House servants.

Lulus?

Lulus were for artists. It wasn't at all unusual for the bride-groom to bring syphilis to the nuptial bed. Gonorrhea might have affected Herzl's children. They wound up basket cases, you know.

I don't want to hear about it.

I don't want to talk about it, either. It's a fucking tragedy.

Good night, Zach. You're a good man.

Night, Kale. I'll take your word for it.

PART THREE

1.

The phone rang at 7:00 a.m. Zachary got out of bed and walked across the room to the thin stand where the phone sat.

It was Wiederspiel. It's early, I know, but it can't be helped. I got a call from Moe Cohen. He asked me to find you.

Why you?

Never mind that. I haven't got good news. Your father died yesterday morning.

After a pause Zachary said, Must have been his heart. Thanks for getting to me, Hal. How did Moe get into this?

The police called the L.A. number in your father's address book.

Why didn't they call my New York number?

Maybe they did. The L.A. number was your agent's, and he said Moe would know. So he called me. Geula said she was sure you were in Paris. My office people called the better hotels. Anyway, it doesn't make any difference now, Zachary. You may want to go home. I'm sure there are things you'll have to sort out.

Yes, thanks. Zachary hung up without knowing what else to say, then leaned his head against the cool glass of the windowpane and tried to understand what he was feeling. There were only a few details that had required immediate attention. Booking the flight—the concierge could attend to that. Luggage—just a small bag with underclothes and socks, a few shirts and a spare tie, slacks, shaving gear, and toiletries.

Twelve hours later he was airborne. The concierge had been able to change his francs into dollars and arrange for a car to take him to Orly. Barthelmes had made a single telephone call. It was to his father's attorney, Walter Morton, who had offered sincere condolences. Jerome Barthelmes had been cremated at Cook's Funeral Home two hours earlier. Zachary said he would pick up the ashes himself. There was a simple will, Morton explained. Jerome's estate, mostly securities and cash, would be given to Trinity Church on Wall Street.

Was my name mentioned in the will? Zachary asked.

Yes. Your father said that you were his only living relative; that you required none of his estate; and that, if you were able, you might dispose of the goods in his apartment. Furniture, bedding, utensils, papers—you know.

Does he mention my mother's family?

No, nothing. I haven't even got an address. When did your mother pass on?

More than forty years ago. Anything else?

I think that's it. I wrote the will myself. It was bone simple—two double-spaced pages.

Keys to his apartment?

I have a set.

Can you have them dropped off with my doorman?

Surely.

By the way, Walter. His death, how did it happen?

Even though he was retired, as you know, he still did some accounting jobs for old clients just to keep his hand in. He was at Jimmy Clark's house—the fellow with the shipyard in Great Neck. Hadn't looked at a sheet of paper when he collapsed, just like that. Heart attack. Massive, I'm told. By the time they got him to the hospital it was all over.

How old was he? Seventy-two?

Let me look. . . . Here we are. Seventy-six. No, seventy-seven.

Barthelmes buzzed the flight attendant and ordered two shots of scotch. He poured the minibottles over the ice, then rolled the cold glass between his palms. He hadn't seen his father for—what?—eight years. Something like that. It was on Jerome's birthday, and that year Zachary had become dutifully sentimental and arrived unannounced at his father's apartment. When Jerome opened the door, he smiled, the same pale smile, which revealed only his yellowed teeth. What a wonderful surprise, Zachary, his father said. What a wonderful surprise!

Happy birthday, Dad! Zachary embraced his father, thinking, as he held him, how small he was, how frail. Zachary presented the gift-wrapped box. You can open it later, Dad. If your liquor cabinet's stocked, let's have a birthday drink or two.

They sat in the living room, Jerome in his favorite chair and Zachary in the corner of the couch closest to him. The furniture, the carpeting, the drapes, the green plants hanging halfway down from the ceiling—everything seemed *House Beautiful* fresh, the good taste of perfect indifference. A living room perfectly suited to a Certified Public Accountant, almost beyond criticism, barely used and wholly unloved, although not inexpensive. Zachary had visited that apartment not more than a half dozen times, and never had he ever seen any room but the living room; even having the need to go into the bathroom and piss seemed almost a violation of his father's privacy. He never did.

Barthelmes sipped the cold drink. Jerome: father, dad, daddy, stranger. There was the other house, the house in which they once had lived. Queens, three stops from Manhattan on the Flushing train and four long, tree-lined blocks from the 46th Street Sunnyside station. An accountant's house, neat and trim. In that house there had been no laughter, except his own little-boy laughter. Jerome and Katherine Anne never laughed. They smiled. His mother's smile, Zachary thought, was very much like his father's, although her teeth were bigger and whiter. Very white with some blue in them. Katherine Anne had no odor, not even of soap, and he couldn't remember if she had used makeup. A very pale touch of lipstick—lip rouge, she had called it.

In that house, the Sunnyside house, Mozart had played at an almost inaudible level. Zachary remembered sitting on the floor with his head close to the mahogany cabinet of the record player. How wonderful was Mozart! Had the music been heard only by the small boy who sat floating on the sea of the beige wall-to-wall carpet? The boy's bedroom, on the floor above, was across the narrow hallway from his parents' bedroom. When he had said his prayers, they each in turn kissed him good night. Smiling, they quietly shut his door behind them. If he awoke before them in the morning, he always would find their bedroom door closed. To keep us nice and comfy in our very own beds, his mother had said, kneeling before him and anxiously patting his cheek.

Once the boy had had a nightmare, coming awake to his own loud screams. It was a long time before his mother came into his room. She held him to her warm breasts. He remembered her warmth. She said, over and over, It's all right, Zachary, it's all right. Just a dream. A dream. A dream, just a dream. He wanted to tell her about the dream but she said, Shhh, go to sleep.

After that she always left his door open a little and hers as well. His nightmare had frightened her, the boy realized. Sometimes he pretended to have a nightmare so she would come to his bed and cradle his head against her breasts. Just a dream, just a dream, just a dream.

Only in the basement of the Sunnyside house did Jerome Barthelmes come to life. Down there the boy remembered his father whistling and the radio playing, a small, brown radio in a wooden case. Down there Jerome had whistled and sung while working with his tools and his lathe, building crucifixes and sculpting the bleeding forms of Jesus Christ, Our Lord. Crosses of many sizes, many of woods (pine, ash, oak, teak, mahogany, and the flesh of other trees) and metals (iron, brass, aluminum, stainless steel, silver, and tin). And for each crucifix a body of Christ (Christ of wood, Christ of bronze, silver Christ, clay Christ, porcelain Christ, Christ of crystal). All made in the ovens, on the worktables, on the lathes of Jerome Barthelmes. Everything done in the basement, where Jerome sang and whistled, except the castings, which were fashioned in the hot foundry where Jerome's clay Christs had been magically transformed into bronze or silver or iron and were then brought back to the basement and lovingly fixed to a waiting crucifix.

On the basement walls these crucifixes hung in their many colors and sizes, and the largest Christ of all leaned forward over Jerome's workbench: an iron Christ, His hands and feet bolted to burnished teak.

The boy had sat on a high stool surrounded by the many Sons of God. Once, smiling a real smile, Jerome had said, What do you think, Zachary?

Good, he answered.

Yes, good. You won't understand this, my son. But this is it: God guides my hands. If I tried to fashion a dog, Zachary, I would fail. Yet because God guides my fingers, to find the form, the pain, of Jesus Christ, it is not so difficult. You see that?

Yes, Daddy. I love my Lord Jesus, Daddy, and He loves me.

The flight attendant, responding to Zachary's signal, brought him a fresh glass of ice and two more minibottles. He could not remember how Katherine Anne Barthelmes had died. He never had asked his father, so he didn't know. Had there been a proper funeral, or was she simply cremated as his father just had been? He did not know. It almost seemed that after Zachary's last nightmare she had left his room, gone down the stairs, opened the front door, and wandered down the tree-lined streets until she was seen no more.

She had left no odor. Where had they left him, the boy, when they had taken Katherine Anne away? Zachary wondered. He did not even know if his father had ever told him his mother had died.

There had been a housekeeper—vague recollections. She had an odor—but what was her name? He recalled that Jerome had spent more and more time in the basement. But the boy had never been asked to accompany him again, nor had he heard any whistling or singing or radio sounds, no hammer tapping or whining lathe. Within a year of his mother's death, Zachary had been enrolled in the North Country School at Lake Placid. The youngest child there, he was frightened by the hoots of the owl nesting outside the window of his shared room. Tears ran down his face, but he had not cried out.

Zachary was quite skilled at drawing and painting, and was able to make up fully rhymed poems. Just name the subject and Zachary will have it down in eight good lines, his teacher had said, as quick as a flash—no moons and Junes, either.

Jerome came to visit on all the major holidays, and once again in the winter and spring. Each time he brought gifts and a little extra spending money, which Zachary stashed in a drawer along with his socks and underwear. Invariably, Jerome would arrive just before lunch and would leave a little before dinner. Each year, for two weeks, father and son were at home together in Sunnyside, and almost from the beginning Zachary would look forward to returning to North Country.

Two events of great importance took place at the school, both in his fourteenth year. First he decided he would become a writer, and then he had a great deal of sex with Adriana McCauley, who described herself as a "revolted Catholic." Jerome had attended his graduation, genuinely pleased that Zachary Barthelmes was valedictorian.

Zachary spent the summer after graduation at a wilderness camp, where he learned to climb mountains. In the fall he entered the Mount Herman School in Northfield, Massachusetts; three years later, Harvard.

A fresh glass of tea, more whiskey.

Jerome's death had rattled him more than he could understand. Zachary did not think he had loved his father, yet he was moved to compassion. For an accountant. For a pale man with a weak smile. For the sculptor of Christ, who once had whistled in his simple, basement workshop. Compassion, Zachary thought, certainly not love. How I wish I'd known you, my father!

2.

Zachary Barthelmes sat quietly on the couch, close to the chair Jerome had always occupied. His breathing was shallow, almost as if he didn't want his breath to rattle the silence. Finally he stood up and walked slowly through the apartment. In the kitchen the cabinets were empty, except for a few water tumblers, a skillet, and a small stainless steel pot with a black-knobbed lid; he found some cutlery in a lower drawer. The refrigerator had two brown eggs, two small jars of apricot and strawberry jam, a small container of milk and, still in the plastic bag, a few slices of bread. Sustenance, Zachary supposed; his father's last meal. As he emptied the contents of the fridge into a brown paper bag, his eyes filled with tears. Jesus Christ! he said aloud.

He opened the door to the bedroom. Had Jerome shut it? The slatted blinds were closed against the light, and the bed was neatly made. The toes of a pair of brown slippers peeked from beneath a floral-quilted bed cover that didn't quite touch the beige carpet. A large desk stood against the wall between the doors of two closets; an oak, curved-back swivel chair with a straw mat on its seat rested in the well of the desk. Above the desk, the iron Christ leaned forward from the wall. In the chambered air, a silent sound of whistling filled Zachary's ear. Leaving the door ajar, he went into the toilet, unzipped his fly, and pissed for what he thought was a long time.

Emptying the rooms, he figured, would be no problem. If Trinity Church didn't have its own thrift shop, one of its deacons might know of one. Taking a deep breath, Zachary returned to the bedroom and seated himself at the blond-finished desk and looked up at his father's iron Christ. A cord of leather hung from Jesus's iron neck, and a small ring was attached to the cord. Zachary stood up and slowly reached toward it; I am inside a B-movie, he thought, *The Talisman of the Mummy*. When I touch it, I'll scream and turn slowly, frame by frame, to dust. He removed the cord from Christ's neck. The little silver ring had its own tiny iron Christ affixed to its surface. Zachary sobbed as he had in Jerusalem, where the Holy City had displayed itself before the window on Ein Rogel Street.

Jerome Barthelmes had fashioned this ring for his small son. How proud and delighted the boy had been! Then, the day it had vanished, terror and shame had replaced delight. Why had he lost the ring, why? *If I die before I wake, I pray the Lord* . . . Without knowing the reason, he hadn't reported the loss of the ring to his father. Now, as he warmed the tiny Christ in his closed fist, he wondered why his father hadn't told him the ring had been found. Had it been discovered by Katherine Anne or by Jerome? Or was it some sort of test? Perhaps it had been expected, or even hoped, that the boy might say: Father, I have lost my Christ.

3.

Barthelmes unlocked each desk drawer. He reached to open the long top drawer on the left side, then hesitated. Even as he lit a cigarette, he realized that smoking was forbidden in this room. He bolted up from the oak chair, walked to the bathroom, and flushed the cigarette down the toilet. He returned to the desk and, without sitting down, pulled the drawer open. On the left-hand side, a pile of pads in descending order: small, medium, medium large, and a large, lined yellow pad at the bottom. In the center, a checkbook as large as the yellow pad, with check numbers 1328, 1329, and 1330 facing up. On the right, the New Testament in good black leather. In the front, a bundle of ballpoint pens in the embrace of two rubber bands; to the rear, nothing. In the drawer below were ten years' worth of date books, and the two drawers below that were empty.

In the top drawer on the right side were copies of Jerome's income-tax returns, another dozen years. In the second drawer down, Zachary found an olive-drab metal box, almost as long as the drawer. He fitted the small, plain key hanging from the ring into the lock, and lifted the lid back on its hinge. Everything was bound by rubber bands. Photographs of his mother as a high school graduate: white dress, hair ribbon, rolled diploma in hand, 1919. At some anonymous beach in a black, all-concealing bathing suit, 1921. As a graduate of Columbia University, 1923. Snapshots of Katherine Anne and Jerome, in a rowboat in Central Park, on a hilltop, and under a magnificent sky. In the latter she's holding flowers as Jerome holds his straw boater aloft; on the back a note read: *Cold Springs, N.Y. I proposed here. Katherine said yes. August 19, 1924.* In another shot, in a Packard touring sedan, Jerome stands before the door to his office, pointing:

Jerome A. Barthelmes, Certified Public Accountant. There were many other snapshots. Several of the infant Zachary in a crib, in Katherine Anne's arms, in Jerome's arms. They seem content, even happy, with their newborn son. The rubber band, its elasticity gone, snapped when Zachary tried to stretch it around the thick packet. Marriage certificate, 1924; death certificate, Katherine Anne Barthelmes, 1936— congestive heart failure. Documents and receipts pertaining to two grave sites at the cemetery at 157th and Riverside Drive. Trinity's, Zachary thought. I'll bury his ashes there. Baptismal certificate for one Zachary Wellington Barthelmes, also at Trinity Church. Papers—papers, the proof of deeds done, of death done, of time, of existence.

Zachary got up from the chair and went to the bathroom to smoke a cigarette. Flushing the butt down the toilet, he opened a window onto the air shaft. He felt heavy—from the trip from Paris, and the emotional drain of being in Jerome's apartment—yet he had to finish this. He returned to the desk and sat before the tin box. A manila envelope was folded in two and strapped in many rubber bands, each breaking at his touch. The glue of the flap had lost its hold, and Zachary emptied the contents onto the desk by the side of the box. Photographs mainly. An unopened letter marked RETURN TO SENDER. In a yellowing paper frame, a portrait of a man in his forties with a short, brown beard sitting in a straight-back chair and wearing a homburg, almost smiling. In another paper frame is the same man, very serious, with a boy sitting on his knee. In the next he stands between two women, their arms linked; here the man is younger, and the women are very young, in their late teens or early twenties, their bosoms large and hair tied back. Hebraic letters beneath each figure. Their names? In another photo, a woman, holding a book, stands before a small building, behind her a painted sign. Hebrew letters and English letters. The English says, Burnside Avenue Central Synagogue. In the next photo, the bearded man again; the beard is longer and white. In yet another, in a heavier paper frame, the boy is now older. The picture is hand colored, the eyes blue and the hair light brown, the cheeks and lips rouged. Here the boy stands on a red-carpeted platform wearing a blue-and-white prayer shawl; behind him is an open, velvet-curtained cabinet. Two Torah scrolls are visible. The boy is smiling. Zachary looks closely at the photograph, touching it gently with his forefinger. He knows this boy. This boy is his father. This is Jerome.

In the oak chair, Zachary trembles and then picks up the unopened letter. It is addressed to Zalman Borenstein, 981 Burnside Avenue, Bronx, New York. The sender is J. Borenstein, GPO Box 67, Boston, Massachusetts. He unseals the envelope.

June 14, 1930

Dear Papa,

Three letters I have sent have been returned by you. I hope that you will open this one and read it. I am writing with good news, Papa. Katherine has given birth to a healthy son. Seven pounds, four ounces! We have named him Zachary. I hope you will let us bring Zachary into your house so that he can see his *Zayde* and so that you can hold him on your lap.

I am enclosing the first photo taken of your Grandson. The woman holding him is Katherine, my wife.

Perhaps you will not send this letter back to me. I hope and pray you will read it and see your Grandson.

With all my heart I wish for your good health. I send you my deepest respect.

Joseph, Your Son

With no thought of leaving the room, Zachary lit a cigarette. He inhaled deeply, holding the smoke in his lungs, allowing it to escape from his mouth and nostrils without directing its passage. It rose upward in an erratic cloud.

Joseph Borenstein—Jerome Barthelmes. Joseph Borenstein had become Jerome Alexander Barthelmes. Borenstein the Jew had become Barthelmes the Episcopalian. Obviously he'd told his father of his conversion. Obviously his father— my grandfather!—wasn't willing to accept this. No evidence of anger, unless you consider returned letters as total silence and relentless anger.

Zachary studied the photograph of the man—foreign born, he thought—with the two women. The one on the left, he guessed, was his grandmother. She was the one standing before the Burnside Avenue Central Synagogue and was also represented in other photos, often with Zalman. What was her name? In his letter to Zalman, Joseph had not referred to his mother even once. Had she died? And why had Jerome written under the name of Borenstein? Was it so difficult to tell his father that he'd given up both Judaism and his name, or was this a weak attempt to keep in contact? Or, along with the post office box, a ploy to keep Katherine Anne from learning that Jerome Alexander Barthelmes was a converted Jew?

Zachary smoked one cigarette after another, wondering what it must've been like, this choosing of God with His Son over a God without child. What was it that had driven Jerome to Christ? And why was it so important to Zalman that he had slammed all doors shut in his son's face. Were other children—now uncles, aunts, cousins—born to Zalman Borenstein, patriarchal Jew? Stern, remorseless, unforgiving.

Zachary now thought of his father with a sense of warmth, and of admiration for the courage it took to defy his father, to commit an act so perilously close to murder. But Zachary wondered how he would ever discover the deep, hidden reasons his father had for doing so. There was only the letter begging for Zalman's forgiveness, hoping he might open the envelope, see his grandson, and soften his heart. Begging for forgiveness but not yielding his new God. What did Orthodox Jews do when faced with such betrayal? Zachary imagined Zalman rending his garment and retreating into the synagogue to wail out the prayer for the dead. *Kaddish*, it was called. *Kaddish*. For Zalman, Jerome was dead. And you can't receive letters from dead men.

Suddenly Zachary laughed out loud. He laid his head down on the photographs spread across the desktop and laughed hysterically, sobbed, jagged into coughing, and laughed and laughed and laughed. I'm a Jew! he shouted. I'm a Jew! He laughed until his abdomen ached and his breath grew short. Then he wiped his eyes, got up, and went into the bathroom.

Zachary Barthelmes studied his face in the mirror. His hair was still blond—his mother's. There was gray in it now, but you'd have to look hard for it. Easier to find in his beard when he didn't shave. Blonder when he was tanner, as he was now. Though not small, his nose was straight—also his mother's. His father's was slightly wide and showed the hint of a curve. Next Zachary looked at his eyes, which were almost artificially blue. He hated them. When he'd been at school, his eyes had attracted boys rather than girls, and he was pretty rather than handsome. When had he become handsome? But Kalia did love his eyes. His lips were thin— Jerome's. His teeth, not counting the dozen-odd fillings, were perfect—his mother's. His jaw, a little too square, perhaps was descended from a relative other than his parents. Could it be Zalman's? A Jewish jaw? Zachary smiled at his reflection. He still was the spitting image of a proper Episcopalian.

Amused, Zachary shook his head. A Jew! Well, half a Jew. That was strange. No, it was fucking bizarre—and amusing, too. Zachary Wellington Barthelmes: a Jew. Jaizus Emmanuel Christ! Yet something was missing. The passion. Barthelmes thought that if he were writing a scene of this kind, surely it would be filled with towering, monumental passion—Harry Bauer playing Beethoven, Laurence Olivier as Lear—but not this mixed bag of emotions: a small initial shock, incredulity, a little amazement, pity for Jerome, curiosity for the Borensteins, and the need to laugh because it was ironic and, yes, it was fucking funny. Zachary Wellington Barthelmes, the well-known Jew. And how did Joseph Borenstein come by Barthelmes, anyway—the phone book, the movies? The old actor Richard Barthelmess, maybe?

If Jews as a people had anything, he thought, it was passion. Passion unto the highest. Moe Cohen had it to spare. In Wiederspiel it seethed. In Theodor Herzl it had raged.

Jerome Alexander Barthelmes would have joined Herzl in his earliest fantasies about the Jewish Question. Solve it through mass conversion. More or less, if you can't beat them, join them. Was that passion?

Zachary sat down at the desk again, shuffled the secret photographs, smoked, and smiled. Conversion, that surely was the last act of passion for Jerome Alexander. To quit Judaism. To live the rest of his life in an emptiness he could not have imagined. Herzl had considered the conversion-solution himself—and that, Zachary thought, would make a good scene. It couldn't be funny; but could it be regal? It was serious, all right. Sad, goddamn it, it had to be sad! But how the hell can you realize that sort of scene? If it didn't work on the screen, it could be easily dropped—a neat, complete edit.

Barthelmes closed his eyes and conjured up a crowd of images.

Vienna, 1895. Sunday at noon, St. Stephen's Square, St. Stephen's Cathedral. Ancient spires reach toward heaven as the carillon peals. The doors of houses open and people emerge in Sunday dress. They walk through the center of the streets inside the Ringstrasse. Clusters of CHILDREN *walk hand in hand toward St. Stephen's, singing sweet little Austrian songs, as gowned* WOMEN *and formally dressed* MEN *greet one another. Close, quick shots of St. Stephen's towering windows, hissing gargoyles, spires, and bell towers. Closer shot of the bronze bells as the ringing becomes even louder. Cut to the street. A skipping* GIRL. *A beatific* OLD WOMAN *on crutches, propels herself rapidly along. Two* PRIESTS. *Cut to the towers and bells. Sudden silence. Butt cut to cathedral doors and the bowed, worn marble stairs. As the doors swing open, a torrent of massed voices leaps from the inner darkness into the sunlit square.*

Hallelujah! Hallelujah! Hallelujah!

The POPE *emerges, his golden miter glistening, his crooked white staff burning the air. Out of a side street comes a parade. On the flanks, wearing prayer shawls,* JEWISH MEN *carry prayer books and chant ancient prayers. In the middle march* CHILDREN *dressed in white, lace-fringed robes. Each wears a large Star of David made of gold. A thousand Stars of David, a cacophony of light flashing, light leaping from Jewish stars. The marching* JEWS *chant and the parade moves forward. The* POPE *turns his face directly toward the parade. The papal face is filled with love. All through the square, people are kneeling. Crossing themselves, praying. The parade of Jews presses forward, slowly, ecstatically, step by step. Forward. The chanting* HEBREWS *weep as they march up the steps of St. Stephen's.*

They stop and a great silence resounds like a thundering chord of music. In his blue-and-white prayer shawl, HERZL *steps out of his file and marches crisply forward. Eyes follow him through the silence. He comes to a military halt in front of the* POPE, *who extends his hand. Cut to the papal ring, then to the eyes of the* POPE *and the Jewish leader.*

HERZL *speaks without looking down at the prof-*
fered hand:
Your Holiness, in keeping with our discussions
and agreements, I am here to present one thousand
Jewish boys and girls to you and the Catholic
Church for conversion to Christianity. Next Sunday
at high noon, the Jewish community will bring forward another thousand children. This open act will
be witnessed by all Vienna, the Empire, and the
world. This act will be repeated each Sunday until
all Jewish children have been absorbed into the
Church. As for the older Jews, we will live in our
faith and in our honor, worshipping in our synagogues, praying to our God in our way, until we
will have finished our lives. Thus, the Jewish Question will have been laid to rest and thus peace without end shall come to the world.
The CROWD *roars. The bells peal. The light dances
off glass and gold. The* POPE *says,* Ora pro nobis, ora
pro nobis. *He chants in Latin.*
*The doors of St. Stephen's open wider, the age-
blackened doors groaning on their hinges. The*
JEWISH CHILDREN *march forward in their white
robes. Row after row they go up the three marble steps
into the medieval darkness of St. Stephen's.*

Now, for the first time, Zachary Barthelmes sobbed out the
connection between himself and the dead man: Daddy,
Daddy, Daddy! After a long while, he went into the bathroom
and dried his face of its tears.

Surely, he thought, his father had known of Herzl, but how
much? Had it not been this fantasy of Herzl's that Joseph
Borenstein had wanted—indeed, had acted on? Yet Herzl
had recognized this fantasy as nothing more than the fevers
of rage. Why had he been born a Jew instead of a Prussian?

Why didn't the Gentiles love him? And of course this solution evaporated before the cold reality of the Church. No public acceptance of the children of unrepented Jews. The Pope would not have it, nor would organized and established Jewry. The Chosen People would remain the Chosen People, by God! And even for Pastor William Hechler, mass conversion was an unthinkable, disastrous act. An abomination! How could Christ rise if the Jews did not return to the Holy Land? Well, God had put a stop to those fantasies, hadn't he? He gave to Hechler, and to the world, one Theodor Herzl.

In the real Vienna, not the one of dreams, Jews who had converted by the thousands had done so in near darkness, not in Herzl's dreamlike daylight. New Jews cloaked in new names, and imprinted with new guilt and shame. And what of Jerome Barthelmes? Had it been so hard to be a Jew that he could risk losing his own family? And how had Herzl's pipe dreams of conversions by daylight and duels at dawn with anti-Semites given way to the ever more fantastical idea of a Jewish state, drawn to his own design and specifications?

As the parade moved toward St. Stephen's, what music played? Bach or Beethoven? Certainly not Mozart. Maybe you could risk having new music composed. But of one thing Barthelmes was sure: it would be one hell of a scene!

Barthelmes replaced the papers and photographs in the long, metal box. He locked it, then tucked it under his arm and left Joseph Borenstein's silent apartment. Down on the street, Zachary's stomach throbbed and ached. Was he a Jew in any real sense? When Joseph had acted, had he acted for his son as well? And had he kept the green box so that his son might discover it? Yes, Zachary thought, his father had left it for him.

As he walked west toward Central Park, he felt feverish. Jesus Christ! he said out loud, though he couldn't tell whether the voice was only inside his head. My name is Zachary Wellington Barthelmes, and I have a few questions to ask.

Why did my father do it? Was it simply because he fell in love with Katherine Anne Wellington? No, my mother must have known. Would she have married a Jew? Had *she* asked him to accept Christ? But why had there been no other Wellingtons in his life? Perhaps his mother was ashamed of her family's attitudes toward Jews. Maybe Katherine and Jerome had agreed: neither Wellingtons nor Borensteins, no families at all. It was a possible scenario. Had Jerome formally converted, or had he walked into Trinity Church one day and sat down? Yes, Zachary thought. Into Trinity's darkness went Joseph Borenstein, and, no questions asked, Christ had come. Joseph Borenstein, a Jew, had entered; Jerome Alexander Barthelmes, an Episcopalian, had exited.

Who is a Jew? *What* is a Jew? And what about a converted Jew or half a Jew? What is a Zalman Borenstein?

The late-afternoon July sun washed across the West Side of Manhattan. Zachary took his sunglasses from the breast pocket of his safari jacket and put them on. Walking he watched the sun touch the gilt, silver, and glass rooftops. The sight of these sun-washed towers made him think of Jerusalem as he'd seen it from the apartment on Ein Rogel Street. Suddenly, filled with exhilaration, Barthelmes stopped on the street corner and stretched his hands before him. They were his hands, tanned, covered with shiny blond hair. He laughed as people passed by, hurrying in all directions. I'm invisible, Barthelmes said to himself. The invisible Jew. Correction: the invisible half Jew! Light headed, he walked west through Central Park.

Back inside his apartment, Barthelmes put the green tin box on the dining room table. Only then did he remember he'd forgotten to stop by Cook's Funeral Parlor to pick up his father's ashes.

PART FOUR

1.

Wiederspiel climbed down from the roof of his house after replacing a dozen cedar shingles that had rotted out. Rain had seeped through and dripped onto the wood stove, whose iron top had begun to rust. The stove was quite large and had come with the house, built in 1829. The house—Wiederspiel had painted it white—faced the Connecticut River from the New Hampshire side, and the front lawn sloped down to the bank where Wiederspiel had built a dock. An aluminum canoe and rowboat drifted with the current, pulling against their ropes. This morning the river was quiet. The fog had yet to burn off.

The day before, Wiederspiel had found several cans of stove polish at a barn sale. The tins were at least fifty years old, he guessed, but the polish was still moist, and he'd polished both the wood stove and the eight-burner gas range next to it.

Geula was already two days late. She'd planned to leave Vienna on Wednesday, and now it was Friday. A telegram had arrived early this morning: DELAYED. WILL ARRIVE AS SOON AS POSSIBLE.

Telegrams weren't exactly her style, and this disturbed him. Why hadn't she phoned? He hadn't heard her voice for a week, when she called from the airport in Vienna. No, it was not like her at all to send a telegram.

Waiting in the freezer were four trout Wiederspiel had caught in a stream in the Vermont woods, thirty miles west. Geula liked trout, and he didn't mind catching them, either. Although it was October, the days were warm, and the vegetable garden was still yielding tomatoes, string beans, onions, zucchini, and cucumbers. In another week there might be a frost, and that would end the garden until the spring, so Wiederspiel harvested all the ripe and near-ripe vegetables. As he did so, he brooded about the delay of Geula's arrival. It made him feel uneasy. Why hadn't she specified the exact day? WILL ARRIVE AS SOON AS POSSIBLE. Did that mean another day, or a week? All that remained of their vacation was two weeks.

A few days before they were to leave for the New Hampshire house, Geula had announced she would have to go via Vienna. Army business. When he had asked what that involved, she just laughed and said, Top secret. Wiederspiel hadn't pressed her, for that was the nature of their lives. Sudden departures, more often than not without explanations. Besides, the army played its own games, conducted by the Moshe Dayans and the Achad Barones, and Hal had made it a principle never to ask Geula questions about her work. If there were to be any discussion, she had to initiate it.

Late that night, the sound of wheels crunching on gravel and the motor cutting into the silence roused him quickly out of sleep. It was after 3:00 a.m. Geula? He slipped into his jeans and went barefoot down the stairs, pushed open the side door, and called her name into the dark. Helmut! came the answer. It's me, Helmut! She emerged from the darkness and ran into his embrace—the racing of her heart, the trembling of her strong body, the tears, warning him that something had happened. He stroked her hair. Shh, he whispered, you're here now.

He held her hand and led her up the stairs to the bedroom. He could hear her disrobing. Helmut? she said. He answered in the darkness: I am here. By the bed. In two steps her naked body was in his arms. Her lovemaking was very intense—no tenderness offered—and he could feel her tears on his chest. When they had finished, Geula continued to hold him tightly. They had not spoken. Only at dawn did she close her eyes.

When Helmut moved to get out of bed, she awoke and cried out. He stroked her body and remained with her until sun flooded the room. In that sunlight Geula slept. Finally Wiederspiel left the bed, put on the coffee, and busied himself sawing and splitting logs for the winter. There had not been a winter when he didn't have the opportunity to spend at least a week here in this rambling house by the river, and guests, too, used the place in his long absences.

Geula, awake now, watched from the window as he split the sawed logs. His shirtless body glistened in the sun.

2.

Let's go in the canoe, she said. I want to talk.

Pack a lunch?

Yes.

You have a lot to say?

Yes. If I can say it all.

Okay. Ten minutes. I'll cut up some vegetables. There's plenty of good bread.

On the river, Wiederspiel paddled smoothly with deep, strong strokes. Geula had not yet spoken, and seemed to avoid looking at him. She looked into the river or over his head at the sky or at the places the canoe had glided past. He could feel her tension; it was so palpable it almost had an odor. He understood that she didn't want him to speak. The canoe was swift and weightless as it moved. The river made its small sound against the paddle. Bird sounds, close and distant, seemed to fall from the trees onto the morning skin of the river. Wiederspiel absorbed the silence.

Quite softly Geula said, I am an assassin. He continued to paddle. Did you hear what I said?

Yes. You said you were an assassin. Vienna?

She nodded and became silent for a time.

Wiederspiel pulled the oar from the water. The canoe gradually lost its momentum, rocked in place for a while, and then slowly moved backward on the weak current.

I shouldn't have said that. I'm not an assassin. I killed a Nazi.

On whose order?

The Mossad. They said I would be perfect. I was army, and I'd served in Vienna before. I resisted the request. It was by no means an order. It was a request. The Mossad made a good case, and I agreed. But I am not an assassin.

Who?

Otto Klimke.

Why should that upset you?

Oh, it's not that. I'd do it again. Maybe not. There were other things.

Would you like to eat?

No.

I'll eat. I'm ravenous.

Can I tell you from the beginning?

Wiederspiel nodded, and soon after Geula began to speak he stopped eating entirely.

Otto Klimke. Maybe it was because it was him that I took the assignment. Klimke. To kill Klimke, what an honor! I thought it might also be a pleasure. There was fear in it, too, but not so great. Really, Helmut, going to Vienna I was happy and even proud. Can you understand that?

Yes, of course. The canoe drifted slowly downriver with a slight movement toward the right bank. Wiederspiel felt his jaw tighten. He didn't want to hear Geula's story. She was going to tell him how she had killed. He did not want to hear that. He did not want to know that she had killed a man. Even Klimke. It made him as uneasy as if she were confessing an infidelity.

It was all very simple, really, she continued. The Mossad knew where he was: in the Hotel Diplomat. Hitler always used to stay there on his visits to Vienna before he had taken power. Always in the same suite. Klimke stayed there, in Hitler's suite. Very proper, no?

Our people not only knew of this but provided me with a key. A room reservation for me, too. They instructed me to do the job between midnight and dawn and to check out in the morning after breakfast. Everything normal. After that an agent was to pick me up in a taxi and take me to the Ambassador Hotel, where I would check in as if I had just arrived from New York that morning. They even made a date for me with a friend.

Who?

Zachary Barthelmes. He was in Vienna again, for Moe's movie. He goes a lot to Vienna. They knew all of that.

Barthelmes is under surveillance?

Maybe, but I don't think so. He's a personality who travels a great deal. A movie about Herzl! I think that made them suspicious. They might have thought it was some kind of cover. Barthelmes was clean, of course.

You could have been recognized, Geula.

Would you like me as a redhead with long hair? I wore a wig. What a pity to have dumped it into the Danube! That part of it was very simple, very efficient.

Wiederspiel smiled.

Do you know I took a shower at two o'clock in the morning and dressed in a blue suit with a white satin blouse and a double strand of pearls? I sprayed myself with Cacharel. Later, I thought that might be a mistake. Could they trace me by my scent? I worried about that, you know, but I had the feeling I wanted to be properly turned out for Klimke. Crazy, no?

The wind coming upriver from behind her floated Geula's perfume toward him, and in its sweet spicy smell the exquisite, painful breath of lovemaking.

The Hitler apartment was on the top floor. My room was

on the floor below. That time of night, the sound of the elevator would certainly have made a racket, and maybe some clerk would notice that it went from my floor to Klimke's. So I walked up. I had the key in my hand as I walked down the corridor. Over and over again I had visualized the suite: a foyer with a mirror over a small table, elegant chairs to each side. Then a very large living room, two couches, several armchairs, tables, paintings in poor taste, and fresh-cut flowers. Then two bedrooms, at opposite ends of the living room. Yes, and one lamp left lit. In one of those bedrooms, the one farthest away from the foyer, Klimke would be asleep. I would walk into the bedroom, put several rounds into his head, and leave.

Was it like that?

No. Some of it was correct—I was given accurate sketches—but when I opened the door, I immediately knew something was different: the air was heavy and stale. Like my father's room after my mother died. He would forget to open the windows and sit for hours in his chair, doing what? Sleeping? Dreaming? Dying, I would think. The smell of an old man. Do you know that smell, Helmut?

Yes, of course.

Also it was very hot. A fire was going in the living room —but the temperatures were quite mild—and all the windows were shut tight and the wooden shutters outside closed against them. You could hardly breathe. In front of the fireplace there was a large—what do you call it in English—wing chair? I saw only the back of the chair, but I knew Klimke was sitting there. I coughed, just enough to clear my throat.

He heard me, of course. I have a visitor, he said. I have expected you for years. I should appreciate it that you are so late.

He was speaking in German, and although my German is acceptable, I told him to speak English. Any language but

Hebrew, he said. In English. I still had not seen him. I walked around the chair to face him. It was quite dark, yet he was wearing dark glasses. Looking at me he said, You are very beautiful for a Jewess. You *are* a Jewess?

Israeli.

Not a Jew?

Israeli.

From the Mossad?

I did not answer. He wore a bathrobe. There was a blanket on his lap. Very beautiful, Klimke said again, very beautiful. You have come to kill me?

Yes.

I attached the silencer to the pistol. He was so pitiful, Helmut. A shriveled little man trying to keep warm when there was not enough warmth in the whole world for him. Imagine! It is stifling hot in his rooms, and he is bundled for a New England winter!

You felt sorry for him?

Not really. But in a certain way, yes.

Wiederspiel took the paddle in his hands and stroked deeply upriver. You see, he said as he paddled, you send a woman to do a job like this and her emotions get in the way. Do I have to remind you that Klimke was responsible for the death of forty thousand Jews? Or that he encouraged the Romanians, who needed little encouragement, to massacre another two hundred thousand?

That included Gypsies, Geula said coldly. I am an army officer, Helmut. I will thank you to remember that.

His pace slowed, and then Wiederspiel stopped. I'm sorry. I shouldn't have said that.

They listened to the sharp birdcalls that echoed in the silence.

Do you want to continue? I said I was sorry.

I want to—I need to continue, Helmut. I *need* to.

The canoe resumed its slow drift downstream.

I had intended to be quick. I had pointed the gun at his head when he said, Just like that? Pfft, pfft, pfft, just like that? I want to confess to you, dear executioner. I want my story to be your story.

I answered to him, What can you tell me, Klimke, that I don't already know? I have your dossier from the Hitler *Jungen* to Paris, to Leningrad, to Romania, to Argentina, to here. We have carefully counted your corpses. I have no need of your story.

Then how can you learn anything?

I have no need to learn anything from murderers.

Hah! There it is: Jews are incapable of learning! That is always the Yid's downfall. You learn nothing.

Helmut, I had to laugh. And I wondered, Was it his contempt or his arrogance? But Klimke had my interest. I thought perhaps he might have something to say.

Wiederspiel's mouth opened to comment, then he restrained himself. He let his hand fall into the water, and the river ran between his fingers.

What do you think I should learn, I asked him.

No games now, he said. There is no time for Jewish games.

I think you do not like Jews, Klimke.

He managed violent coughing instead of laughter. There was a pitcher of water with some tumblers on the end table, but I let him cough until he had finished. His hands trembled, lifting the pitcher, and he poured as much water onto the rug as into the glass.

I'm fond of the dead ones. The rest I hate.

I am aware of that. You hate Jews even more than your comrades.

Quite right. This is because I understand them better.

I said to him, Here you are dying, and your hatred is still hot. If the gates to Auschwitz opened, you would repeat your crimes.

No, he said, I would do better. Ah, the Romanians knew how to do it! They were filled with a mad kind of poetry.

Your dossier says that you instructed the Romanians.

Wrong, of course. They instructed me! I admired them. Marshal Antonescu and his call to cleanse Romania. Dossiers! Credit where credit is due!

Whatever they did, you approved.

Yes, yes. Approved and encouraged. Does the dossier say how the Iron Guard sent a dozen Jews into a slaughterhouse with the cattle? Down the same chutes? When a steer came into the tight space facing the slaughterer with his heavy hammer, it would stand there docile, unsuspecting, unafraid as the hammer smashed down into its skull. Then the hooked chains hoisted it up and the knives stabbed into its belly letting out its guts, its blood rushing into the gutters. Death. Over. Done with. Done.

But Jews, you see, do not have the intelligence of a cow. They resisted! Resisted! They would thrash about, throw their arms before the descending hammer so the blow would smash a shoulder, a collarbone, tear away an entire jaw! Naturally, the slaughterer became frustrated. Swinging the hammer was hard work. So he used a crowbar. It took longer to beat a Jew to death that way, but it was easier. Most times it took five or six blows, sometimes more. They were noisy, too. Then the hooked chain pulled them up. They traveled down the rail with all the other carcasses. But the Jews were not butchered. It was not practical. Who would eat a Jew? The Jew carcasses hung with the rest, frozen in the huge iceboxes. A few were hung in butcher shops once owned by Jews. There would be a naked, smashed Jew in the window where gold lettering said, BOSHER KOSHER. Again Klimke coughed and gasped.

When he swallowed some water, I said, That was a very good story, Klimke. When I fired a shot into his knee, a sound of pain came from his clenched mouth.

Finish the job! he said.

I could see the blood dripping from his slipper onto the rug. I liked that story, I said. You must know others. Tell me stories, and for each good one I will bring you a little closer to eternity.

Finish the job!

No, first you must tell me a story.

Helmut, I did not want him to die. I wanted to kill him bit by bit. He sensed that, and he smiled at me. All right, he said. I will tell you stories, Jewess.

Enough, Geula, Wiederspiel said, his voice hard. I don't want to hear Otto Klimke stories.

I want to speak, Helmut. I *need* to speak.

Geula, I do not want to hear. What stories will you tell me? The one about the beautiful young woman who is used first by Klimke, then by his officers, then by his noncoms, the privates, and then is taken to the stables, tied to a rail, and mounted by a bull? The one about the father told to fuck his ten-year-old daughter or watch all three children and his wife torn apart by killer dogs? The medical experiments for the future of mankind? How about the Jews who threw their bony bodies across the barbed-wire barricades, hoping the guards might shoot them down?

Geula turned angrily away. Wiederspiel dug into the river. The canoe surged forward erratically.

I'm sorry, he finally said. I can't listen to those stories anymore. They're already in my cells, crowding out my life! I just want to do my work, Geula. I want to help build the country! Just that, only that!

Wiederspiel paddled, and Geula looked toward the shore. The trees and shrubs had become a green line. Tears fell from her chin onto her bosom. Wiederspiel, without breaking rhythm, raced the canoe into a cove. It glided over a patch of water lilies and pushed halfway up the bank. Exhausted, he dropped his head to his chest.

Geula looked toward him and finally reached over and put her hand on his bowed head. I'm sorry, too. You're right about the stories, of course. I didn't intend to become Scheherazade. I was reliving the night. For myself, Helmut. To hear these tales from Klimke's mouth! To see his joy, Helmut!

I do understand. I do. But I can't stand it, that's all.

No stories, then. Will you listen if I don't repeat Klimke's stories?

Wiederspiel kissed her cheeks, first one and then the other, several times. I've become so raw! It's all right now, he said. Tell me whatever you want. It's okay.

Just about *der Wigwam.*

Der Wigwam?

They both laughed, immediately and uncontrollably. The canoe tipped over, and they spilled out onto the bank and stretched out on the wild grass. Time passed, amorphous, unmeasurable, shielded from the world by an interlocking canopy of leaves through which pieces of sunlight glared— more than a minute, less than an hour.

Finally, Wiederspiel sat up. What the hell is *der Wigwam?*

There was no laughter in Geula's voice. I will tell you, Helmut, but allow me this much more about Klimke: he presented me with one horror and then another. For each tale he told, I put a bullet in him. Little holes in nonlethal places. I was amazed that he did not die more easily. I am ashamed now to admit it, but I half enjoyed it. You can see what hate will do. He enjoyed not dying quickly because I was the final form of everything he hated. And I enjoyed his pain with regret because I knew he could not keep himself alive very long. He had told me six stories. I shot him six times. Then his voice just disappeared, and his head went to the side. The blanket across his lap slipped into the blood on the floor. My only thought was: too easy a death for the monster.

Der Wigwam?

Yes. This was his triumph.

Yes, but what *is* it?

A nightclub. On a narrow old street near the Ringstrasse. I went there with Barthelmes.

3.

On the sidewalk, attached to the top of a post, was a sign fashioned of rough leather, into which was burned a rendering of a tepee. There was no lettering, just a feathered arrow with a barbed tip that pointed toward a space between two buildings. The alley was less than three feet across.

I guess this must be it, Barthelmes said, looking down the long alley to where a bare light bulb hung down at the far end. Do you really want to try this place?

Yes, Zachary, I do.

Okay, Geula. Put your pearls in your pocket and hold on to your purse. Here we go.

He stepped into the tight alley first. Geula kept her hand on his shoulder as they walked. The alley smelled of urine and feces, and it seemed a long way to the end. Beyond the suspended light bulb, the alley opened onto a small square in the center of which loomed a large, dark form. They stared dumbly until they could see it clearly. Barthelmes laughed. *Der Wigwam*, he said.

Geula lifted the leather flap across the entrance, then smiled back at him. Quite clever, Zachary. Come in.

In the center of the tepee, a rough wooden staircase led underground.

I don't like this, Barthelmes said. We could come to a no-good end.

Don't be silly! It is advertised everywhere. Very clever.

Very.

A recorded voice rose up from the stairwell. The language

was German, so Geula offered a quick translation. Good evening, braves. The Tribe welcomes you to the Native Land. Descend slowly. Food, drink, and joy await you!

The staircase cut three stories down into the earth. On the lowest landing they came to a leather-covered triangular door. Again, *der Wigwam* was burned into the leather. The leather cover was drawn back by a young blond man. His torso was nude, and his buckskin chaps covered his legs but left the cloth-covered crotch exposed. Black and red war paint adorned his face and chest. His headband sprouted a single white feather. He raised his arm and said How! Then, in German, Welcome to *der Wigwam*! Welcome to the Native Land!

They stepped through the entrance into a large, brightly lit room filled with laughter and shouts from the beer- and gravy-stained raw wood tables. Bare-breasted waitresses, wearing short buckskin skirts and loud smiles, their braided hair stuck through with feathers, carried steins of beer on trays held high above their heads. An orchestra of fat Indians pumped out loud oompah music.

Son of a bitch, Barthelmes said.

Americans! the blond maître d' said in English. Enjoy! We will send you an English-speaking waitress. He seated them at a table in the second ring from the stage.

Hi! I'm from Milwaukee! said their pink-titted waitress. Gee, we're getting more and more people from the States!

Have you a menu, Barthelmes asked.

No. Just the wurst, bread, and beer, light or dark.

Barthelmes looked at Geula. Light beer okay? When she nodded, he ordered two steins. You think all the swastikas are Indian signs?

No, Geula said. I believe they're of a more recent vintage.

The room was less than half filled. Some of the guests were on the dance floor. Except for one young couple, they were middle-aged or older.

Sehr gemütlich, Geula said, remarking on the heavy rumps

of the women and the ample stomachs of the men. Picture-postcard people. *Ganz Deutsch.*

The waitress from Milwaukee returned and unloaded her tray. If you need anything else, I'll take your order now. The floor show starts in about five minutes. We don't serve during the show.

This is fine, thank you, Barthelmes said. Have you lived in Vienna long?

Three years. My parents moved back here because you know how it is over there. In a year or two they'll take over the U.S. I think we got out just in time.

You don't say, Barthelmes said.

The lights dimmed with a fanfare of trumpets. A circle of light appeared on the stage. A woman in Indian clothing stepped into the bright circle.

Pocahontas, Barthelmes whispered.

Ilsa Koch, Geula said.

Pocahontas Koch smiled, then addressed the *Damen und Herren* in German. Welcome to *der Wigwam.* Tonight there is a very good entertainment, the second in the series of our modern passion plays. I think you will enjoy it. I would like to greet all the first-time guests and thank our many loyal supporters who have returned. The play will begin when the waitresses have finished serving. *Heil!*

A chorus of *Heils* rustled among the tables. Clear and loud, one or two voices behind them said, *Heil Hitler!*

Let's get out of here, Geula.

No. Now that we're here, I will see the show.

Pocahontas left the stage, the circle of light trailing off at her heels, as the Indian band played a tuba-heavy overture featuring "Lili Marlene" and "Tonight We Sail Against England."

If you see me start doing something foolish, Barthelmes whispered, stop me.

If you will do the same for me, she answered.

The band music faded and the sound of tom-toms gained until the pulse was insistent and strong. Suddenly, mid-stage, there was an artificial bonfire. Entering from right and left, wielding tomahawks, and dancing to the drum rhythms were eight bare-breasted Indian maidens. Breasts bouncing, the maidens performed the standard Hollywood routines around the smokeless flames.

Not bad, Barthelmes said. This I could put it into a Big MAC movie.

The dance continued until another Indian, shaking wooden instruments in each hand, appeared from the bellowing red center of the flames. The sounds of bones rattling, Barthelmes thought, the archetypal medicine man. Holy Geronimo! Barthelmes said under his breath. This character was fully clothed in rough leather, his chest covered with beads and the tiny heads of children's dolls. When Geula noticed these, her body tensed.

The medicine man hooked on to the dance line and awkwardly imitated the dancers' steps. Then he pushed close to the Indian maiden before him, his hips thrusting back and forth in the movements of ritualized fornication.

Swine! shouted a voice behind Zachary and Geula, but other voices quickly responded with loud shushes.

The medicine man broke from the dance line and danced awkwardly to the apron of the stage. On the red and blue paint that covered his cheeks were small, white, six-pointed stars. The medicine man's artificial nose was very large and hooked and had a hairy wart at its tip. He leaned over the stage above the tables in the first ring. His tongue darted in and out, wet and lascivious.

Swine! a voice called from the dark. Jew! Another voice shouted, Don't interrupt, fool!

Geula put her hand on Zachary's thigh. If you are going to make a scene, she whispered hoarsely, I will not be going out with you again.

Don't you see what they're doing?

Of course I do. Watch. Later we'll talk. All right?

After shaking his bone rattle a while longer, the medicine man finally spoke. Geula leaned toward Barthelmes and translated into his ear: Oh, wicked, wicked world! World of filth and vermin! I am here to cast out evil! I am here to save you from the uncleanliness and unholiness of the White Man! The White Man who has told you lies, has raped your women, eaten your children, stolen your wealth, and divided your land!

Loud hisses. Shut up, fools! He's a Jew! Where do these idiots come from? More hisses.

Bring me peace pipe! Everybody smoke! Big magic! Bring victory and peace!

A new Indian maiden entered, carrying a long-stemmed pipe that she handed to the medicine man. He pretended to smoke, then passed it to the maidens. In turn, each of them took a long drag and bolted upright in what Barthelmes thought was *der Wigwam*'s version of a zombie.

The shaman walked among the maidens fondling their breasts, licking their nipples with his flicking tongue, pushing his hands between their thighs, smelling his fingers, and smiling a gap-toothed smile.

A heavy-breathing silence in the house.

Two braves entered, stage left, dragging a third brave with them, his arms bound behind him. They presented him to the medicine man.

Do you confess your guilt?

No, never!

Did you drink the White Man's whiskey?

No, never!

Did you sleep with the White Man's whore?

No, never!

Did you sell *der schönen* Geronimo to the hated Blue Coats for thirty pieces of silver?

No! I am innocent! I am a true Apache!

We will see what kind of Apache you are!

A zombie maiden gives sharp-bladed knives to the medicine man, and the prisoner is brought forward. Holding the gleaming knives above his head, the shaman hisses, This is the true test of a true Apache! Then he laid the blade against the brave's cheek and drew it along his skin. A line of blood welled up. The action was repeated several times on each cheek and the lines of blood flowed down, though the brave showed no sign of pain. The medicine man—using a fresh, unbloodied knife that he brandished before the audience in a gleaming, fire-lit display—drew a long line across the man's left breast and then his right. Blood covered his chest and abdomen in a slow, even flow. The witch doctor emitted a cackle. His tongue darted.

Well, Geula whispered into Zachary's ear, at least it's a good trick.

In an almost normal voice, he replied, That's no trick. Real knife, real blood.

Over the sound system came the pounding of horses' hooves and the blaring of a trumpet.

Cavalry's coming, Zachary said. Hooray!

Three Blue Coats in Nelson Eddy Mountie hats entered, stage right. All the Indian maidens dropped their heads in shame. The bleeding man jutted his defiant jaw at the oppressors. The shaman bowed obsequiously: Welcome, my brothers! I have destroyed the Apache nation, as you have ordered me to do.

But, said the Blue Coat Colonel, I see that some are left alive. Give me your knife! He took the knife and touched the left breast of the prisoner with its point; then he spun the man around and quickly cut the thongs that bound him.

Soft, anticipatory laughter rippled through *der Wigwam*.

What are you doing? This traitor is stirring up revolt among the braves! I tell you, he is a traitor!

You are mistaken. This man is a true Apache and a hero!

No! I tell you by all my bones and powers—this man is a vile renegade!

This man is one of many thousand who will save the Indian nation. You, false medicine man, *you* are the traitor! No more will you steal our treasure and rape our women!

The Mountie trio swiftly stripped off the Velcroed fronts of their uniforms, tossed away their Nelson Eddy hats, and, now in black, revealed themselves as SS officers to loud applause from the audience. They slipped swastika arm bands onto their arms.

Seeing the swastikas, the medicine man shielded his eyes and cried out for mercy.

Kill him! ordered the SS Colonel.

A trial! I demand a trial!

No trials for traitors! Two of the officers seized him and flung him to his knees. They tore off his headdress and his braided hair as well, uncovering two flesh-covered horns. He wept grotesquely, sniveling, begging.

Kill him! repeated the Colonel.

Most of the audience was on its feet chanting. Kill him! Kill the dog! Kill him! Kill the Jew!

The drugged maidens wiped their eyes as their senses returned. They each grabbed a feathered lance from a stack in the corner and danced again around the fire while the exposed Jew howled and pleaded for his life. The drums suddenly stopped, and the Indian maid with the biggest tits plunged her lance into his chest. Each dishonored squaw buried her lance into the squirming body.

This must be a trick, Zachary, Geula whispered.

Yes, that is a trick.

After the victim let out a final shriek, the stage blacked out in a moment of darkness, and then the lights bounced back on. Holding hands, the cast bowed as the audience, except for a handful, cheered wildly. In closing, the cast sang an

Indian parody of "Deutschland über Alles," their swastikas and breasts in full view. Native Land, Native Land, We will serve you.

Pretty neat, huh? the bare-breasted waitress from Milwaukee said as she handed them the check. Slowly the audience filed up the staircase, but Geula found an exit that led directly onto the Ringstrasse.

We didn't pay the bill, Barthelmes said.

Would you want to go back and do it?

No, he said. They had walked in silence for several minutes when Barthelmes stopped suddenly and looked up at the Viennese sky. Jesus Christ! he roared.

4.

The canoe drifted downriver.

Maybe Klimke's stories would've been better.

It was Klimke's gift to me. To all of us. They are rising from the ashes.

Whose ashes, theirs or ours?

They want so much to kill us. Their only regret is that by some miracle we survived. The third bullet I put into Klimke was when he compared us to cockroaches. There were always some of us deep inside the walls, he said. Next time they would have better gas. Klimke was convinced the Nazis were resurging everywhere, all over the world. Here, in the United States, too. In the United Nations. There was blood in his throat, but his last words were clear: We will triumph!

The talk of a dead man, Wiederspiel said. I don't believe that for a minute.

But haven't the Arabs taken up Klimke's cause? Don't they want to exterminate us just as much as Klimke?

No, no, Geula. The Arabs want us out of Palestine, that's

all. But no matter what some of us think, the Arabs are not Nazis.

But it goes beyond Nazis, doesn't it, the mystery of the Jews? We are simply in the world to be hated.

Then so be it, Geula! We have Israel. We will build it. We will defend it. We will survive. And with luck we will find peace.

I want to kiss you. Lean toward me, Helmut, but please don't capsize the boat. They leaned into each other and kissed. I hope so, Geula said.

How can you doubt it? In the next fifty years, no combination of Arab countries can defeat us. And in that time we will find a way to settle things. Peace. Besides, we have our allies, too.

But when I said that to Klimke, he choked and laughed. There will come a day when the United States will have had enough of Israel and the Jews, he said. Then what will Israel be but a place where five or ten million Jews will be caught like rats in a trap and exterminated?

Did he say how?

Yes. Arabs with gas. He said we were nature's aberration. Humanoid, I think he said. Really not human. We were the most subtle of subspecies, who were posing as human beings for the sole purpose of subverting the Aryan pure. Not to kill them but to enslave them, to suck out the essence God had given to them. I asked him whether he really believed we were in league with Satan. Can you doubt that, Jewess? he said. In your heart are you not the Devil's whore?

A little insane, I'd say.

I put another bullet in him anyway. It was then he babbled about *der Wigwam* and bled to death.

The canoe drifted on. Wiederspiel said, And maybe *der Wigwam* convinced Barthelmes to do Moe's movie.

Not that. No. Something happened a few weeks ago. Zachary learned his father was a Jew who had converted. He said to me—you know the way he talks—I'm a little bit confused about being a Jew. Pretty shocking! I told him it was not so easy. His mother was not a Jew, so under the law he is not a Jew either. He would have to convert.

And he said?

He said the Jewish blood in him would do Moe Cohen's film. Of course he laughed. But *der Wigwam* shocked him at least as much as it shocked me.

When Wiederspiel docked the canoe, they could hear the phone ringing up in the house. It stopped as they walked up the lawn but rang again as they entered the house. Wiederspiel picked it up, listened, and then said, Yes, I hear you. Yes, of course, immediately. He put the phone down.

Something bad, Helmut?

Yes. We have to go home at once. Egypt has attacked.

I haven't unpacked, Geula said.

When she suddenly laughed, Wiederspiel said, Funny sad or funny ironic?

Both, Geula said. It's Yom Kippur. The Egyptians have attacked on Yom Kippur.

PART FIVE

1.

My Dearest *Shiksa*,

I try my best not to think of you. I ache when I do. Your perfume sits right under my nose. I can smell your odor, your real odor, all the way across the seas and oceans in my opulent hotel in Istanbul. Yes, my darling, there is such a place. A strange place . . . made stranger by your absence. Take off your clothes, please, and come into my big Turkish bed.

My suite overlooks the Bosporus. I asked for this view because that's what Herzl had. The water's almost as blue as the sea around Jaffa when we were there. I think I made you angry that day. Bosporus. Isn't that the water where Io swam—Juno's gadfly on her tail? Now the Bosporus is filled with noise and boats, freight and commuters. The Bosporus is filled with stains. All kinds of s—— floats on the tide. (Don't want to offend you!) If one has no idea of history and myth, the Bosporus would look about like an industrial canal— even if it does connect or separate Asia and Europe.

Last night, my first in town, I ate in a local bistro. Eeech! The waiter had food stains on his black pants and talked a little Pidgin English. Just enough to gain my trust and proceed to poison me. My gratuity was generous, and I left enough very old mutton on my plate to feed many starving children, of which the Turks have a few. After that I went to a cabaret where the prices were higher and the waiters cleaner. The place was almost empty until midnight—then it was showtime! Two small points. The belly dancers were unbelievably homely—bad teeth, fat bodies, ugly faces with unbelievably stupid smiles—and the prostitutes were no better. They pushed little carts of drinks around. I bought one (very very weak) and when I refused her services, the Turkish hookah (pun!) offered me her ten-year-old brother. By that time I'd caught a cold, anyway.

Why did I come here at all? Herzl's diary was clear enough about his reasons for visiting. In the company of ye olde spy Count Philip Michael Newlinski, he came for an audience with Sultan Abdul Hammid II. I was going to visit one of the cemeteries with a working cabaret among the tombstones. Herzl and Newlinski frequented one of those while waiting for an appointment, but nobody seems to know any disco-graveyards anymore. But Herzl knew, the sly dog.

The doctor came, gave me a shot, plenty of fluids and bed rest, etc. Much writing and thinking. I've made up my mind to get out of merry Istanbul as soon as possible. Once called Constantinople. I always thought they were two different cities. Go know. Please note I am beginning to speak in little Yiddishisms.

I have been thinking a great deal about *der Wigwam*. What I told you when I called that night was the account in full and fulsome detail. I don't think I told you of Geula's re-actions. I know I didn't give you my own. Truth is, the shock was so deep that I simply froze emotionally. This cold and fever has rapidly thawed out something rotten in the depths of my gut. Anyway, afterwards we sat at the hotel bar having drinks. Geula's distress was all over her noble face. Her nostrils were distended and stiff. Every so often, although her low voice never wavered, tears ran down her cheek and dripped off her chin into her martini. I tried to make light of things. Maybe I, too, should have wept! She couldn't speak—neither of us could—until the third martini.

I thought, she said, gin was supposed to do something. Two more and I'll carry you home, I told her. Oh, yes, Kale, she is attractive. But no matter how much booze, I could never do it. I could say this is out of deference to you, but maybe I'm more scared of Wiederspiel. Kidding, kidding!

So anyway, Geula said it was starting to happen all over

again, more to her martini than to me. Kooks and kids and tiny cults, I told her. They come and they go. Kids! They just got over acne. Then she asked if I noticed anything funny about the audience and the actors and the waiters. Like the waitress from Milwaukee who came there with her parents. They must only be in their forties and probably were born in Austria, with Nazi parents. Or maybe they were native Americans. Whatever, she said, they're all coming back. I said that was a pretty drastic conclusion; then she said she could feel it in her bones. Jewish bones, she said. Five-thousand-year-old bones.

Why don't I feel it in my bones? I'm also Jewish. She smiled and patted my hand. Zachary, she said, don't be too disappointed. I have explained why you are not a Jew. Your mother was not Jewish, so you are not Jewish. That's how the Orthodox law defined it. I argued the point. She said she was only giving me information and trying to lift the curse off my back. There I was, getting used to the idea that I was Jewish, and the wisdom of the ages says no—Wellingtons can't be Jews.

I protested. She smiled. Zachary, she said, I am afraid you will have to convert if you are serious. Also, you will have to be circumcised. Of course, I immediately thought of you. I'd never damage it without your prior written consent, since it's as much yours as mine. What a barbaric custom!

We sat at the bar for two hours. Geula didn't get stoned but was pretty withdrawn by the time we said good night. The next day, no good-byes—she was gone. So there I was, alone in the land of Hitler, packing for Istanbul and trying to decide if I were a Jew or if I just wanted to be one. All that day I thought about it. Barthelmes, I asked myself, do you *look* like a Jew. Answer: No. Underlying touch of anti-Semitism there! I look as Jewish, let's say, as Helmut Wiederspiel. Put us in SS uniforms and we'd easily pass. Nazis out of central casting. Come to think of it, dear *shiksa*, plenty of Jews in Hollywood have played Nazis. There's an Austrian-Jewish émigré named Ludwig Donath who did both Nazis and rabbis. He played Al Jolson's rabbi father, what was the name of that picture? No one *looks* Jewish. And that's why, according to the rednecks, they can form conspiracies and take over the world. If, on the other hand, you killed Jews on the basis of physical features, we'd have millions of dead Arabs floating in the Red Sea. Hell, I was always under the impression that half of Ireland looked Jewish. Seriously, though, if there is a Jewish look, I think Moe Cohen has it, even at six-foot-seven.

But even if there is no such thing as Jewish looks, what about a distinct and particular Jewish belief and soul? Here I'm getting into deep water. I've always thought there was a special quality about Jews—but only *after* I knew that the person was Jewish. Little anti-Semitism there. So, *shiksa*, tell me, is there a Jewish soul or not? Maybe, maybe not.

You can see the edge of my razor-sharp mind is dull on the Jewish Question. Herzl, of course, born Jewish, bar-mitzvahed, regrets for a good part of his life that he wasn't born a *Prussian*. Yet he refuses to convert even with the blandishments and bribes of the Austrian government, and in the end he's totally committed. Why, Kalia? He got no visit from an angel with a note from G—d. Biologically, at least, I'm half Jewish, so don't I get half a Jewish soul? But we don't know what that is, do we? It does have a lot of Christian in it, though, doesn't it? Judeo-Christian. Brothers and sisters under the bed sheets.

So why are Jews so stubborn? That's a fact! They're the original stiff-necked people. You spend a night in *der Wigwam*, and you bathe in that putrid swamp of the master race and you say to yourself, why not fuck them all? Convert, convert! Let's all be kindly Christians together, loving God and waiting for Jesus! In Grace and Love let us spend all our days on earth! But we Christians (a slip of the tongue?) can do no such thing! We need to kill, we need to cheat, we need to enslave, we need to rape—we need to destroy the world just so we can rise up to heaven. But most of all we need the Jews! Then we can say we never kill, never cheat, never enslave, never destroy, because the Jews already did it! Behind every perfidy, there is your Jew! How wonderful it is being free to commit every crime under the sun because the Jew is waiting there to take the blame! No mea culpas for the innocent lambs of G—d. The filthy, horned Jews did it! It's a riddle. The Jews know all this and yet remain Jews. Do you think that's noble or stupid?

We sat so calmly in *der Wigwam*. A day later I want to scream! I want to take the bloody neo-Heidelberg blade and plunge it into the throat of the kneeling Nazi brave! Tear the tits off our Nazi maiden from Milwaukee! I would like to set fire to that fucking oompah band! By Divine Intervention I would like to piss in every German beer for the next century. Hardly Christian sentiments at all, and not Jewish either. Just my balls screaming. You can't blame Geula for taking off. Probably in Israel now, bathing her Jewish bones in Shiloh's waters.

I find myself thinking of Herzl all the time. I admire him. I think he pitied the poor Christians and their currents did not turn his thoughts awry, nor did he lose the name of action! Kalia, how I need you now! I feel so raw and violated! I need you in bed with me. I need you naked beside me. No, not to make love but to *be* love. My body, your body, my pain, your balm. God, how I love you, dear, dear *shiksa*! How I hate Vienna! So much that I'm prepared to love Turkey! What a tomb of horrors history is! Moe Cohen knows that. Sing a sentimental song!

Last night I had a nightmare: I was behind a movie camera on tracks in a cold, bleak place. Like a gallery or a museum. The light was a thin industrial white glare. Hanging on the walls were my father's Jesuses, nailed to their crucifixes. A steady drip of blood, from each figure, so the white gallery floor is segmented by red rivulets. A little lake of Christ's blood collects in the center of the floor, and in the center of the lake is a little boat. Its sails are blue, and it's rocking.

Love you so,
Zach

Me, too, Kalia said to herself. It's hard to be a half Jew, she thought. But what isn't hard?

2.

Later Kalia wondered if there had been the seed of commitment in Zachary's letter, some commitment to his Jewish side. But what did that dream mean, she wondered as she reread the letter. She felt very close to Zachary now. And yes, he would marry her. She had made it not impossible but uncomfortable for him to deny her that. But maybe, after all, Zachary was right and they didn't have to stand before court or clergy. Why should I want that random God-appointed stranger to bless our union? She thought of herself and Zachary in all the known and unexplored aspects of love. Sex, as good as it was, was only a small part of their union. That's it, she thought. Union! We *are* fucking well wed. I can yell at him all I want!

Immediately she was troubled by the ease with which she'd surrendered her idée fixe—especially in view of the fact that Zachary had finally agreed to marry her. Maybe his initial resistance was a reaction to her two previous marriages, each solemnly executed in Protestant churches of diverse creeds. Together these two marriages represented three years of her life, from ages nineteen to twenty-two. Neither had lasted two years, obviously, and the second didn't make seven months. She'd had lovers who'd outlasted her husbands. But the pattern was always the same—she'd rush in, pour out her passions, then run headlong away. How vague these husbands and lovers seemed now; their voices had vanished and their bodies, too. She tried to retrieve the images of their penises, erect, ejaculating. She was unable to do even that.

Suddenly she trembled. Daddy was standing in tall, angry silence in a deep corner of her mind. Her eyes filled with tears. Oh, no! she heard herself say. Please! Sitting there at the breakfast table, she trembled quietly. It would be two weeks before Zachary came home, and tomorrow wouldn't be soon enough.

Finally she showered and went to work, which she knew would be perfectly unproductive if not unpleasant. She just couldn't get into the new Murad Hair Color and Conditioner campaign. Just imagine, Kalia thought, a whole company hanging by its fingernails and waiting for me to tell them how to tell the world why it needs this great stuff. The laugh of the day was a many-times Xeroxed sheet Sandra Abramowitz had circulated. Kalia made a copy to enclose with her next letter to Zachary.

WORLD RELIGION SIMPLIFIED

Taoism: Shit happens.

Confucianism: Confucius say, Shit happens.

Buddhism: If shit happens, it really isn't shit.

Zen: What is the sound of shit happening?

Hinduism: This shit happened before.

Islam: If shit happens, it is Allah's shit.

Protestantism: Let shit happen to someone else.

Catholicism: If shit happens, you deserved it.

Judaism: Why does shit always happen to us?

3.

When she returned home that evening, she found a new airmail envelope. Zachary's scenes of Herzl in Turkey.

ISTANBUL/CONSTANTINOPLE 1901

[N.B. I'm fudging Herzl's negotiations with Sultan Abdul Hammid II a little. There are two scenes: The first with Count Newlinski in the belly-dancing graveyard outside Constantinople. The second, the actual encounter with the Sultan, took place five years later, by which time Newlinski had died on a mission to Turkey for Herzl; he had been so ill that he made the trip with a physician in tow. Another fabulous character named Vambery took his place. What a mess! I'll tell you about all that if you want to hear. But for the purpose of the film I'm compressing time and keeping Newlinski alive. Maybe I'll switch to Vambery later.]

TURKISH SCENE #1

The high flight of noisy birds against a gray sky. Slow pan down, close to an INFANT *in a crude wooden pram. The* BABY's *laughing, clapping hands. Pull back to reveal tombstone, then pan along clothesline that runs from one tombstone to another.* A YOUNG WOMAN *hanging wet wash. Cut. Close-up of a woman's mouth singing an Italian aria; then pull back to reveal the* SINGER *on a small stage surrounded by the tombstones. Clotheslines and wet wash undulate. Aria finishes. Small applause, drumroll. Three* MIDGET ACROBATS, *two men and a woman, tumble and flip onto the stage.*

Cut to a rear view of HERZL *and* NEWLINSKI *sitting at a table. Heads turn as they speak to each other. Profiles. Cut to* MIDGETS. *Cut to front shot of the two* MEN *in elegant afternoon dress (gray top hat, brown top hat, etc.).* WAITER *brings coffee. We see the fearless, amazing* MIDGETS *in the long shots. Close-up on* NEWLINSKI:

If you would like to have the soprano, it is arranged.

No, I would drown beneath her bosom.

Well, Dori, there's a new belly dancer after the acrobats. She is also available.

Why haven't you offered me the midget?

Smashing idea! *(*NEWLINSKI *laughs.)* Shall I make an offer?

Philip, you are pimping!

I am a diplomat, *mein lieber* Herzl.

Spy!

Intelligence agent! I do not steal secrets. I share carefully imparted information given to me at one court with a second and third court. Then the process is reversed. How else would Vienna know what troubles London or why the Sultan will slaughter another million Armenians? Newlinski brings clarity.

HERZL *watches in silence as the* MIDGETS *swallow fire and very short swords.*

My money bag is nearly empty, Philip. When will the Sultan receive me?

Soon, Dori. Be patient.

It has been a week! We have already bribed the entire court.

Yes, and we will have results.

You are sure?

Abdul has awarded you the order of the Mejidiye, First Class, Cordon Rouge.

Junk!

That is almost a certain commitment!

If I did not trust you, Philip, I would kill you.

The MIDGETS *take their bows. The* WAITER *brings plates of dates, figs, pomegranates, baklava.*

How do you explain a million dead Armenians, Philip?

They committed the crime of independence.

A capital crime, obviously. Do you think I should speak to the Armenians in London?

Yes. The Sultan wants to make an accommodation. Do it, Theodor! It will be good for the Jews.

HERZL *stares coldly at* NEWLINSKI *as a flight of birds swoops through the graveyard.*

How can I love Wagner, that Jew hater? But he is a god! He towers above the world!

What are you talking about, Dori? What has Wagner to do with the Armenians?

Nothing is good for the Jews. *(*HERZL *shrugs, a Jewish caricature.)* Anything is good for the Jews. Why didn't Wagner know that I loved him?

You are slightly mad.

The BELLY DANCER *takes the stage and starts her act.*

Totally mad! Have you ever considered, Philip, that the world has driven us mad with its sultans, its kings, its prime ministers, and premiers?

Tight shot on the DANCER's *active belly.*

You are certain you have no desire?

I am too tired, Philip.

The BELLY DANCER *is now among the tables, and the patrons touch her hips and belly and stuff currency into her brassiere. As the music grows louder, she dances toward* HERZL *and* NEWLINSKI, *her movements more frenetic. Her belly is almost in* HERZL's *face.* NEWLINSKI *starts to sweat, but* HERZL *merely smiles and looks her in the eye. Then he takes a small gold piece from his leather purse and places it carefully in her navel.*

TURKISH SCENE #2

Close-up. NEWLINSKI *and* HERZL *stand on a balcony above the spacious, manicured gardens of the imperial grounds. It is* semalik, *the hour for prayer. Long shot of a minaret framed against the sky. The* MUEZ-ZIN's *call rings loudly through the eerie, beautiful silence.*

Pan down to a huge, ornate gate of gold. It swings open, and a hundred RIDERS *in glittering costume come through on black horses. Perfect dressage, the music of hooves. Pan to a second gate. A hundred white horses.* RIDERS. *Perfect. Music of high-stepping hooves. Cut back to balcony.* NEWLINSKI *proudly surveys this pageant:*

Best cavalry in the world.

But can they fight, Philip?

It's a matter of history.

No, it's past history. When it comes to slaughter, do they do their work on water?

What?

No matter. Just an English poet.

Cut to a third gate, through which comes a hundred gray horses whose RIDERS *wear even more astoundingly beautiful uniforms. Their diamond-encrusted decorations glint in the sun.*

NEWLINSKI *announces:* The sons of the Sultan.

Six carriages roll in the wake of the gray horses. Close-up of a carriage window, through which are visible the heads of heavily veiled WOMEN.

HERZL *voice-over:* The wives?

NEWLINSKI *voice-over:* The harem, yes.

Pull back to SULTAN *in open carriage. Hawk faced, he seems to be looking toward the balcony where* HERZL *and* NEWLINSKI *stand. Hundreds of* FOOT TROOPS *form a walking hedge on either side of his carriage. All lower their heads as the* SULTAN's *carriage rolls into the gold-domed mosque. The* MUEZZIN *wails.*

Cut to HERZL *sitting in a hip bath in his room. Through the open windows, the blue Bosporus gleams.* HERZL, *lathering himself, softly sings a passage from the Ring Cycle and is interrupted by a* COURIER, *whom he calls inside. He hands* HERZL *an envelope, bows, and leaves.* HERZL *opens envelope and leaps to his feet, naked:*

Philip! Come! Come now!

NEWLINSKI *pushes through the door of an adjoining room.*

Cut to HERZL's *carriage stopping before the ornate gates of the Yildiz kiosk, the* SULTAN's *residence.* HERZL *is elegantly dressed and carries a large package. The high gates swing open, and* HERZL *puts some coins in the outstretched palms of the* GATEKEEPERS. *This action is repeated over and over again with* OFFICIALS *who line the way inside. The last one is* IBRAHIM BEY, *the* SULTAN's *secretary, who receives the package at his desk and opens it avidly. It is a fine silver clock:*

It is beautiful, Herr Herzl!

I pray that it keeps the time.

Oh, yes! *(He gets up from his chair and looks at his pocket watch.)* The Sultan is waiting.

Camera pushes in on the figure sitting on the ornate reception throne. The SULTAN *has a large hooked*

nose. He has a short-cropped beard. It has been re-
cently dyed. A streak of dye has dried on his thin neck.
The SULTAN *wears a cape over his uniform. The cape*
is thrown back. The SULTAN's *tunic is festooned with*
decorations, medals, and diamonds. A very large
sword rests uncomfortably between his knees. Frayed
chartreuse cuffs extend from his tunic sleeves, and his
white gloves are too large for his hands.

Cut to HERZL's *perfect, fashion-plate elegance.*
Looking impeccable, HERZL *bows. The* SULTAN *nods.*

Camera pans to include IBRAHIM BEY, *who acts*
as the interlocutor and translator. He gestures to
HERZL, *who walks crisply forward, stops a few feet*
before the throne, and bows again. The SULTAN *nods*
again and indicates a brocade chair, where HERZL
seats himself. IBRAHIM BEY *takes a less ostentatious*
seat between the two. [In order to keep this simple,
the Sultan's voice will be kept below Ibrahim's. The
effect will be that Ibrahim is doing the speaking for
him. But it will also be clear that Abdul can follow
some of Herzl's French, and on occasion will cut in
and say something. Fucking complicated, but I'll
get it worked out.]

IBRAHIM: His Majesty has been told that Emperor
Franz Josef is very well. He rejoices in that.

HERZL: All the world rejoices for such blessings, as
all the world rejoices in the good health of His Imperial Majesty. I am here to show my devotion to His
Imperial Majesty because history will show that Abdul Hammid has always been good to the Jews.

IBRAHIM: His Majesty likes the Jews. He can only
trust Jews and Moslems.

HERZL: I thank His Imperial Majesty for awarding
his humble servant the Mejidiye, Cordon Rouge.
With this he honors all Jews everywhere.

IBRAHIM: His Majesty says that he has a Jewish jeweler whom he trusts implicitly. He can say some good things to his jeweler and instruct him to say a few words to the press.

HERZL: Will the Sultan allow me to speak frankly?

SULTAN: *Bien sur! Ça c'est bon!*

HERZL: If a jeweler speaks to the newspapers, it will trivialize the great affairs of the Sultan. Moreover, news given in this way will not be received outside of Turkey.

IBRAHIM: His Imperial Majesty says you are very wise. What business do you have with him?

HERZL: I am sure that His Majesty has heard of the fable of Androcles and the Lion.

SULTAN *(nodding vigorously): Oui,* Androcles.

HERZL: I have come to play the role of Androcles. To remove the thorn from the paw of the lion—who, of course, is His Imperial Majesty, Abdul Hammid II.

IBRAHIM *whispers into the ear of the* SULTAN.

SULTAN: *Oui.*

IBRAHIM: The whole world knows of this monstrous thorn, the burdensome debt of the Ottoman Empire. It is a heavy, heavy debt that His Majesty's illustrious, heaven-appointed predecessors have left him. Such a painful thorn! If only it could be removed!

HERZL: Indeed it can be removed! And so the Empire would be free to govern its people in peace and prosperity, to do the good works for which the entire universe reveres this ancient land!

SULTAN: Allah be praised!

IBRAHIM: Allah be praised! *(Confers with* ABDUL.*)* And how, Herr Herzl, would you remove this thorn?

HERZL: In every land I will ask the masses of Jews to establish committees, rich and poor alike. The Jews will lend you enough money to begin to repay this burdensome debt.

IBRAHIM: Begin? But how long before the entire debt can be repaid?

HERZL: Many years. It must be done slowly. For if the great powers learn that the Jews are doing this, it will go badly not only for the Jews but also for Turkey. After all, the major powers and their banks do not want to forfeit the usurious interest His Majesty now pays. The debt must be retired slowly and, equally as important, in great secret.

SULTAN: *Secret, secret!*

IBRAHIM: In the meantime, can the Jews make a loan to Turkey in the amount of fifty million pounds? This loan will be secured from the income earned from our lighthouses, amounting to about forty million pounds per annum.

HERZL: I will propose this to the Rothschilds. To strengthen my hand, His Majesty might wish to make a gesture to my people, who suffer so in many lands less generous than Turkey.

IBRAHIM *(tense, reflecting the* SULTAN's *alarm):* What sort of gesture?

HERZL: An enclave in Palestine.

IBRAHIM *(after conferring with the* SULTAN*):* Let us speak about the lighthouses.

HERZL: A vassal Jewish state under the suzerainty of His Imperial Majesty.

IBRAHIM: Lighthouses!

HERZL: Palestine.

IBRAHIM: We have discovered new oil fields. These, the Jews can develop.

HERZL: Yes. For a small place in Palestine.

IBRAHIM *(after the* SULTAN *nods):* Lighthouses *and* oil.

HERZL: Yes, and Palestine.

IBRAHIM *(looking exasperated, and the* SULTAN *suddenly seems bored):* Gold mines! Railroads! Oil! Lighthouses!

HERZL: In Palestine the Jews will pay great taxes.

IBRAHIM: His Imperial Majesty does not wish to speak of Palestine. Palestine is the jewel of the Ottoman Empire!

HERZL: Without a place in Palestine, it will not be so simple to remove the thorn.

IBRAHIM: You must convince the Rothschilds about the lighthouses. It is an excellent opportunity!

The SULTAN *drops his head to his chest and begins to snore. A tall, gaunt* MAN *dressed in traditional clothing and wearing a tarboosh enters. He places his hands over the* SULTAN's *temples.*

IBRAHIM: His Imperial Majesty is dreaming. This is his dream interpreter.

HERZL: Perhaps he is dreaming of Palestine?

IBRAHIM: Lighthouses.

A dozen WHIRLING DERVISHES *burst into the room and spin at full speed around* HERZL.

HERZL *(shouting):* Palestine!

HERZL's *cry becomes the long scream of a train whistle. Sharp cut to the Orient Express speeding westward. Cut to the dining car, where* NEWLINSKI *and* HERZL *sit at a linen-covered table.*

We accomplished nothing, Theodor.

We accomplished everything. I have negotiated with a monarch as the representative of a state which does not yet exist.

But did he say yes to a Jewish state in Palestine?

He did not say no, Philip. He did not say no.

This works, Kalia. It's real, surreal, and absurd. Of course if MGM were producing this, this scene wouldn't even make the cutting-room floor. It would *never* be shot. But if Moe produces and puts up the money, I promise you, Kale, I'll shoot the damn thing. The question is, Will *I* have the guts to use it?

Further confession, Kale: I'm floundering. Good scenes, sure, but where am I going with them? What's the through-line? The plot? The story, for God's sake? Love you. Love you. Zach. Zach.

P.S. Going to London. Lots of Dori there. Must hear English spoken.

4.

My poor darling Zach Zach,

The scenes are great! Wonderful, really. History in school always seemed so dull, dull, but this is so alive. All these strange, driven people who make our lives! How much of all this are you making up? What I mean is, I guess, how much of it's from the box of books Moe gave you and how much is *you*?

I am not going to forget about Vambery. First night in bed—either before or after—you will tell me Tales of Vambery. But please, don't get rid of Newlinski. I love him! Ask me about casting.

Der Wigwam sounds so upsetting and scary that I can't understand how the two of you just sat there. You should've set fire to the place—to the world, maybe: what an ugly place! Your questions about the nature of Jews are very provoking. I have a lot of ideas on that subject, but I don't know how to write them down. What I mostly write is something short, with a lilt, usually about the glory of hair or fingernails. How to be a Jew in fifty words or less. Tragedy in forty. Comedy in two. (Hah, hah!)

Did Geula really laugh at your half Jewishness? Probably she was laughing at the silliness of the old Orthodox ideas. But I guess you would've liked her to embrace you and say something like, I'm so happy you're one of us! Do you want to be one of them, Zach? Join the tribe?

You're right about *it*. Don't even think about hurting it. How long would it take to heal?

If you decide to join the Jews, you'll have a head start, but I'll do it too. I'm fascinated by them. I couldn't begin to tell you why in a million words or more. If I were doing an ad, maybe I'd say, JEWS ARE GREATER THAN DINOSAURS. Or, SHOW ME A JEW AND I'LL SHOW YOU THE GLORY OF THE WORLD. Or, GOD, HIS SON, AND ALL THE ANGELS OF HEAVEN ARE JEWISH. HOW ABOUT YOU?

I think I'll look into it. I don't want to be a *shiksa*. Seriously. I mean it.

Can you come home sooner than two weeks? *Je souffre.*

> *Dein Shaine Maidel*,
> Kalia

P.S. What's a good Jewish name beginning with *K*?

P.P.S. Am enclosing "World Religions Simplified." Comments, please.

5.

Everything disturbed Zachary Barthelmes. The sensitive stomach he had carried away from Istanbul to London. His sudden doubts about his grip on the script. Kalia's feeling that he was tilting toward Judaism. More to the point, *her* tilting. If he converted, he could point to his polluted bloodstream. But Kalia bemused by Jews? Why such a serious whim? Let me honor my Jewish heritage with a good film.

But fuck you, Moe, you can't trap me into the temple! As for you, dear *shiksa*, one night in bed with me will cure you of these fantasies. Resist! Resist! What I want is to be a good, free, fair, sensitive man in this world. Just that. Biology isn't destiny, and it isn't half destiny, either. I will be what I choose and so will you. But choose with me, Kalia, please.

All of these disturbances had shaken Zachary's confidence just as he felt himself committing to make the film. And now, damn it, Colonel Albert Edward Williamson Goldsmid! How had he overlooked Colonel Goldsmid? Could he afford to omit him altogether? And what about Vambery—not to mention Queen Victoria and her Jewish counselor, Arthur Cohen. Lord Cromer, King Victor Emmanuel, the Pope, Grand Duke Friedrich, the Czar of all the Russias, President Theodore Roosevelt, the toiling Jewish masses of all lands, etc.

Everybody wants in! The whole world wants to get into my picture! A cast of millions! A can of scorpions! Where will we get the money, Moe? It's slipping away! The film is slipping away! Barthelmes's heart pounded, his breath fast and short.

Outside his window, the sun was shining onto the back lawn of the Savoy. For some reason Barthelmes couldn't understand, a uniformed band was playing. Trembling, he climbed back into bed and pulled the Savoy covers over his head.

6.

A light appeared on the wall of the room. Through this halo the figure of COLONEL ALBERT EDWARD WILLIAMSON GOLDSMID *entered the room's darkness. He was in full cavalry regalia.*

My horse is tethered to the concierge desk. A quiet mare, Zachary. She'll be no bother.

There's no part in the film for you, Albert. Over budget.

I think you can't make the film without me, Zachary. There's that whole business with Lord Cromer in Egypt. Why, we almost had Palestine! Missed by a gnat's whisker!

We already have a cast of millions, Albert!

You might consider dropping the Queen, Zachary.

She was in favor of settling the Jews in British Palestine. I don't want to appear ungrateful or rude.

Point there, Zachary. Consider dropping Herzl's Palestine delegation. Greenberg and that crowd. Talk, talk, talk! Herzl, Cromer, and myself, we can do the business without the others. Good scenes, too. For starters, Lord Cromer and I pounding across the desert sands. I tell him we'll turn all this as green as Ireland. Cromer says, If there is enough water, Goldsmid, if there is enough water. Now I look deep into his eyes. Lord Cromer, I say, water is no problem. We shall split the Nile! It is then that my mount whinnies and rears up on its hind legs. Is that not a promising scene, Zachary?

A wonderful scene. But where's Herzl? Shouldn't he be negotiating with Cromer?

Damn it all, man, Herzl's all over the bloody film, and he has the best bits, too. The whole business with the belly dancer—that's a role I'd like.

Albert, you weren't in Turkey.

But you can see to that!

It wouldn't be true. I can't change history, Albert!

Pshaw, Zachary. You've been doing it right along.

I have not!

Do you mind if I smoke?

It's a small room, but have your pipe if you must.

We are like brothers, you and I.

I know that, Albert, but you can't use that sort of thing to get into the film.

You disappoint me, Zachary.

Why?

Jews ought to stick together.

I can't believe you are a Jew, Albert. Jews don't get to be battalion commanders in London.

Cardiff, actually. Born in India of Jewish parents who had converted to Christianity. I was baptized and raised a Christian, Zachary. I am a living Daniel Deronda.

Well, there you are, Albert!

There I was, Zachary, there I was, a young Christian lad who chose a career with the military in India. But when I discovered my true heritage, I did not hesitate. I reclaimed my birthright and reconverted. Circumcision and all!

Did it hurt?

Like blazes, Zachary. But worth every piss and pang! Made the Queen proud of me. Gave me the Cardiff command, she did. Rahel and Carmel, my two daughters, speak Hebrew perfectly. You are aware, of course, that I told Herzl if he required an army, I would raise it and lead it. Find a role for me in the film, Zachary. We are fellow converts!

I am not a convert!

Ah, Zachary, Zachary, that will come in time.

I told you. I am not a convert!

No kicking or screaming, Zachary, or I'll lay the broadside of my sword across your arse!

Goldsmid pulled the light with him and faded through the wall.

Barthelmes leapt out of bed and buzzed the concierge to get him a seat on the night flight to New York. He needed to get his mind off the film, and he needed to be with Kalia.

PART SIX

1.

Egyptian missiles and shells exploded in the sand. General Achad Barone blew his nose and rubbed the sand from his eyes. If the desert is their target, he roared, these bastards rarely miss!

Don't demean the enemy, Achad! Helmut Wiederspiel shouted over the windblown explosions. Show a little respect.

I'm not demeaning *them*, Hal. I'm talking about Dayan, Bar-Lev, Rabin, Gonen—*those* bastards. They're bottling me up!

You left Golda out.

Ahh, she'll do anything Dayan says. That one-eyed pinup boy! If he'd lost his arsehole instead of his eye, he wouldn't be on so many magazine covers!

Listen, Achad, I don't like him either, but he is the Defense Minister, and he's trying to do his job.

He's trying to lose the war! He stinks. They all stink. You and I together, Hal, we could drown Sadat in his canal!

Maybe, but there's no use bitching. You will wait for orders, Achad. They have the overall view.

They have shit. They can't even read a map. I've been to General Headquarters twice. I show them where the Arabs are. I show them where my forces are. I explain to them how I will cross the Canal and begin an encirclement.

And they say wait.

Yes. Wait!

Maybe they know something?

Shit! That's what they know! They're not soldiers anymore. They're archaeologists!

Wiederspiel laughed. You're always too fast, Achad. Always ready to move without thinking.

That's not fair, Hal. If I have a fault—and I'm not admitting to any—it's that I think too much. No, not too much, just enough. You see, if you think things through, really think things through, then you can stop all the mental masturbation and devote yourself to what must be done.

I accept you as a great general, Achad. But as Achad Barone the philosopher? There I have some doubts.

Barone pounded Wiederspiel on the shoulder. You son of a bitch, he shouted, it's good to see you! What is this—the third time since the Six-Day War?

How would I know? Who counts?

Have you heard anything, Hal?

Like what?

Like when they'll let me cross the Canal?

Nothing about that, no. I did hear they'd like to cut your balls off.

Barone roared, then smiled broadly and paused. Listen, he said, they've stopped firing. Probably out of shells again. It will be a half hour before their ordnance trucks roll up. He then climbed out of the trench and strode into the desert.

Wiederspiel shouted after him, Where are you going?

Taking a walk. General Achad walked a hundred yards across the open sand and up a dune. From the top he surveyed the empty desert around him.

Wiederspiel could barely hear his voice, except when the wind caught it and carried it back. We have men out there, he heard Barone saying. Some still alive. Trapped! What kind of bastards will let them die? And they've ordered me not to attempt a rescue—the bastards!

But most of the time Wiederspiel couldn't hear this distant figure howling into the wind. Then the bombardment started again, and sand filled the air. From atop the dune, Barone shook his fist against the incoming fire. Each explosion splashed great waves of sand into the air as if it were the water of the sea.

A shell slammed into the dune where Barone was standing. He vanished. Wiederspiel ran out of the trench, the desert dragging his boots down.

Achad! Achad! he shouted as he slogged toward the dune, where he stopped and listened through the Egyptian barrage. Nothing.

Why the hell are you standing there? came Barone's voice. I've been hit!

Wiederspiel found him, raced down the slope, and pulled Barone free of the sand. Blood covered his arm and chest. Is it bad? Wiederspiel said.

No, Barone said. Just the arm. Shrapnel.

What about the chest?

From the arm. The blood is from my arm. As Wiederspiel unbuckled his belt, Barone snapped, What the hell are you doing?

Tourniquet. You've seen these before, no?

Oh, shut up, Hal. Use your goddamned eyes. The blood isn't even flowing now.

I thought you said they couldn't hit anything.

They missed, didn't they?

Wiederspiel was smiling. Yes, he said, they missed. I'll go back and get a couple of men with a litter.

I can walk, Wiederspiel, Barone said as he got to his feet.

Let's wait until the firing stops.

Arsehole! I told you they can't hit anything. Barone threw his unwounded arm over Wiederspiel's shoulder; Wiederspiel's arm encircled Barone's hard, thick waist. Slowly they walked toward the trench, and the air was filled with exploded sand.

2.

The medics cleaned Barone's shrapnel wounds as thoroughly as they could, then suggested that the general be taken to a hospital in the rear. Only a surgeon could remove some of the metal embedded in his flesh.

Barone snorted and shook his head. Bastards, he said.

Achad, Wiederspiel said, you can fool around with General Headquarters, but you can't avoid the doctors.

Listen, Hal, once they get me away from the Canal, they won't let me come back.

And why is that, Achad?

Because they know I will cross, with or without orders.

Will you?

Maybe. They're just waiting for Kissinger to tell them what to do. You know it's true, Hal. The Washington gang is telling them what to do.

Wiederspiel did not reply. You need a doctor. I'll order an ambulance.

You will order nothing.

Yes I will. I outrank you, Achad.

You're a retired general!

No. Active duty.

If you pull me out, Hal, I'll hate you forever.

Wiederspiel smiled. All right, he said, I'll get a surgeon to come here. The mountain comes to Mohammed.

Two hours later, a surgeon in his twenties pulled a dozen pieces of metal out of Barone's arm. Then he asked if the helicopter was ready. Told that it was, he turned to Barone. The next time you get hit, General, you come to the rear. I have a couple of hundred men in the hospital who have more than scratches.

So who asked you to come?

It was on your direct order.

No, Wiederspiel said softly, it was mine. I apologize.

The doctor turned and left the bunker. After a moment of silence Barone said, He was right, Hal.

No, he was not right. I didn't order him here for your convenience. There was something in what you had said. Maybe they wouldn't let you return.

Do you know why?

You frighten them.

Why?

They can't trust you.

Why?

Stop playing games. You're a fucking loose cannon. They almost court-martialed you over the Golan business.

What stopped them?

I appealed to Golda. I will never do that again.

The two men stared at each other, and neither would look away. Finally Barone said, All right. Thanks.

I don't want your thanks, Achad. I did what I thought was right. You're a great soldier, but what you did on the Golan was murder.

Your opinion. You cannot control the passions of battle.

But letting your commandos wipe out an undefended village?

In the first place, I didn't *let* them. I *ordered* them.

It was undefended, you son of a bitch!

Barone laughed. My dear comrade, how did anyone *know* it was undefended? How many of our good men have we lost in these *undefended* villages? How many Arab houses have blown up in our faces?

That doesn't give you the right to treat every Arab like a time bomb.

Well, I would prefer that they were Germans, but that's the way it is. My job is to defend Israel and to win battles.

Not that way. Not by killing women and children.

Barone lowered his dark-blond head. I did not know that women and children were there. There were also armed men there, Hal.

You didn't know that, Achad, not when you went in.

No, I didn't. But my order was correct. I would give the same order again.

Then you're a butcher!

That may be, but Israel can use a few more like me. It will never be said of Achad Barone that he gave Israel to her enemies because they also bleed, because they also die, as Jews bleed and as Jews die.

Wiederspiel paused for a moment, his teeth clenched. I don't think we should continue this, Achad.

Will it cost us our friendship?

It could, Achad.

Why? Because I do the job everyone wants done, but that no one will admit to or talk about? Oh, no, here's trouble—send in Barone! An impossible situation on the Golan—send in Barone and his commandos. The Arabs are massing troops on all fronts—send Barone to all fronts! What did your American general say? War is hell?

Oh, shut up!

All right, I'll shut up. But only after I say this, Hal: I make you angry because you are, after all, an American, a Judeo-Christian humanist. A *Bill of Rights* Yankee. And I am, after all, a biblical eye-for-an-eye Jew. I will do anything, you hear, *anything* to keep Israel alive. All Israel. All we have and all of the land of Israel we will have.

Do you know what you're saying?

Yes. Do *you* know what I'm saying?

Yes. I'm sad to say I do.

Am I so wrong?

I can't answer that.

There will never be peace for us, Helmut. You think that negotiating with the PLO gang will achieve peace? It has not happened yet, and it will never happen. No peace for Jews. You must know this is the truth.

Barone's aide, a Yemenite sergeant, brought in a cut-glass decanter. Taking the brandy from him, Barone said, Aha, it's exactly five o'clock! Thank you, Ezra. He poured two glasses and handed one to Wiederspiel. Don't be angry, Hal.

Wiederspiel swirled the brandy in the glass, sniffed it, and sipped some over the lip of the glass.

Good, isn't it? A gift from Nixon.

Very good. Don't cross the Canal without orders, Achad.

Barone shrugged.

What does that mean, Wiederspiel asked.

It means I do not know what I will do. Besides, if I said that I would cross, I believe you'd have me court-martialed. Correct?

Correct.

Yet if I do cross, all Israel will stand and cheer—even the Chasidim.

Probably.

They drank in silence. Pouring refills, Barone became mellow. His pale-blue eyes filled with tears. You also think I am a loose cannon?

Yes.

Hal. Hal!

Aren't you?

Yes, of course. But what does it mean—Barone the loose cannon? That I will not make the same mistakes we have made for two thousand years?

Who decides that, Achad?

Me. Not Dayan, not that whole bunch. They are politicians.

You said archaeologists.

Archaeological politicians, then. Didn't Dayan try to sell you that damaged mummy, the one with the missing leg?

Wiederspiel laughed. Barone laughed. Don't cross, Achad, I beg you. Wait for orders.

Sure. I'll wait for orders—if they come in time. Well, at least we know where we stand. Thank you for that, Hal. Please, I love you. There is not another soldier—

I am not a soldier.

Flyer! You like flyer better? Give me a little concession, will you? You are a soldier. With you I would go to death and hell for Israel. In your heart, Hal, you know I am not wrong.

Achad, please.

All right, put your heart to one side. Just let me speak a little.

Give me some more, Hal said, extending his glass.

Barone poured. Here is my whole belief, he began, my whole belief! Almost two thousand years ago we lost Eretz Yisroel. We wanted to return. We cried for Israel, but there was no way back. There it should have ended. The Jews and their memory of the Old Land should have perished in the Diaspora. Some say that we did not perish because the old Orthodox kept the faith alive. But that was not it, Hal, that was not it at all! The *goyim* kept us alive. They kept us alive to punish us, so we could be their repositories of evil. It made no difference to them that we brought them gifts of the greatest stature. It is enough to say we brought them God! God, Hal! Could we do more? Before Pharaoh, they killed us. After Pharaoh, they killed us. Before Jesus they killed us. After Jesus they killed us. Before the Inquisition they killed us. After the Inquisition they killed us. Before the Czar they killed us. After the Czar they killed us. Before Hitler and after Hitler. The only time they didn't kill us was when we lived on these holy lands. And that is all I believe. If we are to stay alive we must control this land and we must control Eretz Yisroel, the Greater Israel—all of it. Then, only then, will we not be killed.

And what about Arab rights?

I am not a soldier to fight for Arab rights.

Wiederspiel swallowed the rest of his brandy. I think you're a little crazy, Achad!

That I acknowledge. But am I wrong?

How many Palestinians will you destroy for Eretz Yisroel?

All of them, if I have to. Let them go live in Jordan with the dwarf king. Let them live and be well in Jordan.

And how many Lebanese, Syrians, and Iraqis?

As many as I must. I am tired of dying. I will not be pushed into the sea.

And nuclear bombs, Achad?

Barone drew a quick breath. If it must be, he said.

Wiederspiel hit Barone in the face with a closed fist.

Barone's head snapped back, but his expression did not change. Am I wrong, Hal? Say I am wrong.

You are wrong. How can you think of bringing down the world for the sake of a Greater Israel?

Syria can do that? Iraq can do that? The Soviet Union can do that? The United States can do that?

We are Jews! We cannot—we *must* not—do that!

Masada, then? The whole nation must leap from a mountaintop or wade into the waters of the sea?

There is a point, Achad, when we must be willing to die.

You mean a point when Jews must leap from the mountain? That is not a possibility, Barone groaned. I'm not asking Jews to die, Hal. I'm asking Jews to live. To take destiny in their own hands and live! I don't want our fate to be decided by Arafat or Brezhnev or Nixon. Or by you!

Why not me? I'm a Jew. I'm as good a Jew as you are.

When the time comes, we will see, he said, taking his silver pistol from the holster around his waist and handing it to Wiederspiel. Tears now ran down his face. Listen, Hal, if you ever think, even for a minute, that I'm an enemy of Israel, you are free to shoot me. Anytime you like. Come to me with the pistol in your hand, and I will kneel at your feet and bow my head.

Then the sergeant came into the bunker, carrying a field phone. It's Dayan, he said.

General Barone put the phone to his ear. Moshe, what's the news? He paused. Yes, of course. I have a hundred rafts and eight hundred men. . . . In four hours. Done! No problem.

Then he called in his officers and gave the orders to cross the Suez Canal.

3.

Wiederspiel climbed into the Cobra that had brought him to the front and ordered the pilot to follow the commandos. He watched as they inflated their rubber boats and pushed off into the twilight; they stroked deeply with an easy, synchronized rhythm. Wiederspiel spotted Barone in the third boat, seated starboard with his good arm to the outside.

When the rubber armada was halfway across, Egyptian fire took out two boats. Dead bodies floated away, while the living and the wounded swam toward the Egyptian shore. The other boats rowed ahead almost as if they were unaware. Once they landed, Barone directed the troops with his good arm, and they disappeared into the Egyptian night.

Soon after, two rolling metal bridges were floated across the Canal, followed by Israeli tanks. Above his Cobra sounded the boom of IAF Phantoms. Wiederspiel gestured to the pilot to move forward. Now the Suez desert was illuminated by gunfire as Egyptian planes exploded and burned. Several hundred tanks formed a wide, iron arc around the enemy's armor, burrowed into the sand a few hundred yards ahead of them, while Barone's men put forth a paralyzing curtain of fire. The arc of tanks tightened; the fighter bombers swooped down and loosed their missiles. Egyptian tank hatches popped open, spitting out men who hoped to be able to surrender. After a few disastrous encounters, the Egyptian Air Force flew in retreat beyond Cairo.

The Cobra hovered a hundred feet above the front line. Barone looked up, waving his good arm and shouting something that Wiederspiel couldn't hear. With their general, the commandos stood in the open, burning desert. When Barone stuck a cigar between his teeth, one of his men lit it for him.

The Cobra broke to the right and flew toward the rear. Wiederspiel felt the weight of Barone's silver pistol in the pocket of his worn bomber jacket. In the face of this great victory, how could he not feel relief and joy?

4.

The Yom Kippur War ended on October 24 with a cease-fire declared by the U.N., with the strong backing of Washington. Golda Meir's government acceded, pulling its troops and armor back across the Canal and putting its planes, aside from those that monitored the border, down on their bases.

General Achad Barone returned as the hero of Yom Kippur. In dozens of interviews, both domestic and foreign, his bloody arm sling prominently displayed, he condemned the cease-fire. Filled with passion, his steady voice excoriated his government for caving in to the United Nations: Had not Anwar Sadat rejected the first call for a cease-fire? Egypt had complied only when the Israeli Defense Forces were on the verge of complete victory. Neither did Barone spare the United States, and Henry Kissinger in particular, for the political meddling that saved Sadat's neck. But his most bitter attacks were reserved for his government's obsequious relation with the United States. We have a right to defend our nation from attack, he argued. We have a right—an obligation—to defeat and punish any enemy who attacks us. No proud, independent nation would do less. So why are these special demands made on Israel? Why must our sons die without being avenged? Because we are Jews? Because we are still regarded as a ghetto state? Never again! We must say, Never again!

As his celebrity and popularity soared, Barone further proposed that all Arabs living in Israel be deported. That preemptive strikes be undertaken whenever Israel felt threatened. That the PLO be programmatically hunted down and destroyed so that no more innocent lives would be lost to terrorists. Finally, on an American television show, later broadcast in Israel, General Barone resigned his commission. This should not be interpreted, he cautioned, as a return to his family farm to grow turnips. If the politicians will not let me win on the battlefield, he announced, I will win on the floors of the Knesset, where the real decisions are made. Long live our boys, those who will give their lives, those who stand between us and destruction. Long live Israel!

How much of this was bombast, or was Barone entirely sincere? Wiederspiel's hand trembled as he turned off the television set and then sat and stared at the blank screen.

5.

A few weeks later, David Ben-Gurion died and was buried at Kibbutz Seder Boker in the Negev.

Helmut William Wiederspiel was at the grave site as the rabbi prayed. Standing alongside him was Morris Albert Cohen, whose massive head towered above the other mourners. He wept and chanted the prayer for the dead along with the rabbi. Geula, standing across the open grave from Wiederspiel, was glad when it was over; though the ritual was short, it had seemed interminable.

Then Ben-Gurion's body, small and almost shapeless in its linen shroud, was lowered into the sandy pit. The rabbi

threw the first handful of earth into the grave, and the rest
followed. Wiederspiel, transfixed, let the desert sand trickle
from his fingers. The slapping wind carried most of it away.
He had visited Ben-Gurion only the week before. Outside
his desert house, the old man had been asleep in his wheelchair in the fading sunlight. Wiederspiel sat down opposite
him, well aware that this might be the last time he saw him
alive.

Was it a good life, Ben-Gurion? Wiederspiel said softly.
Did we do what we set out to do? Have we come to the end
of our dreams? Is this our Israel, old man? Have we finally
come home? Anyway, I want to tell you you did a good job,
a very good job. Only because you are asleep, David, I will
say this: You are the greatest Jew since Moses.

The old man awoke smiling and looked intently at Wiederspiel. Who are you? he said.

Helmut. Hal Wiederspiel.

Do I know you?

Yes. We have served together for many years.

In the Haganah?

There too, Ben-Gurion.

Stand up. Walk around. Maybe it will remind me.

Wiederspiel stood up, walked toward Ben-Gurion, and
then leaned over and kissed him on the cheek.

Ach, Helmut! Why, it *is* you!

Yes.

It is strange how the mind works. At first I didn't know
you at all, so I was sparring with you. I thought maybe it was
the Angel of Death standing there. Except you were so young,
so handsome, and there was a warmth in you. What a relief,
Helmut!

An army nurse came from the house carrying a tray with
a teapot and cups. She poured and gave one to Helmut.
Another, half filled, she gave to Ben-Gurion. He may spill
it, she said under her breath and retreated to the house.

Sipping his tea, Wiederspiel looked at the old face. Not too many wrinkles, he thought. The white hair stood up wild in the wind that found its way into the sheltered area where Ben-Gurion sat.

They tell me we have won the war, Helmut. Is this true?

Yes, David. We have won.

Was it a new war or an old one?

New, Ben-Gurion. An attack from Egypt on Yom Kippur.

And we won?

We crossed the Suez and trapped their armies. But the U.N. called for a cease-fire. We stopped.

Was Barone there?

Yes. He was wounded.

Ben-Gurion laughed. Barone doesn't mind that, so long as the wound is not in his head, he said and laughed again.

He has gone into politics.

Who has gone into politics?

Barone.

Into politics? That is serious, Helmut. See him. Talk to him. Explain things, Helmut.

What things?

He's a hothead. A good boy, but so hotheaded.

Can he be right, Ben-Gurion?

But the old man's head was nodding, and soon he had fallen asleep. Wiederspiel removed the teacup from his hand; within a few minutes, the nurse returned and wheeled Ben-Gurion into the white-stucco-fronted house.

Well, Wiederspiel thought, at least I got to see him once more. The last sand spilled from his hand into Ben-Gurion's grave. It was November 29, 1973.

PART SEVEN

1.

Kalia was in Zachary's arms, her cheek pressed against his chest, as Guy Lombardo's orchestra played. I'd do this only for you, darling, Zachary said. And you *know* how much I hate it!

Thank you, my sweet. I'll make it up to you later. I'll do your favorite things.

You're bribing me. But it's all right. I accept. Can you stand dancing with me?

Sure. You're a hell of a lot better than you think. Awkward but on the beat. And you wear a tuxedo beautifully. I love it. Kiss me behind the ear.

If you ever tell anyone, *anyone*, that I took you to the Waldorf for New Year's, I'll kill you.

I promise I won't tell.

They danced to "They Can't Take That Away from Me." Do you know how much I love this song, Kalia asked.

Tonight you love everything.

That's right. Tonight I do indeed love everything.

Will you explain again why you changed your mind?

About what?

Marrying me.

Oh, that! Okay, Zach, one mo' time. In Old Yafo, remember you said that marriage wasn't such a big commitment, and I got angry?

You sure did. But I've changed my position. I'm determined to make an honest woman out of you.

Thanks. I appreciate it! But not until I've converted. I want—insist—on having a proper Jewish wedding.

You can't have one of those if you marry a *goy*.

What makes you think I'd do that?

I'm a *goy*.

That's the point. I won't marry a *goy*. Once you convert, I'll consider any serious proposal.

Well, then, we'll just have to live in sin.

Great! I love sin. Sin's great.

Forgetting his self-consciousness about dancing, Zachary pulled Kalia closer as the orchestra played a tune he knew but couldn't recall the title of. When you become a Jew, we'll talk, he said. Which, given your luck with rabbis, may be never.

Just one rabbi, with Dov Schechter. You know what they say: it's hard to be a Jew. Well, it's harder to get to be one. But I'm up to it. I'll earn my Jewishness. The real question is, Will *you* convert?

The trouble is, I'm half Jewish on the wrong side. If I had a Yiddish mama—even if she had been an amoral, mentally deficient atheist—I would be, of course, a full-blooded Jew. What have you got to say to that, my dear *shiksa*?

I love you. But I won't marry a *goy*.

Sin then.

Sin then.

Guy Lombardo played one cheek-to-cheek memory after another, songs his father and mother had known. Then the orchestra played a fast tune. Everybody except Barthelmes knew what to do, so with Kalia in tow, he left the whirling dance floor and bellied up to the nearest bar. It was ten minutes before eleven o'clock on the last night of 1974.

2.

Films, Zachary Barthelmes thought in a reflective moment, are the noblest form of lying. They rely on omission and compression; whereas his script, he realized, had gotten hung up on inclusion and expansion. Goldsmid was, after all, correct: he did have a right to be in the film. So did Vambery, but Barthelmes's loyalty to Newlinski was unwavering.

After returning from London a year ago Barthelmes had done more walking through Central Park than writing. He had, as a matter of fact, written only one scene and then nothing at all for almost three months. Maybe the project was just too big. Maybe it had been easier to write *Geronimo* because he hadn't really known anything about him; of course everybody said he'd won the Oscar because of the scope and depth of the script. But Herzl? Herzl was a whale, and Barthelmes felt like a minnow trying to swallow the big fish. Or, perhaps, like Jonah, the whale had swallowed him and would not spit him out. In February he'd called Moe Cohen to confess he was stuck. Wait a minute, Zach, Moe had said. Tell me, how do you *feel* about it? Do you want to do it? I mean, in your *kishka* do you want to do it?

Zachary had answered, with my *kishka*, with my heart and soul, with my balls, Moe, I want to do it. I lose sleep. I lose weight, Moe.

Cohen laughed. That goes with the territory, Zach. So long as you don't lose your beautiful Douglas Fairbanks, Jr., hair. Do you need some more money?

At this point, I'd pay you. Help!

Don't worry, you'll break through. Moe paused. Zachary listened to dead air in the receiver until Moe said, Can I make a little contribution?

I told you, Moe, I don't need money.

Not money. I thought of what to call the film. Can I tell you?

Sure. Fire away.

Maybe you can call it *The Beggar's Cup*.

Now Barthelmes was silent. I like it, he said, but what does it mean?

It was in a dream I had once. It has to do with a *pushka*. And what's a *pushka*?

When I see you, I'll tell you. Anyway, it's an idea.

That night he'd asked Kalia whether she knew what a *pushka* was.

Yep, she had said, it's one of those little blue-and-white tin boxes. Jews still do use them to collect coins for the Jewish National Fund, to build roads and plant trees in Israel.

Son of a bitch! How'd you know that?

Crossword puzzle. No, I'm only joking. Sandra Abramowitz, in my office, has one on her desk. She keeps pencils in it. But it does have a picture of Herzl on it.

Jesus! It *is* a beggar's cup!

In a manner of speaking, I guess.

Finally the Guy Lombardo forty switched back to slow sentimentality, and Kalia led him back to the dance floor. She was accustomed to Zachary's brooding silences, but tonight was, after all, New Year's Eve, and somebody was singing "Impossible" in a voice like Perry Como's.

3.

It was difficult now to remember why she had called Dov Schechter on that particular day. She could not recall it, but the month had been April. The beginning or the middle, not the end. Why had she called him at all? Was it because Zachary was so deeply involved with the film, with Herzl, and with his lengthening parade of Jews—the Jews she had come to love so much? That and a growing loneliness. Aside from Zach she felt that she belonged to no one and to nothing. Unless you considered the advertising agency something to which one belonged. She was convinced she no longer belonged to the Christian church. Yet how that alienation had evolved, Kalia did not know. The separation was there like a chasm—deep and cold and endless. Would Judaism fill it?

Was Judaism the warm road back to God? Perhaps Zachary did not need God. She did, or she thought she did.

From her makeup case—where she had put it, where she had seen it every day—she removed the scrap of paper the Jerusalem butcher had given her. As she looked into the mirror, her eyes stiff and wide for the mascara brush, Kalia Wiggins decided to call Rabbi Dov Schechter. He agreed to meet her the following Tuesday at the Famous Dairy Restaurant on West 72d Street.

After the phone call she had felt neither excitement nor elation, only concern and anxiety. What should she wear? And should she pick up the check? Zachary was no help. He'd taken to smiling constantly whenever Kalia expressed her fears. This is *serious*, Zach, she finally said. You could be a little supportive.

I am being supportive. No matter what disguise you wear, I'll still love you.

Very funny. Please, Zach.

You are serious, aren't you?

One of the most important decisions of my life. I've thought about it for years now. I want to become a Jew. I want to die a Jew.

So you not only want to have a proper Jewish wedding, but also want to be buried in a proper Jewish cemetery.

You're teasing again.

I'm sorry. I just couldn't help it. Zachary had held her in his arms.

When the appointed day came, Kalia was standing in front of the Famous Dairy ten minutes early. It was a raw spring morning. She wore her black Burberry raincoat over a black Anne Klein suit. Then a twinge of doubt: why all this black? She was going to a happy, if serious, meeting, not a funeral. But her blouse was white, she assured herself. It was all quite proper.

Then she wondered whether she should stay outside on

the sidewalk or wait inside, near the door, until the rabbi came. And how would she recognize him? It would be better to seat herself and wait, she decided, to pretend to be at ease. The burden of recognition would then fall to both of them. She went inside and waited for a waiter to notice her, but it was Dov Schechter who came forward from his table. He wore a gray, boxy suit and, on his head, a velvet *kippah*. His thin face was fleshed out by a neat, wiry black beard. Miss Wiggins? he said.

Yes. Rabbi Schechter? How did you know?

Not too difficult, he said, leading her back to the white-topped table where he'd been waiting.

Was I that obvious, she asked. I admit I'm nervous, but *still*.

Oh, I saw that. But excuse me, Miss Wiggins, you don't look especially Jewish. Dov Schechter handed Kalia a menu. It's all very good. Very traditional. *Glatt Kosher*, if you understand the expression.

Yes, I do, Rabbi.

Good! Here we hardly know each other, and we already have plunged headlong into Jewish culture.

She laughed. Yet behind the man's smile and wit, Kalia sensed a certain hostility. Maybe black was the wrong color, or perhaps her hair was too blond. Maybe he had a toothache. She ordered some potato *latkes* with sour cream and a little applesauce on the side. The rabbi chose a chopped pickled herring salad.

Listen, the rabbi said, I never really know how to start these things. I've done it maybe six or eight times, but I always feel awkward. You want to break the ice?

Well, I want to be a member of the Jewish faith. I guess that why I'm here.

Any special reason?

I've always enjoyed being with Jewish people. They seem more sensitive, more cultured, more compassion—

Thanks for the compliments, Miss Wiggins, but simply because you love elephants doesn't mean that you have to become an elephant. You can enjoy your Jewish friends —that's no sin. But there must be more to it, don't you think?

Yes, of course. I just don't know exactly how to start.

Calm yourself! There still is dessert and coffee, and the noon rush is over. Their cheese Danish is terrific.

They chatted about all manner of subjects over lunch, passing the time at once amiably and awkwardly. Then, over coffee, Kalia said, Perhaps it was being in Israel for a few weeks. All the things I was vaguely attracted to in the Jewish people suddenly seemed very real and concrete.

How was that, do you suppose?

Kalia could feel the tears in her eyes. I can't really explain. At the Wailing Wall I cried like a baby. Why should I do that? I was brought up as a Baptist in a small town in Georgia. I was crying because at that moment I felt that I'd always been a Jew. A thousand years ago. Eternally. I was crying because I'd been reborn.

Rabbi Dov Schechter lowered his coffee cup. Reborn, he asked over the thin smile that split his beard.

Oh, I'm sorry. That was an unfortunate choice of a word, wasn't it? But I don't mean I was finding Christ in some other form.

What were you finding?

A longing for something, something I'd lost.

That simple? A longing?

Yes.

Are you married?

She had hesitated before shaking her head. No, not really.

Dov Schechter smiled again. You know, Miss Wiggins, when a Christian wants to convert, most often there's a Jew in the woodpile. A boyfriend, a *chupah* over the horizon. The intended happens to be Jewish so they decide maybe it's better for her to be Jewish also. And it's better for the children, as they always say.

The boyfriend—it's serious—is half Jewish. His father was Jewish but he converted to his mother's denomination. Episcopalian.

The rabbi shook his head.

I'm aware that he's not even half Jewish, technically.

That's right. So it has nothing to do with him, your wanting to convert.

It does and it doesn't. I'd like it if he also decided to become a Jew.

If he doesn't, then what?

It doesn't matter, Rabbi. I know what I want. And Judaism will give me the spiritual life I want so badly. Will you help me?

Rabbi Dov Schechter sighed. We'll make an appointment, he said, taking out a small leather-covered date book.

4.

Barthelmes stood before the urinal; it was a long letting out. To his left and to his right were more than a dozen other New Year's celebrants, and the flushing was constant. Three urinals to the left a portly man with a beet-red face sighed loudly with relief—and this brought the image of the Grand Duke Friedrich to Zachary's mind. Friedrich of Baden, uncle of Kaiser Wilhelm, who in 1871 had placed the crown on the head of the Kaiser's father, the first ruler of the newly unified Germany. Zachary knew the Grand Duke had a grand set of white muttonchops and a flowing, well-barbered mustache, and Zachary had given him a ruddy complexion as well as the habit of sighing constantly and dramatically clearing his throat. In fact, Friedrich had dominated the last scene Barthelmes had written.

Karlsruhe, April 23, 1896. The Orient Express hisses into the station. In their compartment, HERZL *and* HECHLER *note the commotion on the station platform. His hand cupped above his eyebrows,* HECHLER *peers through the train window:*

It is here, Dori! The Kaiser's private car! They are joining it to the train. Everyone must believe it is for the Kaiser.

Does the Grand Duke often use the royal car?

In truth I don't know.

Do we go to his car?

No. We must await word.

The wheels revolve slowly as the Orient Express hisses into the night. HERZL *lights a cigar. His hand trembles. Trees, houses, and an occasional light flash by as the express whistles through the darkness. There is a crisp knock on the compartment door.*

HECHLER: Come!

CAVALRY LIEUTENANT *(saluting):* His Royal Highness Friedrich, Grand Duke of Baden, expects the pleasure of your company in his car.

Interior: an ornate stateroom with a small, flat crystal chandelier pressed against the ceiling. In the center of the room stands FRIEDRICH, *a man in his early seventies. He walks briskly toward* HERZL *and grasps his hand.* HERZL *bows.*

FRIEDRICH: None of that, Herzl, none of that. This is an informal meeting. Man to man, you see.

HERZL: I am honored.

FRIEDRICH *(circling* HERZL, *regarding him):* Good, very good! A fine figure of a man, Hechler, just as you said. In the flesh, Herzl, you look better than in your photographs.

HERZL: Photographs?

FRIEDRICH: Oh yes. My aides found a good like-

ness of you in an old theater program of your play
I Love You, Kate. Amusing, but not as good as
Schnitzler. Your photographer on the Ringstrasse
provided us with two others. I studied them carefully
before deciding to have this informal meeting.
Informal! I must say, Herzl, you don't look too,
well, too—

HERZL: Jewish?

FRIEDRICH: Well . . . harrumph . . .

HECHLER: He looks like a Syrian king, Your
Highness.

HERZL *turns his head slowly, displaying his profile.*

FRIEDRICH: Exactly, William! Would you care for
some slivovitz? (HERZL *raises his hand in demurral.*)
Not a drinker, eh? I hear you are good with swords.

HERZL: When I was a boy.

FRIEDRICH: The dueling society?

HERZL: Yes.

FRIEDRICH: Scars under the beard?

HERZL: Only one, Your Highness, a very small
one.

FRIEDRICH: Have you ever gone into battle,
Herzl?

HERZL: I have not yet had the good fortune.

FRIEDRICH: Do you know why men on the battlefield pluck up their courage and take arms against
the foe? It is for a good flag. A good banner. Nothing
more than that. Harrumph.

HERZL: I have designed a flag for the Zionists.
White and blue, with seven stars of gold.

FRIEDRICH: You are profound, my good fellow.
A rag on a stick with a star that will get a bumpkin
to charge every time! Would you like to use the
Kaiser's commode?

HERZL: I have no need, Your Excellency.

FRIEDRICH: And you, William? Would you like to make a wee-wee for the Kaiser?

HECHLER: I would be honored, sire, but I'm quite depleted.

FRIEDRICH: Well, lads, I must use the commode. Heavy-duty stuff. Can't control it for too long at my age. When nature calls I must obey.

FRIEDRICH *pulls open a door, and filling the closet is an exact replica of the imperial throne, topped by an eagle gripping a crown in its claws. Above it is a large glass tank filled with water, in which a dozen large goldfish are swimming.*

FRIEDRICH: No other commode like it in the universe! To sit here is to call forth all corruption.

FRIEDRICH *raises the purple-cushioned seat and drops his side-striped military trousers to the floor. He lowers his long white drawers, seats himself on the bowl, and begins to sing "Heidenroslein," gesturing to* HERZL *and* HECHLER *to join in. He closes his eyes as they sing.*

FRIEDRICH: You have a lovely baritone, Herr Herzl. William's tenor I am familiar with, and I have introduced you to my basso profundo.

He pulls the velvet-covered chain, and the water drains from the tank. In the emptying space, the goldfish swim frantically in a tightening pack. Once the water has completely drained, they thrash about violently in the now empty reservoir and gasp for air—as fresh water begins to enter the tank. Soon the fish are covered in their element and swimming without concern in the glass tank.

The red-faced stranger flushed his urinal. Better get back, he said, before the old year runs out.

Barthelmes smiled, and for a few seconds he was alone in

the Waldorf pissoir. I'd like to use that scene, he thought, but how does it fit into the overall design? As Kalia had said, The writing's super, Zach, but I still miss Lulu—you know, the actress who was in bed with Herzl. For all the kaisers and sultans, I find myself wondering when I'll meet the wife and kids. After so much power and pomp, doesn't Herzl ever go off in a corner and cry?

She was right, Barthelmes decided as he zipped up. That's where the film was. Who the hell was this Herzl, anyway? Not a stylish suit of clothes, nor an erudite bag of manners. He was a man. Something like himself. Like Moe. Like Hal.

5.

Great night, the man said. Tell you, I'm celebrating but I hate to see '74 go down. More than doubled my gross assets, and that's a great year! You care to dance?

I'll sit this one out, Kalia said. I'm waiting for a friend.

Allow me to buy you a drink. Dom Pérignon '63. Now that's a great year!

Better than '74?

He laughed. Sharp, the man said. You're really sharp. Ever try the St. Regis on New Year's Eve?

Nope. Can't say that I have.

Well, it's better than the Waldorf. They should ask another ten, twenty dollars a head and thin out some of the riffraff. Say, is your friend as good-looking as you?

I think so.

Also a blond?

Yes. A little gray at the temples, though.

Hey, I like older gals. It takes time to get the experience.

There was a long silence between Kalia and this bald stranger who, finally, said, You think we have a future? Either you or your friend, know what I mean?

Speaking for myself, Kalia said, I'm looking forward to it. But my friend will have to speak for himself.

At this the man smiled and cocked his head. Well, nice speaking to you. You're a good conversationalist.

Thank you, Kalia said and then realized she was mildly flattered by his ludicrous attempt to pick her up. This, on the whole, had not been a good year. A rotten year, 1974. Good riddance to bad rubbish, as her mother used to say.

If there had been a positive feature, it was the deepening of her relationship with Zachary. But *The Beggar's Cup* had gone slowly. Zachary had rewritten constantly, and, what was even more unusual, he'd required endless support and encouragement. Then, of course, there was the business with Moe.

Last, but not least, her conversion had foundered on the shoals of Rabbi Dov Schechter's disbelief. In this she had failed, but felt more like a Jew than ever before—a feeling that was deep and without rational explanation. Why couldn't she run back to Jesus or put on buckskin and beads and chant with the Hopi? Religions of the World Simplified. She was angry about her failure to be properly converted, and she directed this against Dov and then against herself. Finally, only later, she had discovered why she had wanted to become a Jew in the first place, and this was truly shattering. Now she was trying to rethink her needs—not to mention her actions and feelings—but suddenly all her universes seemed to have become unmoored. Zach was her only rock, and she lifted her neck to look over the madding herd. When would he stop pissing?

Dov Schechter, Kalia Wiggins thought, was not happily married. His wife, Estelle, seemed older than her early thirties and was worn out by their six children. Everything she said seemed to be a complaint directed at the world in general and at Dov in particular. When Estelle's eyes had met Kalia's, the complaint had been shared: Does he care? Look at me?

If the rabbi ignored his wife, he was always combatively alert when Kalia arrived for her weekly visit—too beautiful, too blond, too long legged, and too good a student. He'd given her a list of more than thirty books, and she'd purchased all of them; some were hard to acquire, and for those she'd gone down to Biegeleisen's on the Lower East Side. The Pentateuch had especially fascinated her, these five books of Moses in the Torah. How personal it was! Moses taught the holy words to Joshua. She could see them sitting together, flames flickering from the caldron-bearing fireplace, Joshua's eyes burning with awe. God speaking, God speaking through Moshe, not Moses—Moshe! Joshua then teaching the Elders, who then broadcast the Torah to the world. When she explained her interpretation to Dov, he was moved. And he was more than moved when Kalia wept as they discussed the Zohar.

I work with words, as you know, Rabbi Schechter. You can imagine what it means to me to find it said that the words of the Torah have no meaning until God, as His children look at the words, gives the words their meanings, their light! So even as you study it, a word might emerge with a new meaning—God's meaning. And is this true of the words we use and say in profane life? Is God behind our daily words?

Rabbi Schechter had never thought of this before. For days this idea of Kalia Wiggins had stayed with him. Does God invest all words in all languages with meaning? She had said with light, *with light*! He was shaken by her insight, yet he did not trust her and could not quite figure out why this was. It had nothing to do with her beauty. This was in self-defense; he did feel attracted to her, but so might many men. After ten years of marriage and six children, these random feelings often welled up. No, he was sure that his distrust of Kalia was not based on physical attraction. But on what, then?

Three months of visits with Rabbi Schechter passed. Kalia had read the recommended books, added a few titles of her own discovery to the list, mastered a basic Jewish cuisine, and assembled a vocabulary of almost four hundred Hebrew words. She felt she was achieving Jewishness if, indeed, she were not already a Jew. Any week she expected Rabbi Schechter to say: Kalia Wiggins, you are ready for the *mikveh*, the ritual bath, the final step.

Instead, at their next session, he had said, I cannot continue with you. Kalia felt herself shrivel, hiding inside herself, as if she'd been struck. Her eyes filled with tears. Why, Rabbi? she finally asked. Have I done something wrong?

No, no. Not at all.

I have done everything to the best of my ability. Have I been insincere?

No, Kalia, not at all. It was the first time he had used her name.

God, Rabbi, these months have been among the happiest in my life. Why are you doing this? Why? She broke into tears and sobs.

Rabbi Schechter went to her and put his arms around her shoulders. Control yourself, please. I would like to explain. It may not be your fault at all. It may be my fault. Control yourself, please.

How can it be your fault? You have been a good teacher. You have been such a good guide, and I thought I was reaching into the—

Let me explain, please.

Spare me the explanations, Dov. I laid myself on your altar, and you've cut my throat! Goddamn you!

Will you let me explain?

No! You're destroying me! You're only a rabbi, not the Almighty!

Kalia, let me explain!

Oh, you don't have to explain. I've lived this long as a *shiksa*; I can handle that all by myself. She blew her nose several times into some tissues and then looked up and saw that the rabbi was weeping, tears rolling down into his black beard.

Maybe it's my fault, he said. I want to explain. I must, Kalia.

She didn't speak, and for several minutes they just sat there.

Finally Schechter said, I have confused and complicated everything.

I really don't see how. You've been as direct as a punch in the mouth.

Give me a moment, please, to find the right way to begin. Kalia nodded.

You see I am weeping? I weep easily, but at funerals, weddings, bar mitzvahs, good sermons—not like this. I'm weeping because I don't know if I'm doing the right thing by not bringing you to conversion. There was a thermos on his desk. He poured two cups. Excuse me, but there is a Yiddish expression: On the lung, then on the tongue. In Yiddish, too, it rhymes. If you feel it inside yourself, then spit it out. I will start that way: I just don't trust your motives. There, it's out!

Kalia's head bobbed with rapid little nods. If you feel that way, Dov, then you are right. But you must tell me why. Otherwise I'll go crazy—I mean really go crazy!

My problem is this: I don't know why I don't trust your motives. Still, I can't deny what I feel, and it's a strong feeling. Though I'll admit it's not as strong as when I first met you.

You had that feeling from the start?

Yes. I said to myself: What have I here? A blond beauty in dark clothing. A *goy* who says she wants to be a Jew. Something strange, strange.

Just by looking at me?

Yes. My gut feeling was that there was something not kosher.

Kalia laughed almost hysterically. Of course something

wasn't kosher! It was me! That's what I needed—to be salted and seasoned and koshered. That was the whole idea!

Yes. My gut—

Stop it, Dov. I don't want to hear about your gut.

That I can understand, but I don't understand your motivation, Kalia.

I explained my motivations!

But what I'm looking for is your *essential* reason.

Now you're getting too Talmudic.

Please, your boyfriend is not a Jew.

Half.

Not even half. Look, Kalia, there's no pressure to convert. It's just that you *want* to be a Jew.

Of course! What's wrong with that! Yes, I just want to be a Jew. I'm a lousy Baptist.

Do you believe in God? Do you believe in *Christ*?

I have explained that as best I can, Dov. I was brought up believing in God. I am imprinted. God lurks inside me somewhere.

The God of Baptists or the God of Jews?

There's only one God, right? I told you a thousand times, Dov, I believe in the historical Jesus, but I don't think he's the son of God. I don't want to be a Jew for Jesus. I want to be a Jew, a complete Jew. I want to have a Jewish wedding.

Maybe becoming a Jew is just a kick?

That's cruel and cheap!

There have been plenty of such incidents. Someone is bored, needs a change. How quaint, be a Jew! Wear a Mogen David.

Kalia fingered the gold Mogen David around her neck. It had been designed on Rodeo Drive and commissioned by Moe Cohen, who had sent it as a gift to celebrate her impending conversion. The six-pointed star had six tiny stars at each of its points, and in the center of each was embedded a seed pearl. The Mogen David had arrived inside a *pushka* of gold, from which the faint, matted image of Theodor Herzl looked out at the world. Are you implying something? she said.

No. I'm saying it all wrong!

Is there sexual tension between us, Dov? Is that it?

He caught his breath, blushed, and recomposed himself. I would lie if I said no, he said. You are a beautiful woman. You must turn heads without provoking. Yes, I have noticed you. But believe me, I don't feel involved.

Am I a threat to Judaism?

No, of course not!

For Christ's sake, will you say something that makes sense!

I'm trying!

Now Kalia laughed. What am I going to tell my friends? That the Rabbi Dov Schechter would not see me through to conversion because I'm too blond, too sexy, too Christian, too sincere, too diligent in my pursuit of Judaism? That the rabbi simply couldn't understand why a person like me wanted to become a Jew?

Enough!

What do you really think, Dov? That I'm not good enough for Judaism, or that Judaism isn't good enough for me?

That's enough. Please leave. I'm sure you can find another rabbi who will be happy to help you. I don't want to do it! I will not do it!

Because you suspect my motives?

No. Because I don't know what your motive is, and I am convinced that you don't either.

Kalia's cheeks burned. Again, the feeling of a hard slap—the feeling of her mouth filled with dirt. Stunned, she walked from the rabbi's apartment. Not until she reached Columbus Circle did she sit down. On the green bench near the entrance to the subway, she said aloud, almost shouting, I know what my motive is! But how could Dov Schechter ever understand that motive?

Her handsome father standing in front of the coffee shop on Main Street filled her mind. You were the motive, Daddy dear, you bastard, she said, her voice loud enough to attract the attention of people going toward the subway stairs. Her head had filled with noise, her brain twittering like an old radio that couldn't find a signal. There was Daddy's voice, her brother's voice, her mother's heavy silence. When she looked down, her shiny black pumps seemed an Alice-in-Wonderland distance away. The sun was setting and Kalia Wiggins was shouting: I'm a little Baptist slut! I'm evil! I suck cocks! Then, at the top of her lungs, she sang "Amazing Grace."

Over and over again, she said, I caught you, Daddy! By now a small crowd had gathered. A policeman pushed his way through and took hold of her arm. Can I help you, lady?

Kalia stared into the cop's face. After a moment she said, Did you know my father? Edward Wiggins? Then she began to weep. Crying steadily, she sounded exactly like a small child. The policeman walked her to the hospital a few blocks away. In the emergency room he signaled, twirling a finger, that she was cuckoo.

6.

Kalia knew it was Zachary's kiss on the back of her neck. You were away such a long time. I missed you.

Slow music! Zachary said as he led her onto the thick, turning floor. Wanna dance?

After three consecutive, passable dances, including one well-executed dip, Zachary Barthelmes realized that he hadn't really gained control of *The Beggar's Cup* until August.

This did not mean the entire film was clear; he still had to select scenes from the great spread and variety of Herzl's life. But now the script had both a design and good pulses, beats that testified to the truth of each scene in its rightful place. And he knew the end: Herzl's death, or perhaps the day before, when Julie had concluded her visit and he was left alone with the Reverend William Hechler.

Wake up, Zach, Kalia whispered in his ear. You're falling out of tempo.

Barthelmes regained the rhythm and Kalia's head nestled back onto his shoulder. Until a few weeks before, the very beginning of the film had eluded him. Barthelmes was fairly sure it was the right opening, yet he remained cautious about it. How many scenes, good in the reading, turned out to be trash in the shooting? But maybe this would work.

Meanwhile, Guy Lombardo's voice counted down the time till New Year's. Twenty-three minutes to 1975! Synchronize your watches, folks!

Pelikan Strasse, Vienna, home of JULIE *and* THEO-DOR HERZL, *1897.* HERZL *in shirt sleeves, Prince Albert coat thrown across an armchair, his tall, athletic figure outlined by the dying flames in the fireplace. Squinting as he reads a letter, he holds it at an angle so the dim light from the fireplace catches it. He rubs his backside.*

Cut to upstairs bedroom door. It is ajar. JULIE *emerges in a nightgown, her good figure apparent. Camera tracks back, holding her in full frontal view. She is barefoot. Red polish on her toenails, matching polish on fingernails. Quick close-up of hand sliding along bannister. Point of view over* JULIE's *shoulder.* HERZL *reads at fireplace.*

You didn't come home last night.

No.

I wish you would tell me. Hansie had a bad dream and he called for you. I told him you would see him.

You might have noticed my bed.

I pay little attention to your bed.

Is Hansie all right?

JULIE *goes to the fireplace and holds her hands out toward the warmth of the flames.*

Yes. Frightened by something in his dream.

Quite natural. I hope you don't mind if I avoid bringing any more dinner guests.

I can survive that. *(She hitches up her nightgown, backing closer to the fire.)* They were bores.

I don't think so. Israel Zangwill is a very prominent English novelist. And Rabbi Guttman is the most important Jewish religious figure in Vienna.

Boring. Boring, boring, boring. Talk, talk, talk.

(After a silence.) Why did you serve crabs for dinner? I told you they were Orthodox.

Oh, dear, I forgot. But the crabs *were* delicious. You didn't eat any either.

Have you no brains, Julie? You insulted them! Crabs in the home of the Zionist leader!

Are you truly the Zionist leader? *(Laughs.)* You made up all this silly business, didn't you? It's a big game, this Jewish homeland. Isn't it?

If you would read my book—

Is it a novel? That's what I read, Dori, novels. *(Silence.)* They liked my fingernails, you know. Mr. Zangwill couldn't take his eyes off my hands. I told him I was the first, the very, very first woman in Vienna to use nail polish. *Rouge de rouge.* Did you make love tonight?

No.

Would you consider me?

No. A streetwalker would be preferable.

(Flirtatious.) There's nothing a whore can do that
I can't.

They don't talk like idiots.

She slaps him hard across the face. HERZL *smiles.*
JULIE *moves toward the staircase.*

I will fill this house with pork. None of your crazy
Jews will come here again. And everyone knows that
you're crazy, too. Promised Land! *(Ascending stairs
as she speaks.)* Homeland! You'll die before you ever
see Jerusalem.

(To the empty room.) Good night, Julie. *(Returns
to reading letter.)* Cut to sunrise over Vienna. Crawl
begins.

A Big MAC Production
The Beggar's Cup
Written and Directed by
Zachary Barthelmes
Executive Director
Morris Albert Cohen
Starring:
Names, names, names, etc.
Credits, credits, credits, etc.

Long shot of HERZL, *top hat, Prince Albert coat, gray
gloves, silver-topped walking stick, walking jauntily
through the streets, greeted by merchants and pedes-
trians. He arrives at the* Neue Freie Presse *building,
pauses for a deep breath, and then goes inside. He
ascends in the elevator and walks through a warren
of desks until he reaches his office,* HERR THEODOR
HERZL *painted in gold on the translucent glass of the
door. He enters and seats himself. When the door
opens, a* WOMAN SECRETARY *pokes her head inside:*
Herr Herzl, Herr Bacher begs your presence in his
office at once. He said for me to emphasize *at once.*

Cut to BACHER's *opulent office. He is talking hard and fast to* HERZL.

I thank you very much for your appearance at your desk today. How would you calculate it, Theodor, the first day in three weeks? Ordinarily, I do not concern myself with your whereabouts. However, we have been beset by rumors. One is that you have perished, which I can see is not based in fact. The other is that the Burg theater is presenting your new play—whatever it's called—and that you are there from sunup to sunset watching rehearsals and giving ardent private instructions to the prima and—

Herr Bacher—

Please, dear fellow, call me Eduard since you are taking my money for what services I do not know.

I am doing my work, Eduard. You know that. I have not missed a deadline.

Yes. How in the world do you manage it? What is your secret? How can you be King of the Jews and a journalist, too? Each of these is a full-time job.

For the salary you pay me, you have not bought my entire life.

If I did not pay you that paltry salary, how would you stay alive? Who would support your wife and children?

A silence. BACHER *lights a cigar.* HERZL *looks at him calmly:*

I do my job.

Your job? It is a job now? Less than three years ago it was your career. Theodor Herzl of the *Neue Freie Presse.* Creator of witty and penetrating feuilletons. Arbiter of the arts and the lesser sciences. An illustrious career for a gifted young man.

I am indebted to you for the opportunity, Eduard.

It was Paris, wasn't it? If I had not assigned you to Paris, this Jewish-state business would never have happened. I am responsible! Dreyfus turned you into a lunatic! All of Austria, all the *Jews* of Austria, know that Dreyfus is innocent. But only one Jew is demanding a Jewish state!

I am not the only Jew demanding a Jewish state, and it is not even a demand. At this moment it is a prayer.

Oh, next year in Jerusalem! How religious we have become!

I am a Yom Kippur Jew, like yourself.

Exasperated, BACHER *raises his arms toward the ceiling, lowers them, points a finger at* HERZL, *tries to speak, then finally, calming himself:*

All right, all right! Man to man, *kedves Tivadar* [Dear Theodor, in Hungarian]. In simple language, how did you manage to start all this nonsense?

I dreamed it.

Don't provoke me!

I have no intention of provoking you, Eduard. It is the simple truth. It came to me in a dream. In dreams awake and asleep.

I also dream, but I don't go about advocating Jewish states. Why, Theodor, why?

If we do not find a land of our own, soon, the Jews will vanish from the earth.

You believe that?

In my heart and soul.

We are respected. We are protected. We are the loyal servants of Austria, Germany, Hungary, of the Emperor and the Kaiser. You know that.

Eduard, with or without Dreyfus, anti-Semitism is just below the skin of France. It waits to erupt like a pus-filled boil. In Russia the Czar's policy is

to export one-third of his Jews, to keep one-third—
the best and the brightest—and to kill the last third.
Here in Austria, we have von Schoenerer in the
countryside and Leuger in Vienna, screaming for
our blood.

Stop!

I will stop.

There is a silence and a change in BACHER'S *attitude.*
He is gentle, patronizing:

Tivadar, I disagree with you. Totally. But even if
we were in perfect, complete agreement, how could
it be done? No one supports you. Not the poor Jews,
nor the rich Jews. Baron de Hirsch and the Rothschilds have dismissed you, while the Jews in the
middle think only of their careers. No one is rallying
to your banner except the anti-Semites because they
say Herzl is our man: he wants to get rid of the Jews,
too. So who will help you?

The Kaiser.

BACHER *is startled into a brief silence.*

I see, the Kaiser.

In a short time. First I must see the Grand Duke
Friedrich. It will be up to him to arrange things with
the Kaiser.

Of course!

I am meeting him tonight.

I see. And where will that be, this meeting?

On the Orient Express, Eduard, outside
Karlsruhe.

You arranged this?

No. The Reverend William Hechler has arranged
it for me.

That madman? The lunatic of the Ringstrasse?

He is not mad, Eduard. He is eccentric. I am mad.

BACHER *parts the window drapes:*

He sits on that bench across the street. I have watched him take off his shoes. He wears no stockings. He wraps his bare feet in old newspaper, probably the *Neue Freie Presse*. So, Hechler arranged this meeting with the Grand Duke of Baden?

Yes. He is a close friend of the Duke. The Kaiser knows him as well.

You may leave, now.

Am I fired?

No, Theodor. You are reprieved. And I am the one who is crazy.

I will be absent for a few days, Eduard.

Get out! Get out!

HERZL *exits, and the camera pushes to the translucent glass. For a count of three the screen is milky white.*

7.

Are you enjoying this, Kalia? Zachary said, as they stood on the endless line to the buffet table.

I really am. But you must let me tell people we did it. New Year's Eve at the Waldorf!

Not before February. In February it will be less humiliating.

You're loathing it. We're snobs, you know.

Displaced people, maybe. I'm not looking down on this multitude, but we don't really fit in.

The beginning of the buffet table suddenly appeared. Zachary opted for the fricassee on rice; Kalia was served a scoop of Swedish meatballs the size of marbles, also on a bed of rice. When they finally found an empty table, they pushed aside the clutter of soiled dishes and sat down to eat.

I know it's been an awful year for you, darling, Barthelmes

said. But in a few minutes we'll burn it. And next year will be great.

Don't insist on how lousy it's been for me. If it's been lousy for anybody, it's poor Moe. And for me, it has been a good year, a very good year. All that childhood stuff's behind me, and I feel great about it. Don't you believe me?

I do. Of course I do. But it was scary. You walk out of the house to meet the rabbi, and then you end up in the—in the hospital.

Psychiatric ward, Zachary. The nuthouse. Hey, give me a kiss. Don't wipe your mouth. Just give me a sloppy fricassee kiss.

He kissed her, and she held him close. I know that scared the shit out of you, Zach, but it's over. Really, I'm elated. I'm filled with joy. I'm free. I'm happy. I love you, and I've told you every single detail. Can you imagine how it felt when you cradled me, fed me, bathed me yourself?

No hero me, my love.

You hero. Me Kalia.

Hey, another week and I would've done it.

Committed me?

Yes. I was so fucking scared, Kale.

I love you.

I'm telling you I was a coward.

She smiled. I know, she said. Every time we talk about it, you tell me what a coward you were. What was it, three weeks? And you never left the apartment once.

Well, you're okay now, thank God. Really and truly okay.

Only if I get another kiss, please. And only if we don't have to talk about all that any more. It's finished.

In the psychiatric ward, they had tied her down to the bed. We'll learn more, the doctor had told Barthelmes, once the sedative wears off. It's some sort of breakdown. Quite spectacular.

Zachary had been looking at her face, far more peaceful than when she slept at his side.

It has to do with her father, the doctor had continued. Do you know him? Sexual abuse, actually, beatings, all that. And her brother, too.

She never mentioned a brother, Zachary said, looking away from her.

Oh, yes. Named Tim, evidently. He beat her and abused her sexually, too. Children who suffer such things tend to block them out, understandably. It's their way of burying what they can't live with. You're her husband, aren't you? Maybe I shouldn't have told you all this right now. Does it upset you, Mr. Wiggins?

Of course it fucking upsets me! I want her out of here! Discharged. Now!

That wouldn't be very wise, Mr. Wiggins. She must be treated for a week or two. My guess is she should be sent to Manhattan Psychiatric on Ward's Island.

I'm taking her home.

You can't do that!

Watch me. Barthelmes found Kalia's clothes and dressed her. A group of hospital employees had gathered around the bed, and a woman in a white coat presented him with a clipboard of papers. If you don't sign these, she'd said, she will not be permitted to leave. He signed them and said, Will someone help me get a cab?

A young black nurse's aide brought a wheelchair to the bedside. I'm with you, she whispered to him. If she ain't crazy now, they sure gonna make her crazy. You know what you gonna do?

No, not exactly, Zachary said. Except that I won't leave her here. He wheeled Kalia through the ward, where patients shuffled and drooled like zombies. Some howled. Others sat on the floors, leaning against the green walls. Why, he wondered, were the walls always this puke green?

Outside, at the taxi, the young aide gave him two bottles of pills.

Go light on the Thorazine. Just a little. The Valium's to keep her down. Very little Thorazine, hear?

For five days, Kalia slept. She did not eat. The three times she awoke, it was to go to the bathroom, and Zachary had to support her. Urine ran down her legs. Aside from a little apple juice, he couldn't get anything into her. He had his doctor, Reuven Lowenstein, come over. His advice was, Get her into a hospital.

What will happen if I don't?

She's dehydrating. Keep a wet cloth on her lips.

What will happen?

Kidney failure. Heart attack, conceivably. She could die.

How long will that take?

Two, three days. Depends a lot on her basic health.

Later that afternoon, Reuven returned and, hanging the plastic bag from the bed's headboard, fixed an IV into her arm. He left six bags of sodium dextrose solution and instructed Barthelmes in the art of bag replacement. If the flow gets impeded for any reason, he said, or if the needle pulls out of her arm, call me, okay? I shouldn't be doing this, Zachary. Just change the bags when they're empty. She'll be all right.

Thanks, Reuve.

Just don't sue me.

On the fifth day, Kalia had sat up and looked at the unshaven Barthelmes asleep in the chair by the bed. She smiled. Zach, she called softly, Zach, repeating his name until he stirred.

His heavy eyes opened, and he stared at her. You feeling all right?

Yes, but so weak. I have no body.

You've got me, babe, he half sang.

Please, Zach, don't. If I laugh, I'll die. And I have a splitting headache. What's sticking in my arm?

Reuven fixed that up. A little lifeline.

Ooooh, Zach, can you see my ribs? They're sticking out all over.

Your tits have lost a little weight, too, Barthelmes laughed. You're talking, Kale! he said.

I'm hungry. For a great big steak!

How about some Jell-O? Cherry, orange, strawberry, lemon, lime—your choice. I have them all in the fridge. Got to go slow on the food. You're talking! You're hungry! He rose from the chair, leaned across the bed, and took her light frame into his exhausted arms. He rocked her gently. What happened, he asked after a few minutes. You were in the psycho ward, you know.

I knew I was in a hospital. Was I tied to a bed? I thought I was.

You were, and drugged to the eyeballs. Want to tell me what happened, Kale? If you don't want to that's okay, too.

The most wonderful thing in the world—the primal vomit. I let go of a belly filled with terror and shame, Zach. It just exploded. I purged. All came out black bile, black blood of guilt and shame. It was all inside me, eating me, and I didn't know, Zach, I didn't know! I must have that Jell-O. Cherry, please.

Barthelmes watched as she slowly spooned up the red gelatin. He was smiling.

I am sated and bloated, she said once she'd finished. What have you been feeding me?

Prayer, mostly.

Poor Zach! I'm so sorry. I'll make it up to you, I promise. But can I sleep now?

You've been sleeping forever! If you go back to sleep, I'll turn back into a frog.

When I wake up, I'll kiss you back into Zachary, she said and immediately fell asleep, snoring lightly.

I hate you when you snore, Wiggins. He lit a cigarette and kept smiling.

When she awoke, she told Zachary what she thought had happened. You know, I have Rabbi Schechter to blame. Or to thank. Here I was, sailing along over the high seas of conversion. I was so happy, Zach; I was going to be a Jew. Then, Dov—Rabbi Schechter—pulled the rug out. He didn't want to continue because he couldn't understand my motives. He allowed that, on the level of logic, he couldn't quarrel with my desire. I was sincere, and he knew it. He just felt that something wasn't quite right, an intuition. He felt it in his gut. And he dumped me!

It felt like a blow, a kick in the stomach. No, no—it was a hard slap across my face by a big, calloused hand. My father's hand. I walked down Central Park West. I was dizzy, reeling, so I sat down on a bench. God, Zachary, it was like I was in a Bugs Bunny cartoon, and then—boom!—I exploded. I heard voices. I saw my father. I saw my mother. I saw my asshole brother. I mean, they were there with me. They were yelling at me, and I was yelling back. No idea about what. Jesus Christ was walking toward me carrying a knife. I knew he meant business. I started screaming.

Suddenly I was six years old. I mean really six years old, Zach. I was wearing sneakers and blue jeans; my hair was in these two ratty braids. My voice was a little squeak. I was six—Jesus, *six*—and I was fighting for my life!

It really was Dov Schechter. That blow was exactly the same as my father's hand across my face. I was bringing love, and he smashed my face. Knocked me down to the sidewalk. I was bringing love to my rabbi, and he smashed me, too.

Kalia wept softly. Her crying was that of a child's. Her face that of a little girl in pain.

Zachary realized, then, how tense he was. He wanted to embrace her, but knew he must not touch her. After a while he said, Darling, it's okay. You don't have to say anything. Whatever it is, I love you.

I want to, she said, still weeping. Please, I have to! I love you so much! Are there any tissues? I need a whole box.

Zachary found some. She blew her nose forcefully and wiped her eyes so hard she was almost scrubbing them. Are you all right? he said.

She nodded vigorously. I'll go on, Zachary. Please don't stop me. Even if I cry a lot, even if I scream, don't stop me!

All right, he said, then waited for Kalia to resume.

I'll call it the incident, she said. Before the incident I had vague dreams, dreams of myself in the crib. I really didn't know these were dreams. Sort of an image flash. I can't explain it, Zach. Dreams will have to do. Am I a year old? Maybe less than a year. I can see the bars of the crib. Everything beyond the crib is pale yellow, probably the color of the room. Hands reach down, and I'm lifted up. High, high, high into the air. I giggle and burble, whatever you do before you can laugh. Big hands descend into the crib. Hard hands. They play with me. One of the big fingers strokes my vagina, and the tip of a finger enters me. I burble some more. That's the earliest memory.

How much time elapses? Many months. Years. Probably a few years. I'm playing with his penis. This part isn't a dream, Zach, it's a memory. A lost memory, a buried memory.

I am kissing his penis. It isn't very big or thick. It's like a fleshy finger. My father's middle finger is bigger than his penis. He puts it in my mouth, and I suck at it. Do you like that, Kalia? I nod. I love you, Kalia. Do you love Daddy? I nod again. This is our secret. You must never tell anybody. Not Mommy. Not Tim. Do you understand? So I nod. If you tell anybody, Daddy will not love you. Daddy will die. While his penis is in my mouth, his finger's inside my vagina. It feels good. It's exciting. He withdraws his penis from my mouth. It's purple red. He ejaculates and some of it falls on my face. I laugh. He cleans me and himself with the wet cloth he brought with him.

Enough! I have the idea. I don't want to hear any more!

Kalia breathed heavily. Don't stop me, Zach, please. I don't want to remember it by myself. Please?

He squeezed her hand. All right, all right.

When I was four, around then, he had me on his lap and was entering me. He came inside me. When his sperm dripped out of me, he cleaned it up with his washcloth. At the end he would always say, I love you, my little darling. Daddy loves you more than anybody in the whole world. Give Daddy a kiss. This is our secret, isn't it? Nobody knows. Nobody will ever know.

The change in my mother, her relationship with me, told me she knew or at least suspected. My brother certainly knew. But even when Tim had begun to use me—he told me he'd tell my secret if I didn't let him—I kept my secret. Tim was violent. He would beat me. He called me a little Baptist slut. He told me that Jesus would get me, that I'd burn in hell. And I shouted back that I wouldn't because Daddy loved me and didn't love him! Then a real beating! I was seven or eight. Tim was six years older than me. His penis was bigger than Daddy's.

Zachary continued to grip Kalia's hand. He felt weak.

I remember it all now. But you have it now, too. There's just a little more, Zach.

Barthelmes nodded deeply.

It came to an end about that time. One Sunday after church, my mother asked me to go to the coffee shop to fetch Daddy home for lunch. I was still wearing my ruffled pink go-to-church dress and my black patent-leather shoes. I was so happy skipping down the sidewalk. When I came to the coffee shop, Daddy was standing outside, laughing and talking with a bunch of his friends. He was the handsomest of all. The tallest. He laughed the loudest. I could see they all loved him. I wanted to show them that I loved Daddy, too, so I ran up and put my hand on his crotch. On his penis, our secret.

I hadn't even seen his hand move when the rough palm crashed against my face. I was literally lifted off the ground and sent flying through the air. I landed in the gutter. Daddy's face was red, and his hatred and anger was so intense I could *feel* it. His friends didn't say a word.

For a long time Kalia was silent. Zachary thought she was just remembering things now, no longer needing to share her memories. His grip on her hand relaxed slightly.

It was a small town we lived in, Kalia continued, and of course everybody knew what happened, what I'd done. At least the adults did. I couldn't tell if the kids at school knew about it, or if they figured *something* had happened but weren't sure what it was. Mrs. Lattimore, my teacher, probably knew. I think she tried to be helpful. She gave me special books to read. I became a bookworm and spent all my spare time in the library. It was wonderful, just me and the librarian. I can't even remember her name.

I had no friends. I didn't want any. I felt ashamed and guilty. Daddy must've had a good reason for hitting me like that.

Yet I still loved him. His sexual activity with me had ended that Sunday—not only his but Tim's. It was almost as if they'd spoken. My mother—oh, she knew all right! Now she seemed haggard and very old, and at meals she hardly spoke. Daddy asked the blessing and would talk about church activities— he was an elder—but always to Tim, never to me. I was so confused. I broke things deliberately, missed meals. A regular truant. I wet my bed, which only Mother knew about. Daddy punished me for each misdemeanor, hard slaps on my palms or my buttocks. This was always followed by my being locked up in the hall closet, which was filled with clothing and smelled like camphor.

My salvation was the library. At home I read under the porch or in a corner of the garage behind the lawn mower. But not in our parlor, not in my room. I didn't want them to know I was reading. That was my territory, my happy place. Reading made me more than them. I knew more. I was stronger.

At meals, especially on Sundays, Daddy was always railing against the Jews, the evil of the world! The world which God had made good and for which Christ had died. Satan had spawned the Jews with mud and offal and sent them onto the earth to corrupt and destroy good Christians so he could collect their souls. Jews never let you know they were Jews until they already had you in their power, and by then you were going to their secret rituals where they drank the blood of kidnapped Christian babies. Jews owned all the banks— except the one in our town, which James Kelton ran—and all the newspapers except ours. But you could recognize kikes by the small horns they had beneath the skin of their fore- heads. Big Devil Jews, of course, had great big horns and only came out at night. And in Rome they even had a statue of a Jew with horns displayed on an important street to in- struct and warn the local Christians.

Nothing in all the universe was so evil and rotten as the Jew, so unworthy of love or pity. So by the time I was ten, I figured I might be one. I was always feeling my forehead for little bumps. In the library, I read what little they had about the Jews. They were people. They'd given the One God to the world. The Old Testament was theirs. Basic things like Joshua fought the battle of Jericho, Moses and the Ten Com- mandments. I already was convinced Daddy was evil, so the Baptists were evil too. That meant that Jews were good. Every night I prayed to God to grow me horns.

By the time I was twelve, I had breasts and was menstruating. Tim, when we were alone, would feel my breasts and say pretty soon I'd be big enough to be a whore. One night he came into my bedroom and got on top of me. I stuck him with a pair of scissors, and he bled all over the place. Daddy beat me with a belt. I was in the hall closet for a week. I'd already blacked out the sexual things, but I knew I hated Tim. I still loved my father, no matter what he did, and wondered why he was so mean to me. I fell in love with Jews, to spite them. To threaten Daddy—if you don't love me, I'm going to love Jews, grow horns, you see.

I was quite tall and very mature at fifteen. I had read almost the whole library. About that time the thought came to me: I could run away. I could leave this horrible place. I got odd jobs. I swept and mopped the library floor twice a week, even when it was clean. This was the librarian's way of helping. I ran errands for the pharmacy and delivered newspapers on Sundays. I stole money from my mother's cash box in the kitchen—she knew but pretended not to. A small kindness built out of awful guilt.

One night, when I thought I had enough money, I packed a small suitcase and, without knowing why, bought a bus ticket to San Francisco. When I got there I had enough sense to read the want ads in the *Chronicle*. I got myself a job as a waitress. My real life had begun.

Barthelmes had gone through half a pack of cigarettes. They sat in silence.

The first words spoken were Kalia's. Her voice was relaxed and content. Oh, she said, do you know it's dark outside?

Zachary turned toward the bedroom window. Yes, he said, it is.

8.

At 11:52, Guy Lombardo's singer paused in front of the microphone. It's time for some circle dances, she announced happily. Everybody Conga! Everybody Hora! Everybody Hokey-Pokey! Everybody Chicken Dance!

This, Barthelmes said, is where I sit down.

Come on, don't be a killjoy! Let's go!

No way! Hey, didn't I do a great dip? That's it—there ain't no more.

Then hold my purse and watch my smoke. With that, Kalia cut into the Conga line and soon was lost in the concentric circles of dancers. One, two, three—kick! One, two, three—kick!

Kalia had found the bright side of her breakdown, Barthelmes thought as he watched, but where could Moe Cohen even look for his silver lining? Poor Moe. It had been the day after Christmas when Archer Doty called. Bad news, Zach, he announced. Moe had a stroke yesterday.

Oh, Jesus! Bad?

Looks awful, but it's too early to really know.

Is he conscious?

Yes. His eyes are open.

Anything else?

They're doing tests. They have the best brain guys in L.A. looking at him.

Where did it happen? In the office or out in the Valley?

Neither, I'm afraid, Doty said. It actually happened in Cinci Adams's apartment, he said and giggled.

What's funny?

I'm sorry. The whole thing was a mess. Moe and Cinci were celebrating life, you know, and right in the middle— pow—he blows his fuses. So there he is, naked on Cinci's double king-size bed, and there's Cinci screaming and crying.

How the hell did you know that, Arch?

She called me. Screaming, hysterical. She didn't want to call the cops or even an ambulance. She didn't want Moe to be found naked in her bedroom. I went over with my wife. What a mess, Zachary. Anyway, it took the three of us to clean him up and get his clothes on. God, he's a giant!

Didn't anybody have the brains to call for help right away?

I didn't want EMS turning up when Moe still had cum all over his crotch. Would you?

Archer! His life was at stake!

Maybe, but that was my judgment. Cinci agreed, and my wife. Look, I know the guy. He'd rather die than be embarrassed that way. Cops, ambulance, Moe Cohen naked in an actress's apartment? It's next day's press.

Which hospital?

Cedars of Lebanon.

Visitors? Does his family know?

I called his daughters. Nobody can find the son.

Have they flown out?

Not yet. They have to make arrangements.

When do you think Kalia and I can visit?

Give it a week or so.

Tell Moe we'll be there as soon as you give the word.

He'll be glad to hear that, Zach.

Out on the dance floor, the revelers were doing the Chicken. Scratch, scratch! Peck, peck! Flap, flap. Cluck, cluck! Barthelmes shook his head. Kalia, he thought, you are lost in a silly dancing barnyard! I'm very happy I can't see you pecking and scratching. God, Kalia!

The lights flash. The mirrored balls turn. The trumpets sound. The hour strikes. *Should auld acquaintance be forgot . . .*

PART EIGHT

1.

Barthelmes hesitated in the hospital corridor. He looked again at his wristwatch. Kalia was fifteen minutes late, and he didn't want to go into Moe's room alone. How should he handle it—stride in boldly with a big smile and a loud greeting? How're you doing, Moe, baby?

Shit! Barthelmes hated this. He and Kalia had been briefed on the phone by a nurse. Moe was totally paralyzed. His arms and legs were immobile, and he couldn't turn his head. But he could hear and understand. He could open his mouth and swallow. He could see. He could move his eyes, open and close his lids. One blink was yes, two was no. No eye response meant he wanted you to repeat the question or that he was displeased; the context would indicate which. Closed lids meant, I want to be left alone, so leave. Also, the nurse said, You don't have to speak loudly or treat him like a moron. He can hear quite well. His intelligence is unimpaired.

Barthelmes decided he couldn't wait any longer, so he took a deep breath and pushed the door open. The bed seemed endlessly long. Moe lay flat beneath the broad, white sheets. His great head with its curved nose was solid and still as a boulder. His eyes were closed. Zachary could detect a slight pulse beneath his hooded lids, and he cleared his throat: Moe?

Cohen's eyes opened and rolled toward Barthelmes.

How are you, Moe? It's me, Zachary. He positioned himself at the side of the bed, the alert eyes staring up at him, and tried to think of a sensible question.

Behind him, Kalia's voice said, Push that button, Zach. Sit him up.

You're late. What button?

She came to the bedside and pushed a button on a set of controls. The mattress lifted itself and Moe Cohen into a sitting position. She kissed Moe's cheek. I hope you felt that, Moe. Should I kiss you again?

His eyes blinked once.

Kalia kissed him. I like your after-shave. Do you want the bed higher, Moe?

Single blink.

Kalia pushed the button again.

I'm glad you got here, Kale. I was scared to come in alone.

Afraid Moe would bite you? I wish he could. Would you bite him, Moe?

Two blinks.

Okay, Zach, relax. Moe still loves you. You love him, Moe?

One blink.

You know why I'm late?

Two blinks.

Chicken soup. I picked some up on the way over. Would you like some?

One blink.

Can you swallow noodles?

One blink.

Jesus, Kale! How'd you know to do that?

Common sense, Barthelmes, common sense. Right, Moe?

Blink.

Kalia took a container of soup from her shopping bag, spooned out some of the yellow broth, and brought it up to Cohen's face. Open, she said. Slowly Cohen's jaw lowered, and Kalia moved the spoon into his mouth. Too hot?

Two blinks.

Pretty good?

One blink.

When you get out of here, Moe, I'll make you some home-made. Puts this store-bought stuff to shame. Kalia chattered away as she spooned the soup into Moe's mouth. When he'd had enough, Moe blinked twice.

She's terrific, Barthelmes said. I think I'll leave her here to take care of you.

Blink. Pause. Blink.

Zachary and Kalia laughed. The mask of Moe Cohen's face remained its frozen self. When the silence among them became uncomfortable, Kalia held up a three-ring binder so Cohen could see it. I took this out of Zachary's fancy Gucci briefcase, Moe. And he's going to read it to you. It's a scene from the forthcoming Big MAC production, *The Beggar's Cup*.

Cut it out, Kale!

Moe, would you like the great Barthelmes to read this great scene?

Blink.

What have I ever done to you to deserve this? You read it.

You want Zachary to emote—right, Moe?

Long blink.

Moe says yes, by all means. So read, Zach.

Barthelmes sighed and took the binder from Kalia's hand. He cleared his throat. You know, he said, except for the last scenes, I've more or less finished the first draft. The bad news is, it's running to about four hours.

War and Peace, Kalia said. Talk about artsy-fartsy!

You know how complicated it is, Moe. All these sets and locations, not to mention costumes. It could bankrupt you, Moe.

Two blinks.

What do you mean, no?

Two long, hard blinks.

Thirty million, conservatively. The banks won't give you a dime for a picture with a Jewish hero, especially one that jumps around like this one. Who's the audience? Under thirties won't buy tickets even if I make the sex scenes torrid.

Jewish sex is hot, hot, hot! A guy with a big black beard will really turn the kids on—am I right, Moe?

Cohen's eyes fixed on Kalia. There was a pause, then a blink.

You wanted to laugh?

Blink.

From now on, if you're laughing, three quick blinks. Okay?

Blink, blink, blink.

This project will bankrupt you, Moe.

Cohen's eyes did not signal.

Barthelmes smiled. Do you care if you go broke?

Blink. Blink.

If you do, Kalia said, I'll give you back that *pushka*.

Blink, blink, blink.

All right, Barthelmes said, you don't care about money. Anyway, this scene's one of the many extras I've written. I keep saying I have it all, Moe. I don't need any more. Then I think of something. You know how movies go: in the cutting room we'll need something else, but it's not there and the budget's already gone . . . shit's creek. So this is an extra scene—of which I have thousands—but it's a train scene and part of a pattern. I can shoot it with a gang up of train scenes. The Orient Express through the night of history.

Read it, Zach, Kalia said. It works, and I think it belongs. Ask Moe, after you've read it.

He put his hand on Cohen's shoulder, wondering if Moe could even feel it. Let me set the scene for you. If I use this, we'll need a couple of others right before it. So I'll just tell you what those might be. *Gewalt!* This is a complicated business, Moe. Maybe the whole thing runs you forty mill. Anyway, here it is.

Herzl, through a Polish woman of high standing, has gotten an introduction to Count Sergei Witte, the Czar's finance minister. This is a few weeks after the Kishinev pogrom. You know of the Kishinev pogrom?

Moe's eyes blinked once, sharply.

Well, okay, I don't have to recount the killings and rapes, the sacking and burning of the town. It was a big Cossack do. What's important about Kishinev isn't just that it had happened, not that it was the biggest pogrom, but that it was the first time a pogrom made worldwide press. Until then pogroms were myths, Jewish propaganda, always denied as poppycock by the Russian government. Well, now, in the Year of Our Lord 1902, here's the Kishinev massacre on the front page of the *New York Times* and even on the front page of the *Neue Freie Presse*. Was the world shocked? Yes sir, Moe, the world was shocked.

But Dori saw beyond the shock. I tell you, Moe, Herzl was nothing if not a political animal first-class. He knows the Russian government, the Czar, the whole Cyrillic pack, don't want the world thinking it was their fault that a few hundred Cossacks got drunk and pillaged a town. You know how it is when a Cossack has a little too much vodka! So Herzl decides this is the time to pay a visit to the Czar. And maybe trade the dead of Kishinev for the Czar's support for a Jewish state in Palestine.

Not only is Kishinev on the front pages but also some cockamamy Russian ambassador in Constantinople has been assassinated by a hashish-crazed Turk. At least that's the Sultan's story. He's moaning and trembling that the Czar might pour his navy right up the Bosporus and blow away the Yildiz Kiosk. What a great confluence of events! Herzl thinks, probably with a smile under his beard: Ask the Czar to tell the Sultan that he will forgive the Turks if they give the Ottoman half of Palestine to the Jews. This makes up for the assassination, and at the same time shows the *New York Times* where the heart of the Czar lies when it comes to the

Jews. Of course, as we all know, it was never going to happen. But he did get Count Witte to agree that it was a great idea. He even got Witte to give him an introduction to the Czar's foreign minister, Vyacheslav von Plehwe—a first-class Jew killer, also much embarrassed by Kishinev. In that one chink in the wall of time, Herzl got both Witte and Plehwe to say they supported a Jewish state in Palestine, and he even got Plehwe to write a letter he could read at the next Zionist congress in Basel! There it is, Moe: our boy Dori, ambassador plenipotentiary of a state that didn't exist, shaking up the great powers.

Anyway, did the Jews all stand up and cheer? No sirree bob! There was a great outcry on the one hand that Herzl was selling out to the czarist butchers, while, on the other hand, the great majority of Jews, especially in Russia, recognized Herzl as the one man who could stand up and speak for them and get the leaders of the whole evil world to listen. Jesus, I'm getting carried away here, Moe.

Kalia leaned close in to Cohen. Are you getting tired? We'll be here for a few days, and Zach could continue tomorrow. Shall we leave?

Two blinks.

Would you like Zach to continue?

Blink.

The floor is yours, Mr. Barthelmes.

Anyway, that's just the background. Here's the scene, straight through. It's not that long, so don't worry. Then Barthelmes took a deep breath, expelled it, and began to read.

With great bursts of steam, the train pushes down the tracks. Slowly the grandeur of St. Petersburg slides past the compartment where HERZL *sits, looking through the window. The architecture begins to blur and the buildings get smaller. The sky becomes more present as the train speeds along. The whistle sounds*

*repeatedly. The train races toward the darkening ho-
rizon until it is deep into the vast night of the Russian
countryside.*

A uniformed WAITER *rolls a small table into*
HERZL's *compartment. He lays out the silverware on
the heavily starched linen cloth and serves the soup
from a small silver tureen. He bows and leaves. The
train lurches violently, splashing soup into* HERZL's
lap. The train is slowing. HERZL *peers out the window
but can see nothing but night. The train comes to a
dead stop.*

Cut to the engine of the train, where the ENGINEER
*leans out his window. On the tracks below, bearded
faces look up at him. Pan along the faces to the tracks
in the front of the engine. The engine pants and the
dense steam thins and parts. Now we can see hundreds
of people standing on the track—men, women, and
children. They are absolutely silent.*

Cut to HERZL's *compartment. The door opens as
the* CONDUCTOR *enters:*

Your pardon, Herr Herzl. The train has been
brought to a stop.

So I see. Trouble?

I don't think so, sir. They are poor people. Jews
from the village, I believe.

I see.

Well, sir. They are carrying banners *(lengthy
pause).* Your name is on the banners in Russian and
also, I believe, in Hebrew.

Oh.

Sir, they will not permit the train to proceed unless
you address them. The police have been informed.
They may well arrive soon.

*(*HERZL *stands.)* The police are not needed. I will
address them. *Cut to* HERZL *descending from the car*

to the trackside. Bareheaded, he walks toward the front of the train as a great cry goes up from the crowd:

Hedad, Hedad, Hedad! Herzl Hamelech! Herzl Hamelech!

HERZL *is helped up onto the train's rectangular cowcatcher. The words of the cheering become an indistinct roar.* TRAIN CONDUCTORS, ENGINEERS, *and* PASSENGERS, *now on the trackside, look on. An* OLD MAN *with a white beard leads the crowd in a Hebrew prayer:*

Our leader, our king, our savior! May God protect you and keep you safe from all harm. We have come here to see you, to touch your hand, and to give you a gift, this prayer shawl.

The OLD MAN *hands the prayer shawl to* HERZL, *who puts it around his shoulders. He takes a white handkerchief from his coat pocket and covers his head with it. He looks out across the crowd:*

My people, I am honored that you have come out on this night and have asked me to speak. I do not know what to say to you. I ask you all to listen only to my heart. I know you can hear every word of my heart, every drop of its blood is speaking. I will remember this occasion all my life. I know that you, in your prayers, ask God for Jerusalem. Perhaps, some of you ask, why is it that God takes so long when his chosen people are hungry, maligned, beaten, and, alas, murdered in their homes. I cannot speak for God. I am blessed that God has allowed me to speak for His people. I am blessed because I can give my life for the return of the Jews to the Holy Land. Pray with me that next year we will all pray together in Israel.

A great Hebrew song arises from the people. They parade past HERZL *where he stands on the cow-*

catcher. They kiss the braids of the prayer shawl. They kiss his hands. Then, without warning, POLICE *on horseback charge into the crowd. People are sent sprawling. They keep singing. There are some bloody heads.* HERZL *holds his hands in the air:*

Stop this at once! Stop!

A mustachioed OFFICER *blows a whistle and gestures to his troops. The* POLICE *rein in their horses and back them away from the crowd. The* OFFICER *turns toward* HERZL:

You are Theodor Herzl? I apologize, sir. We were told there was a riot here. *(To the police):* Retreat! Pull back immediately!

The singing continues. Pan slowly over faces in the crowd—expectant, hopeful. Cut to HERZL's *compartment.* HERZL *lowers the heavy window shade. He sobs. He beats his chest with his fist. Tears flow into his heavy beard.*

Moe Cohen's eyes also filled with tears, which trickled from the corners of his eyes onto the bed cover.

Zachary and Kalia, fighting their own emotions, waited for several minutes. When Cohen's eyelids didn't open, and his breathing was regular, they quietly got up and left.

2.

Later that afternoon, Barthelmes met Archer Doty for a drink at the hotel bar. I think I'll have the script finished in a few weeks, he told him.

Well, I'm glad you've got paid for it, Zach. Everything at Big MAC's on hold. The medical reports are not good, you know. His daughters have gone into court—guardianship and all that.

What does that mean?

The kids will take over.

Then they'll rely on you, Arch. You know what Moe wanted better than anybody.

Yes and no. Yes, he wanted a script from you. But no, I have no idea what he wanted to spend on the production.

I kept him advised, Arch. He knew this was a big-ticket item.

How big is big? He never discussed bucks with me. Never asked me to draw a budget. I'm in the dark.

He wanted this film very badly.

Out of my hands, I'm afraid. Everything's on hold except Big MAC's next wide-scream horror. Tell you what, Zach: you direct it, and I'll try to get the family to okay your thing.

Are his daughters here now?

No. And we're still looking for Marcus. All we have is a P.O. box number in Majorca. He hasn't even cashed the last two checks we sent him.

I thought you said the daughters were coming?

Not yet. They have an attorney who calls. Marty Bressler. You know him?

Yes. I've worked with him. Good man.

Tough! He'll find out what the daughters want, and that's the way it will go.

Yeah. Have you got a phone number for them?

Just Bressler.

Cut the crap, Archer. I have to speak to the girls, not Bressler. I know you have the numbers, Arch. You talked to them right after Moe had the stroke. Archer?

Okay, okay. I'll get you the numbers. Just don't tell Bressler you're working on the kids.

Of course I won't.

Will you direct *Dracula's Final Secret* for me?

Maybe. But not under my name.

I'll think about that.

After I see Moe's kids, I'll let you know. You won't help otherwise?

I would, Zach. Of course I would. But I'm not here for too much longer. I'm going over to Disney after *Final Secret*.

Barthelmes laughed.

From horror to Mickey Mouse. I get the joke, Zach. But in my book, everything's budgets and management. A film is a film is a film—ninety minutes, more or less, of someone or other's ego. Creative guys come and go. Old films go into vaults in New Jersey. Doty goes on forever. I wish you luck, Zach. You know something? Moe never told me the name of this picture. You got a working title?

No, Barthelmes said. We just call it "the film."

He left Doty sitting at the bar and started up to his room. Why hadn't he told him the title? Maybe because Doty already belonged to Disney. Or maybe because *The Beggar's Cup* belonged to Moe, to himself, and to Kalia. And for the first time, Barthelmes felt it might never belong to anyone else.

3.

From Los Angeles he called Moe's daughter Carrie in Westport, Connecticut. Of course I know who you are, she said. I've seen several of your films. I'm a big fan—*Geronimo*, especially.

That was an auspicious beginning, Zachary thought; then he explained the background in a general way.

So let's have dinner, Carrie said. I'll make sure Emily and Wallace can come, and we'll try for tomorrow night at seven.

Kalia would remain in Los Angeles. Well, Zach, she said, we had planned on staying a few days, and I think that's what we told Moe. I'll take care of him if you'll take care of his kids.

Why, Zachary wondered, was he rushing off? But with Archer moving out and Bressler picking up the reins, the meeting with Carrie and Emily couldn't wait. He had to know what they were thinking, and he especially wanted them to know what their father wanted. Time was now important.

Barthelmes caught an early flight to New York and by 7:10 that evening he was pushing Carrie's doorbell, setting off a Westport equivalent of the B-minor mass. Throughout dinner they spoke of Moe: what a tragedy it was for such an active man to be so unlucky! Emily attributed the stroke to his drinking, her husband, Wallace, to lack of exercise.

Except for sex, Carrie added. I swear Moe was the horniest man I ever heard of. God, his exploits could fill every tabloid in the supermarket!

You can't believe everything you hear, Barthelmes demurred. Your father was a man of great accomplishments.

Horror pictures? Emily said with a porcelain laugh that matched neither her dark complexion nor her voluptuousness.

I'm not that critical, Carrie said. After all, look at us. He's made sure that our lives are comfortable—whether we deserve it or not. Three cheers for Big MAC, I always say.

Money is always money, Emily said. I would have preferred a few more visits. His grandchildren have grown up without the frequent pleasure of his company. Except when Wallace Junior got to be twelve. Then he was at my house once a month, at least. Bar mitzvah time! It didn't matter much to my father that Wally hadn't been raised as a Jew. Wallace and I had agreed before we married that the children wouldn't be raised Catholic or Jewish, that they could choose for themselves when they grew up. But I thought my dear father was going to keel over on the spot when I said we weren't having a bar mitzvah.

No way, Wallace said. I'm still a practicing Catholic.

And I recognize my Jewish background, Emily added. I have not converted. Do you think he appreciates *that*?

Carrie laughed. Well, he hasn't cut you off, has he? As I say, we owe him.

Don't do that dutiful daughter crap, Carrie. He just happens to be a lousy father with a track record to prove it.

Our mother might've had something to do with it.

Shit!

Don't get yourself too excited, Em, Wallace said. Turning to Barthelmes, he muttered, High blood pressure.

I just don't care for her attitude. Was her Marshall bar mitzvahed?

No, he wasn't, Carrie said. But I didn't put Papa through the wringer because of it. I told him I wasn't about to burden Marshall with being a Jew. I told this to Papa when Marsh was four years old.

He took it from you, Carrie. And he wouldn't take it from me.

You played cat and mouse, Em! What did you want: a million-dollar bar mitzvah grant?

Abruptly Emily pushed her chair back from the table and glared at her sister. What a bitch, she snapped. Big Moe's little girl!

Carrie laughed.

Wallace looked away and coughed. I think we're embarrassing our guest.

It's okay, Barthelmes said. Typical family night, the same the world over.

Maybe, if the sisters can get it under control, we can talk about the business at hand. More coffee, Mr. Barthelmes?

Zach. Please.

Wallace poured.

Let me try to get to the point, Barthelmes said. I've heard

you're in the courts, petitioning for guardianship of your father and his affairs.

That's right, Wallace said, looking guardedly toward the two women. I think we've been granted guardianship. Isn't that right, Em?

Yes. Mr. Bressler called to tell me—and I suppose Carrie, too. We'll get some sort of document soon.

Carrie looked at Zachary and smiled. My sister's too discreet, she said, to mention that our brother isn't much interested in these affairs. Doesn't give a shit, I believe is how he put it. Just mail the check, he said; he lives in Majorca. So anyway, we're Moe's guardians, she said. Is that important?

It means, Wallace said, that we're in charge.

We? Emily said with a hard look at her husband.

I mean, you and Carrie.

Thank you, Wallace. As I was saying, Zachary, is guardianship important?

It means that until Moe gets well, you run Big MAC. You make policies. Sign the checks, all that. So it's very important to me—and in this instance, I can say, to Moe also. You see, there was a project he wanted me to develop. I've been working at it for some time now.

A film, right? Carrie said brightly. But if Moe was so interested, it must be a Stephen King story or something.

Barthelmes smiled. No, he said, not really. It's a film your father would call artsy-fartsy. Perhaps a bit beyond that. It's about a Jewish leader named Theodor Herzl. Is the name familiar?

It makes a slight tinkle, Carrie said.

Em shrugged, and Wallace added, Not one of my saints, I guess.

He wrote a book called *The Jewish State* in 1896. He founded the political Zionist movement to win a homeland for the Jews. Moe asked me to write a script about him.

Doesn't sound very sexy, Emily said. A movie has to have a touch of porn to get people out of the house.

I can't argue against that, Barthelmes said, smiling. But some movies make it for other reasons.

Name two, Wallace said.

Barthelmes felt a twist of anger in his stomach. There's a lot of tits and ass these days, that's true. It might be the style, but Moe didn't follow patterns. He built a major studio on another set of premises.

And what might those be? Emily said. Blood and gore, cannibalism and zombies with electric-light eyes?

Well, yes. But he brought it to a new level.

Emily snorted. I saw one. It made me want to vomit.

Carrie laughed. I've seen all of Daddy's flicks. I like them, really I do. Not for my kids, though. I mean, I wouldn't let them see them when they were little, and now they're into triple X.

That's not so bad, Wallace said. At least we can skip sex education.

For whatever it's worth, Barthelmes said, trying to keep the conversation from drifting further from the point, Moe wanted to make this film about Herzl as a way of celebrating his own Jewish heritage. A payback to his family and friends who died in the Holocaust.

News to me, Emily said. I know he gives lots of money to Jewish causes and Israeli hospitals and the like, but I think that was a matter of form. With a name like Morris Cohen you support the UJA, not Catholic Charities or the Fellowship of Christian Athletes.

That's not entirely true, Wallace said. When I asked, he made a donation to a Catholic charity. But Emily's right—the big bucks went to Jewish things.

He was very Jewish, Barthelmes said. He felt very deeply about his heritage.

I can't judge that, Carrie said. I was seven when he decided to go Hollywood. I felt like, and indeed I was, a deserted child.

You can count me in on that, Emily added. But okay: he was a Jew right down to his black lisle socks. Why do I remember his socks? Isn't that funny? His socks!

Ah, the laundry and lisle of family life! Zachary said with a sigh.

Carrie laughed. I like you, she said.

What did he say, Emily asked. Did I miss something?

I'm sorry, Barthelmes said. Long plane ride. I'm making bad jokes.

Carrie looked at him with a warm, frank look. Did you say you were married, Zach?

Barthelmes smiled. More or less, he said.

No luck! She laughed. Here I am, freshly divorced. . . . Oh, well, shall we get back to business? So, Moe really wants to make this picture about Theodor what's-his-name.

Yes. I guess I've come to see you because I would like your support.

Why? Emily said. Does our father have a little blond bimbo he wants to star in it?

Look, it's public knowledge that Moe didn't like to sleep alone. Sometimes he used his clout to warm his bed. It's typical Hollywood, but it has nothing to do with this movie.

Not to get personal, Zachary, but do you use your clout? Carrie said, raising her eyebrows.

I have been known to answer the unsolicited knock at my bedroom door. He shrugged, then grinned. Hollywood, thy name is temptation!

Very good! Carrie said, laughing.

But why-oh-why must every attractive man be tied up? Emily added with a cold touch of sarcasm..

Very good, Em, Carrie said. Touché.

Can we get back to the film, Zachary asked.

I'm all ears, Carrie said.

Hmm, Emily said.

I do know that being a Jew was important to your father.

All right, Carrie said. Moe Cohen was a Jew, big time. But you didn't come here to convert us or anything, Zachary.

No. I came to tell you about the film and why Moe wanted to make it.

I can understand that, Wallace offered. Considering his life among the stars and starlets, he probably felt guilty as hell, wouldn't you say?

Probably. Anyway, this was intended to be the film that would cap his career.

But what have we got to do with it? Carrie said.

You'll be taking over Big MAC. You'll decide which pictures get made.

Pictures! Wallace blurted. Zachary, we don't even know what the company is worth. He paused. Do you?

No, I don't.

Also, we're not remotely film people. We'll have to rely on Mr. Bressler and Mr. Doty for all that.

The thing is, Doty will be leaving Big MAC after the next film is completed.

I don't get it, Wallace said. You haven't come here looking for a job, have you?

No. I was hoping I might get your blessing for Moe's wish to do this movie—not to be melodramatic, but to complete his life.

I don't think it's as easy as that, Carrie said, her voice taking on an edge. This is the first we've heard of this film, this wish of my father's. We've heard nothing from Bressler. Nothing from Doty. And double nothing from Big Moe. Such an important film and never once mentioned to us! She wiped her eyes and looked up at her beamed ceiling. Why am I getting so damned emotional?

Yes, Emily said. Why are you?

Don't get bitchy, Emily.

Shut up, Wallace.

Wallace stood up, walked into the next room, and walked right back again.

We're really not film people, are we? Emily said.

I'm sorry, Barthelmes said. You're right. You're not film people. I don't want to give you the impression that I've come to your home to take advantage of you. Martin Bressler is the best attorney in the world. He'll guide you and do it well.

Maybe you should speak to him, then, to Bressler? Wallace said.

That's a good idea, Emily added. Zachary, I'm not against Papa's movie. You said you wanted our support, but how can we give it? We're absolute amateurs.

After a silence, Barthelmes said, I visited your father yesterday. It was a bad stroke. I think you might want to see him as soon as possible.

We will. Early next week, Carrie said, nodding at Emily. There's a lot to do. He's not dying, is he?

No. But I do think this is the time when a visit from his family might help. Psychologically, that is. You could bring the children.

That might not be practical, Emily said. They have their own lives.

I can appreciate that, Barthelmes said. When he lit a cigarette, his hands trembled. I'd like to leave you only with this request: think about what Moe had in mind. I'm really afraid I must go. Thank you for your hospitality.

Stay for a drink, Zachary, Wallace offered. One for the road?

Okay, thanks. But a very short one, please.

Wallace poured. Cheers, he said. You know, it's funny hearing you talk about Moe's Jewish thing, his heritage and all. You're Christian, aren't you?

Wallace! Emily said. That's rude.

Sorry, he said immediately. No offense intended.

None taken, Barthelmes said, toasting him with his glass and then draining it. Really, I don't mean to rush, but I do have to get back into town. Thanks for everything.

Carrie asked, as she escorted Zachary to the door, What's the name of the picture?

The Beggar's Cup.

What's it mean?

I'll have to explain that another time. He smiled.

She smiled back. You'll find me at home, Mr. Barthelmes.

The taxi he'd kept waiting through dinner pulled up to the front door. Next time, Carrie called as he climbed into the back seat for the short ride to the Westport train station.

4.

In bed with Kalia at the hotel, Barthelmes said, I don't think we'll get any support from them.

You can't be sure of that. They've just been plunged into the situation. It must be confusing.

Maybe, but I don't think so. Let's say the company's worth a hundred million.

Two hundred, easy.

Two hundred, then. I still don't think the daughters will spend twenty million to honor their dad. They don't know him. They're angry at him. They don't like him, especially Emily.

Maybe they're right. He did desert them.

He deserted their mother, Kale.

In their minds, he deserted them at the same time.

Okay, so he did. He also made them rich.

He paid them off. Wouldn't that you make angry? They wanted love and got checks instead.

He didn't have to be so generous, though. He's really set them up. You could smell the money on those two.

Guilt, Zach, guilt! Moe was filled with it.

Wallace said Moe gave money to Jewish causes because he felt guilty. I said no, Moe gave because he was a proud Jew.

I'll bet there was a little guilt in there somewhere. Isn't there always, when it comes to charity?

You cynic! Come on, Kale, Moe's so Jewish you can hear the shofars blow when he passes by.

I had some great talks with him while you were away. I had him blinking up a storm. Got him to laugh a lot. You know what I did, Zach?

I told him all about my so-called conversion. Not about my father. Just about my ideas and feelings about wanting to be a Jew and how I'd flunked out with Rabbi Schechter. I asked him in the end if he thought I should try again. Blink. Pause. Blink. Pause. Blink. These were very hard blinks, Zach.

He kissed her gently. You're going to kill me. You really are.

She smiled. Why? Are you getting too much?

I'm getting to love you beyond reason.

Me, too.

I'm not going to tell Moe about his daughters and the guardianship.

You have to tell him sometime.

Let them tell him. I'm not about to tell Moe Cohen he's the ward of his children—that he's an incompetent, a legal idiot.

I think you should. But if not, get his daughters to stall, not to tell him unless it becomes absolutely necessary.

What difference does it make?

He loves the film, Zach. You have to keep telling him about scenes, progress reports, whatever you've got.

Jesus, Kalia, there isn't going to be a film. His daughters will take the money and run.

You sure?

Sure I'm sure.

Well, Moe doesn't know that. So share the film with him. Read to him. Discuss casting. You know, what about Olivier?

What about him?

As Herzl.

Barthelmes lit a cigarette and blew a cloud of smoke toward the baby-blue ceiling. You think so?

Oh, I don't know. But Moe would like it. Think of it! Laurence Olivier as Theodor Herzl.

I don't think I can carry it off. No, I'd flub it.

No you won't. I'll read scenes myself. And as far as I'm concerned, Zach, there's going to be a picture.

No. His damned kids won't do it.

Then sell it to Orion, to Paramount, to somebody. They're always calling you up.

Okay, Barthelmes sighed, it's worth a shot.

Lots of shots, Zach. This wouldn't be the first time you had to hustle a little. Hey, you know who came to visit? Cinci Adams.

Jesus!

Yep! She was very nice, but she told me she couldn't—wouldn't—visit Moe again. It was breaking her heart. I have the feeling no one's going to bother coming after a while.

Except you and me, you mean.

5.

After she had fed Morris Albert Cohen some chocolate pudding, Kalia patted some of his favorite cologne on his cheeks. How's that, good?

Blink.

It's a super day out, Moe. The smog's at half-mast, and

you can see practically all the way to the ocean. We can wheel the bed out onto the balcony. Would you like that?

Blink. Blink.

Barthelmes came in from the corridor, where he'd smoked a cigarette. He patted Moe's shoulder and began pacing at the side of the bed. Okay, Moe. One of the biggest problems I have is the balance between the historical and the personal. Mostly I've gone lightly on the personal—Kalia says too lightly. What do you think?

Moe's eyes remained fixed on Zachary's face.

All business today, Zach. But you have to give Moe a question that fits his blinking system. Isn't that right, Moe?

Blink.

Well, this is too complicated. I can't get it down to yes or no. Barthelmes paused. I'll fill in with my considerations. Then we can get it down to the blinks. Okay with you?

Blink.

Do you remember Lulu—you know, the actress Dori had a thing with in Paris?

Moe stared at him without blinking.

Something wrong? Is that a yes or no?

When Moe's eyes remained fixed, Barthelmes realized his faux pas: Cinci!

After a lengthy pause Moe blinked. When no one spoke, he blinked three times in a row.

Zachary and Kalia both laughed.

Lulu, of course, Barthelmes continued, is personal. Her scenes give us one insight into Herzl, and those with Julie another. Yet in a peculiar way, he keeps his distance with both of them—except that Julie burns his ass. Those scenes work for me, and they're extremely personal.

And I've thought a lot about involving his mother, but I've decided against it. Some writers, historians, and psychologists believe that Herzl was dominated by her. That he adored her and spent more time with Jeanette than with Julie. Really

Oedipal, right? Julie hated Jeanette and wouldn't even let the kids visit Grandma. The only time they saw Jeanette is when Herzl managed to bring them. There were lots of fights over this. At one time Herzl tried to work it so that his parents would move in with them. No dice. Julie was ready to pick up the kids and move to Shanghai, if not farther.

So, an absolutely middle-class house cloistered with woes. Blood seeping through all the walls. A Viennese *Doll's House*, maybe. But some say Julie was extremely neurotic, even a touch psychotic. Some of the same observers say there was a trace of mental illness in Herzl's family, too. One son of a bitch wrote that in 1694—get that, Moe, 1694!—Eliazer Herzl had a religious quarrel with his twelve-year-old son and beat the kid to death. Put in prison, Eliazer hanged himself with his own phylacteries!

You don't say!

I swear, Kale, God's honest truth! The fact is, I don't know how to deal with Jeanette Herzl née Diamant. There are speculators without evidence—not enough for me, anyway— who say it was her dream that Herzl should crown her life by becoming King of the Jews!

But, Zach, in that scene with Herzl on the train bumper, the villagers called him King of the Jews, didn't they?

Sure. But the whole point there is that Herzl responds to the pity of it. He is beyond ambition at that point. Don't you agree, Moe?

Blink.

Also Herzl's father, Zach—you haven't dealt with him either.

Barthelmes stroked his chin. I've blocked him out, he said. That's interesting.

I need more personal stuff. Okay, not everything. I can live without the venereal disease, thank you. But I'd like more on his family.

You're probably right, but I don't know how to deal with

both his mother and Julie, who stole the darling son away. If I overdo it, I feel—I really know, Kalia—that I'd be doing another film. Or at least losing control of this one. So I drop Mom and Pop from the film. Filmmaker's prerogative. What do you think, Moe? Am I right?

Moe stared.

Dropping the mother's crucial. She'd be distracting, don't you see? Not too different from Herzl's gonorrhea. Here's the scene. He goes into the fashionable Ringstrasse haberdashery to buy a linen sleeve for his dripping member. The clerk, a young woman, presents him with the requested sleeve. Herzl sends it back: too small!

Blink. Blink. Blink.

It's funny, all right. And true. But I don't want scenes that unfocus the Herzl I'm creating. Little by little, I'm creating a hero. I want a hero, Moe!

Blink.

Maybe what you're creating is a Herzl who conforms to your movie ideas.

Now that's not fair, Kale.

If you want a hero, Zach, you'll find him in the personal stuff. Not just in ideas.

I'm not afraid of the personal or the intimate, Kale! You know that! Even the scenes that put Herzl in the dead center of spectacle, I think, keep it personal.

Well, yes. They do. You've done such a good job so far.

So far? Barthelmes said with a rising voice.

Oh, Jesus! Do you think I love him, Moe?

Blink. Blink.

You son of a bitch! I'm not feeding you any more!

Blink. Blink. Blink.

Enough comedy! Barthelmes took out a pack of cigarettes. Let me say this; then I'll go out into the corridor to smoke. I'm absolutely, positively, for exploring the hero's underbelly. But I will not do anything that demeans him. It's not that I don't want to do Mama or the clap. It's that I do not know *how* to handle either one without demeaning or distorting him. Tell me you agree, Moe.

Blink.

If you want to kill him, Zachary said, the easiest way is with his children. Consider what happened to them! Pauline becomes a compulsive back-alley prostitute. Hans converts to Christianity under two different flags and then commits suicide. Little Trude bounces from psycho ward to psycho ward, marries, has a son, gets carted off to Theresienstadt, where she regally announces that her father is the great Theodor Herzl, and she expects the other Jews to pay her high respect. In three months, like thousands of lesser Jews who aren't gassed, she dies of starvation.

That's horrible, Kalia said.

But there existed a grandson! Trude's son, Stefan Theodor Neumann. Educated in England, graduates from Cambridge with degrees in law and economics. Changes his name to Norman. World War II, captain in the British army. In 1946, after some official business in the Far East, his plane stops in Palestine. He meets some old Zionists and learns about his grandfather's importance for the first time. And he's emotionally impressed by Palestine. Later he gets appointed commercial councillor at the British Embassy in Washington, D.C. So one day he gets up from his desk, tells his staff he'll be away on a short trip, takes a folder of papers with him. He walks down the street to the Jewish Agency and hands the folder to an Eliahu Eilat. Walks down to a Potomac bridge, walks halfway across, and jumps into the river. Finis. *Finito*. End. Done. The Herzl line is blotted out. All that's after Herzl's death, of course. His children, his grandson, all after. It isn't part of the film. Thank God and the prerogative of directors!

What was in the folder? And why did he go to the Jewish Agency?

Don't know. No need to know.

But it's fascinating! That's the stuff I'd really like to know.

Not from me, Kale. But if you find out, tell me. Would you like to know, Moe?

Blink.

There, sweetheart, hie thee to a library and dig it out. In the meantime I go to yon corridor to smoke, perhaps to burn. I leave you with this scene I've written but cannot use, do not know how to use, and will not use: Dori with Mama and children.

Zachary put the papers in Kalia's hand, kissed the top of her head, and left the room.

I think, Moe, that Zachary has become a *bisel mishuga* with your Herzl. Don't you feel guilty?

Blink.

I don't have to burden you with the scene. Or do you want me to read it?

Blink.

Sure?

Blink.

Okay, then. Kalia glanced through the pages. I haven't read this one, but here we go, Moe. Do I feel nervous? Answer blink or blink blink.

Blink. Blink. Blink.

Moe, you dog! She laughed, then cleared her throat, and began to read.

> The large gray-stone house of HERZL'S PARENTS *in Vienna.* HERZL *and his mother,* JEANETTE, *are seated at a small, skirted table laid with demitasse cups, a silver coffeepot, cakes neatly stacked on an oval platter. Intense sunlight fills this area of the room and makes the scene seem very white. We don't see the entire room, but we can feel its opulence. We do not hear the voices of* DORI *or* JEANETTE. *The only*

sound in the scene is a tense, lush, sensuous music,
fin-de-siècle. JEANETTE *fills her son's cup. Girlishly,*
she throws her head back as she speaks. DORI *laughs.*
She responds. He laughs.
 Pan through the window to a very manicured gar-
den. PAULINE, HANS, *and* TRUDE *are discovered.*
Only music is on the track. TRUDE, *the youngest, is*
on a swing. HANS *pushes the swing higher and*
higher. TRUDE *laughs silently as the swing arcs up.*
PAULINE, *the eldest, silently claps her hands, and*
HANS *laughs. No voices. We sense danger, but the*
intense white light makes the garden magical.
 Pan back to JEANETTE *and* DORI. *No sound except*
music. From behind his chair, she puts her arms
around DORI. *She kisses the top of his head. She is*
laughing. He speaks rapidly. He laughs. He kisses her
hands. Music continues with a fast pan to the garden.
HANS *is standing on a tree stump. He is making a*
robust speech, but no words can be heard. Finished,
he leaps down from the stump and marches through
the garden. PAULINE *and* TRUDE *follow, imitating*
his rhythmic, high-stepping stride.
 Pan back inside. DORI *is pacing back and forth in*
front of the window. Uncharacteristically, his hands
and arms make big gestures as he talks. Same music.
JEANETTE *reacts thoughtfully. Sometimes she inter-*
jects, sometimes she laughs. Her eyes gleam as DORI's
brilliance makes the room seem even brighter. Fast
pan to the garden. The soundtrack holds on the single
high note of a violin. The three CHILDREN *are on*
their knees. They are looking into a declivity, a little
grave. Lying in the bottom is a dead bird. HANS *is*
speaking, clearly a prayer. At the end he crosses him-
self. PAULINE *crosses herself.* TRUDE *crosses herself.*
All together they push earth over the dead bird. PAUL-

INE *pats down the earth of the grave.* TRUDE, *wiping her eyes with the back of her hand, lays a crudely made cross of twigs on the grave.*

Well, that's pretty personal. It's good, very good, isn't it, Moe?

Blink.

Just then Barthelmes pushed through the door and looked toward them.

You should use it, Zach, Kalia said. Moe and I agree— and Moe's the producer. You have to!

I'll think about it. I promise.

What doubts?

I don't want Jeanette to look like a doting Jewish mother and Herzl like the mother-fixated son.

Well, maybe Jeanette's just convinced that her son's a great leader. And maybe he enjoys and respects her intellect.

Barthelmes sighed. I don't know what kind of feeling the scene would have. It might play badly, negatively. I don't know.

Casting?

That would help.

What the children do is very clear. It's a real flash-forward. We almost know something unfortunate is going to happen to them.

I hoped it would just make you feel uneasy.

It does that, Zach.

Barthelmes turned to Moe, then walked to the bed and sat down on the edge. Okay, boss, do I shoot it?

Blink.

If it doesn't work, we blame it on Wiggins.

Blink. Blink. Blink.

I don't mind, you bastards.

It's true that Jeanette gets a bad rap, Barthelmes said. I think she knew what her son was about, and she supported him. Maybe, I'm speculating now, without her support, Herzl would've given up. Anyway, it's a thought.

Shouldn't mothers support their children? Cheer for them? Do it, Zach!

Let's see what happens in the cutting room. Barthelmes got up from Moe's bed and embraced Kalia. I wish I had a mother like Jeanette, he half whispered. Mine had no warmth, no *life*. Maybe because she'd learned that the man she married was nothing but a Jew. Maybe that's why she died so young.

Moe's eyes had closed, and silently they left the room.

PART NINE

1.

In an Arab quarter of Tel Aviv, Wiederspiel took Barthelmes to lunch—ordering the food in his usual mixture of Hebrew and Arabic. He listened patiently to Zachary's account of Moe's stroke. Will he live? he asked after a long pause.

Who knows? If Kalia flies out once a week for a few days, that seems to keep him involved. She knows how to handle him. She even has the blink signals up to ten or twelve different meanings. An amazing amount of combinations, almost a new language. If they exercise him enough . . . The key thing is Moe, really. He has to want to live. The one thing we can't tell him is that Big MAC is in his daughters' hands. I suppose he always expected to live forever. Never made a will. No instructions of any kind.

You've finished the script?

Effectively, yes. It could go into production right now.

Can't Moe make it happen?

Zachary shook his head. His daughters have legal control, and his son isn't available or interested.

A sonic boom cracked the air outside the restaurant, and the window glass vibrated.

F-15, Wiederspiel said. Good plane. There was a second boom, softer than the first. Wiederspiel's head turned in the direction of the diminishing trail of sound. Mirage, he said.

You really can tell the kind of plane it is by the sound?

Any mechanic can do that. If two Phantoms are flying by, a good mechanic can tell which one's running best and who's flying.

And you're a good mechanic.

I used to be.

Barthelmes continued speaking as if he had Wiederspiel's

complete attention. You know, Moe never told his daughters about *The Beggar's Cup*. And as far as they know, it might just be an ambitious writer-director trying to swing a deal over their daddy's corpse.

Wiederspiel commented with a grunt.

They know nothing about the movie business, but they'll learn soon enough. *The Cup* would cost a fortune. And it isn't a market picture by a long shot. It was Moe's to do. And while Big MAC has plenty of cash in the bank, the girls can figure out that the real payday comes by selling the whole thing.

I see.

Hal, Barthelmes finally said, you're not listening.

Oh, sorry. Something on my mind. You were saying something about Moe's daughters? He rubbed his forehead, his hand trembling slightly.

You okay, Hal?

Yeah, I'm okay. Just a few things that need sorting out. I always get things sorted out, you know. Suddenly, he smiled, reached across the cracked marble tabletop, and slapped Barthelmes on the shoulder. Thanks for asking. When do you go to Jerusalem?

Tomorrow or the next day. As soon as Motti Amit calls. He has the script now. Do you think he might help?

He should, but I can't say. Mention my name, anyway.

You know him?

No. Maybe he knows me. Don't expect too much. They're just starting to build a film industry, and I hear they've fucked it up already.

A long silence followed. Abruptly Wiederspiel got to his feet, put some money on the table, and walked toward the exit.

Barthelmes trailed after him onto the street. Are you sure you're all right, Hal?

Oh, yes. No problem. I'll sort it all out.

2.

Motti Amit called Barthelmes early the next morning and asked whether he could come to Jerusalem that afternoon— anytime between one and seven. Zachary said he would try to be there by three.

Traffic was light getting out of Tel Aviv, and the road to Jerusalem was nearly empty; from modernity to antiquity in less than two hours. By 2:20 Barthelmes was pushing through the tall, old doors of the building where Amit kept offices on the third floor. He walked up the widely curving staircase. The domed ceiling, cracked and peeling, was held up by a latticework of beams and struts; inside the lobby, scaffoldings of different heights faced curved walls that were pocked with white plaster patches and ready for painting. Barthelmes wondered how old the building might be. A new structure, he thought, not older than five hundred years.

At Amit's door, he knocked and a gray-haired woman poked her head out. She looked carefully at Barthelmes, from his moccasins upward, until she stared into his blue eyes. Yes? she said in English.

I have an appointment with Mr. Amit. My name is Barthelmes.

Oh, yes. She opened the door wide and walked away. He stood there for a moment, then entered. She gestured to a chair. Please sit. I'll call him. The woman walked painfully across the large room to a closed door at the other end. She opened it without knocking and announced, Motti, it's the Barthelmes.

Motti Amit came out quickly, smiling broadly. Ah, Mr. Barthelmes, I am so pleased you came. Come in, come in. Chana! Make some coffee! You do drink coffee?

The woman reappeared with an unplugged electric percolator and two small cups and saucers on a wooden tray.

The script of *The Beggar's Cup* lay on Amit's desk. He tapped the blue cover of the script with his forefinger. Well, it's plain you have connections—*proteksia*, as we say. So, you know Morris Cohen?

Yes. And Hal Wiederspiel also asked me to give you his regards.

I never met him, but in Israel everyone knows who Wiederspiel is. I never met Morris Cohen, either. He is in good health?

Unfortunately not. He's had a stroke.

I'm very sorry.

We all hope for the best.

Is the coffee all right?

Hits the spot.

So, shall we talk business? First let me say I'm flattered that you have come here. You're the first Academy Award winner to come to talk to us about a film. You know what my office does?

Yes.

Well, it's not much. Certainly nothing on a Hollywood scale. It comes down to facilitating a producer. Are you doing the producing?

No, but with your cooperation it will be much easier to get a production together.

Cohen is interested?

Very much so.

Motti Amit's eyes narrowed, and Barthelmes was quite sure that he understood something was not correct. If Cohen wanted something done with a film, he would've called the Prime Minister and Amit would've been told to roll out the red carpet.

Motti Amit picked up the script and held it to his chest. Standing, Amit rocked up and back on the balls of his feet. The knotted cords of his *talith-katan*, a prayer vest worn under the shirt, dangled down. It is, he said, a remarkable scenario. Remarkable! I have only one trouble with it. A serious concern. It is with Herzl.

I have been very careful. The facts—

Oh yes, the research is exquisite. In the scenes you give pictures of history that are quite breathtaking. Some are very beautiful. A few are moving, very moving indeed. The problem is Herzl, Mr. Barthelmes. The core of the film is Herzl, no?

Yes, of course.

He is a hero to you?

May I smoke? Barthelmes said and offered Amit a cigarette. He accepted it. Barthelmes inhaled deeply and let the smoke flow slowly, thickly, from his nostrils. I suppose that's a fair question, he said. He has become a hero to me. I also think he actually was a hero. A great man.

I cannot blame you for that. All through Israel, maybe nine out of ten will agree with you. Herzl is a hero. The spiritual founder of the state. His portrait hangs in the Knesset, his face on every hundred-pound note. But sadly, Israelis know very little about Herzl. A hero to many, perhaps—but not to me, not to truly observing Jews.

Barthelmes laughed softly. You've taken the wind out of my sails, Mr. Amit.

Forgive me, Barthelmes. I'm not saying that he did not play a part in Jewish history. Yes, of course he did. But a hundred years later we are free to examine his role objectively, no?

Meaning?

For example, wouldn't you say that he had a huge ego? That, frankly, he was an egomaniac?

He had an ego, yes—a large one. That is not uncommon among leaders, I don't think.

I think he thought he was the *Meshiach*.

You're exaggerating, Amit.

You don't explain in the film how a man who was already assimilated—

I don't buy that! He had religious training, a bar mitzvah.

But he didn't practice.

Practice what? Religion isn't practiced in Israel very seriously, so far as I can see, and Israelis are still Jews. Herzl was like most of the middle-class Jews of his time. Maybe he went to the synagogue on the High Holy Days.

It is a fact that he ate pork. Shellfish, too.

I see, Barthelmes said and smiled. A hundred years later you are accusing Herzl of being a false Messiah for eating *treif.*

You have a little Yiddish, Amit said and smiled back. These are not petty things, Barthelmes. They are indicators of larger inadequacies.

For example?

Wouldn't you say that Herzl was a shameless opportunist who was trying to climb to fame and power on the backs of the Jews?

Certainly if someone wanted to diminish him, that could be said. The counterargument might be, Amit, that an opportunist doesn't squander his health and family fortune for a cause very few people believed could possibly succeed.

Proving his egomania! As for opportunism, he even threw his wife's dowry in the pot of his high-rolling political gambling!

You might also say he threw the lives of his children into the pot as well. You know about his children?

They did not turn out well. I've heard the stories.

They were not stories, Amit.

I see I'm not going to win this kind of argument.

Why not, Amit?

Well, because you're a professional. You gather up the books and you read for a few years. And because you are filled with facts, you assume you can make judgments.

Forgive me. I had also assumed that you had read the books. Even more books and documents than I've read. Certainly you have read his diaries?

Quotes and critiques, but no, I don't have to read everything to grasp the essence of something.

If I've made any judgments at all, Amit, they're cinematic. I'm after what will make a good movie. I select.

Aha! There is where you fail!

I don't understand.

In movies there is either the hero or the antihero. To do your job with Herzl, he *must* be the hero.

Pretend, for a moment, that you were portraying Herzl. How would you deal with him?

Amit walked away from the desk. He lit a fresh cigarette and stood before the tall, narrow window, looking down at the busy street. He returned to the desk, sat down, and said, quite softly, As a charlatan.

Barthelmes stared at him. And here *you* are in the Israel he brought to you!

Amit smiled, shook his head slowly, and picked up the script from his desk. Would you mind if I read to you one of your own scenes?

If you like.

As drama it is very good. I'll read it and then I'll make my point. All right with you?

All right with me.

Amit had no trouble finding the scene, which he'd marked by a paper clip. He cleared his throat and read.

August 22, 1903. Basel. The Sixth Zionist Congress. High shot of the main auditorium. Except for a few delegates, the large room is empty. HERZL *sits alone at a table on the dais, writing in a notebook.* MAX NORDAU *walks quickly up the stairs, and the wooden dais echoes with his footfalls. The ocean sound of distant voices filters into the empty room. Close shot of* NORDAU *speaking into* HERZL's *ear:*

Do you understand a rebellion is brewing? It is very serious.

I am very much aware of it. How many will vote with me?

A majority, but the minority is formidable. Listen to them!

The sound of voices outside the auditorium swells into a roar. The camera pushes forward with great speed into the crowded corridor and closes in quickly to the mouth of a MAN *wearing a Russian blouse:*

Traitor! *(a hoarse shout)* Traitor!

Swift, swinging pans to individual delegates.

SMALL MAN WITH PINCE-NEZ: We must hear what he has to say!

RABBI: Uganda! *(bewildered)* Did Herzl say we should establish the state in Uganda?

YOUNG MAN: He will not leave this hall alive!

BEARDED MAN: Clay god!

DARK-SKINNED MAN: It will be Palestine or nothing!

MAN ON CRUTCHES: Uganda! He wants to feed the Jews to the lions!

REPORTER *(pad in hand):* Let's hear his report, you idiots!

The YOUNG DELEGATE *punches the last speaker in the face. He falls to the floor, blood running from his mouth. Cut to the auditorium, which is overflowing. Camera picks out the* MAN WHOSE MOUTH IS BLEEDING. *Now seated, he dabs at his mouth with a handkerchief. Cut to dais, where* NORDAU *stands at the podium. He raps sharply with a large gavel.*

NORDAU: Order! Order!

SHOUT 1: Order in the courtroom! The monkey wants to speak!

SHOUT 2: Make way for the King of the Jungle! *(Laughter.)*

SHOUT 3: If the socialist delegates from Russia will shut their *shtetl* mouths, we will be able to proceed.

SHOUT 4: Whenever the waltzer from Vienna likes.

(Laughter.)

NORDAU *(pounds gavel):* Order! Order! If there is not order this instant, I will adjourn this convention! *The noise rumbles into silence. We can barely hear a voice calling* Traitor! *The silence beats over the hall like a pulse.*

NORDAU: I am honored again to introduce our great leader and spokesman, Dr. Theodor Herzl.

YOUNG DELEGATE: We know the traitor's name!

NORDAU: Remove him!

Three burly JEWS *close in on* YOUNG DELEGATE, *lift him off his feet, and carry him toward an exit. He struggles as they disappear through a door. Meanwhile,* HERZL *has taken his place at the podium.*

HERZL: The monkey's going to speak. The King of the Jungle has a few words. I will not be long. I will not cite my record in the service of Jewry to this body. You know it well. The Rothschilds have endowed a few agricultural settlements in Palestine. Very few Jews go there. It is not a return to Eretz Yisroel. Baron de Hirsch has endowed a few agricultural settlements in Argentina. Very few Jews go there. It is not a return to Eretz Yisroel. Many Jews think that the United States of America is the place to go. But it is also not Eretz Yisroel. As you all know, I, myself, have always been a Jewish-state man. A Jewish-state man first and last, but the state I most prefer would be built in Palestine. You all know this. England, which first offered us Palestine but could not deliver, has offered us, with no conditions attached, Uganda.

VOICES: No! No! No!

HERZL: I am not advocating that the Jews of the world pack up their goods and their children and go to Uganda. I am saying that, out of respect for the only country which has offered Jews a land of their own, we must form a committee to go to East Africa to see if this offer has any merit.

MAN ON CRUTCHES: The door to disaster is being opened!

DARK-SKINNED MAN: No! No! No!

HERZL: Consider this, dear delegates: the masses of Jews in Europe are in great danger. If we have a place of refuge, does that mean we reject a return to Eretz Yisroel? I think not. I ask you to appoint a committee to evaluate the English offer. Then, at the next Zionist convention, you will vote to accept that report or reject that report. *(A long silence as* HERZL *gathers up his papers, then looks up intently at the* DELEGATES.*)* If I should forget thee, O Jerusalem, may my tongue cleave to the roof of my mouth, may my right arm wither!

HERZL *leaves the podium and descends the dais stairs. In the corridor outside the auditorium, he braces himself against a wall. He is perspiring heavily. He throws up.*

Motti Amit closed the script and put it down on the desk. A very clever Jew, he said, manipulating and gambling. Although you have put the best face on it. To satisfy his sick ego, he was playing dice with the future of the Jews. That's my opinion, my conviction. The question is, if Herzl had lived another year, wouldn't he have tried to build the new Jerusalem in Uganda? By the way, Barthelmes, there is no point in saying to me that Herzl brought me here. I trace my lineage back to King David. We never left this land. The genuine Israel will be established only when the *Meshiach* comes.

I think I've lost the argument, Amit.

So easily! I'm sorry. I shouldn't have burdened you with my beliefs. Better I should act like a proper bureaucrat. I should have mailed the script back to you with a short note.

It's okay, Amit. I think I'd better go.

I'm sorry, Barthelmes. It is an excellent scenario. But the help I might have been able to give would have been little by any measure. It is a film of epic proportions. Too big for a little country like Israel. Tell me, why doesn't Cohen just go ahead and produce it?

That's exactly Moe's intention, Barthelmes said. But he thought, given the nature of the film, it would be good to have Israeli involvement.

That will have to be arranged by someone else, someone above. I feel very strongly about this.

I understand.

With all due respect, Barthelmes, explain to me why a man of your standing in the motion-picture industry would become involved with such a film?

It's a powerful subject.

Ah, but a subject you can't understand. You can be impressed. You can hero-worship. But you can't understand. Herzl was a Jew by birth, but not in his heart. As for yourself, not even a Jew. How could you hope to understand, Barthelmes?

He took the script from Amit's desk. I think if a man wants to understand, he will understand. I know this: Herzl was the greatest Jew since Moses.

Who told you that?

David Ben-Gurion. Who's your candidate?

Amit's face hardened. Ben-Gurion said many things which were not acceptable.

Barthelmes left without shaking Amit's hand or saying good-bye.

3.

Zachary Barthelmes walked aimlessly through the narrow streets of Jerusalem. How the hell would he get this film made? No help was forthcoming from blinking Moe. Archer Doty was happily placed in Disneyland. Moe's daughters would cash out. And if there was another producer in Hollywood who'd even touch *The Beggar's Cup*, Barthelmes hadn't met him.

Under his breath, he heard himself muttering, Alms! Alms! Alms for the love of Allah! Had he heard an Arab beggar say that in front of one of the great gates to Jerusalem? No, it couldn't be. Arab beggars didn't say *alms*. It had to be from a movie he'd seen long ago, and he had a hunch it was set in India. Victor McLaglen, Cary Grant, and David Niven were in it. And Sam Jaffe. That was *Gunga Din*. Or maybe *Beau Geste*. Then Jaffe was out. Robert Taylor? But there had to be a Muslim beggar somewhere. Alms! Alms!

Excuse me, a man said, brushing past where Barthelmes stood on the narrow sidewalk. Ahead of him was the Wailing Wall, where a dozen or so Jews were praying. Most were Orthodox men in black hats and coats, with beards and side curls. Facing the wall, praying fervently, was a young man who wore a green, tie-dyed T-shirt, blue jeans, and army boots. A *kippah* sat precariously on his head.

Barthelmes walked a few yards closer, wanting to go down from the street to the level of the wall. But he did not.

4.

Walking toward the Mann Auditorium in Tel Aviv, Geula Renan laughed bitterly. Oh, you can be sure that Helmut is in there. Wherever Barone is making a speech, he attends and comes home to bed depressed. I am worried, Zachary.

Does he talk about it?

No.

No clues?

There are many clues. You know Helmut. He wants to be the perfect Jew. The Jew who can stand up before God and say: Lord, I have served you with my heart and soul. I have done Your Will.

Jesus, if anyone has, it would be Hal.

You tell him! Barone also thinks he is doing God's Will.

Barone?

Of course he thinks he is. He's as fundamentalist as the Ayatollah. Barone raises questions which Helmut can't answer. He wonders if Barone might not be right about certain things.

Well, what if he is? Everybody's right about something.

Barone would not allow that. All right. All wrong.

Who cares!

Helmut cares. In a certain way Helmut, too, is a fundamentalist. He is no politician. But he needs always to be right, Zachary, and Barone is tearing him apart. If Barone is right, how can Helmut be right? How can Helmut stand before God? For Achad Barone, as for Helmut Wiederspiel, God is not—what is your movie word? Technicolor! God is not in Technicolor. God is in black and white.

They're not that simple, Geula. At least Hal isn't, not by a long shot.

All right, that's true. They are both aware of subtleties,

colors, and tones, yet they are annoyed by them. Each of them wants to sift through the Technicolor maze—haze?—and come down to the black and white of the bottom line.

Maybe that's why they are doers. I live my life among the hues, in the gray areas.

I try to do that, too, but for Israelis it is very difficult. We need more black and white to survive, Zachary, simply to survive.

He laughed. It's ironic, Geula. Two passionate fundamentalists who see two entirely different blacks and whites.

Don't laugh, Zachary; tragedy is made from this.

Together, with hundreds of others, they walked through the stately entrance of the Mann Auditorium. No tickets were required. There were no reserved seats. Geula couldn't find Helmut, so she and Zachary sat down in the fourth row. Although the event was scheduled for eight, it was already 8:15. At war, Geula said, we make split seconds count, but in everything else we are approximate.

A few minutes later a small orchestra in Israeli costume, carrying flutes, drums, and hand-held harps, entered from the wings of the stage. The music was Israeli, mainly traditional. Soon the instrumentalists were joined by dancers. In the middle of the dancing, the theater lighting switched on.

The electricians, Geula whispered, made a little mistake about the time.

I see, Barthelmes said. But as he studied the light designs, he added, But they're very good!

Once the dancers left the stage, a tall blond man wearing a *kippah* made a strong speech in Hebrew. That's Gad Eliav, Geula explained. Went through many campaigns with Barone. Hal knows him. A good man.

He's introducing Barone?

Yes.

What's he saying?

In essence: he's a great hero. He's done this. He's done

that. He is the right man to come at the right time to help Israel achieve its destiny.

Does he say what that is?

He must leave something for Barone.

Behind them someone said, Shhhh!

Finally, to thunderous applause, Gad Eliav introduced the main speaker in a voice that was almost a shout: General Achad Barone!

Is he religious? Barthelmes whispered. He's wearing a *kippah*.

Political gesture. Barone gets strong support from the religious parties.

Barone seemed to Barthelmes a powerful speaker. His Hebrew sentences were short. His arms pierced the air with strength. On occasion he pounded his fist into his palm to make a point. The audience was an instrument he played with great skill. They applauded, sometimes shouted their approval, and laughed at his jokes. Even without understanding the language, Barthelmes knew that this man was a natural orator. Brief me, he said to Geula.

In Zachary's ear, her steady voice said, He's traced the history of the Jews since the Roman victory at Masada. The vanquished Jews—men, women, and children—leapt from the high plateau to their deaths rather than face capture and slavery by the Romans. No more Masadas! No more Masadas! Never again! Never again!

Now he's condemning the Rabin government. Weak appeasers in the pocket of the United States. Israeli policy is made in Washington, D.C.

Round up all of the Arabs in Israel and deport them to Jordan, Egypt, and Lebanon. Israel is for Israelis.

Jesus! Barthelmes said in a loud voice, and voices behind him hissed.

The solution is secure borders. Secure borders mean building the Greater Israel. Judea and Samaria were given to the

Jews by God, and only God has the right to take land away from His chosen people.

Thunderous applause. Great approving shouts. A powerful speech extended by powerful hand-clapping, foot-stomping approbation. Barthelmes's *Jesus!* was lost in the final tumult of the standing audience. Barone held up his hand for silence.

He thanks them, Geula translated. Now he is saying it's no surprise that his friend Wiederspiel is attending.

Behind them and to the left, Zachary saw Hal standing in the bright glare of a spotlight. He was wearing his old leather bomber jacket, and his head was bare.

A second microphone was brought out, and Barone beckoned to him. Briskly, Wiederspiel walked onto the stage. *Shalom* was his first word. A polite applause rippled through the auditorium.

Geula put her mouth directly against Zachary's ear: Achad, my comrade, you know how much I disagree with you. I am sure I cannot make you agree with me. It is the people here, your supporters, to whom I speak. I think the heart of General Barone's argument is the concept of a Greater Israel. What that means is not only settling and annexing Judea and Samaria but driving the Palestinians and all Arabs from those places. Most Israelis disagree with this.

Barone cut in. My dear comrade Helmut, I am always glad when you come to hear me speak. You do me a service by contesting me. It makes me think over what I have said and believe. Your arguments make me see even more clearly what the true and shining path for Israel must be. Yes, Helmut, I stand for a Greater Israel. You are a general, like myself. Will annexing Judea and Samaria not secure our borders? I believe in this land which God has given us—he held up his hands for quiet—and even if I did not believe that it is God's will, as a general I want that land so that Israel can be properly defended.

As for the Palestinians and Arabs, I bear them no ill will.

As you know, I grew up among them. My wet nurse was Palestinian. I suckled at her breast. She was my second mother, Helmut. It is not so unreasonable that I would send all Arabs within our borders to Jordan, to Lebanon, to Egypt. Have they not sent their Jews, except for those they hold captive, to Israel? And those they keep prisoner, have we not pleaded to have them sent to us? I ask you, Why will these countries not accept their brothers? I answer, Because they want turmoil in Israel. They want Arab and Jewish blood spilled. Such a situation, and I agree with them, gives the Arabs a political and military advantage. Israel without Arabs will be more secure and more peaceful. God's design will be fulfilled. This I believe. Barone paused to accept the applause. In one sense, he continued, I agree with Arafat and the PLO: we are at war with each other. Wars are to be won or lost. Certainly they are to be fought. We must fight and we must win. Only then will we have peace in the land!

Wiederspiel waited patiently for the applause to stop, then looked directly at Barone. You are making the same speech, Achad. I repeat, the majority of our people disagree with you.

One day they will change their minds—perhaps tomorrow.

Land can be traded for peace. Peace depends on political agreements.

And you would sit down with Arafat?

Yes, and with his mother. At this the audience laughed. Smiling, Wiederspiel continued. I don't have to kill him, Achad. We need to have political agreements with the Arab world.

They will never give it. You know that!

I don't know that, and neither do you. First we must sit down at the table.

And what if you are rebuffed?

We will sit down again. There are many Palestinians who want peace as much as we do.

Helmut, Helmut! Every time such an Arab opens his mouth, he is killed.

You're talking too fast, Geula. I'm missing too much of what you're saying.

Well, Zachary, now you've missed a little more. Let me catch my breath.

You are counting too much on the United States, Helmut. I count only on ourselves.

A good idea! But how will we build airplanes, guns, and tanks without metals? We are rich in scientists and engineers, but we haven't got the basic materials.

I know you, Wiederspiel. You can build airplanes out of sand.

Unfortunately, this is not true.

You know, there are many countries aside from the United States that will sell us raw materials. With pleasure!

Without America we are in great trouble. I would say terminal trouble. You know that, Achad.

All right, all right, I concede the point. Barone bowed to Wiederspiel as the crowd applauded.

Thank you. To me, being locked into the United States means that we are locked into the world. We must settle the problems of Israel in the world context. That means settling with the Palestinians in the first place. That means peace.

You have a fairy tale there, Helmut. One hundred and fifty million Arabs surround us. They can wait. One day they will build armies as efficient as ours.

That will take a very long time.

Hah! Not if the United States and the Soviet Union supply them with planes and missiles and train their men. And the Arabs have oceans of oil to trade.

You have a point there, Achad. Wiederspiel returned Barone's bow, and again the audience applauded. But that's exactly why we need to build bridges now. The wars of the future will not be so easy as the wars of the past. The Yom Kippur War was a warning about that.

Yes and no. If Kissinger had kept his hands off and had let me finish the Egyptian army, there would be far less danger of future wars or PLO blood games. Our enemies respect strength above all. Barone raised an arm to quiet the burst of approving shouts and clapping. Helmut, you will make a point, and then I will make a point. Your point will be good. My point will be good. We can continue to argue with each other forever. We are like that, we Jews. But it is the ultimate truth that you are afraid to face.

And what is that?

We are not wanted in this world. Jews are not wanted in this world.

Nonsense, Achad!

Barone shook his head slowly. No, not nonsense, Helmut. You know it is true. The United States will not always support us. While we are their outpost against the USSR, their dollars will flow. Dollars flow also to our enemies. And hardware and warplanes. Why? Because the United States needs the Arabs as much as it needs the Jews. More. There is no oil here. One barrel of oil is worth more than one Jew.

It is not that simple, Achad. With America we have a common culture, a common bond.

But didn't we have a common bond with Germany? How often have we given our lives and souls to a host nation only in the end to be slaughtered?

Wiederspiel was silent for a moment. Is there no world for you except Israel?

No. Israel is the only world for Jews. If you don't know this, you are a dreamer. The only bastion for the Jews of the world is Israel. If there is no Israel, one day there will be no Jews.

Achad, you have condemned the suicide solution of Ma-

sada, but look at what you're doing! You are turning all of
Israel into one single, great Masada!

Not at all. My life as a soldier shows me—all of *history*
shows me—that if you are prepared to fight, if your enemy
knows you are determined to win, he will not be so ready to
meet you in the field. Only then is there peace and survival.
Only then is there victory! Am I right, Helmut?

Peace through strength, Achad? Peace through blood? It
always works for a while. For the winner.

You want peace through love, Helmut?

Hal was quiet for a moment, and the silence reverberated
through the auditorium. Yes, he finally said, peace through
love.

Barthelmes was startled by a smattering of laughter.

You can't have it, Barone said. It's not a solution allowed
to Jews.

It is the only solution allowed to us. We are chosen to be
a light unto the world.

So what shall we do if love fails?

But it must not fail!

Where is your reason, Helmut? It's not love we need. It's
respect!

We've already won the respect of the world. Who else do
you wish to impress?

I won't argue with you anymore, Helmut. It does no good.
Your spine has lost its stiffness. You no longer have the resolve
to smite your enemies! General Achad Barone turned away
from Wiederspiel and spread his arms to the audience. Toward the Greater Israel! Toward a Jewish Israel! Toward the
final victory!

During the loud, prolonged applause, neither of the men
spoke. They embraced each other with their eyes. Then
Wiederspiel put his hand into the pocket of his jacket and
pulled out the silver pistol Barone had given him during the
Yom Kippur War.

Several people in the auditorium leapt to their feet. No! No! It's a gun!

The pistol gleamed in the light as Wiederspiel handed it to Barone, smiled once more, and walked off the stage.

Geula and Zachary left their seats and went quickly outside through the nearest exit. But there was no trace of Wiederspiel.

5.

Geula raced the jeep across the sands of the Sinai. Neither she nor Barthelmes spoke. The vehicle bounced over the sand ripples made by the wind. She brought the jeep to a sharp stop. Where is he? she shouted, looking up at the sky. Why are you doing this, Helmut?

Are you sure he's up there? Barthelmes's eyes, too, scanned the vast sky.

Oh, yes. He's up there. They've been tracking him from the base. He can be a hundred, two hundred miles from here—a few minutes' flying time.

Again they were silent. The dawn gripped the rim of the horizon, where the mountains assembled themselves in soft, purple forms.

He just walked onto the base, Barthelmes said, and commandeered a plane?

It's not so difficult. He's taken planes up before. Who would question Helmut Wiederspiel?

Dawn faded. A thin daylight took its place.

Listen, Geula said, turning to look behind her. I hear something from the east.

The Phantom streaked above the mountains. In less than a minute it had split the sky. The air clapped together, and the desert seemed to move. The Phantom raced away from them.

Geula lifted the radio microphone to her face. Helmut! Come in, please! Talk to me, Helmut!

Another silence.

The sound of the Phantom returned—at first soft, even purring, then whining and screaming. Boom, boom, the Sinai filled with echoes.

Am I reaching you, Helmut? Don't do this to me, Helmut. Come in! Come in!

The fighter banked sharply to the north, racing up to the dome of the sky. It barrel rolled, once, twice, three times.

Come in, please Helmut, come in!

The radio receiver in the jeep crackled. I'm in, Geula, Wiederspiel's voice said. What are you doing down there?

I've come to get you.

Beautiful up here.

Why are you doing this? Geula said, struggling not to sob.

Barthelmes took the microphone from her hand. Hal, it's me, Zachary. Geula brought me out for the ride. What have you got in mind up there?

I'm looking things over, Zachary. It's fabulous. You know Moses and his flock camped out here for forty years?

I've heard.

In forty minutes I've crisscrossed this desert ten times. There's progress for you. Now that the sun's up, maybe I can find some footprints.

The radio went dead as the Phantom maneuvered some high, languid rolls; then Wiederspiel's voice came back on. Somewhere out here we were worshipping the Golden Calf, Zach, and being promiscuous. Moses was exceedingly pissed off. So I've been looking for a trail into the mountains. Where did Moses go?

Geula grabbed the microphone. Helmut, if you love me, don't do this. Go back to the base. Please.

I love you more than any person on this earth. But I can't

return to base. My compass is lost. I don't know what's right any more.

Radio silence as the Phantom clapped across the sky.

Wiederspiel calling. Come in, my colonel.

I'm here, Helmut. I love you. Come to me.

Some of the days I loved best, Geula, were on the river in New Hampshire. They were great days.

And in the fields near Jerusalem, when we touched each other under the almond tree. The blossoms fell on us. Oh, Helmut, come to me, please come to me. I beg you—come to me!

When we first started out to build our land, it was so beautiful. So right. What happened?

We're still building it, Helmut. It's still beautiful.

No. We are lost in wars, in righteousness. Do you think Achad is right?

No, I heard what you said: Peace through love.

Wiederspiel's laugh sounded full. I want it that way. But Achad is not all wrong. Maybe we are not wanted in this world.

Helmut, please, we have made our world. There is our Israel. It exists!

But will they let us keep it, or do we have to be at war forever?

It does not matter, Helmut. We have Israel for this generation, perhaps for many generations.

I want it forever, Geula.

Come down to me, Helmut. *Please!*

Zachary, Wiederspiel said, can you understand this? I can't sort things out any more. My mind is filled with cobwebs. Barone is right, I'm a dreamer.

Barthelmes took back the microphone. Nothing wrong with being a dreamer, Hal.

And if there is no dream? Would you believe this,

Zachary—I'm scared shitless. What if there is no dream? Over and out, as the little boy flyers say.

But there is a dream, Helmut! Geula cried into the microphone. There is a dream!

The Phantom climbed vertically toward the sky; then the engine stalled. Plunging down toward the desert, the plane pulled out of its dive and leveled off. Then, screaming and booming beneath the heavens at twice the speed of sound, the fighter pointed itself toward Mount Sinai.

Geula Renan and Zachary Barthelmes watched the explosion and the brilliant ball of flame.

PART TEN

1.

Slowly, very slowly, she read the poem again:

> From grave to grave
> From sky to sky
> They flew.
> One turned the earth
> One burned the air.
> For each there was
> The pulsing moment
> Of an undefined time
> Which throbbed.
> Now they are gone
> In the blink
> Of a sand-blinded eye.
> No monuments.
> I thought this on a morning
> When you were above me like the sun.
> A soft, warm monument.
> Defined, throbbing, pulsing.
> I would say eternal.
> But I close my lips
> Knowing that death blinks,
> That life bursts and burns
> Above the sands.
> The secret buried Sinais
> Of our lives.

She kissed Zachary's forehead. When did you write this?
I guess when Moe died.
He killed himself, too, you know. When he knew he was

the ward of his children. It was clear to him then there would be no film. He stopped blinking for me. His eyes were almost always closed. I think he must have ordered his heart to stop.

There will be a picture, Zachary said. Somehow.

I love you, Mr. Barthelmes. Also loved your new film. How did you get Wayne to act?

Pretended he was Gary Cooper. He won't win an Oscar, and neither will I. But I did get close to Scott Kincaid. He has guts. I gave him *The Beggar's Cup.*

Don't expect anything, darling.

I don't.

I see that light in your eye. Don't! You hear me? Don't expect anything! Every refusal means two weeks of depression. *The Beggar's Cup* is busted.

Can't lose anything.

Are there any producers in Hollywood who haven't passed?

New players are always turning up. But there's also England, France, Italy, the whole Soviet bloc. Maybe Al Broccoli, Bobby Maxwell . . .

Kalia sighed. I don't mind your persevering. Just don't get depressed. Kills our love life.

You really like the poem, quote unquote?

Yes, very much. I'm going to frame it.

Now you're teasing.

No, really. I'm going to frame it and put some of my dried almond blossoms on the page. Little pieces of Israel.

Zachary kissed her and held her close.

2.

No way, Zach, Kincaid said. Even if the script were a virgin, and you've shopped the mother all around the industry. Big fat no's from every major and minor. Too special. I've known you—followed your work, anyway—for ten, maybe fifteen years. *Admire* you. And you did one hell of a job for me on *Buried Guns*. Under budget, too! But the last couple of years, you've been too earnest with this other thing. One of my colleagues says the impression is that you've been on the brink of begging. I know he's full of shit, but that's the impression he got.

Do I get the impression, Scott, that you're not interested?

Zach, you're as bright a director as we've got, but this is simply a nonstarter. I'd be happy to entertain any other project you may have. I can suggest a couple for you. I'll send you the scripts.

To my New York apartment. I'm going East tomorrow.

Kincaid barked instructions into the intercom, then leaned back in his chair. Can I ask you a question?

Zachary nodded.

Why are you doing this?

I promised Moe Cohen.

Moe's dead. We owe dead men nothing.

I owe, Scott.

Okay. But beyond that. There has to be a deeper reason, Zach.

It's a good script. I put a lot into it.

Okay, I agree. One of the best you've ever done. I even asked myself, how can I take the curse off it? One thought was to blow up Lulu's part. Two or three scenes of what's-his-name in the sack with Lulu.

I have one of those scenes.

No, I mean the whole way. A guy with a full beard fucking his brains out. Something else, Zach—the guy's name. Hard to say. Sticks in my teeth. You know, if the audience can't say it, they won't buy it.

That was his name, Scott.

Okay, now we're getting to the heart of it. It doesn't have

to be about what's-his-name as a historical figure. Use him as your model. Turn it around. Use his political side as color. Blow up the personal side.

The Lulu side?

That's the ticket! Also, why does he have to be a Jew?

He was a Jew, that's all.

Makes it hard. You'll have the Anti-Defamation League all over the thing.

Barthelmes laughed softly. I take it, Scott, this is a firm refusal?

Rock hard, as they say. Another question: all the Jewish producers nixed it, right?

Right. That's why I brought it to you, a super-*goy*. My reasoning was something like this. Since the Jewish producers make all of those big religious films about Christ, Christmas, and Easter with lots of leprosy but no sex, maybe a stand-up Christian like Kincaid would do a Jewish turn.

Kincaid laughed heartily. You're a fucker, Zach! You know there are plenty of films, big ones, about Jews. Off the top of my head, the first talkie, Al Jolson's *The Jazz Singer*. Charlton Heston as Moses, not to mention Ben Hur.

Lots of leprosy, no sex, plus he converts.

Kincaid laughed again. Okay, okay. Those pictures weren't about Jews or Christians. They were about box office. Your thing really is about Jews. No box.

Jews *can* be box office, Scott. Israel's big news.

If you do it as cops and robbers—Entebbe, Nazi terrorists, Yassir Arafat, machine pistols blazing! That's sex, fella!

So the answer's still no?

Zach, you know it's no. It's gotta be. Come on—was Moe really going to make it?

Yes, cross my heart.

Good thing he died. *The Beggar's Cup* would've killed him.

It did.

One thing I don't get. Why you, Zach? You're not a fucking Jew! I don't get it.

You're a movie man, Scott. It's a good script. I tell you, it would make a good film.

Yeah, but it's about *Jews*.

Hey, those pictures you rattled off were big hits.

I know. But this one's too Jewy.

Too Jewy?

You know what I mean. It crosses the line. Both of us know lots of Jews. There are lots of Jews in the industry.

They invented it.

I thought it was some frog or the light-bulb guy. Jews are not technical. Great ideas and finance. There was a movie about the Rothschilds, right?

Also *The Jew Süss*, Barthelmes added. *Professor Mamlock*. *Gentlemen's Agreement*.

I didn't see the first two.

So, *The Beggar's Cup* is another one about the Jews.

It's too political, too ideological.

Too Jewy?

That's it. Crosses the invisible line.

Subtle.

Subtle, all right. You can't invest twenty, thirty million bucks in subtle.

No, I guess you can't.

I'll tell you this, Zachary, Jews are a strange crowd. They walk like us; they talk like us. You can bring one or two to a party or a dinner at your house—only very tuned-in people would even know. But bring a dozen and the air changes, the feel of things. *Everybody* knows. I have no problems with Jews here, but I don't invite them to the ranch.

Where's that?

Utah.

Nice state.

God's country.

God's Christian country.

Kincaid's eyebrows lifted. Well, he said, we all have places we like to keep clean, you know.

No argument there, Scott. Barthelmes held his eyes in cold contact with Kincaid's.

Anyway, you're one hell of a writer, Zach, Kincaid said and uneasily looked away. Then he turned back. Know the scene I liked best? In Vienna, when what's-his-name is leading the young Jewish kids to the church to be converted. Great fantasy, but it'll never happen. There will always be Jews. I admire that! Bastards stick in there, never quit. At least we had the good sense to join the right side.

Scott Kincaid laughed and lifted a long, dark cigar from the humidor on his desk. He clipped it and toasted the tip in the flame of his lighter before lighting it. The smoke sat heavily in the space before him, and he waved it away. In that moment Kincaid reminded Barthelmes of Cohen.

Let's keep it simple, Zach. Answer's no, but you can direct for me any time. If you write a film, chances are ninety-nine in a hundred I'll buy it. This is the one I won't buy.

3.

Why didn't you just tell him you were a Jew?

Because I'm not. And I wanted to sell the film.

You didn't have a chance, darling. You know that. You should've nailed the bastard. You can't deal with that kind of Waspy anti-Semitism. It seems so light it's almost not there. I almost prefer the neo-Nazis. You can fight them. God, you should've kicked him in his Aryan tinseltown balls.

It would be all over the industry in twenty-four hours. Say, did you know Zachary Wellington Barthelmes is a Jew? No, who says so? Barthelmes himself. I can't deal with that, Kale.

If Sammy Davis can cope, so can you.

Shit! Now I wish I really had blurted it out! Maybe I was dishonest. Do you think I was, Kale? But I kept thinking, Maybe Kincaid will buy it. I knew that it wasn't possible, so the best I could do was to give him a twinge of doubt.

About what?

I'm not even sure. Why am I so fucking confused?

Depressed?

Probably.

Kalia hugged him, holding on for a long moment. Finally she released him. Feel better?

No, Barthelmes said. I should have blurted it out! He paused. I can't bring it off, Kalia. I just can't bring it off!

4.

Zachary Barthelmes awoke in the middle of the night, slid away from the warmth of Kalia Wiggins, and went into his study. He pulled *The Beggar's Cup* from the large gray envelope. The cover of the manuscript was worn, and one corner had been torn away. There were two neat purple rings in the center—did the drinker of the wine put his glass down after reading the script, or had he not read it all and used it simply to keep his desk clean? Barthelmes smiled at the blue cover, thinking of how many readers and producers had touched it. Kincaid had it last, and two years earlier Motti Amit had pressed the same copy to his chest. Each of them had made the same assumption: he was not a Jew. Why, for what arcane reason, should Barthelmes go out of his way to set them straight?

And what if he had been? Would Amit have thought any differently about *The Beggar's Cup*? Or Kincaid? Not likely. Amit's quarrel was with a Herzl he'd already disowned. Kincaid's with what's-his-name went beyond the box office,

Barthelmes thought. It was probably deeper than Kincaid's desire to kill the hero by making him kinky, and perhaps even Kincaid couldn't understand it. Little Jews, powerless Jews, are easily handled, but maybe the tall, elegant, powerful Jew was Kincaid's secret, unarticulated nightmare.

It all came down to the same thing: *The Beggar's Cup* would never open its pages to the camera. Moe Cohen, of course, had known this and, having accepted it, had retired from the scene. Helmut Wiederspiel had chased after Achad Barone with his own beggar's cup until there was nothing to do but smash everything into the mountains of Moses; his dream had been challenged by other, unacceptable dreams and dreamers. Hal, too, would never gain the Promised Land.

Zachary flipped through the manuscript. The ending, he thought, was also right, yet he wasn't sure it was positive enough. Although he had avoided the cheap denouement of bands of angels coming for to carry him home, maybe it should've been more realistic. Barthelmes read it again—after how many times?

Franzenbad, Austria, July 3, 1904. Small, sunlit room in the spa where HERZL *is trying to recover. His strained heart is failing. He wears his nightclothes and a bathrobe. The sound of his breathing occupies the soundtrack—the shallow, rapid breaths of a swimmer fighting a sea that will soon overwhelm him. He rises from the edge of the bed and moves with great effort to the writing table. His pen scratches erratically across the pages of his notebook, and he stops frequently to gasp in the air. The bright sunlight has woven itself into his beard. His skin is pale and chalky, almost translucent.*

The door opens. WILLIAM HECHLER *enters. The silver crucifix around his neck glitters in the light, swinging in a slow arc.* HERZL *notices it: Christ rocking.*

William, please tuck that away.

I came as quickly as I could. *(Slipping the crucifix inside his shirt)* The moment I heard you call.

I didn't call, William.

Are you certain? I heard your voice. I was out in the meadow. Here, I brought these flowers for you. HECHLER *offers a small bouquet of wildflowers.* HERZL *takes the flowers in his hand. He brings them to his face and smells them.*

Beautiful! Thank you, William. *(He slips the flowers into his notebook.)*

I could swear you had called me, Dori.

No, but perhaps the wind carried my thought to you. I'm glad you came. I'm so tired of writing these damned letters. There is always someone in the world to whom I can write.

Would you like me to wheel you out into the meadow?

No. No, thank you. Who would think it is an effort to be wheeled out into a field filled with wildflowers?

It can wait until you feel better, Dori. The job now is to gather up your old strength. The world is waiting for you.

(Laughing weakly) I didn't expect a clergyman of your standing to exaggerate. The world, William, is waiting for me to die. I will not disappoint it.

Dori!

I have always been afraid of drowning, you see, of suffocating. This, unfortunately, I will have to endure. I cannot breathe. My heart is drowning me, William.

I'll call your doctor.

Why disturb the poor fellow?

Because I must call him.

HECHLER *exits, leaving the door open. The light in the door frame is intensely bright.* HERZL *dips his pen in the inkwell. Close-up on his hand, which trembles as his writing becomes wide and indecipherable. The hand turns palm up. The wildflowers fall to the floor. The raspy soundtrack is silent.*

The roar of a crowd. High shot of thousands of people following the black, horse-drawn hearse. Sobs and shouts fill the air.

Herzl, our king! Herzl Hamelech!

JULIE *and the* CHILDREN *follow in an open carriage. Behind them, alone in another carriage, is the widowed* JEANETTE HERZL. *Hundreds of hands reach to touch the hearse. Sobs and shouts, faces of figures we've met before. Mounted police, pushing against the crowd, keep order.*

MOUNTED POLICEMAN: Who died? Not the Emperor?

SECOND POLICEMAN: The King of the Jews, they say.

FIRST POLICEMAN: I didn't know the Jews had a king. Move on, there! Move on!

The camera pulls high and away. The cortege is enormous, extending beyond the panning camera. The soundtrack is filled with sobs, cries, and the Hebrew prayer for the dead. Music until the end.

Barthelmes thought the scene would serve. He might have depicted the thousands of Jews arriving for the funeral on trains and in wagons from Russia, Poland, and the rest of Europe. But what would it add? He also could have filmed the massive funeral service in Union Square in New York. But how could the film justify tens of thousands of Jews mourning for Herzl in Union Square, even if that's what had taken place? Herzl had never been to America, and the scene would have to be explained. Services in London and Paris as well. Too much. Almost the passing of a god. The ending as written, with luck, would do.

The scene that made Barthelmes particularly unhappy was one set in a *shul* in a Polish *shtetl*. The details were probably right, but it had no flavor—no *tam*. Barthelmes smiled as he thought the word. For some time now, Yiddishisms had been creeping into his English. He credited this to Kalia, for whom Yiddish had become almost a second language.

It was then that Barthelmes realized he could get the feeling of a Polish village synagogue by going to the Bronx, to the Burnside Avenue Central Synagogue, which his father and grandfather had attended. If it still existed.

5.

Kalia made weekly calls to Geula. She was, Kalia felt, over most of the pain of Helmut's loss. She had resigned her army commission to return to Hazorea, the socialist kibbutz where she was born. For the first six months, she'd worked in the central kibbutz kitchen. Then, at Geula's request, the administrative committee had assigned her to the children's nursery. Her feelings about these little Israelis, as she explained it to Kalia, were a mixture of awe and joy. She kissed and embraced them, wondering who among them would become artists, farmers, scientists, technicians and, God forbid, politicians.

She did not sing well, Geula confided to Kalia, and the children seemed to know it. Oh, they laugh at me with my croaking voice! The choir director had confirmed this to her: Geula Renan was a monotone. So she had avoided singing, although it was an important part of kibbutz life and the children enjoyed it. Her compensation for this vocal failure was the discovery that she could paint and repair toys, making them seem almost new. With delight she told Kalia that she'd begun to create and construct her own toys. And the children actually preferred them to most of the manufactured ones! They called her toys *geulas*.

Kalia had come to consider Geula a true Israeli—the kind of Jew who needs never think of her Jewishness. What for other Jews might be religious holidays were for Geula simply national or historical events. She never mentioned Helmut, and she had distanced herself completely from Israeli politics.

The most recent news was that Geula would be in the New Hampshire house for a month that fall. The leaves, Kalia! The leaves! she'd said. They are a miracle! The real burning bush! When I get old, I will live there. But believe me, only while the leaves fall—and then back to the sun. Kalia agreed she and Zachary would come visit in October.

Whenever Kalia thought of *The Beggar's Cup*, she became anxious. Anxious for Zachary. He would not, perhaps could not, grasp that it was hopeless. Moe was dead. Helmut was dead. Hollywood had always been dead. Yet Zachary pursued the project with more energy than it took to direct a film. What Kincaid had said was right: Barthelmes was regarded as a beggar. A special beggar, a loony beggar, who went door-to-door in La-La-Land shaking his *pushka*, his little tin cup.

Zachary, however, dismissed that notion. He had told her, not without anger, That's Hollywood, darling. But if you like that, try this one on: If I'm ever up for another Oscar—and that's very doubtful—I won't get it because I keep pushing *The Beggar's Cup*. Which might also reduce offers to direct.

That's silly, she'd said, though she wasn't sure it was silly at all.

I make them nervous, Kale! It's like I'm sawing away on an off-pitch violin.

He often awoke at night and went silently to his writing

table, where he read and reread the script. Kalia could hear the light clicking of the word processor and the noisy rattle of the printer. Why couldn't Zachary see that *The Beggar's Cup* had become like the heavy crucifix his father once had hung over his neck?

PART ELEVEN

1.

Zachary Barthelmes wrote and directed another film for Double Scorpion, Scott Kincaid's company. It was, for Barthelmes, his first mystery, an adaptation of *The Keys to Billy Tillio*, an award-winning novel, and he was surprised when it received two Oscar nominations, one for Best Screenplay. Although none of the nominations became victories, he felt no disappointment. It was clear that *The Beggar's Cup* hadn't caused him any loss of respect or esteem. Besides, the trip to the coast was a pleasant break from work, routine, and worry.

Kalia in her gown had caught the attention of fans and Zachary's peers alike. On Zachary's arm, Kalia was assumed to be an actress, however unknown as of yet; and the instant rumor was that she would star in Barthelmes's next film. According to another rumor she was his mistress, born out of wedlock in India to a royal British couple. However did they guess? Kalia shrieked. That's simply mar-vellous! However, it was Barthelmes who received the most adoring gazes from the crowds. His clothing embraced him like a soft, black skin, and his blond hair glistened. His face, weathered by time and worry, if not by the great western plains, was made intriguing by a restrained smile.

I never knew you were *so* attractive, Kalia whispered without moving her lips.

But I am, dear *shiksa*. You're making me look good.

And you do look good—for a Jewish gentleman, that is. A regular Douglas Fairbanks!

Junior or senior?

The women are drooling, Zach! I want you out of here—with me!—on the first post-Oscar plane.

Robert De Niro came in right behind them. Listen, Barthelmes, if you come out in front of the camera, I'll kill you. How can you do this to us wage slaves? Come on—you're crushing my frail psychosystem.

Zachary pinched his cheek. Just don't touch the suit, Bobby. If you were a little taller, I'd have a hell of a part for you.

So I'll grow, Zach. My man will call your man. He looked at Kalia, then back to Barthelmes. Does she come with a name?

My name, sir, is Kalia Wiggins.

That's a next-season name if I ever heard one! I won't let my man call your man, Miss Wiggins. I'll do it myself.

You're too short for the part, Barthelmes said, and they all laughed.

When the best-director Oscar was announced, Barthelmes was the first to his feet to applaud. Later, pushing through the crowds on the way out, smiling and answering greetings, Barthelmes seemed happier than Kalia had seen him in months.

You're pretty damned slick, Mr. Barthelmes, she said through a fixed smile. I didn't know this side of you.

Haven't I invited you to my shoots? Zachary replied through a stiff smile of his own. But did you come? I wanted you to see the lion in his lair.

I have a steady job, Mr. Barthelmes, Kalia said.

I don't know if I ever told you this, darling, but I used to be afraid of letting you out to see me here. My impression of myself, before you, was that I was an impostor. Sure, I had a reputation—you know, always on schedule, always under budget. The truth is, I worked like a demon so that I could get back to New York to be with you. You gave me a real life.

Stop it, Zach. She daubed at her eyes. Don't say things like that, not in public anyway.

They had slept well. They had not tried to make love. He heard Kalia say in the hotel dark, Why is this night different from all other nights?

Barthelmes laughed and had answered, Don't tell me, please.

2.

The sheet from his memo pad was Scotch taped to the edge of his desk: SYNAGOGUE, BURNSIDE AVE., BRONX. It had been attached there, yellowing, for more than a year, and he hadn't once thought seriously about going. But maybe, Barthelmes told himself, this would result in the final revision. The last nail in the coffin. He still didn't want to admit to himself that it was over and bury the blue-covered script in the long green box.

The warm part of May had arrived, and there was nothing on his schedule except a few unimportant choices. Another mystery for Double Scorpion, a new comedy for Paramount, or a trip to the Bronx. This was a no brainer, Barthelmes figured. The Bronx was more important. Kalia was right—it *was* over—but what he wanted was to tie up the loose ends and wrap a ribbon around it. Just one last revision.

He left Kalia a note: I am embarking on a journey to the Bronx. Even the phrase *embarking on a journey* made the hairs on his arms stand up, and he hurried down to their parking garage to get his car.

3.

An eternity passed as Zachary Barthelmes stood on the sidewalk in front of the Burnside Avenue Central Synagogue. Finally, he walked toward the high picket fence, each iron bar topped by a gold-painted sphere. He paused, then gripped the bars of the entrance gate as he had at the École Militaire. He breathed deeply and the gate creaked open, gathering momentum and crashing against the inside of the fence. This place, Barthelmes thought, is falling apart.

The building itself had a red-brick front, patched in several places with gray concrete. The bricks had been stained and worn by the corrosive air of the Bronx—like the great edifices of Rome, except that no intervening centuries were required to bring this facade to such a fragile state. Ah, America! He walked up the steps to the wooden double doors; a heavy steel chain and lock was hanging from one of the wrought-iron handles. Barthelmes looked at the chain and felt a sense of pity rise up. Jesus, he said under his breath.

He pulled one of the doors open and entered the small vestibule of the synagogue, then passed through a second set of doors. Suddenly the smells of the synagogue filled his nostrils, and his heart raced. The air was a mixture of fading tobacco, old cloth, traces of old perfumes. Weighing heavily on top of these odors was the strident presence of a strong detergent. He was in the *shul*, Barthelmes told himself. It was small, certainly compared to Trinity or St. John the Divine. The entire *shul* could fit into the Poet's Corner of St. John's. One hundred people, perhaps a few more, at the most.

In the exact center of the rectangular space was a square dais, with a high-legged table pressed against the rail facing him. The square was the place from which the rabbi led the congregation in prayer, where boys became bar mitzvah. He heard Kalia's voice telling him, Hey, *goyisha kopf!* You must learn these names even if you're only half a *yid*. It's called a *bima*.

Barthelmes looked upward. The white ceiling had recently been repainted, and a shallow balcony ran along the side and back walls. Was the balcony merely decorative, or did it have a function? On the wall behind the *bima* was the ark in which the Torahs were kept. Barthelmes recognized this as an important, if hokey, prop in many movies. In a production sense, he thought, the cabinet holding the Torahs might be a very distant cousin to the great blue whale which slaps the sea with its flukes: one prop offers the heart of Judaism; the other, the mysteries of the oceans. Perhaps each one would make an impression on some kid in Ames, Iowa.

Before, behind, and to each side of the *bima* were the long, high-backed benches where the worshippers sat—very much the same look as in every church Barthelmes could recall. Probably, he thought, smiling, there was one manufacturer who'd cornered the market on praying asses.

A small, thin man wearing an old black homburg got Barthelmes's attention by clearing his throat. They regarded each other for a moment before the man said, with a Yiddish accent, Can I help you, mister?

I'm just visiting. I'm a writer. It has to do with a project.

You're writing about *shuls*? Synagogues?

Yes. For a film. I'm a screenwriter. I wanted to see a *shul*, a real *shul*.

You speak Yiddish, the small man asked with a smile.

Well, only a word or two.

So, you picked out Burnside Avenue! When you write it down, please make some good words. Will you mention the name from the *shul*?

I don't think so. I'm writing a scene about a synagogue in Poland or Russia.

The little man clapped his hands together. My God, mister, I'm telling you this is the right *shul*! I'm from Kolkowicz! Burnside is like the *shul* when I was a boy! But bigger, bigger!

I thought it might be. Did you know my grandfather? He was a member here.

The old man spoke rapidly in Yiddish, then switched to English when Barthelmes indicated that he couldn't understand. I'm excited! A new person comes here and he has a connection with the *shul*! Again he spoke in Yiddish before halting the flow of his words. All right, all right! English. Your grandfather, what was his name?

Borenstein. Zalman Borenstein.

The man clapped his hands softly, keeping them together, putting his hands to his chin. Zalman Borenstein, he said, with the tenderness of a long memory. Thirty-seven years ago he died. It was a Thursday. The heart. He was on the *bima*. Studying Torah. Borenstein! Borenstein! He came forward and stroked Barthelmes's arm. What is your name, he asked in Yiddish, and this Barthelmes understood.

Zachary, Barthelmes answered. Zachary.

So you are named after Zalman!

Yes. After my grandfather.

Such a *mitzvah*, such a *mitzvah*! Your father? Joseph, that's his name! Joseph, no? Yussel Borenstein!

Yes.

How is he?

Barthelmes shook his head slowly. Six years ago, he said.

Such a young man!

Seventy-seven. I think he was seventy-seven.

That's how it is, Mr. Borenstein. Everybody dies. My mother used to say to me, Shaoul, the young *may* die, but the old *must* die. Ah, we have lost so many! In a few years we will not be able to have a *minyan*. Everybody moves away. The children—doctors, lawyers. Scarsdale, Palm Beach. The grandchildren, Tucson—what kind of a place is Tucson? You've been to Tucson?

Only once.

The grandchildren! All right, some marry Catholics, some with *schwarzes*. Trouble! Trouble! If only a few would become rabbis! Never mind that: if they would come only for Rosh Hashanah, for Yom Kippur! Tell me, Mr. Borenstein, you think God knows what He's doing?

A very loud snore interrupted itself. From one of the benches another old man rose up and rubbed his eyes.

Rosenfeld, you're up? the small man called in a loud voice. We got a visitor. What do you think, Rosenfeld, Borenstein's grandson!

No! Rosenfeld said, now standing up. Zalman—a grandson? He struggled up the aisle and came directly to Zachary. He looked into his face, squinted, and said, It's a Borenstein, all right. A *lang luksh!* Taller even than Zalman. If you grew a beard it would be red with yellow like your grandfather. What's your name?

Zachary.

Did you see your grandfather's name on the memorial panel? Come take a look. Rosenfeld gestured for Barthelmes to follow as he shuffled in his slippers toward a great white-marble plaque bolted to the east wall. There! Fourth down in the first column. Zalman Borenstein. A great man! A great man! You are blessed to have had such a wonderful grandfather!

His father, Yussel, the small man said, you remember him?

Rosenfeld nodded. Of course, he said. I always wondered why he wasn't tall like his father.

Also dead, Horowitz said. We should put his name up also. There's plenty room.

Listen, Horowitz, the name should go up but I'll have to go to the board. There's no funds.

Everything is the board! said Horowitz. You're the treasurer, Rosenfeld. Isn't there fifty dollars for a name?

Those are the rules. This *shul* goes by rules.

Would you allow me to pay for it, Barthelmes asked. After all, it's my father's name. Would that be all right?

Rosenfeld shuffled his feet.

Horowitz said, Certainly, for the father!

Barthelmes wrote out a check and handed it to Rosenfeld, who studied it carefully. Five hundred dollars?

There may be other times when a name must be put on the panel.

You sure this check is good? On the check it says Barthelmes. Zachary Barthelmes.

That's my movie name. I write for the movies. I use that name for work.

I see. But you're Borenstein, the grandson?

Yes.

Rosenfeld, be hospitable! You know everybody uses a special name in the movies. Who is Tony Curtis? Who is Kirk Douglas? Even, they say, maybe Marilyn Monroe. They have Hollywood names.

That's right, Barthelmes said. It's part of the business.

Don't you think I know that! Rosenfeld snapped at Horowitz. To Zachary he said, I just wanted to make sure everything is regular. I'm the treasurer.

He's a *farbissener*, Horowitz said. He retired from the job too early.

What did you do, Mr. Rosenfeld?

Men's clothing. For forty-one years. For Three G's. I was a cutter. It was a good job, good pay, but it poisoned my life. I wasn't born to be a cutter. I had an education. An accountant. A scholar. A teacher. Not a cutter!

I'm sorry, Barthelmes said.

Don't be sorry, Horowitz said. It's the way Rosenfeld is! Is he satisfied that he has a beautiful family?

Don't talk, Shaoul! How does it make me feel? Even you, a man with no education, becomes a success and I'm wasting my life.

Why do you always say I'm a success? Family I ain't got! Money I ain't got.

You've got health!

So God has blessed me! Is that success, Rosenfeld!

You know what I mean. Arthritis is for failures.

You see, Borenstein, he said to Zachary, he turns everything into bitterness. If he wasn't the last friend I got left, I wouldn't talk to him. *Mishigas!*

Are you denying you are famous, Horowitz?

Well, no. But it was not such a big thing!

Mr. Borenstein! Believe me, ten years after he's retired, they still say his name!

What did you do, Mr. Horowitz?

What did I do? I was a *pikla.*

A what?

A *pikla*, a *pikla.* I had a little store. I made pickles. Cucumbers. Tomatoes. Peppers. Cabbages. Once I pickled cauliflowers. It went good for a while, and then it fell out. It was a fad.

Rosenfeld cut in. You see he's complaining about the cauliflowers. Everybody copied the cauliflowers! Did you ever have pickled cauliflower? The truth!

Barthelmes smiled and stroked his chin thoughtfully. Thinking about it, Mr. Rosenfeld, I must admit that I've often had pickled cauliflower.

You see? Even his failures were successes! Famous, he was famous! Schmulka Bernstein bought from him! Luft's! Junior's! Lindy's! Out of a pickle he made a name. I give him credit. Cutters get nothing. Not even a thank-you.

Max, please, Horowitz said. Don't keep it up. Five more minutes and you'll hate me.

Rosenfeld lit a thin cigar.

Such a big shot for rules, Shaoul Horowitz said. It's against the rules to smoke.

Nobody's here.

I'm nobody? Borenstein is nobody?

It doesn't bother me, Barthelmes said.

Max Rosenfeld smiled triumphantly. He said to Barthelmes, Come with me. I'll show you something. Zachary followed as he walked slowly to the first row in front of the *bima*. He shuffled to the aisle. Here, he said, Sit down! There by the end.

Zachary seated himself on the bench.

Your grandfather's place, Rosenfeld said. The place of Zalman Borenstein.

Zachary cupped his hand over his mouth and suppressed a sob. Horowitz and Rosenfeld nodded, almost in unison, and walked away. It was more than five minutes before they returned.

As if he and Barthelmes were in the middle of a long conversation, Rosenfeld said, What do you think of Begin giving away the Sinai to Sadat?

Max, you just now got acquainted—don't get into politics!

Please, it's Borenstein's grandson. With him I can talk politics.

I don't mind, Barthelmes said as he turned to Rosenfeld. I think Begin did a great thing.

Rosenfeld snorted. He's taking you in, Borenstein. Achad Barone broke with Begin over that. And he was one hundred percent right. Instead of the Arabs driving us into the sea, Begin is leading the Jews out of the desert down to the beach. He's making it easy for them. He's a *farblonget* Moses going the wrong way.

I don't often agree with Begin, Barthelmes said, but he seized an important moment. Barone just misses the point. It's my impression that he only has confidence in military solutions.

There's no other solution, Borenstein. We need to break their backs. Then we can have peace.

I don't want to argue with you, Mr. Rosenfeld.

Call him Max, already.

Max, I follow Ben-Gurion's idea: land for peace. I don't want to argue.

All right, all right. I am one hundred percent for General

Barone. I am one hundred percent for the Greater Israel. I am saying, Never again. Never again!

Never again *what*? Horowitz shouted. What, what? Always never again and never what!

Go make pickles!

Go cut pants!

You think you should fight in the *shul*? Barthelmes asked.

No one's here!

I'm here, Horowitz shouted. Borenstein's here!

Please, Barthelmes said.

The two old men became silent. They sulked. Rosenfeld walked to the front of the *shul*, grunting with pain. Horowitz plodded around and around in a circle.

Examining the door frame without looking back, Rosenfeld called out: Shaoul! You didn't put the *pushkas* on the door!

What's the hurry? Let the paint dry.

The paint dried two months ago.

Nobody puts money in the *pushkas* any more, Maxie. There's rust on the bottom with holes. If you put in two quarters they fall down on the floor.

Barthelmes laughed, and then couldn't stop. Then Shaoul laughed. And Max.

Jews! Barthelmes said, almost choking.

They laughed some more.

All right, Horowitz said, there's a box of *pushkas* in the basement. They've been down there for fifty years. Maybe they have bottoms. I'll put up two.

Four, Rosenfeld said softly. There used to be four before the painting. You forgot already, *shamus*.

You know something? I forgot! I'll put them up before *Shabat*. He turned to Barthelmes. Tell me, young Borenstein: can you join us for *Shabat* services?

Barthelmes opened his mouth to reply, but Rosenfeld was already speaking. It's a small congregation and if Lebenthal is not over his flu, and Kaslow has to take his wife to the hospital again, we may have to look for a few men for a *minyan.*

I'm honored. Of course I'll come.

You have a wife, a good-looking man like you?

Barthelmes nodded.

I'll tell you this, mister, Horowitz said, the Borensteins, they were always good-looking! Zalman, he was like a god with the yellow beard. And the Borenstein women! Oh, boy!

As Barthelmes drove back to Manhattan, he was filled with joy. He beat rhythms on the steering wheel—rhythms to songs whose words he could not recall. Kolkowicz! Of course the Burnside Avenue Central Synagogue was like those in Poland. It *was* Polish!

Now there was a discovery, Barthelmes thought. Zalman Borenstein was a Polish Jew. Zachary Borenstein Wellington Barthelmes! And the Borenstein women? Oh, boy! Where were they now? Were there aunts and uncles and cousins? Were there any Borensteins left in the world?

4.

Oh, it's you all over again, Kalia said testily. You simply slide into things or slide out of things. You don't think! You don't commit! You should've told Kincaid and that Orthodox yahoo in Israel that you *were* a Jew. You should've told the Burnside Avenue guys that you *weren't* a Jew.

In both cases my defense is the same. I'm only half. I can't be sure if my cup is half full or half empty. Am I half yes or half no?

Oh, Zachary. Maybe this is a big joke for you, but it's driving me nuts! They think you're a Jew, and they'll assume I am.

You'll do better than me, Kalia. Your Yiddish is good and

you know all the *Shabat* liturgy. I'll be an absolute idiot. You'll have to hold my hand.

Hah! You'll have to hold your own hand. It's Orthodox. I'll be segregated with the women.

Shit!

And what will I wear, Zachary? Services are tomorrow evening, and I have nothing to wear.

There's a lot of nothing in your closets.

This is for *shul*, Zachary! *Shul!*

Okay, so don't wear a bikini, and don't wear slacks.

I won't wear a *sheitel* either! Goddamn it, Zachary, suggest something.

The gown you wore to the Oscars?

Jesus Christ, Zach! We're going to a poor *shul* in the Bronx! Kalia stormed into the bedroom. He could hear her banging doors and drawers. I have murder in my eye, Zachary Barthelmes, she shouted. You'd better pray to God I find something to wear.

Then there was a long, smooth, deep silence. After a few minutes, Barthelmes tiptoed to the bedroom door and peered inside. Kalia was standing before the full-length mirror and holding a suit, still on its hanger, against her body. Nice, he whispered. Perfect!

I haven't worn this in almost four years.

Oh, really?

I wouldn't expect you to remember, but it's the suit I wore when I met Dov Schechter at the Famous Dairy. I also wore it for my famous breakdown.

Barthelmes hesitated. It does look good, though.

You're right, she said. It's perfect! It's my one and only go-become-a-Jew outfit. It's the Kalia Wiggins jinx suit.

Maybe three times is a charm?

But I feel like someone's vestal virgin on her way to the rim of the volcano.

If you feel that badly, Kale, let's call the whole thing off.

No big deal. They'll wonder what happened to Borenstein's boy, then they'll blame it on Hollywood. Film people! No better than *goyim*.

No. The die is cast. Destiny. I'm terribly anxious about it, but I'm going.

Okay. We're going. If it helps any, think of it as a tryout. We're going to the Bronx. It's only the Bronx. The press won't cover it.

I don't know if I love you or hate you.

I love you, I know that.

When they went to bed that evening, Kalia pressed closely to Zachary. Do you believe in God? Why should any of this have any meaning at all?

What kind of question is that?

Just answer me. Do you believe in God?

I want to.

Do you?

I really don't know. Maybe I *don't* believe in God a little less than I used to.

Oh, get off the fence! Come over here and kiss me. Where are you?

5.

As the Friday hours fell away from noon, Zachary found that he, too, was anxious, although he didn't have a problem about what to wear. There were three appropriate dark suits in his closet. The problem was the other stuff. The *yarmulka* that religious Jews wore in deference to God, who was looking down from on high. The striped prayer shawl with its inscribed collar and knotted, tasseled fringe dangling down, to be pressed against the Torah when it is paraded through the synagogue on the shoulder of a worshipper. How do I know that? Barthelmes wondered. From the movies, of course.

Ludwig Donath playing the rabbi father of Larry Parks in the remake of *The Jazz Singer*.

Zachary removed his father's prayer bag from the back of the bottom desk drawer and brushed the maroon, velvet bag with his hand. In it, long unused, were the silver-embroidered *yarmulka*, the prayer shawl, and the prayer book. His throat tightened. Services were to begin at 5:30. Sundown would be at 7:42.

Kalia and Zachary didn't speak much as they descended into the basement garage and got into the car. As they rolled toward the Bronx, the stereo played Mozart as red and green traffic lights pierced the crumbling gray city.

Say something, please, Kalia said. I can't stand it.

Barthelmes laughed. This will sound crazy, but I've been trying to think of my mother. Why would I do that now?

No clue?

Who knows? First I tried to remember her face. Vague, pale, far away. She had no odor. I remembered that—I *always* remember that. Why did she die so young? I was only six, and I know I felt guilty. My fault, that sort of thing. Now I'm wondering if she didn't die because she found out that my father was a Jew or because, knowing that, she wasn't able to live with him and hated herself. Maybe because her blond, Wellington son had the secret Jew disease. Something like that.

You can't think that, Zachary.

Of course not. But here's a piece of the puzzle I couldn't make fit until now. I have never known a single Wellington. I know why my father didn't want me to know the Borensteins. But why did my mother keep me from her family?

You think she was ashamed?

Maybe, Kale. I just don't know.

At the George Washington Bridge, they turned right onto the Cross Bronx Expressway. And Burnside Avenue lay a few minutes ahead.

6.

As they walked the two blocks to the synagogue, people were entering. Kalia followed two women up the wooden stairs to the balcony, where she took a seat at the rail. Zachary felt around in Jerome's prayer bag, found the *yarmulka*, and put it on; then Rosenfeld guided him by the elbow to Zalman's place on the front bench. Seeing the other men wearing their prayer shawls, Barthelmes took his from the bag and draped it over his shoulders. Like other worshippers, he lifted a fringe of the shawl to his lips, kissed it, and opened his prayer book.

The rabbi was talking to Horowitz, who pointed in Barthelmes's direction. The rabbi nodded. He had a short, black beard, and his *yarmulka* was of a simple, unadorned black velvet. He was slightly taller than Shaoul Horowitz and less than half his age. His deep nods to the little *shamus* indicated a genuine respect, combined with the deference youthful authority visits on the elderly. Horowitz clearly appreciated his attention. Then the rabbi looked at his wristwatch, took leave, and ascended the *bima*. His voice rang out, a surprisingly rich baritone, and filled the synagogue. The Sabbath service had begun.

A light sweat broke on Zachary's forehead as the Hebrew prayers rustled through the *shul*. He stared down at the prayer book in his hands as if it were miles away; the strange letters leaped and bounded beneath his watering eyes. He heard the turning of thousands of pages as the worshippers moved on through the text. Barthelmes tried to focus on the English text printed on each left-hand page, but the English had become as runny as the Hebrew. He tried to hear and to mimic the sounds issued by the worshippers, but what entered through his ears would not form on his lips. The pace of the praying, led by the rabbi, seemed to become faster and faster. Barthelmes struggled with stiff, clumsy fingers to turn the pages in his prayer book as the worshippers around him suddenly broke into full-voiced song. He could almost feel the eyes of those behind him poking into his back.

Don't be so nervous, chanted Maxie Rosenfeld, now standing alongside him. We're already finished with the *mincha*. Soon *mahrov*. Then we'll have *kiddush* and *fertig*. Fine, fine, Zachary, you're doing fine.

I'm dying, Barthelmes said.

I never heard of such a thing, Rosenfeld sang. Turn the page.

I feel like an idiot! Barthelmes sang in reply.

Turn the page. We're getting to the part where we all face the entrance to the *shul*. The *Shabat* bride is about to enter. We are greeting her.

The Bride of the Sabbath enters the synagogue, Barthelmes thought. We pray to her. We bow to her. We embrace her. The missing scene—the *Shabat* bride entering the *shtetl shul!* He looked up to the segregated balcony and smiled at Kalia, where she sat at the rail. Her fingers waggled toward him in a demure response.

Rosenfeld plunged into a robust burst of praying. Zachary noticed, out of the corner of his eye, that Rosenfeld was praying without referring to the prayer book.

Turn the page, he sang to Barthelmes. *Shuckle* a little.

Zachary rocked up and back.

Very good, very good! Rosenfeld sang. Now, Zachary, in a minute, you keep an eye on me, there will be a big *Awmein*. Yell like hell. Then we sit down. One, two, three! *Awmein!*

Zachary, sweaty and drained, seated himself.

So, you're rusty, Rosenfeld said. Two years ago, my son the psychiatrist did me the honor of attending one Rosh Hashanah. He didn't look in the book once! He didn't say even one *Awmein!*

Everybody's praying, Max, and you're talking to me!

Don't worry. I'm praying in my head. God only cares if you're relating to Him. My son couldn't relate to a lamppost! Rosenfeld put his hand beneath Zachary's elbow and pressed upward. Together they both stood up and the sea of prayers washed around them.

The praying continued. The rabbi lifted a cup of wine.

The *kiddush*, Rosenfeld said. If we had children here, they would rush up to the *bima* at the end of the service and sip a little from the cup.

The prayers rushed on, then *Awmein!* The service ended with the soft sound of prayer books closing.

The rabbi stepped down from the *bima* and approached Barthelmes. You did very well, Mr. Borenstein. It is not exactly like getting on a bicycle after a long time. My experience with ritual is that, depending on your involvement, you can draw blanks.

Thank you for your understanding, rabbi. Max saved me from being a total *klutz*.

And the Hebrew text, the rabbi added, goes much more rapidly than the English; one never seems to coincide with the other. English readers are always in one place while Hebrew readers are in another.

I wasn't in another place, I'm afraid. I was just lost.

The rabbi laughed. I suppose, he said, your Hollywood work has given you the experience of an actor?

It depends on how you mean that. Hollywood is filled with actors, of course, and maybe it's true that producers or directors are the best at making believe. But I wasn't acting— at least I don't think I was. Guided by Max, I was imitating the others.

You *shuckled* very well, the rabbi said.

Trembled, maybe. *Shuckling* calls for control, I believe, and I was just shaking. But thank you again for your help.

My pleasure. It is very good to have you in the temple your grandfather helped build. The rabbi shook Barthelmes's hand. Please forgive me if I raced through the service, but Shaoul reminded me that we were ten minutes late in starting. The soup was on the stove, and everybody wanted to get home before dark for the Sabbath dinner. *Gut Shabos!*

Waiting in the vestibule, at the bottom of the stairs, Barthelmes watched Kalia descend. Beneath her black straw toreador hat, her face was flushed with excitement. She spoke in Yiddish to the women around her. When she kissed Zachary on the cheek, one of the women asked, Is this your husband?

Yes, Kalia answered in Yiddish. But he cannot understand what we're saying. He's no better than a *goy*.

Grasping the meaning, Barthelmes frowned.

Kalia turned and spoke in English. Show your sense of humor, Mr. Borenstein. Let me introduce Mrs. Kantrowitz and Mrs. Schwimmer.

Zachary nodded and smiled as the vestibule was filled with good wishes for the Sabbath.

Outside, the sky was shedding its light. He held Kalia's hand as they walked away from the temple. At the corner of Burnside Avenue they had turned to the right, toward the parking garage, when Kalia stopped in mid-stride and laughed, pointing her finger at him. It was then that Zachary realized he was still wearing the prayer shawl and the *yarmulka*.

He smiled, then stopped and turned. My prayer bag! I left it on the bench. Smiling, he turned around again and led Kalia toward the parking garage. Shaoul, he said, will save it for me.

The black and Latino faces of workers returning home moved by them, and none of them seemed to notice the tall blond man in religious garb. Zachary tightened his grip on Kalia's hand. What an evening, he said as he looked toward the sky above the uniform rooftops of the Bronx.

In the darkness of the parking garage, still wearing his

shawl and *yarmulka*, Zachary unlocked the car and then stood upright, placing his hands on the roof. He bowed his head for a moment, then threw it back and shouted, God Almighty! We have become Jews! Then, for a long time, Zachary Barthelmes wept.

Kalia put her arms around his waist. Zach, she said, please stop. If you cry, I will. Please!

I can't help it, Kale. I want to cry for joy. For the lousy things in the world, for everything we've done. I know it's crazy. But I *feel* so crazy! Am I making any sense?

Yes, Kalia said. She lifted the corner of Zachary's prayer shawl and wiped her eyes. Then she reached up and, with the same corner, wiped Zachary's eyes.

PART TWELVE

CODA 1980–90

Zachary Borenstein accepted the invitation to join the Board
of Trustees of the Burnside Avenue Central Synagogue. In
Hollywood, though, he used Barthelmes as his professional
name. Zachary attended the Wilshire Boulevard Temple.
Asked by the press why he had converted, Zachary had replied, I have not converted.

On Sabbath eves, Kalia lit candles and said the Blessing
in Hebrew. She was, Zachary knew, more comfortable with
Jewish practices than he was. Kalia had taken on the job of
educating him in the traditions, rituals, and lore; Zachary
had taken on the task of questioning the meanings of Jewish
philosophy. Why should we be a light unto the nations? Does
a Jew have to believe in God? Is Israel the homeland of all
Jews? Kalia said that his endless probing—at once exploring
and doubting the mysteries of Judaism—proved beyond
question that he had become a *Talmud Bucher*, and a student
of everything Jewish. To doubt, to question, to wrestle with
angels, and in the end to believe, wasn't that the meaning
of being a Jew?

When Kalia became pregnant, Zachary said they should
get married. Kalia refused, saying she already had committed
her whole life to him. They argued. They didn't marry.

Maxie Rosenfeld died. In his eulogy, Shaoul Horowitz
called him a man of high learning and accomplishments,
educated, an outstanding Jew, and the best cutter who ever
worked for Three G's.

Zachary accepted the post of treasurer, replacing Rosenfeld. The balance in the synagogue account was ninety-seven dollars and thirty-four cents until he replenished the funds.

Moe Cohen's daughters sold Big MAC Pictures to Paramount for three hundred million dollars. Marcus Cohen, in Majorca, gave power of attorney to his sisters. Paramount, with all due respect, turned down *The Beggar's Cup*.

A letter from Tim Wiggins was delivered to Kalia's office at the advertising agency. She opened it a week later and read that her father, now dying of cancer, would like to see her. It was important to him. She tore up the letter and dropped the pieces into her trash can.

Citing that only nineteen members, with an average age of sixty-six, remained in the synagogue, the Board of Trustees ordered the temple to terminate its activities as soon as possible. The task of selling the building and properties was given to Borenstein.

Achad Barone controlled nine seats in the Israeli Knesset and was appointed by Begin to a post in the cabinet.

Kalia gave birth to a son: Zalman Helmut Borenstein. When he's old enough to understand his name, she said, he'll kill us. But until he gets married, Zachary said, we'll call him Hal.

After Begin resigned and Yitzhak Shamir became Prime Minister, Geula Renan wrote and illustrated a children's book called *Two Dwarfs and an Ogre*, which the Israeli press immediately recognized as an allegory. For months the book was the subject of massive coverage in newspapers and magazines, on radio and television, throughout the Middle East. Shamir, reportedly, was angry and upset. In Geula's drawings, his arms were stunted, his feet tiny, and he always carried a mirror in which he could admire himself. Barone was infuriated to be depicted with the huge behind of a hippopotamus and a rhinoceros horn for a nose. As the ogre, he spoke only in red capital letters. No reaction was credited to King Hussein of Jordan, said to be the inspiration for a creature, even smaller than Shamir, who barked continuously like the tiniest of Chihuahuas. Geula dedicated the book to Zalman Helmut Borenstein.

With the stony approval of the Board of Trustees, the Burnside Avenue Central Synagogue was sold to the First Holy Korean Baptist Church. The proceeds, roughly two hundred and forty thousand dollars, were divided among American and Israeli educational and charitable institutions.

Zachary had the marble memorial plaque removed and shipped, with Geula's permission, to the house in New Hampshire, where it was bolted to the wall of a large room facing the river. The workmen had to reinforce the wall to which the plaque had been attached. Zachary also removed the *pushkas* left in the basement of the *shul*. He fixed two of the blue tin boxes, with their bearded images of Theodor Herzl, to the door frame of his study in their apartment on Central Park West. Two others he brought to New Hampshire.

Barthelmes took fewer directing assignments. Kalia, noting that his income had not diminished, observed that in Hollywood, the less you do, the more you're worth.

Shaoul Horowitz called to tell them he was moving to Del Ray Beach, Florida, to live with his sister. Kalia took his address and phone number.

A year after Hal, Kalia gave birth to a daughter, Gerryanna Geula Borenstein, whom they immediately called Two G's.

Geula called from Kibbutz Hazorea to tell them she had married a blind air force veteran.

Zachary decided against revising the *shtetl shul* scene. Unfinished, he felt, the manuscript would remain alive. Completed, and placed inside Jerome's long green box, *The Beggar's Cup* might lose its urgency; this way he would think of it often. Whenever Kalia urged him to push it out of his mind, he just smiled.

After a long search, Zachary discovered there were Borensteins in Boston, Houston, and Cleveland. He wanted to write a poem commemorating this, but after several months he had been able to write only the first two lines:

> We are dancing in the Temple
> Which has never been destroyed . . .

FINIS

A NOTE ON THE TYPE

The text of this book was set in Walbaum, a typeface designed by Justus Erich Walbaum in 1810. Walbaum was active as a type founder in Goslar and Weimar from 1799 to 1836. Though the letterforms of this face are patterned closely on the "modern" cuts then being made by Giambattista Bodoni and the Didot family, they are of a far less rigid cut. Indeed, it is the slight but pleasing irregularities in the cut that give this typeface its humane quality and account for its wide appeal. Even in appearance, Walbaum jumps boundaries, having a more French than German look.

Composed by PennSet, Inc., Bloomsburg, Pennsylvania. Printed and bound by Fairfield Graphics, Fairfield, Pennsylvania

Designed by Peter A. Andersen